JAGGED PIECES OF A FEARFUL PUZZLE

The forbidden inner sanctum of CIA Headquarters in Virginia, where the fate of the nation was being decided by men free of all control . . . a top security project in Hawaii protected by high fences, armed men, and savage dogs . . . a mysterious linkup between American secret agents and top Russian operatives . . .

As the man named Grove moved ever deeper into the corridors of twisted ambition, deception, and insane violence the whole incredible picture began to come together . . .

"A fantastically devious plot . . . readers will thrill to the unexpected and ingenious twists"
—*Hartford Times*

"A shattering climax" —*Library Journal*

"Will keep you reading far past bedtime . . . Wylie is a master storyteller"
—*Springfield News & Leader*

PHILIP WYLIE studied at Princeton, worked on the *New Yorker*, and has written thirty books, innumerable magazine pieces, and many movie scripts. A lay scientist, agnostic, and consistent critic of contemporary society, Wylie has enthralled and irritated three generations of American readers. Long interested in marine biology, Wylie is a director of Lerner Marine Laboratory in the Bahamas.

THE SPY WHO SPOKE PORPOISE

PHILIP WYLIE

PYRAMID BOOKS • NEW YORK

THE SPY WHO SPOKE PORPOISE

A PYRAMID BOOK

Published by arrangement with Doubleday & Company, Inc.

Doubleday edition published October 1969

Pyramid edition published October 1970

Library of Congress Catalog Card Number: 74-79970

Printed in the United States of America

PYRAMID BOOKS are published by Pyramid Publications
A Division of The Walter Reade Organization, Inc.
444 Madison Avenue, New York, New York 10022, U.S.A.

1

JOKE

The night watchman at Sea Life Park pedaled his bike from the Oceanic Institute, which was part of his beat, to the park office area. There he smelled trouble.

He did not identify it as trouble, right away, or even as a smell. He stopped his bike on the road between the park and the institute because he had sensed an alien event, or presence, or sign. So he dismounted and stood motionless in an effort to discern the cause.

He was in his fifties, a huge man, wearing a blue uniform with a .45 on a wide belt. Half Hawaiian and half Chinese, the watchman was Buddha-faced with black hair under his visored cap, eyes near black, and amber skin of remarkable smoothness except where scars were hidden by his clothing, scars that were proud mementos of Italy in World War Two and of Korea or of his later but zealous career as a detective on the Honolulu police force.

People who claim to have premonitions of danger tend to be mystical; however the park watchman felt his inklings, his sudden sensations of unnamable threat should be heeded, not trusted. Most such pricklings came from an unconsciously noted phenomenon that was normal and merely unexpected or disturbing when sensed. But Jerry Gong knew that every such sudden flash, nameless tocsin, could be traced by introspection; and he knew some were danger signs. Sound, scent, movement or a tactile phenomenon—such as the delicate tremble of a floor, showing another presence in a dark room, needed interpretation. You therefore stopped as Jerry had done to reconnoiter your nerves, testing each sense organ in turn while keeping under cover if possible.

He quietly moved out of the gleaming lights in Sea Life Park. Had he seen anything or anybody, glimpsed some odd movement, heard a peculiar sound or faintly sensed a strange odor? He rushed through that checklist-for-survival. A sniff of some sort, he decided.

The delicacy of that effort would have surprised most people, for he did not look sensitive—at six foot three and two hundred thirty pounds, with a face as relaxed and as friendly as it was open, a face he'd disciplined to seem least alert when the utmost vigilance was needed.

His ability to dissemble was among the qualities that explained his many military decorations, his scars and his present occupation. The Honolulu police had turned Jerry out to pasture after a huge ceremony, where a thousand people from all parts of Oahu stood up to cheer.

Another, greater number had cheered for a different reason. They were the criminals in the state of Hawaii. Jerry's compulsory retirement had been meant as an act of mercy: a man of his age should not risk more beatings, stabs and bullet holes; so the governor of Hawaii and both senators had attended the parting ceremony. Jerry had tried his best to act pleased but within a month his enforced leisure palled. Restless, cross, prone to argument, given to heavy drinking—and that, for the first time—Jerry changed from celebrity to scourge. His wife, Puuani, his four sons and four daughters, along with at least a hundred relatives, tried everything. "Everything" didn't work. Not being a detective, or a soldier of his special breed, or even a man with a job, made Jerry a skid row candidate.

Then he heard Sea Life Park was looking for a night watchman. Its office safe had been the target of three burglaries, all failures, even though the third gang (after grabbing and tying up the night man then on duty) had hauled the safe out of the park grounds and down the highway. Then they'd pitched it over a cliff where, to their humiliation, it lay, dented and gouged but not open or openable, at least by them.

After that, "Tack" Abbott, who, with his wife, "was" the park, the institute, the Makai Range and so forth, decided he needed a different breed of watchman. Tack mentioned the requirements to Mrs. Abbott, who wrote the ad. Jerry saw it as he sat on the beach near his home in Waimanalo with a fishing rod, trying angrily to discover the joys of doing nothing. The conditions stipulated were those one might find in a paratrooper who was also a guerrilla fighter, an Indian scout and a space age Sherlock Holmes.

Mrs. Abbott's copy plainly showed her vexation at inept night watchmen.

Jerry responded. Roy Hedges, boss of the park's front office, received the application and called the Honolulu police chief to ask if it would be wise to hire Jerry Gong. Chief Hosea Ikkyo knew Jerry's record as a soldier and a detective; he also knew the HQ gossip about Jerry's decline.

"For Lord's sake," he half yelled and half laughed, "get him! There's only one Jeremiah Akaka Gong. I fought like hell to keep him. But people thought he'd had a bellyful of being hurt. He didn't. You'll save the man's life with that job—unless he loses it on duty. How are things?"

"Good," Roy replied, by which he meant marvelous and referred to gate receipts.

So it was Jeremiah Akaka Gong who stopped his bike, slid himself and it into a shadow and set his sense perceptors to work as if they were antennae. What had he smelled that was alien?

Not smoke, the first item to be checked; not people, sweat-stealthy people; not a car or its exhaust, moving in the vast grounds with no lights. And not something even more probable, such as a fish out of water, becoming spoiled. He had smelled something sweet, like a flower. Then he had it.

A flower. *Ylang-ylang.*

So far as he could recall he'd never seen an ylang-ylang tree in Hawaii. Probably there were some. But missionaries had given a bad name to that particular tropical tree and its yellow, iris-like blooms. They'd outlawed it, Jerry guessed, while they had the power, simply because ylang-ylang flowers, night-blooming and exotically scented, were worn in the hair of certain ladies in Southeast Asia as a sign of their profession, that oldest one.

Jerry now recalled more: ylang-ylang blossoms smell only at night and live just one night, perhaps. He wasn't sure. But, if so, it meant someone had brought that blossom, or several, into the park after closing time: 5 P.M., in January, on a Wednesday.

Yet no one could be in the park legally, now. The cleaning people had left at twelve. The last scientist at work in the institute had gone right after. Every scrap of trash and even every cigarette butt left by the past day's thousands had been gathered, put in containers and carted away. It was possible that an ylang-ylang blossom had been overlooked and so showed its ability to perfume cubic acres of air. But the rarity of the scent made him decide to seek its source—in the park.

Jerry was about to mount his bike when he heard a well-known vehicle coming from Waimanalo; Mr. Grove's machine—a custom-built motorcycle that was unlike any other. With that, Jerry biked slowly down the road toward the highway . . . the Kalanianaole, called "Kalan" by almost everybody except tourists, who never could pronounce the royal name or even remember it.

Mr. Grove was a friend of Jerry, of the Abbotts and everybody else. A retired gentleman with a house on the seashore about a mile from the park, he was popular because, if people could invent an ideal or favorite uncle, it would be Mr. Grove. One of Mr. Grove's pastimes—he said he had insomnia—was to come to the park at night and wander among the vast ponds and exhibition tanks to admire their denizens. Occasionally, too, the Abbotts brought visitors at night; and sometimes other executives and scientists did so, or returned late to check their work.

After ten in the evening when Jerry went on duty, one had either to be escorted by someone known to Jerry or provided with proper credentials. Photographers had occasionally spent hours taking shots of the aquatic marvels in the park—after dark for science or for magazines. But few loners cared to wander about enjoying things. Mr. Grove was one, however, and the most constant.

His smooth-running, quiet motorcycle turned in at a one-car-wide curve—the only entry not cut off by heavy chains. It purred up to the parking row beside the high wire fence and the motor died as the watchman coasted into view.

Grove nodded. "Nice night, Jerry."

"Sure is."

For a time they joined in a ritual act.

They listened to the sea as it came ashore beyond the Kalan Highway, broke softly and ran among the black lava rocks, kissing all in turn. They swung in the opposite direction to look at the steep slant of talus behind the park, a great, frozen avalanche of rock and a cliff towering to a crenelated summit, holed through in places and ornamented with senseless sculpture. That skyline was silhouetted by the lights beyond, the effulgence of Honolulu, Waikiki, Hawaii Kai, Kahalo and other suburbs. They drank in the gothic heights and their eyes lifted to the sky above, where the trade winds shunted clouds across stars to hide and disclose them at random: Cassiopeia gone and back; Orion cut and emergent; the Pleiades now sharp and soon shawled—a coming-going of the rigid-spark array men called the visible universe but few take time to watch and still fewer can put names to.

Next, they turned half around to note a pair of beacons above Makapuu Point which seemed to hang in the sky since the mass beneath was blacked out by the park lights: two sky-hung lanterns in effect, signs of a radar station there; and they noted the lighthouse, far below, keeping its rhythm like a drugged metronome. After that they gazed seaward again as if to check the abiding presence of pale and looming Rabbit Island, a near-mile offshore, and Black Rock, a smaller isle. With that they had completed a rite Grove had followed from his first nocturnal visit.

"Beautiful," he said softly.

"It is. Hawaiians, and even half Hawaiians," Jerry mused, "never lose their awareness of the beauty their Polynesian ancestors found in these islands and understood. Others, some of you haoles, have the same perception, or part of it, anyhow, but not many white people."

"All quiet?"

"Absolutely. Pacific, like the sea." Jerry said it, knew it was a little overdone, knew why—and wondered if Mr. Grove had noticed.

He had. He smiled with his wide and smile-designed mouth. "So? What's *wrong?*"

Jerry laughed and explained his theory about subconscious observations. "So, what's wrong is only a smell," he concluded. "I'm a nut to even notice these things. But it's a flower I don't recall seeing around here. Common in Bangkok; one called ylang-ylang."

Afterward, Jerry thought Mr. Grove did something. Perhaps he flinched a millimeter or changed his eye shape. Or, maybe, he altered his breathing for one inhalation. But that memory came later and possibly was a projection. All he was sure of was that Mr. Grove nodded, kept the smile and said, "There must be trees on Oahu."

"No doubt." Jerry paused a second as if some business was unfinished. He thought of none. "Going to the Reef Tank?"

"Yep. Guess so. See you later. When you eat, mebbe."

The watchman agreed and unlocked the big gate in the park fence. Mr. Grove walked through. Jerry followed, relocked and rode on—past the five-eighth scale model of the sailing ship *Essex* in Whaler's Cove, past live whales in that huge salt pond and porpoises that made both splashy and squeaky efforts to get his attention. He pedaled from there toward the Hawaiian Reef building and saw Mr. Grove dimly as that pleasant gentleman entered the bottom ramp. He smiled to think Mr. Grove was considered a little odd simply because he lived alone in a house he had rebuilt, had a great deal of money, kept his own hours and preferred the company of ordinary folks, especially kids, to the society rich men usually chose.

Jerry also thought, cycling onto the gift shop and restaurant level, his friend should get himself a pretty wahine for company because the housekeeper Mr. Grove employed, though recommended by Mrs. Abbott, wasn't that sort of companion. The Hawaiian half of Jerry was a little miffed at that; the Chinese half, sad. Grove's Genevra Oopani was not a nubile lass, however serene, lovely and intelligent. A huge woman as old as Jerry but not one for any man's love, since Prince Kuakuaki had died, long ago. So loving a man should be loved very much and in every Polynesian way, Jerry believed.

Meantime, Mr. Grove had come into the vast, circular building and started up the spiral ramp which ran inside the walls and was lined on the opposite side with glass windows, top to bottom—a gigantic aquarium some seventy-five feet across and several fathoms deep. Into it, every hour, flowed three hundred thousand gallons of clean, unfiltered Pacific water, an incessant river engineered to flow with so little disturbance that the great submarine wonderland was not blurred or distorted. That technical feat permitted Sea Life Park to display myriad forms of life not to be seen in other man-made ocean exhibits; live corals grew there, for example.

All other oceanic displays were limited, since they could not supply unfiltered sea water to such inhabitants. Fishes, sea turtles, sharks, rays and sundry sea-beings could be shown anywhere. Corals, however, along with many associated forms—painted fans, rainbow sponges and their gaudy or grotesque relatives—require a tidal river to bring the microscopic food such mandatory filtration removes, elsewhere. Thus the park's Hawaiian Reef edifice was unique; like nature's coral ranges, it supported a multitude of fixed feeders besides those that pass by. Had a chunk of the gaudiest, most populous, living reef been taken up by a titanic cooky cutter and set ashore unchanged, the effect would have been similar.

The huge, round walls of the building and its conical roof dimmed the glass-walled interior even in daytime. The result was that a person going up or down the sloped ramp that encircled the aquatic habitat had the experience of a scuba diver though without risk of getting wet, not to mention drowning or shark bite, though sharks might eye him through the succession of windows, at a distance of an inch or two. Countless park visitors returned over and over to follow that dramatic incline; and numberless scientific observations were made there, since it offered opportunities difficult or even impossible to find in the sea itself.

Mr. Grove reveled in the slow trip, up or down, day or night. To him, the show in its day and night variations, with constant subvariations at either time, was like a masterpiece of art, but with a difference. This was a work in which perpetually shifting forms and hues were never twice the same. His fascination with the park centered here and his frequent night visits—Jerry knew he also came by day—were understandable. Many more such nocturnal seekers of the spell were gratified when the park was open on certain evenings in the summer.

Now, however, Mr. Grove did not follow his regular procedure, his hour-consuming pilgrimage on the ramp, taking one window at a time and each for a lengthy look. As he entered he noticed a new occupant: a foreign one. He stared up, whispered, "Gosh!" and then swiftly made sure Jerry had proceeded on his beat—which would have included cycling over the walkway to this place, if Mr. Grove hadn't been there. When he found that Jerry had moved beyond the park, this rather ordinary-sized man with the rather commonplace appearance ran quietly up the ramp, glancing only for a second into passing windows until the intruder came into full view on the surface. It was a man, a dead one.

Ylang-ylang, he mused; strange that Jerry had noticed. But Jerry noticed a lot; maybe too much, he thought.

Grove's excitement was intense but, like the watchman, he reacted to stress with its opposite look, one of near boredom, the empty face of a professional.

Standing, staring, he remembered snatches of a conversation from long ago: ". . . Life Park . . . early January . . . no, a year from next . . . be an ylang-ylang lei . . . more when the time arrives. . . ."

From that had come an interpretation by Mr. Grove that led to his move to the windward side of Oahu, in Hawaii, and the purchase and reconstruction of his house on the beach near Waimanalo. After that, he'd spent an unrewarded year. His long vigil, though not yet quite abandoned, had begun to seem futile. The critical date had gone by without incident. He was relieved he'd hung on.

The corpse half floated above the fishes and the other creatures swimming both at random and merry-go-roundwise. It was stranded on a replica, in concrete, of offshore rock formations, legs extended in water, toes down.

Mr. Grove had gone up the ramp as if it were downhill and he a track star. His age might have been fifty or even more. His hair was brown but with silver intrusions, his chunky body seemed ordinary and his height appeared less than it actually measured—owing to his unusual breadth of shoulder and the thickness of his torso. He wore sneakers, an aloha shirt and baggy slacks. His ascent of the ramp would have astonished strangers. But his friends and neighbors in South Miami, Florida, and Warsaw, New York, where he also owned a house, would not have batted an eye. Mr. Grove was an acrobat . . . among other things.

At the nearest possible approach, however, the corpse was not ideally visible in the night lighting under the broad, conical roof. Grove stopped to peer from behind a concrete rail. The half-beached corpse wore a trench coat, belted. A gray, snapbrim felt hat was aground on the same lava-like concrete outcrop. The dead man's suit was a pinstripe sort; chalk on grayish blue. A sag of the jacket and a cant of body, Grove guessed, was caused by a .45 in a shoulder holster. The man had been drowned, perhaps; but not here. In and out of the open mouth came a tiny and regular tide of something that wasn't water and more was visible in a small depression in the "rock ledge" under the man's face.

Grove's initial reaction was self-reproach: this scene was set because he had failed. But all men fail sometimes and only lesser men linger on their defeat. Grove had a moment of bitterness, only that.

He did not know for certain who the man was but he could make a very good guess: Jarvis Menly of the CIA, already reported lost or missing, a datum Grove was certainly not supposed to know. He was not supposed to know anything more about the CIA than the public learns from radio, TV, newspapers, magazines and books concerning America's superspy organization.

Grove nonetheless did know. And he now recalled an ancient, top-secret fact. Another American, an agent like this dead one, had perished—soon after the Second World War when Grove had been somewhat similarly employed. That one, Arthur Allening, had been in the OSS and was executed, so to speak, in Marseilles, France, on its famed boulevard, the Canebière. They'd killed Art Allening in a café where he sat in a rear corner, assaulting him from behind, through a paneled portal. That had implied a strong man, or men, and the result was that the poor jerk had actually drowned in his large (hot) bowl of bouillabaisse. It couldn't be proved that Art hadn't fainted and drowned himself since the strong boy or boys had left no useful evidence.

But Grove had been OSS himself at that time and was relatively nearby. He had looked over the scene and found the panel; so they knew: not who; but how. And who, they thought, related to Reds in the supposedly dissolved French Resistance. The Commies were trying to take over France, then, as usual.

So Grove was one of maybe six men still living who would remember the incident in detail and, consequently, would note that what flowed out of (and back into) this man's open mouth was saffron-colored and contained bits like onions in bouillabaisse. Besides, and even before noting that, Grove had observed the man's costume (it was a costume, now) precisely resembled what many American agents wore in the late forties.

He had to know more. It might even be the long-deceased agent's clothing. He moved out onto the broad wooden bridge that led to the park's entrance plaza, keeping in the shadows to see if Jerry had stuck to the expected routine. He had. Jerry was cycling now, toward the Makai Range area, beyond the institute, where Martian edifices awaited further and overdue activities of titan machinery.

He dropped down the side of the plaza embankment, knowing he had at most a half hour. He entered the men's toilet and ripped masses of toilet paper from their rolls. With that, he re-entered the Reef Tank at its base and stripped. Naked, he ran up the ramp to the surface where, after a glance to be sure of an unencumbered bottom, he slipped in and waded, then swam over to the carefully stranded, nicely arranged corpse.

It took a little more than ten minutes to complete his examination. He was careful not to make a splash, since he wanted no sign of his effort to show and, especially, wished to keep his hair dry: Jerry would notice even one wet strand.

The clothes on the body, he felt, were probably those of the long-departed hero. Art Allening; not the garments he'd died in, but others, taken from his supposedly secret hide-out prior to its inspection by the OSS minion, a day later—by him, in sum. He briefly wondered if this charade was addressed to him and decided not: his visible park visits weren't predictable.

He found exactly what one would expect in the pockets and on the person of an OSS agent active in the era that followed the Second World War: a gun in the period-piece shoulder holster, a few thousand francs in bank notes and some coins, a hundred dollars in American money—forbidden but usually stashed away by an agent at that time as insurance against adversity—several tokens of the sort cafés supplied to girls who persuaded their customers to buy drinks prior to further exchanges, a snapshot of somebody female who signed herself, "Your adoring Bébé," three telephone numbers, all in the Marseilles area, with names: Francette, Marie-Chantelle, Yvette-La-Vrai-Rêve, a partly used packet of *jaunes*, French cigarettes unsmokable even when fresh, and, in the expected outside tuck, a z-pill. This was provided against any extreme instant—which, in Allening's case, had occurred; but, Grove reasoned, a man couldn't reach it, even if he was conscious, while held in hot soup, face down.

He returned these items exactly as they had been, swam back across the tank with his head out of water and dried himself enough to prevent lingering tracks. He finished the paper toweling near the bottom entry and went outdoors in deep shadow to hide the soggy bundle behind a sea lavender clump so he could dispose of it later. Re-entering the dim, circular structure, he dressed rapidly, checked his face and arms in a tank window—an adequate mirror at the right angle—making sure no telltale bit of paper adhered to his face and arms. Twenty-two minutes had been consumed.

Jerry would by now be on his return trip, somewhere in the institute area. He might wonder how Grove had managed to ascend the ramp for what would ordinarily be two thirds of a normal tour, without himself noticing the alien silhouette on the surface. It was, however, not very prominent and could well have been deemed some addition, or piece of gear, that a fascinated spectator on the way up would not see, or seeing, would not have reason to suspect as what it proved to be.

In a very deep sense, the discovery was gratifying to this pleasant-looking but not imposing visitor. It proved the time and the money he'd invested in a chancey enterprise were well spent. Nothing more than that was sure; but at least something had given authenticity to a long and private (not to say complex and covert) endeavor.

As he stepped from the sloping spiral to the level, walled walk around the summit, he grinned. For the man who was dead and the nature of these odd arrangements were intended as a joke.

The violent reaction of certain persons, of one of them in particular, would be that sort; the costumed cadaver would seem like the "sick" humor in recent vogue, and, Grove thought, *meant* for that and also for an added reaction, a wrong one.

The Man in Moscow, he told himself, or in Peking, or wherever he was at this moment, had taken the measure of his opposite number in USA.

Probably, Grove added, still to himself.

Compliments of—Moscow? Or a Chinese puzzle?

The cops would be there first, he knew—the CIA much later, and never sure, in consequence, of what the cops might have missed. Or sure of anything else, if, as was quite possible, Washington didn't get wind of this event till after a few thousand people had trampled through Sea Life Park on the next morning.

Grove chuckled a little. Then he went out to yell for Jerry.

2

WHITE HOUSE

The careful man smiled as he responded to the President's question.

"That, sir, is information I cannot give you."

"What?" The President said "What?" as if he *meant* "What?" He did.

His sole visitor in the just completed Gold Room, repeated the statement: obviously, the new Chief was a little slow.

There was a pause. Then the President spoke again, calmly but with a sort of anti-calm effect. "Mr. Cagg. You mean that there is information in a federal bureau which cannot—or will not—be given to the President of the United States?"

"Exactly so," Cagg replied.

When he offered no more, the President simply stared at the assistant director of the CIA for a sufficient interval to cause that man soaring discomfort. Cagg thought to amplify. "It—what you just asked of me—is material classified as Zed."

"Zed?"

"Zed." Rollo Cagg realized the new President hadn't been briefed, yet, on "Zed." He undertook the deed. "Prior incumbents of the White House have gladly assented to Zed. That is to say, they've been only too happy, after one of your predecessors set it up, to be *able* not to know about certain—acts—of our outfit. Duties execu—uk—carried out."

"Why?"

Mr. Cagg was finding this very difficult and he did not like any difficulty—at the top, especially. To be sure, the recently inaugurated President was noted for fairness and candor, for his detestation of secrecy in politics, his moral courage, integrity, and blah-blah-blah. But Cagg had presumed that noble reputation was only his "image"—the product of campaign rhetoric. Now, he realized with alarm, there might be truth in it.

He put on a look of strong and patient amiability, one of his best expressions for certain ends. "*Why*, you ask, Mr. President? Simply so the head of the government of this nation can remain peacefully unaware of certain acts—necessary for national security—that we at CIA must be ready to perform—acts that, well, multitudes of our more naïve citizens regard with—say—zero approval. After all, ours is a rather deadly enterprise. Sometimes. And that is why certain minor things need not be known to the White House. Not knowing, the nation's Chief Executive cannot be badgered into embarrassing cover-up efforts by, well, the press, say. Radio and TV. Snooping liberals."

"And my predecessors, as you call them, assented?"

"So far as I know, they were glad to. Certain sorts of information would tend to make them seem—say—as if culpable. Even make them *feel* culpable, if they were dubious about covert policy. And so, ever since the Zed Classification was designed, they all have concurred."

"Which," the President replied in a gentle tone, or one sounding gentle, "explains why Kennedy got caught in the Bay of Pigs sack? And Eisenhower was given the lie on that U2 thing? And why Stevenson, maybe, was double-crossed at UN? Because the CIA got between him and Kennedy? And which may partly indicate why LBJ had his 'credibility gap' trouble?"

Mr. Cagg listened with a scowl. "No, Mr. President. The Zed files relate to matters of far lesser scope. Eliminations of enemy agents—to invent a sample—when they have valuable data and cannot be prevented from carrying it to the enemy by other means. Well, as you say—to 'antagonistic' nations. Operations of that nature, sir." The invented example was unfortunate.

"Murder." The President looked off beyond his visitor into the deeps of his mind, infinite space or merely at the bare treetops outdoors. It was a compellingly effective attitude and completely unconscious. Anyone above the level of cretin would, could and did interpret that faraway look of those greenish-brownish eyes as a sign of immense intellect and also the very visage of justice, patience, boundless courage. Actually, such interpretations were correct.

At last he spoke, almost idly. "There was a car crash last week, I recall, involving people attached to the embassy of a Red-controlled power. Poland? Hungary. On the National Highway, below Alexandria. All four passengers killed. And—if I read an early account accurately—a brief and rather annoyed complaint was made by the Virginia State Police about evidence that somebody—aside from the motorist who first saw the wreck in the woods—and aside, too, from those necrophiles who came up after that—*somebody else,* the police thought, had been at the wreck even before such persons arrived. Somebody who'd rifled pockets and stolen brief cases the embassy said the passengers carried. Somebody who'd gone through all the luggage and, perhaps, finished off one not quite dead victim. That, as I further recall, was later denied by the same State Police. Called, the *Post* reported a 'fantasy of overworked, inexperienced new troopers.' An item, perhaps, now having a Zed Classification?"

"To answer," Cagg murmured, "would be to violate my oath, sir. But if what you have described *were* a CIA bit, and it was not, it might then *be* Zed. The category exists simply to save the Chief Executive from himself. Nerves. Upsets. Nightmares. The very essence of our own occupational hazards. Not knowing certain—counterespionage necessities, say, is one less weight for the man who carries the greatest burden of any man in all time."

"Thanks. *My* problem, however. Not *CIA's."*

Mr. Cagg took that as dismissal and stood. He shook hands with his new Chief and went, which left that Chief alone for some minutes.

Finally, he rose. A tall man and lean: a strider. At a door he paused and then swung it open. Outside were secretaries, Secret Service men and George Doanne. Doanne was usually outside when needed and George was the man the President trusted most of any. He beckoned and, when Doanne was inside, closed the door, staring at his friend for a time before he spoke. Fat, bald, lazy in seeming, Doanne was a brain and a steel arm, a passionate reverer of the new President and a man whose veins ran not with ice water but with lox.

"I just learned the ferrets at CIA have a classified division called Zed. All information in Zed is kept from the President."

George gasped, a rare thing. "You've got to be fooling!"

"Find out about it. Snoop. Talk to the FBI in confidence if that's feasible. And if you don't make progress, speak to Jim Tate, at Justice. Obliquely. For, by Jesus, there are not going to be any secrets the White House, meaning me, isn't allowed to know!"

When, after ten days, George reported no progress, the President was more angry than he remembered being in his entire life. George had established the existence of the category. He'd even had a promise from Cagg's boss, Eaper, to "send over the recent stuff." It was a promise glibly proffered when George said the President had heard of the special files and ordered samples. But nothing came. The CIA stalled. Their computer couldn't locate the storage number, it was claimed. After some further and subtler effort, all to no avail, the President decided to put that problem in his own, very secret file—his mind—for study and hopeful solution. Of course, he could order the Zed files brought to him. But he surmised that if he did so there might be a warehouse fire—or the like.

He arrived at a solution owing to the fact that, some weeks after his talk with Cagg, his plane, White House Alpha, ran into bad weather en route from Boston to Chicago, where the President was due to make a speech for a national convention of communications executives. Chicago was socked in suddenly. Airports nearby were closed too. The smog and snow began to appear in a wall which soon enveloped such vast areas east of Chicago that the pilot, after consulting his most august passenger, sat Alpha down at Buffalo International Airport. Almost immediately it, too, was shut down.

The President had some phoning done. His Chicago speech could be put off to the convention's closing day. It seemed to the President a good idea to use the interval in a way he rarely could: go, that is, to a good hotel and loaf for an afternoon, sleep for a night, breakfast at leisure and, while doing that, skip all but the essential people, guards, gadgets and so forth. He was booked in at the new Cosmos-Plaza and soon got comfortable in his suite—robe, pajamas and everybody else outside, red and gold phones at hand, the Box, too, and a highball even closer. The Secret Service stayed clear of the rooms and even George went off on his own in the cold, the wind and the snow—girl-hunting, the Chief supposed.

He chose a divan and fixed cushions to suit his favorite

posture, feet up, head up, a shambling but comfortable way to read which he hardly dared use in the White House as it looked unpresidential and, even, slightly loutish. Thus set, he began to read the Buffalo *Evening News,* but not its national or international reports—the mere headlines gave a measure of the paper's prejudices, there. He read the local stuff—for fun. And that was how he learned about the thirty-four-hour locking of the main or downtown Buffalo Public Library.

The closing had been ordered by federal authorities, something done a week earlier, or nearly, since the strange event was reflected only in the "Letters" column. And every one of five printed missives on the subject was enraged. Three women and two men were enraged. "Why," a lady asked, "was the library shut, if, as is the official excuse, federal agents were merely looking for a document that *might* be hidden in some book?" The search for it needn't have interfered with regular users of the library, she went on. And why, at the start, she asked, was *force* used? "I, for one, refused to leave and was carried bodily from the Main Reading Room to the outside staircase by a man in no uniform whose credentials I asked for but never saw. It's getting to be like a dictatorship, our once free land."

By the time the President came to the last and longest letter he was both fascinated and indignant himself. For it was clear that this was a CIA thing—clear because so unclear—highhanded and comic, as well, evidently, as a failure, since, as he had seen, "scores of document-hunters quite abruptly left the large and handsome building in a defeated manner."

The last letter was read by the President three times. It was signed by "R. W. Grove" with an address in the hotel where the President now lounged. It began with a vigorous protest against the library closure. It went on to note that if the searchers were, indeed, hunting for a document they would have to hunt through every book in the building. Their numbers, though large to start, and added to hourly, were never great enough even to shake out a third of the volumes on hand, as a simple test and some easy arithmetic made clear. They emerged—Mr. Grove was on Seneca when that happened—"obviously downcast."

It followed that their unfinished search had been called off although incomplete because their mysterious chiefs had found that the so-called document could not have been hidden in the Buffalo Library. It had reached whatever was its intended destination, probably.

Grove continued on the note that, as a man with wide experience in intelligence work, and also as a citizen, patriot and lover of liberty, he was sore. The fumble, he said, had the look of a CIA operation—the miserable look characteristic of that bungle-bureau. It was fascistic and un-American. He had lately become more and more outraged by the secrecy in government and the lack of needed facts which the public suffered. If there had to be a CIA, he went on, it ought to be an organization that was more effective, better understood and more effectively operated by an improved breed of people—not a closed zoo that surfaced only when it flubbed, which was too often and too gruesomely.

All more or less true, the President thought, and sometimes truer than Mr. R. W. Grove knew. He had a warm feeling for the man; and, with a long afternoon ahead, in which he had arranged to loaf, it occurred to him that it might be pleasant to see what this furious gentleman (with "wide" intelligence experience, too) was like. So he picked up the house phone—one he was not supposed to use and that should have been disconnected but had not been.

He asked for Grove and a phone began to ring. Then a very pleasant, deep and easy answer came. "Hello? Grove, here."

The President said he was that and had read Grove's letter. And what was Grove doing, now? Busy?

Mr. Grove proved rather amazing. He said he'd heard the President was in the building. He added that he'd been in Buffalo for two weeks on business and was about to go back to Warsaw, New York, where he lived, when the blizzard began. He seemed unawed by the event—which was puzzling, since few private citizens take a sudden, surprise call from Presidents with instant aplomb. Could Grove come up to 2255? the President asked. For a chat? And would he, perhaps, when he came through the outside guards, try to keep from being a memorable person?

Mr. Grove would, given a few minutes to change his clothes. (Agreed.) Was he right in thinking the President didn't want his guards to recognize him? (He was.) Then, perhaps, he should be a Mr. Tree? (Good.)

"Fellow named Tree coming for a private talk," the

President told his minions. "Old friend. And—by the way—get me a room across the hall. Send him there. I'll be in it. This is one of those old-pal things. Okay?"

A room across the hall and down a bit was arranged. The President moved into it promptly, for he had a hunch about Mr. Grove. In due course the man appeared, knocked and entered, a person reddish of hair, gray-eyed, stooped, with plump cheeks and a Santa Claus potbelly. He was not what the President had hoped for and utterly mystifying to the people on guard duty. But clean of weapons, they ascertained.

The door shut on the two. Mr. Grove had spoken in a tweaky tone. His overcoat, which he'd worn needlessly since he'd not had to go outside, was wet. He'd been in the snow, then. The tall, disappointed President, as he looked at his odd-ball guest, wished he'd not had that hunch. In a minute the wish vanished because the man piped a question! "Not your suite, Mr. President? Plainly! I assume you just took this room to insure privacy? No bugs here? No 'protective' listening gadgets? Am I right?"

"You are."

"So I thought, owing to your word about being careful to make no impression. If you'll pardon me, I interpreted it rather fancifully." Grove walked to the bathroom and remained there for a few minutes. When he reappeared he was another man: brown-haired, broad, erect, wearing a handsomely tailored gray suit and a smile, expansive and heartening. "This is me, sir. I gathered you wanted a very private talk—though I could only guess about your reason."

The President was both astonished and amused. He felt suddenly excited, too. "Your letter in the paper," he began, "suggested a possibility. But first, would you like a drink?" Grove shook his head and watched the President sip a transported highball before he went on. "Tell me who you are, your history in brief and all about your intelligence work."

For nearly an hour, with few interruptions, the President listened; listened to as strange an account of a human life as he'd ever heard of or even read:

> Grove, Ringling Wallenda; age fifty-four; semi-retired; with considerable wealth—several millions.
>
> Born, Sarasota, Florida, Both parents born in Russia.

Father, Igor Grovidnskovsklovi (or something like that). Mother, Ilena Bekovskil, or about that. Father had owned a small traveling circus in Russia before the Red Revolution and was a trapeze and slack-wire performer in his show. Mother, animal trainer. As European Communist regime became increasingly unbearable, the father, mother, family, and their circus in its vans moved across Siberia, giving shows en route and finally went into China—Manchuria.

Three Grove (et cetera) children with troupe, all performers. During the next years (in China and Malaysia) all three died of epidemic diseases and the circus was finally disbanded. Parents reached USA and sought circus work. Their hoarded money and valuables about exhausted when they reached Sarasota, Florida, winter quarters of Barnum and Bailey; they were taken on immediately.

Boy born Sarasota and named for circus czar, Ringling and the Wallendas, famed for high-wire acrobatics. The President remembered them. Young son was educated in Florida during winters, when not on the road. He'd become an acrobat, clown, and aide in his mother's animal acts, also. She performed in side shows—as a snake charmer for some years. At sixteen, Grove entered college; his parents wanted their surviving child well educated. Graduated with engineering degree. Popular at school (not stated but obvious), athletic, and began to develop a hobby, stage magic. Young Grove liked doing magic tricks even better than his circus acts. University of Miami.

Served as infantry officer in Second World War. (Didn't mention decorations but admitted, when asked, field promotions to the rank of major by VE Day. Recruited for postwar intelligence by "Beetle" Smith; the major spoke perfect Russian (parents used it at home) and knew local dialects; also German, learned from circus people. And Italian (the Wallendas). Very valuable work (check if possible to do so without calling attention to Grove) especially in areas behind Soviet lines.

The President was almost speechless as the man went on.

Returned USA late 1948. No funds. Parents dead. No desire to go into circus again. Refused what he called "desk job" in re-formed intelligence, in Washington. Turned his long-time hobby of magic into a professional act and traveled for years as "Zeno the Wizard." (I even *saw* him, in a musical! Wonderful tricks!) Tiring of show business and wanting financial security, Grove moved to a village in New York State (Warsaw).

A friend, an old circus performer, lived there and had built a small factory nearby to manufacture joke toys and party gags, the most profitable of which, he'd written Grove, was a cigar that did not explode, but once well lighted, poured forth a roomful of black, harmless smoke, astounding in its sudden volume.

Grove had gone to the village in western New York State to see his friend, a man crippled by his big-top act years before. Grove was, if anything, ingenious. He did not much care for his friend's callow products but he did, on that first visit, suggest a few novelties that were produced and made a profit. In time, Grove bought a house in Warsaw. He liked the Northern summers and the unusually hospitable spirit of its people. He became a partner of the factory owner; his fertile mind originated an endless series of games and toys and jokes which were a success and (the President first inferred and then certified, as he thought of the toy series lately presented to his grandnephews and grandnieces) the firm, by then, Grove, Inc., had pioneered in toys and games that did not involve the violence which had always been anathema to Grove, on TV, and as advertised products for young kids.

"Grove Games" were now available everywhere and their inventor had achieved the security he'd longed for—many times over. He spent winters in South Miami, still. The firm's founder had died years ago.

Grove had never married—a regretted admission—for his love for children and young people was great. Questions showed he had contributed to children's welfare organizations and his homes, north or south, were, the President gathered, kid-swarmed. The man had even run away with himself a little in talking about young America, its needs, lacks, narrow and inadequate education, alienation from nature, and its hopefulness.

Grove was also a physical fitness buff who went so

far as to assert any man up to age seventy ought to be able to do a back flip or walk on his fingertips, feats he demonstrated, with quiet ease.

All the rest of that interval the man and the man's past beguiled the Chief Executive. He lay awake till late telling himself that, unique as Grove was, all human beings are unique. Yet he couldn't dismiss casually what he'd heard and seen. Pictures ran like movies from the entrance to the exit of his guest and his use of the bathroom again to emerge as the fat, reddish-haired, high-voiced nonentity in a still-damp overcoat who toddled down the hall tossing idiotic salutes, to the disdain and unspoken amazement of Secret Service men. Presidents don't ordinarily spend half an afternoon with such a jerk—old friend, old classmate or whatever.

Grove had done it though the Chief faked a slight embarrassment when he went back to his suite. The house phone, he then found, with a grin, had been cut off: *no more whimsical calls allowed*. He had dined with several Buffalo notables and excused himself early. But even reading didn't stop his memories of the afternoon: not even the work of his favorite essayist, Joseph Wood Krutch, whose books he read and reread, keeping one always at hand. The clear, rhythmic and acutely perceptive prose blurred. Time after time he saw, not print, but Cagg, telling him about the Zed Classification. And the self-consciously elegant décor of his suite turned into a room down the hall and a man doing a somesault in the air, who landed without a palpable thud.

A man who had suggested, after that was in order, a means by which he and the President would communicate, secretly. One who, if he were checked out (by very devious means), might volunteer for the task the President had in mind.

Should such an enterprise be suggested to *any* person, he wondered—when it might lead to death—and an unseen obit in Zed?

While snow buried Buffalo and spread white camouflage on the filthy ice of Lake Erie the President debated what he so much desired, so truly felt he needed, and was so reluctant to define even to himself.

A *personal spy,* he finally acknowledged, *whose target would be the CIA.*

At last, tired, his conscience still hurting, he told himself that Grove, after all, would decide for or against, granted the mission materialized.

Then the President slept.

Three weeks later, as arranged, the President took a rather rare early morning walk, trailed by Secret Service men, of course. It was a cold and dull day. The Chief Executive wore an overcoat and carried a newspaper. It appeared to be a bother to his arm swing so, as he came up to a trash can, he tossed it away.

The parade went on and his tagging guard didn't think of retrieving the cast-away newspaper. But a man who looked unlike the real Grove, and nothing like the Grove who'd visited the room in the Buffalo hotel, came up, by and by. He plucked out the *Post*. He did not open it till he had returned to his big brick house on the hills above Warsaw. There he found seven sheets in the presidential handwriting—between some added pages of notes for a speech.

The next time the President took his walk in the direction of the first paper-dropping, he noticed that somebody, kids, likely, had spilled a daub of white paint on the trash can he'd used to dispose of the paper. The daub had a shape vaguely like a fish. But with feelers, or antennae, where the blob ran down in two streaks. Nobody else gave attention to that trivial result of seeming vandalism —which might not even have been that, anyhow; pigeons could have produced the same effect.

After he saw the white blotch the President relaxed, in a way.

Grove was going to try.

3

AXE

The room was twenty-six stories under the ground, in Maryland, not far from the Baltimore-Washington Expressway. The earth's surface above the buried building was tree-covered. Beyond it stood another government edifice with a parking yard, all in plain view. The parking yard was large enough for a bomber take-off and had been used for that (occasionally, at night).

Thousands of people turned off the expressway to their jobs in the visible structure. The route was well marked by signs, saying: *Federal Computer and Computer-Computer Building*. Its employee horde used those big and bizarre machines to collate data on the citizens of USA, all the data available to all governing bodies, to all corporations and credit bureaus, to nearly all sources that had data on people, true or hearsay—checking and then cross-checking the mass of material so its sum could be put on easily retrievable microtape.

This monstrous place wasn't related to the one deep beneath the adjacent woods except in one way. The FCCC building was entered from three ramps, at three levels. Banks of elevators took myriads up and also down. Of those arrivals who went down, many boarded tram cars that conveyed them to the subterranean edifice. So the Computer and Computer-Computer building had not only a data-processing and data-storing function but it was a blind, serving as the major entrance to the buried and equally huge structure. That fact was supposed to be secret. And of the morning people who went up or down, none cared to mentioned that many went deeper down and then elsewhere: to do so was to risk losing one's job, or worse. The so-called "moho-scraper" was thus kept secret from the general public, at least.

Such, then, was the location and nature of the headquarters of the CIA, or Combined Information Authority. In a big room on its twenty-sixth floor *down* (and the last but one) sat the director, Arthur Xavier Eaper, a man of medium height and weight, white-haired, but not from advanced age. Almost everything else about him save the snowy hair was average. His eyes, for example, were not blue, yet not quite gray and certainly not hazel. They were the color of gristle and had an empty look, as do so many eyes of that uninteresting tint. His left thumb was missing but a prothesis made so excellent a replacement that few knew of the loss.

His age was fifty-nine. He was a pin-stripe addict and a chronic attaché-case carrier. His feet were small. He wore loafers in the office, handmade, British and black. At home, alone, he preferred elkhide slippers. His nose was his only superb organ: Roman, thin to near cutting edge and small of nostril. His eyebrows were heavy and black, a cosmetic effect, perhaps. (Or had he admired the looks of Warren Gamaliel Harding, as some asked but no one knew?)

He had graduated from Harvard, Columbia and MIT—a Bachelor of Arts, an M.A. in languages and a Ph.D. in physics. He spoke eleven languages; six like a native, the other five, well enough to pass if he were not interrogated at length. He had risen to deputy administrator in the OSS (Office of Search and Security) after the Second War. He had missed out in Korea owing to a five-year bout with skin trouble—a period he'd used to advance special forms of knowledge and esoteric skills, in a planned manner and for a purposeful end; to gain the post he now held.

His desk was huge, a kneehole type, anything but executive-nude. Upon it were many objects—a cigarette box, several ash trays, three sacks of Bull Durham and a gold holder for cigarette paper (he rolled his own), along with at least twenty mementos of his past: thumbscrews from Dachau, a human eyeball in a decanter of alcohol, a scalp—red hair and female—with the rest. Many had two functions and only one of them was to distress visitors.

The room, forty by thirty feet, had been carpeted from wall to wall in blocked-red nylon and the walls, a dilute shade of that hue, were bare as walls of an operating room. The lighting was indirect and bright at the time because the administrator (or director) was reading. As he read he often clucked with disapproval. The book, entitled *The Cadmium Caper,* had been compared by critics to the works of the late author of the James Bond stories. Arthur Xavier Eaper disagreed, and, being the top American exponent of the same trade, he may have been right and the reviewers wrong.

He sat in a beat-up swivel chair on a thin cushion of foam rubber covered with the belly-hide of an oryx. There was one more nearby chair, across the desk, for a visitor—a rather heavy article of oak. It bore some resemblance to the conventional electric chair but was more comfortable and lacked, of course, visible electrodes. Beyond the grim souvenirs on his side of the desk was a bank of buttons and another of lights. On his side, also, were certain levers and control knobs not visible from a visitor's angle.

Now, as the director read, a light glowed. Arthur X. Eaper was in the middle of a passage about an effort of the agent-hero to escape pursuit on a glacier, aided by vacuum cups handmade while he'd been captive in a secret Red cave, one hundred and eleven feet below Lake Lucerne. He did not see the light.

Ten seconds passed.

A chime sounded.

"Nuts!" said the director. He pressed (unnumbered but memorized) button fifty-four. A drawer slid toward him at his right and he dropped the book into it, on top of three others of a similar sort. The drawer slid back of its own will, in three seconds and without a sound, coming or going. Eaper pressed another button in another series; these were pink.

Now the office intercom was operational and he growled, "Whicket?"

"Yes, sir. Sorry to disturb you. We're having a bit of a problem. Chap here insists on seeing you. Got to Seventeen Purple on his own."

"Good God!"

"Seems to know the routine, up to that point. Colonel Garboyle's on duty at Seventeen purple. Holding, there."

The administrator, or Axe, was vexed. "Who the hell is he?"

"We aren't sure. Checking in CX. Says to tell you his name and you'll see him."

Suddenly the director's voice froze. "I am *waiting,*

Whicket, for the *name*. Any reason to withhold the only essential information?"

"No, sir." But the outer office hesitated before it went on, anxiously. "He calls himself Mobile MacB. Forrest. Has a card to that effect, engraved by Tiffany." A description began to flow, nervously.

Abruptly, the administrator was glad of his assistant's verbosity. Had Whicket not talked on, he might have ordered the invader tossed out. But the interval reminded him of an incident he rarely recalled and then only with chagrin: the time when he'd been holed up behind the Russian lines, as Berlin was about to fall—holed up in Schrekdamham, as it had then been. Now it was Leninskovosk. He vividly recalled the accursed, vacant brewery where he'd gone to ground—with the NKVD hot on the trail and Soviet Naval Intelligence (Skisvovkolt) only blocks away, besides: a house-to-house search. *Doomed.*

It had been *that* man, code name Mobile MacB. Forrest, who'd gotten Eaper out. His real name had been—*what?* Something related to trees, of course. Woods? Thicket? No. "Whicket" had suggested that. Which brought him back to the open line:

"Give me five minutes for a decision. And skip the checking. I know him. And I do not believe he is a playboy." "Playboy," naturally, referred to "enemy agent," which made it possible to discuss certain people in public with an easy disguise of lascivious looks and robust guffaws.

"Check and out, sir."

Eaper rocked back in the swivel chair and remembered, much against his wish.

The dank stone emptiness and the smell of mildew, the rotting wood and spider webs came clear from long ago. Oglethorpe coming in—through the storm sewer route, reporting that the search had reached Goering Plaza—and then falling dead, aware, certainly, while he'd reported, of the lethal hatpin that had been fired from an air pistol into his back. *You know we French stormed Ratisbon.* It had been Eaper's thought at the moment of the chap's death and he prided himself in that. But not the rest.

Forrest—Mobile MacB. Forrest—what the hell *was* his

real name?—had crashed through the front doors—in a Soviet truck!

Eaper shuddered, remembering.

It was like an explosion—that roar of engine and scream of burst portals. He could see the vehicle now—a beat-up, two-ton Zotz loaded with four huge hogsheads. And this—damn it!—Grove, right! *Grove!*—at the wheel . . . alone. He could even remember the words on the truck's body, printed in battered cyrillic. The Russian escaped him but not the translation.

People's Soft Drink Cooperative
Giantgorsk, Rostov-on-Don

Trembling, he recalled how nearly he had bit down on his suicide capsule, sure the wrenched-open door meant capture. But that Grove fellow had yelled in time. "Hold it, Pop! I'm taking you out!"

He had leaped from the cab after the shout, dragging scuba-like gear he'd stolen from the Soviet naval base at Pleek, stolen from the cruiser *Stalin,* in fact. (How the hell did he even board her? Eaper had never asked. And there had been little enough time, then or later.)

The man, always a happy-looking type, had explained swiftly: "I'm on my way to the Luxembourg Soft Drink World Fair. Russia is exhibiting some stuff—orange pop and lemon, also cider—to show off the Soviet victory spirit. You'll ride in a barrel, with the breathing gear. Papers are all set. I'll nail you in while we get clear of this hellhole and let you out again—till we approach the border. Nail you back in when we're near the checkpoint. Okay?"

Dazed, Eaper had still functioned. Another matter for self-congratulation. "You mean, I'll be in a hogshead of cider? Orange pop? With Soviet frogman gear? But, man, when we stop, I'll bubble!"

"Sure All four barrels will bubble! We'll go out near Ponz, two hundred-odd kilometers from here. I'll explain to the muzhiks about the trip; and about breakdowns, and the result: the whole cargo fermenting. It'll be hilarious!"

"My God!" He recalled saying that, or the equivalent.

Grove hardly noticed. He was already dragging Oglethorpe's body toward a long-unused vat, wooden and rotted. He lifted the corpse and threw it in. No splash or rat squeal followed. Weeks later Eaper realized Grove had picked up and tossed, literally, a dead, 185-pound man into an empty beer vat higher then he was.

"Hop in!" Grove had thus easily and swiftly disposed of the fifth best man they'd placed behind Red lines.

Still, Eaper had hesitated. Grove understood and smiled!

"They're two streets away: NKVD, in civvies," he said. "Navy lurking too. But they all might as well wear uniforms. Got any better idea?"

So Eaper had clambered aboard the truck and been helped into a hogshead three quarters full of what smelled like rotten apples (and was, in part). The lid came down, a hammer whacked and soon the motor revved up, missing a few beats. The truck backed and rattled on cobblestone streets, still loudly fecund of dangerous engine sounds: of skipping, par for USSR vehicles.

He was let out when they reached an empty plain as immense as the sea. There was plenty of such unused and weedy terrain in the People's Paradise.

He emerged sticky, soaked, stinking and shivering with cold. He passed that night on the truck bed: rusty steel. Toward dawn, and after two tire changes, Grove put him back in the oversize barrel, topped it off from a muddy stream, and checked out his passenger for the critical events to come.

The Russian gear was unfamiliar but Eaper managed to use it, with Grove's help.

As he remembered the next part, the director rose to walk about the bare, red-hued room, not stepping on certain areas of carpet with the automatic precision of long habit. *That ride!* The temporary frontier was reached after a thousand years he'd spent gargling in mud and water with a rotten apple flavor. But now the other three casks, like his own, were hissing, burping and glugging—their seams open and the chemical Grove had added working with gassy effectiveness.

At the border, it was "hilarious": for the Soviet guards, at least; and, possibly, even for Grove, who'd predicted that condition.

Eaper couldn't hear the words but he dimly caught some of the soldierly laughter. And he shook as the casks were rapped.

It was, as Grove had prophesied, a successful gambit. Nothing that outrageous could surprise the soldiers, not even the idea that Stalin, or somebody near Stalin, had decided to make a premature victory gesture by sending vats of soft drink to a Luxembourg fiesta.

That the cargo had been en route too long, owing to the ricketiness of the conveyance, and was now fermenting, was also accepted and even condoned as a usual mishap. The fermenting of the fruit juices would, moreover, disqualify them as "soft drinks"; but one expected such trials. The border guards were sure, too, the truck would never make that far-off and only vaguely recognized and soon forgotten country. But maybe, they said, by this time, the load might be potable? Like hard cider? Would the driver let him have a sample?

If they liked, Grove said. But at their risk, he added. Because there had been a preservative in the stuff which had somehow failed to prevent fermentation. It might be a toxic thing, for all he knew, since it plainly was a mistake. Besides, he had something a bit better; safer by far. Eaper hadn't noticed a smaller cask in the truck, one made for nails, presumably, but half full of vodka now. Grove suggested it; his sly camouflage was complimented. His authenticity as a Soviet citizen was now complete. The keg was sampled and appropriated after Grove, who had a pronounced Don Cossack accent, got one shot.

He had argued for a while. The truck went on when he lost. For some miles, distant artillery could be heard.

An hour passed before Grove dared unnail his colleague, who by then had mere minutes of air left. Unable to stand, vomiting apple-scented muck, Eaper finally saw a British jeep there, waiting. That was the worst bit of all: two British officers *not* laughing, at a visible cost similar to the paroxysms of angina pectoris. And he had two more days of travel before he was able to bathe.

Yes, he remembered "Mobile MacB. Forrest."

As seldom as possible.

The Bank C light went on—Amber in Ten.

Grove would be in Holding Two, then: Ringling Wallenda Grove. R. W. Grove—which rang another bell: a name seen in the past five—six years. R. W. Grove Products? Stock Exchange? No. Newspaper ads? Eaper got it: *Grove Games.* He pressed through to Whicket and looked up at the bare, pale rose wall he faced. On it, suddenly and from no discernible source, an image was projected, along with shining words in flowing type.

The image was of a skeleton—Grove's—with what additional, opaque items he wore and had in his pockets—keys, the eyes for laces on his shoes, a fly zipper, bill clip and buttons. The words ran along, name first, and finally:

X ray clear—not chemical-sensor-positive—radiation nilnormal—any further?

Eaper signaled to bring the man in.

Grove came smiling—always had grinned, the fool, Eaper mused; wore a cheerful expression in the worst times. Wide-apart, gray eyes made the smile, mainly. He had broader shoulders than Eaper remembered; looked pretty young for—mid-fifties—in good condition, smooth walk, and not quite a fool, either. Grove's eyes took in the bare room swiftly, fixed on the visitor's chair a split second and glanced from it to Eaper with an increased smile. Mocking? Eaper wondered. Perhaps so. A devil of a hard guy to euchre into a serious state of mind, Eaper recollected. Full of fun; and the hotter it got, the merrier he grew: the hotter or colder.

"Well, well . . . !" Eaper put on his second-best welcome face.

"Tutti-frutti," Grove said.

Eaper's response was automatic. "Beeman's."

"Nabisco."

"ZuZu."

"Trade and Mark Smith."

"Katzenjammer Kids."

They laughed, Grove with real amusement; they shook hands, taking care to do it gently.

"Hell, friend, it's good for sore eyes!"

Grove chuckled. "Happened to be in DC and thought of you. I've thought of you often, lately, in fact."

"Take the electric chair." Eaper still played the game. But what did Grove want, since he'd been thinking of CIA's chief? Eaper sat as his guest did and his geniality, or his feigning of it, diminished like a receding taillight: a job, probably. The old boys get sentimental; get to wanting to try their hand again. Dated and obsolete, all the old lads who'd retired.

"You did damn well, getting—as far as you managed before you were stopped."

"Seventeen Purple?" Grove laughed.

Eaper flinched but not, he decided, visibly. "That's classified, Ring. It evidently leaked. We'll have to change."

Grove watched as Eaper slid cigarette papers from a tooled leather box and separated them. He rolled the excess tissues into pellets and snapped them at the floor. One bounced under the desk and stopped on Grove's side. Another followed. With a third, in a lifelong and vain way, Eaper made, one-handed, a cigarette—tobacco-sack string in his teeth, cowboy style, eyes above, wary, annoyed, as he put a kitchen match to the final product. Grove patiently waited out the exhibition and then explained.

"No leak, Art. Got it from Thinbutter."

Thinbutter was Army: four stars and due to be one of the chiefs of staff, next month. If Grove knew the general, he, Axe, had better be careful. "Glad to hear it. Like to keep our—entrances and exists—as Shakespeare had it—in the family. Shifting Seventeen Purple would louse us up for a while." He added, "You look fit."

Grove reached for a pocket. Eaper reached for a paper knife and toyed with it while Grove got out a pack of Chesterfields: regular. He lit one with a Zippo, which had been checked *as* a Zippo. He blew smoke and eyed his one-time colleague.

"I'm fine, Art." The use of that truncated first name irritated the director. He hadn't heard it from anyone but the President, lately. But he took it with a graceful expression, in order to end this soon but urbanely. "What can we do for you, Ring?"

The other man studied his Chesterfield in, apparently, unconscious imitation of Eaper's scrutiny of his now-shedding homemade butt. "Well—nothing, perhaps."

"Friendly call? Dam' decent of you! Like a drink?"

"Thanks. No." Grove seemed unhurried. He smoked. Eaper did, too, being gingerly with his remnant and worrying behind his unworried look; noting, however, that Grove's suit was custom-made, as was his shirt. He recalled more of Grove's singular history: the circus parents; his language skills; others, odder. But he didn't have any use for the man, he felt, not probing into that, much.

"You—retired? Living up there at—what is it—in western New York State?"

"Warsaw. Yes. Much of the time. Have a South Miami place too. Not exactly retired. I own a small, you'd call it, manufacturing business. Quit the stage magician trek years back."

Eaper recalled that period—spoke of it, hiding his disdain.

"I know you're busy," Grove finally said. "Or should be, in seeming. Guy runs a thing like CIA must at least fake being busy. Though I remember your saying, oh, during the time we had to kill, waiting, before that Bandol bit—'44, was it?—that the bigger job a true executive held, the more time he should have for his personal interests; his pastimes or hobbies or even a nap. Sign of good organization, you said."

Eaper didn't remember any such statement. But he nodded. What came to mind was an endless wait during a cold mistral in a cowshed overlooking the Mediterranean. What Grove said he'd stated gave a fairly good posture. "Right," he murmured.

"Kind of reverse Gresham's Law," Grove grinned. "As Tintetta Pollack would say."

Eaper was discomfited by "Tintetta Pollack." That was the name of the heroine of the book he'd been reading, *The Cadmium Caper*. And his copy was an advance one; so Grove, too, arranged to get spy yarns, prepublication. He couldn't have known what Eaper was doing when interrupted. But Grove knew a great deal about Eaper's eccentricities, the habits that hadn't changed over the years, at any rate. A pretty cute guess, he decided, and he tried to figure out a connection between Gresham's Law and the lady spy whose sexual "sacrifices" so intensely preoccupied the—exceedingly explicit—spinster author. They discussed fictional espionage for a few professional, and so, very amused, minutes.

"However," Grove went on, his humorous glow fading into a sleepy-eyed shimmer, "I didn't drop by to reminisce, sell anything, covet imaginary females in books or borrow money. I merely—well—wondered, say, if, perhaps—with the world the way it is—you could use an old duffer who, once—"

There it was, as feared and anticipated; as feared, because Eaper owed this avuncular-looking man a debt: his life, and not once but three times, minimally, with only a single pay-back, when he'd gotten Korslivsky just as the Ruskki was about to blast a clip at Grove.

But he did not want Grove in the "shop"; his word, shop; because, he suddenly saw, Grove could tell many a true tale that would not advantage the director, if Grove would tell—though, on reflection, he rather felt Grove was not that sort of boy. The risk, however trivial, remained: a motive concealing any possible other motives.

He began his usual talk for this situation, one that sounded like a tape recording. Appreciation of patriotism. Measureless value to his country of past efforts. *Past* efforts. And so on, topic by topic.

The finale sounded regretful.

It wasn't 1942 any more. Or '48. The business of information gathering had changed. Cloak and dagger stuff was now a minor factor. And where it had to be used, it was highly mechanized and technical, demanding young men, with the reflexes of youth and years of training behind them.

A disarming smile, and the demonstration followed. From Grove's standpoint that was quite vivid, although scarcely unexpected. He saw Eaper tap with his letter opener—not, as hitherto, on the desk blotter—but against a cigarette box, lightly. With that, a tremendous, instant glare blinded him for a second; he thought the room then went dark and knew, later, that was so. In the glare or dark came a whooshing sound, a stir of air, a hushed thud—and everything returned to normal. Grove blinked away the strobe-light dazzle. Eaper was where he'd been, smiling with apology and saying, "For illustration." But his voice now came through a loudspeaker. He reached out with the letter opener and tapped a glass barrier, then a pen set.

A sound came next, an ear-bursting scream that seemed to emerge at Grove's brow level. He jumped. The act was involuntary and automatic but it would have interrupted any hostile move on his part for long enough to allow Eaper time to do whatever Eaper might have in mind. The strobelike flash had been identical in its effect. Even a man who could draw a weapon at record speed would falter in either situation. Even a man with the cool of a Grove would freeze or flinch briefly.

Grove's first reaction was anger. Eaper had been a gadget buff in the OSS days but Grove had mistrusted automated devices and relied, as far as he could, on his own faculties and abilities. As a scientist, a man entitled to be called "doctor," and as an inventor of harmless toys and games, he could imagine the mechanical resources of people now in Eaper's employ.

He realized Eaper was talking, then—and still through a loudspeaker. "Between us is a bulletproof wall. It descends in three tenths of a second. I am now shielded and could, touching appropriate studs, paralyze you, knock you out for a predetermined time, and, of course, kill you. The chair, desk and shield, among other, up-to-date devices, have those capabilities. Sorry to throw a scare into you. But it's the quickest means of showing the differences between old and present—call them, tricks of the trade."

Grove's anger was useful in a long-perfected fashion. His eyes continued to glow amiably. His mouth half smiled. He gave an oboe chuckle and with a slightly trembling hand again produced his pack of Chesterfields. In trying to take one, he dropped it on the blood-red carpet. He glanced, then, at Eaper, who nodded to permit retrieval.

The act put Grove's hand briefly out of the administrator's sight. Or presumably did, he thought. Grove's cigarette had fallen within inches of one of the tissue pellets Eaper had rolled and flipped, part of his trademark—a dexterity he did not display outside secure areas; his home, and his office if no one, or only "X-cleared" persons, were present to impress.

Grove swiftly picked up the pellet and snapped it toward Eaper's feet on the other side of the desk, a sleight-of-hand trick very simple for a professional magician. The tiny wad stopped at Eaper's loafer sole, proving the director's instant glass barricade did not cover the kneehole.

Grove grinned as he pretended to fumble momentarily over the dropped Chesterfield: Eaper's self-protective device was flawed. Any would-be assassin allowed to recover a dropped cigarette, dropped glasses or whatever would have access to the director's legs.

That discovery took two or three seconds. Grove straightened up, lit the Chesterfield and continued to fake a tremor, which increased Eaper's pleasure. A vase was moved, and the glass barricade whooshed away as the loudspeaker was cut out.

"I'm trying to explain—"

Grove nodded. "Made your point! Very ingenious!" He frowned quizzically. "Ever needed to *use* these—devices?"

"So far, three times." Eaper's vanity led him to explain.

"One lunatic—in my own outfit. Next, a colonel, who wanted G2 to sit over CIA. I merely pacified those two. But Bulganov got in here—as an American electronic wizard with some devices he claimed would be of interest to me—and, in a sense, one was. He had a mergator."

Seeing his old colleague's bafflement, Eaper used a patronizing tone. "A plastic thing. A no-show on the X ray and other sensors. He was unrecognizable, give him that! Almost managed to activate the merg when I set the light on. It's a thing firing a needle loaded with aconitine. Lethal. Having seen him produce the merg, I decided Bulganov had to go. He was in your chair and he died in seven seconds."

"Marvelous." Grove made a mental note: Bulganov was dead; and a welcome riddance.

Eaper nodded. "Be a rather dramatic scene in my memoirs. Eh?"

"When you can publish a next volume, you bet! Incidentally, I greatly enjoyed your latest. All three, in fact. By far the most authoritative personal accounts of intelligence work." To that, Eaper bowed.

Grove's mission was now complete. He dallied, however, to conceal his sudden and keen interest in learning that Eaper was still keeping his ultra-secret diaries from which, when clearance was feasible, he produced his conceited and abominably written "true tales" of espionage. In them, he was the sole hero. All others were less clever and resourceful. The masterpieces, in sum, were incomplete, and inaccurate.

Eaper had grown restless by the time his visitor rose, apologized, admitted that modern "black" work was too complex for him, and departed—with a souvenir: a replica of an NKVD "death dart," solid silver, bearing an engraved note stating that the original had been taken from an enemy agent by Arthur Xavier Eaper on August 9, 1944.

Eaper had evidently forgotten it was Grove who'd thrown Arvlov after a furious fight and Grove who'd used his special skills to grab Arvlov's dart, on that August afternoon in Lvov. Grove it was, too, who'd turned it over to the OSS for study: entrusting it to Eaper, as a matter of fact.

4

HAWAII

Arthur Eaper's residence was in Virginia, near the Potomac River and not far from George Washington's birthplace. The house, however, in no way resembled the colonial mansion of that great gentleman and active admirer of females. It was a modern edifice. There were no windows on the first floor. Those on the floor above were large, horizontal and set high. The director's offices and bedroom would be there, Grove guessed when he carefully surveyed the place from the side of a fairly well traveled road. Eaper liked windows, when they were safe to have. Bulletproof, Grove was certain, of the ones he studied.

Around the building lay a peculiar landscape: lawns that undulated gently and contained several free-form fish-ponds: Eaper liked fish, too. Was one, nearly, Grove thought. The area of mowed grass and shining ponds was considerable—perhaps twenty acres—giving, of course, a clear field of fire. He could not see any machine guns (and probably, mortars, gas-shell cannon, etc.) but he could see where they were doubtless mounted, on the roof and beneath certain green hillocks.

It looked difficult, by day.

At night, however, with a fairly powerful telescope, it seemed easier; easier, because Grove chose a Sunday night for his survey—and Sunday night was the time Eaper had routinely used, in the distant past, for dictating his diary. The diary consisted of notes on the major happenings of the prior week, dictated to a tape recorder nowadays, Grove presumed; it had been a dictating machine in the OSS years.

A tree would help, Grove thought, after another night of surveillance. There were thick hardwoods of adequate growth just beyond a picnic area on the main road nearby.

Grove selected and climbed the most likely tree. His study of the times when lights went on and off in the very "functional" residence made him certain of the room in which Eaper did his Sunday night recording. The tree, however, wasn't quite high enough. He could see the far wall of the room where his man apparently worked along with part of some chairs and a collection of framed citations, awards, what not. He was disappointed. He'd be obliged to erect a tower if he wanted to look straight at the Axe.

He mused on ways and means as he perched on the highest crotch steady enough for scrutiny. Then he noticed a slim and slanted reflection of movement, of a person, that reached him from one of the largest framed awards, honorary degrees, or the like.

Some time afterward, a mustached man with a limp was allowed into the administrator's home. The man had been inspecting neighboring mansions in behalf of the American Fire Underwriters Brotherhood. Eaper's staff had become aware and reported the fact. The man was to be admitted, they were told, and his study would not be out of bounds: Eaper would prepare it.

The inspector showed his badge in a few days and began an expert room-to-room survey of electrical equipment. A butler, so claiming, accompanied the underwriters' expert until a ruckus outside took him away. He was sure the man was bona fide, by then; he had made fairly sure by inquiries among neighbors before then.

Several hogs, it now seemed, had escaped from a broken-down truck and were rushing about the baize-smooth Eaper lawn. They had to be rounded up. Two, moreover, were wallowing in a fishpond; acting crazed, so the butler was told. Grove listened to that and nodded vague understanding, absorbed in checking electrical outlets, wiring, circuit breakers and related matters.

The butler hurried out and Grove moved into the study, hoping he hadn't overdosed the pigs with LSD. And hoping the time-release device on the rear end of the "broken-down truck" wouldn't be noticed while he was busy in the Eaper house.

He gave the director's study a general survey and no more. The desk was bare and its drawers were certainly locked. The tape recorder was on a table at its side—without tape. Grove knew that the vault where Eaper's weekly notes were stored could be found behind a tidy panel opposite the entrance: a good safe, beyond doubt—purchased by the taxpayers (like the house and the landscaping—or its lack). He paid no heed. What concerned him was the arrangement of framed documents on the wall opposite the oddly high windows. The light had been such that, from his tree and with his telescope, he'd been unable to read these treasures of vanity.

He was slightly surprised to find his goal was an engraved, large scroll presented to Eaper by the International Game Fish Association in recognition of the man's "near miss" of a world-record tarpon catch. He took the thing down and withdrew from an inner-thigh sheath of foam rubber (a hiding place detectable by a stripped search, and only then by trained personnel) a small Aerosol container. Swiftly, he sprayed the glass and then wiped the traces from its frame. He replaced it, after gluing a long strip of wood to the upper, rear edge of the molding, altering the angle at which the trophy hung. The difference was not noticeable. Grove had been relieved to find that the wall awards were not often or perhaps ever changed; the rectangle behind this and associated objects was slightly darker than the beige wall itself.

When the butler returned, the inspector was finishing up his chore in a guest bedroom. The two parted amicably. As he drove off, however, Grove noted in his rear-view mirror that the butler, doubtless a karate expert (and other things), was writing down his license number. That made him glad he'd taken the trouble not only to duplicate one of the underwriters' Chevys but to borrow the license plates of a real car of the organization, one he located in a Baltimore garage, awaiting repairs.

He now hid the car in a tunnel, long unused, as the railroad tracks formerly above it had been taken away years ago. Next he recovered and drove off the truck that had carried the drugged hogs. Later he replaced the borrowed license plates.

None of these efforts was ever to become known.

For he next several Sunday evenings he climbed his chosen tree. After reaching a perch (modified for comfort) he pulled up a very powerful telescope. That, he fixed to a stable arm already attached to a tree limb. Then he watched. He knew, of course, that in these modern times a man like Eaper would have a device that probably could hear and see all for some part of the distance, nearly a mile, over which he merely peered. But a mile was too sound-loaded for such metal ears and too full of tree and traffic motion for electric eyes.

Grove was satisfied with his obsolete technique of distant survey. He had learned shorthand in high school in Sarasota. Besides which, he was an expert lip reader as all OSS men at his level had once been trained to be.

Through his scope he could clearly see a reflected Eaper. The spray he'd used to treat the glass on the IGFA "award" intensified its mirror-like capability. The wooden prop he'd glued behind the frame made its angle perfect.

Thus, for a series of Sundays—Eaper missed only one—Grove sat in a tree and copied what he lip-read as Eaper dictated careful notes on his principal acts and those of all major CIA departments. Moreover, Grove could and did, also, transcribe Eaper's muttered comments on that amazing data, as well as his intruded plans, intentions, comments, oaths and his memos on highly placed persons, usually uncomplimentary.

Even a man as sanguine as Grove would find himself startled by those discoveries. The CIA was engaged in operations that were unknown to the State Department, unheard of in the Pentagon, often contrary to the policies of both, and, of course, completely secret in so far as Congress, the Cabinet, other security bodies and even the President were concerned. Eaper was playing Supreme Ruler.

One matter, especially, bemused Grove. It appeared in the third week of surveillance as a mere trifle, surrounded by Eaper impatience.

"Callubon, in Area Limbo Six, concerned with offshore Soviet fishing vessels, especially in Upper Two."

The next week, "Callubon" was mentioned again, along with "Upper Two."

Eaper told his recorder, "Sent Billiger to Upper Two. Think Callubon's anxiety is deliberately provoked and has nothing to do with Neptune One, save as diversion. Soviets not as foolish as original report implies. Sure that if there's anything in Neptune One idea, diversive acts will be major. Like the fishing ships—watch C reports. Top One, Middle Eight, Nine and perhaps Seven the only reasonable areas, providing Neptune One is not a rumor—floated also to misdirect us. Me, mainly. I know Solentor. Tricky. Will increase guarded watch in areas noted and wait. If our info real, Neptune One not slated till early days in January of a second year. Ample time. Hawaii—scrub—Upper Two, worst possible site for Nep. One, if a big deal is planned. Pearl Harbor command is vigilant now. Radar tops. Hydryphonic watch at Two in process of planning. Kauai Range operational. No threat of rumored magnitude conceivable, that area. In my view, whole plan only a hazy drift of planted snow from (unreliable—question mark—) Anna Al and Carla TG. Wish Ball's bints weren't inherited when I took over. Dangerous. Unstable. Purchasable. Easy marks for false suggestion."

More came in the following weeks.

There was, for example, another "shaky report" from a "bint" that, sometime in January—a year from the next one—something would "begin" at "park." A meeting, apparently. Any evening, early in the month.

A few other details set Grove thinking hard. After many tree sessions, Grove acted. He was among the pedestrians who watched the President take his occasional morning stroll—his word. Reporters trotted to keep up. The disguised Grove, as seen in Buffalo, sat on a bench eating an apple.

The President made no sign of recognition.

However, three days later he retrieved a felt hat "somebody" had lost in the White House grounds. He turned it over to nearby Secret Service men, none of whom saw him slip a folded, thin bit of tissue from under the sweat band. "New hat," he grinned as he handed it over. "Might fit one of you boys."

The guard who took the hat muttered, "You're not supposed to pick up things, Mr. President. Might explode. Poison you."

Everybody laughed: the man was new on the job.

Grove never learned exactly how the President got off the telegram. It came a week after the "lost hat" incident and so a week after the President had read Grove's summary of his findings, with Grove's suggestions. They filled three pages, microtyped on tissue, both sides, which the President had read with a magnifying glass, after chemically bringing out the invisible ink. That had been an extreme precaution. But the Secret Service men might have seen the report first and might not have assumed the apparently blank tissue had been used by the hat owner to reduce a size too large for his head. What he'd learned about Eaper made the President wary. Eaper had men in the Secret Service, for one thing.

The wire to Grove said, merely, "Endless thanks. Yes. Go. Do. My blessing."

Grove soon left for "a year in Europe," as far as his friends and business associates knew or ever learned. Mail came to them from there—France mostly. He phoned them, now and then, from abroad. At least, a "secretary" with a French accent put him on the line. And he gave interviews to the press, occasionally, in France and twice in London. It was an effort that distressed Grove.

He had flown to Hawaii after getting the President's signal and bought and rebuilt the house near Sea Life Park. When it was ready he'd done a bit of devious smuggling to complete the furnishing. And he had enjoyed a very pleasant year—save for the actual trips to England, France (and, once, Yugoslavia) where he again gave newspaper interviews and made phone calls. It was a tiring thing, especially the flights back to Honolulu, from Paris via Beirut, Calcutta, Bangkok and Tokyo, a backward route taken to conceal his destination, Hawaii.

Occasionally a special letter came to Grove, handwritten, adroitly posted and not on White House stationery. These missives kept Grove up to date on Eaper's dictating. Another man, suggested by Grove, was now maintaining the telescopic, lip-reading vigil in the tree. These communications indicated that the President was both enraged, almost cosmically enraged, by Eaper's activities but, also, far too fascinated to stop Eaper's ploys . . . yet. Nothing of much interest had appeared on Project Neptune. However, the President arranged, at Grove's urging, a system for future communications less liable to interruption than direct mail.

Grove's year was perfect, save for the essential flights to other lands. He hated every interruption of his Hawaiian idyl, his pleasures in a growing group of friends, his gang of kids, his enjoyment of the halcyon weather and the beauty of the islands. He shared the "aloha spirit" which was very real on his windward side of Oahu though it had become commercialized in the Honolulu area.

Jenny, the huge but graceful, middle-aged but beautiful housekeeper took care of his wants, coming and going six days a week. The ground floor, however, was out of bounds for the Hawaiian lady. Grove had workrooms there but when he was not at work he often forgot the purposes of those rooms, forgot their odd contents, and became unmindful of other matters such as bulletproof glass at one place, and soundproofing, everywhere: soundproofing, to quench various odd noises made by animals, but not by domestic species.

5

QUANDARIES

It began to rain in Sea Life Park—without a beginning, which often happens in the state of Hawaii. First, it was not raining and the park glittered in the dark under the scattered beads called stars. Then it was pouring and white, pounding cliffs enclosed the little world of everybody caught out, including, at this moment, the park watchman, Jerry Gong, and a park visitor in a great, round building in which a body half floated. Grove looked across the gently murling surface of the Reef Tank and beyond its roof: speculatively, Jerry thought.

Grove turned back and said, "Lucky."

Deliberately, Jerry allowed faint suspicion to form on his brow: no sense in feigning complete trust of this man, though he was a friend of the Abbotts.

"Lucky for them," Grove added. "Or him. The killer, I mean. Killers. Rain washes out evidence. If they left any."

Jerry nodded. He had examined the body as much as was wise. "I've got to go call the police. Would you—?"

"Sure." Grove lightly hoisted himself onto the outer wall of the super-aquarium to sit, Jerry realized, in plain sight while he went out and used the phone. From that act Jerry could be sure that Grove was not going near the body. But Grove could have had the opportunity for that prior to yelling. He wondered why that notion had entered his head. Grove certainly could not have been the killer. Theoretically, yes, Jerry realized; but actually? He was sure . . . not.

He went quickly to put in three phone calls.

Jonathan Kitrick was first to arrive. He had been on patrol in a prowl car with its blue roof light turned out, creeping along Laumilo, Kalanianaole, several connecting streets and into the labyrinth between the main highway and the pleated mountains. It was a new thing, this police patrol, set up because some few of the local teenagers had commenced to rob the residences along Waimanalo Beach. The policeman received the murder news in coded words, drove the mile and odd to the park, siren searing, roof light a deep cobalt revolving in the skidding rain. He stopped hard, ran to the Reef Tank and recognized Grove. . . .

"Jerry?" the cop asked.

"Still phoning. Honolulu chief, I believe."

"Good!" Kitrick had merely glanced at the partly floating figure. "This is a Honolulu matter. Homicide."

"At least."

The policeman stared down at Grove, for he was six-seven, thin as wire, as hard, and about as full of love for man as he seemed empty of any quality save an electric tenseness. Kitrick was a displaced Yankee, third generation in Hawaii and the one white cop on Waimanalo's small force.

"At least?" He was puzzled by that remark.

Grove nodded pensively, looking at the dead figure. "Kind of costume you don't see around here, isn't it? Mainland type, just arrived, maybe. FBI, then?"

Kitrick walked over then and peered. Presently he pulled a monstrous flashlight from beneath his dripping slicker, aimed it and moved it about. "Maybe you're right. What's the story?"

Grove gave it in six sentences. He could summarize as tersely as any Yankee, first generation or thrice removed. He, too, was a professional but with far more experience in such reports than the local cop's.

The rain stopped. Both men now could see Jerry, still on the phone. Kitrick said, "Ungunh." Meaning, Grove interpreted, What the hell. He ventured to explain further.

"After alerting your people, Jerry must have called Honolulu. Next, I'd think, the Abbotts. *Maybe.* And then, the FBI—if he didn't tell Honolulu to do that."

The thin-harsh, deadpan face of the officer suddenly became a smile—one the world generally had felt compelled to share. "Jerry's quite a boy."

"Yes."

Jerry came out of the glass booth at that moment and called up, "The circus is on the way. I'll remove the driveway chains. Some of those people could turn in and flip over one, way they handle cars." He added, as he mounted his bike, names of those he'd alerted.

"Abbotts?"

Jerry called back. "No. Tack's in Washington. Sapphire gets up at six on school days. No need to bother her now—and plenty of time, before the morning mob arrives."

Sirens began to echo among the black escarpments of Makapuu Point. Beam-up headlamps swung into the park, sashaying on the final curve. The law was arriving in force. Honolulu's police chief, a large and largely Japanese man named Hosea Ikkyo, was among the first. The last was Warren Coy, FBI. The sequence took some of the zest out of the drama since Grove was obliged to repeat this account of events four times, with his biography, false, in part, but false by omission.

R. K. Grove seemed very near the name of an earlier R. W. Grove. The slight change of an initial was his idea of a disguise. To disappear, he'd found, it was best to move only a few blocks, change your name slightly—and dye your hair just a few shades. The nearer you cling to what you were the better the effect; because the pursuit will expect gross alterations, hunt other cities, and usually dismiss a visible, somewhat similar man with a similar name. That will seem coincidence.

Grove had proven his formula, often.

The Waimanalo police, soon in the background, gave Grove a complimentary bill. Chief Ikkyo obviously felt that since Grove was permitted to roam at night in Sea Life Park by the Abbotts he must be reliable. Also, the man was rich and exceedingly popular, even beloved—facts conveyed by the local officers in asides.

The FBI man was unimpressed, however.

Coy, a vain individual, also felt a need to exhibit his superior methods. "Your business, Mr. Grove?"

"Retired, mostly."

"The rest?"

"Oh, I own a factory on the mainland."

"Reason for moving here."

Grove waved at the now-clear night. Warren Coy followed the wave and frowned. "Own stock in the park?"

"Wasn't what I meant. But—yes."

"What the devil *did* you mean?"

"I came here, Coy, for the banal reason that Hawaii is a wonderful place to live."

"Mind being searched?" Coy didn't like to be called Coy by anybody he ranked.

Grove smiled. "Any citizen would."

"Suppose I insist? After all, you, and you alone, have a direct connection with this murder."

"Visual only. You'd need a writ. Or—need to claim I'm a suspicious character."

"*Your* claim might be grounds enough—that you merely saw the dead man." Coy was angry now, and had, Grove thought, possibly been born that way. Coy, moreover, was genuinely upset by the situation owing to causes not stated by him but easily adduced by Grove: the FBI man knew, or suspected, that there was more to this killing than the police had realized. "Ever been fingerprinted?" Coy demanded.

Chief Ikkyo and several specialists from homicide were examining the body which now lay on the concrete floor. Coy's tone was hardly proper as procedure unless its object was to panic a probably guilty person.

Grove kept smiling, however. He moved toward the FBI man before he replied. "Fingerprinted? Hasn't everybody? Quit making like God."

Too late, Grove realized he had overreacted. Out of practice, he thought—unforgivable. Still, he forgave himself. There was that about Warren Coy which repelled him—an Eaper-like quality, not physical but overly official and so, as if omniscient.

Coy now grabbed Grove's aloha shirt. His later explanation was that the other had moved "threateningly."

The rude grab was an error. Chief Ikkyo said sharply, "Lay off, Mr. Coy. He's okay."

Grove later, and with technical truth, said the grab was an unprovoked assault. Grove was not under arrest. Coy was simply showing off—and with no sense of hazard; he stood five-eleven and was thirty-five years old, in standard FBI condition, with standard training, while Grove was inches shorter and two decades older.

Under those circumstances, he confidently grabbed a handful of the shirt of the allegedly "resisting" man. "Drastic," he was to admit later, "but sometimes a little roughness, early in the game, gets the best results."

And it *did* get results.

Behind Coy was the wall around the aquarium, high enough to prevent kids from falling in. Warren Coy had grabbed the shirt with the intent of shaking its wearer, a simple scare measure. He pushed Grove backward and then hauled him forward, intending to continue the moves. But on the inward course the pattern changed. The old man crouched; his shirt tore free. Then ensued a sort of blast, with Grove the agent and Coy the object. The object rose in the air, pivoted on the rim of the wall and splashed into the tank. Grove grinned as the startled police—and he—were doused. The water was about four feet deep where Coy landed so he was able to find footing. He did and bellowed, "Hold that man!"

Nobody budged. Nobody wanted to miss Coy's part in the show.

This was viewed silently until Ikkyo began to laugh in a high, thin way. Coy charged back toward the wall but stopped, just as he reached it—stopped cold, stunned and somehow horrified. Then he howled.

No architect, engineer or park employee had anticipated the Reef Tank's use as a wading pool by unauthorized persons. Not one of the millions of visitors had fallen over the wall. Those who did enter had requisite knowledge; but there is nothing about spiny echinoderms in the FBI training program.

Coy yelled, or, accurately, screamed. Pale, shaken, in agony but trying not to panic, he was helped over the wall. "Thank God there's a doctor here!" he gasped, eying the medical examiner who had been summoned by the Honolulu police. "Get a tourniquet on me! A sea snake bit me!"

Grove said loudly, "No snakes here. Probably you stepped on a starfish." He sounded very unsympathetic as he peered over the wall and added, "It was a starfish. You tipped the damn thing over. Luckily it's not a lethal critter. Exceedingly painful, I know."

The tired-looking doctor examined the wound. Coy ground his teeth audibly in an attempt to contain his agony—and rage—or both. A really nice try, Grove had to admit, but not a success. Unable to keep his teeth clenched, Coy screamed again and rolled his eyes interestingly. Several pinpricks on his sole were rapidly causing the foot to swell as a ruddy and then purplish aura spread from them. Coy's eyes continued to roll up till the whites showed, only. He passed out.

Kitrick, back from a park search, had the decency and speed to catch the man. The Honolulu chief, barely able to speak between high and banjo-like bursts of mirth, faced

Grove, pointing, to clarify his intent. "Go home. Go get drunk. Find a girl. Anything. We'll take a statement, tomorrow, if we need more."

Grove insisted on being searched, as Coy had demanded. Ikkyo obliged but when Grove said, looking ruefully at the sodden Coy as he came back to consciousness and pain, "I should have chucked him somewhere else," the pent-up mirth of officialdom gave way. The Reef Tank reverberated and fish darted about in alarm. Coy alone failed to join the laughter.

It would rain again soon, Grove saw, as he crossed the bridge to the entrance plaza.

He went down broad steps to the public walk and on toward his parked motorcycle. Jerry overtook him, however, and jerked his head. Grove followed and the watchman took him to a minor path where he stopped and beamed his flashlight on something at the side: a lei of wilted ylang-ylang blossoms, a lei broken apart. The perfume was pervasive, alluring, mnemonic—to Grove.

The night watchman eyed Grove carefully, then picked up the lei, raised the lid of a refuse can and dropped in the yellow, lavishly scented garland.

"Nobody else," he said aggrievedly, "was interested."

"No?"

"So some dame lost, or threw away, her lei. So who can get fingerprints off flowers? Five to ten thousand people were here today. Meaning yesterday. And a thousand had leis? Dames, guys, kids? So what if ylang-ylang leis are rare?"

"Well?"

Jerry shrugged. "Guess I must be losing my grip. I *did* have a feeling—that *you* had a feeling—"

"Yeah. Took me back. Had a place, once, with a tree in the yard. Brazil." Grove yawned. "Kind of a rugged night. I'm whipped."

The watchman's sense that Mr. Grove had reacted to the first mention of the flowers in a more meaningful way than this wasn't quite erased. Jerry filed it and changed the subject. "I'll go see Mrs. Abbott if the chief okays it."

"I'll tell her, if you like, Jerry. Or go with you. After all, she's got to know and she'll want to get word to Tack. Reporters will nail him in Washington."

"It won't be good publicity for the park," Jerry replied somberly.

Grove stared. "Are you out of your mind? They'll storm the place!"

Then Jerry laughed. "*People!* You sometimes forget how they are!"

"You *sometimes*," Grove replied, "can't properly guess, when you *do* remember 'how people are.' "

"So right! Well, *I'll* tell Sapphire since I'm on duty still, and you're beat."

Grove nodded and moved again toward his cycle; he straddled it and stood that way, looking east. A low light would soon appear over the Pacific, faint warrant for what was coming: the sun.

And with that thought, an answer came to a misty question he'd had no time to examine for answer in the past hours.

Dawn. And ylang-ylang.

Bangkok—Jerry had hit that place on the nose, by chance.

The *Temple* of the Dawn! Wat Arun; Grove remembered.

And as he rode away he recalled vividly Mavis Hampton wanting to watch the sun rise, with him, from that near obelisk. Mavis, wanting more—wanting to see him fall, crumpling and spinning, down those hundreds of feet of narrow stone steps that were as near vertical as is possible for a staircase.

Mavis Hampton, he almost spoke the name—alias Francine LaMer, and born Navna Kvolsk—a vital detail he'd learned long after that gaudy gidget had come so near to getting her two wishes granted. For it had not been Grove (then Robert L. Bush) who'd made the arcing, thudding, bone-cracking and blood-spattering tumble down the vertiginous stone stairway. The one who did was Nikolai Rolski, a great loss to the OGPU. But Mavis had seen that dawn, after all: it had taken the Thai fire department to get her back from the gallery at the summit.

Nikolai, presumed to be a White Russian refugee, was not the first man, or even the first lover, to have slipped or been pushed from that lofty temple, that near needle in the Marco Polo skyline of Bangkok. And the firemen plainly believed that the lady hadn't pushed the deceased: her shock was too genuine to be faked by a murderess. But her poor state, as Grove had known in the end, was real enough, though not due to what the Thai police presumed.

Her employers would exact an unthinkable price for her failure and, by it, the loss of Rolski.

Was it in . . . '46 Or before?

From back then to *now?* he asked himself. *Still* in business? And still a woman who could put a trained agent in the way of sudden death?

He rode on slowly, cutting to the highway shoulder to permit an ambulance to pass—one that would take Coy to a hospital or, it might be, collect another corpse in Grove's carcass-spangled record.

He was still thinking of Mavis when he turned in at his garage, dismounted, pushed his cycle inside, relocked the doors and removed certain accessories from the vehicle. It was growing lighter, though he did not notice. His mind was busy with details of an old relationship—with memories of Mavis. He thought of her apartment, overlooking the Chao Phraya River; her pet cat; and the exquisite Siamese maids who served her. She had a manservant, too, a battered and menacing former Thai "boxer," which was the nastiest of sports, Grove had felt then. There was, also, Mavis' child—whom he'd never seen but had heard, once or twice.

A girl, he'd gathered; her daughter, he'd imagined, who well might grow up to inherit, or acquire, her mother's duplicity and also her special taste for ylang-ylang blossoms, since, Grove suddenly realized, they might have a neat use. In lands where they would not be flaunted by every doxy on the street, as advertisements, a woman wearing them would be identifiable. Shipped anywhere by air, now, they would mark their wearer's presence in pitch-darkness and without a sound from or the sight of their wearer.

Grove reflected on that in a self-deprecatory way as he crossed to and unlocked his front doors. He ought to have realized, at the critical time, the purpose of Mavis' ylang-ylang penchant. He scanned the room beyond the last door. Things looked okay. He used more keys and stowed the auxiliary items he'd removed from his motorcycle in their regular and accessible place: on a shelf behind some books and a panel behind them.

He ought to have got onto the flower sign.

It was lucky, indeed, that when he'd found Mavis' passionate embrace tended to edge them both along the wall atop the high tower, he'd been sufficiently alert to use what knowledge he did possess. Kissed girls close their eyes and some men do. But one who entertains, however reluctantly and slightly, a sudden sense that he is being both kissed and maneuvered toward a very hazardous spot should take care to keep open a slit of eye. That way, he can notice if his inamorata also slightly cracks open her lids and possibly has done so to make sure her lover is blinded by her behavior—and its immediate promise. Certain of that, however then mistaken, she can glance away briefly at something, which, if she does so, will indicate that she is not, perhaps, about to arrange herself gracefully on a stone floor hundreds of feet above the ground and reward her escort totally even if unconventionally, as here, in the exotic capital of what used to be called Siam. A furtively caught eye-shift may thus suggest to a lover that he is not about to be wrestling for love, or even with her, but with a nameless and hitherto unsuspected person, surely male, an enemy and no doubt muscular.

You have to watch things, he mused, crossing his living room and settling in a comfortable red leather chair, then reaching for a cigar. The staircases of the Temple of the Dawn had been built, he recalled, to supply a very risky penance for sinners against an ancient creed.

You have to watch things, he repeated.

And *smell* them analytically, too, this revelation added.

He sighed as he took the cigar from a humidor and unwrapped its foil cover. But his sigh became a faint grin even before he lifted a handsome lighter and dialed it to flame. Cigar, foil and briquet were, *apparently*, just that. And all three were just that.

"Opportunities" Eaper would regard as overlooked.

And certain others, also—hopefully.

Grove's gaze went from the first ghost of smoke to the innocent telephone stand and the flameless humidor, at hand with a Directory, beneath, in which, if one looked, one would find listed the CIA and a number; but no address.

The *cunning* of it, he thought, chuckling as he turned to the night's event.

The question now became, who'd be first to call?

Eaper's boys? FBI? Police? Or the others?

The next new question was, when? Its answer seemed to be, soon.

For the game had begun with a vengeance—a literal vengeance. What sort of game?

Chess? Go? With Russian or Chinese players? Grove was bad at games, even checkers. So, whatever game they chose, he'd have to play it his way: by ear, so to speak; and by the hand that's quicker than the eye.

Until now, he had "heard" nothing, he reflected. And even now, he had gained no inkling about Project Neptune—what it might be or where—or even if it existed. He was to continue in that ignorance for a long and often worrisome time.

6

SEARCH

Grove smoked his cigar till his fingers were hot; he stubbed it out, then, and lit another. For some while he went over the preparations made in the period since he'd come to Hawaii—come here on what, till this moment, had increasingly seemed a false lead and might still be that. The preparations he now considered were many. . . .

Grove's house was very close to the high-tide line; it furnished spectacular views of the sea and the nearby islands and, opposite, of the mountains. It was a two-story house; but the upper level alone rose above the grounds. The entire floor below was visible from the ocean side only, and windowless from there. It was walled with glass on the rear, and its several rooms could be entered by sliding glass doors. All of the chambers were equipped for the special hobbies and the business of the owner: a carpentry shop, metal-working room, another for chemical experiment and a larger one fitted out as a gymnasium. At one end of the house, on that lower level, a glass-roofed conservatory had been added and in it grew a collection of tropical plants, some, rare specimens that had been present on the islands before the Polynesians arrived—then the Europeans, serving God or seeking whales—the people who had brought the alien vegetation which had by now almost wiped out earlier and indigenous flora.

At the end of the house opposite the conservatory a shed stood, part of the original structure and meant for boats; but Grove had no boat and the lean-to contained odds and ends: discarded boxes, stored cartons and trunks and half-completed toys that had been intended for his business on the mainland but abandoned as unsuitable or set aside for alteration. Among them was a box of many-colored plastic pieces in as many shapes, intended as a do-it-yourself kit, with which youngsters could make their own mobiles. It was a good idea that Grove had set aside because it was based on Calder's originals. He'd forwarded the toy version to the artist.

The glass-walled lower floor was separated by a flagged walk and flower beds from a little cliff of stone cut long before by a then-deeper sea. That gap was spanned at one place by a bridge with wooden sides. Entrance to the upper floor was gained that way; but tall palms on both sides of the bridge largely concealed the miniature canyon and the glass walls and doors. This feature had amused Grove. When he'd first perceived it, he'd thought of Eaper. With such a facility, Axe would have turned the walk into an automated drawbridge. Grove, of course, had no such intention.

The garage was as close to the Kalan as law permitted, with room for three cars and three electric doors. It could be entered from the house by way of the street or the bridge. Grove had added concealed staircases and a tunnel as a third means of passage between his residence and his vehicles.

All other changes were as well-hidden as the accesses to his tunnel. Some alterations had been expensive and were novel. Of them, several had been devised and installed by Grove. They were not what Eaper might have dreamed up; but Grove was, after all, a master of theatrical illusions—who could make live girls in gilded costumes vanish—or saw them in half—and materialize them, too, from thin air.

The grounds were beautifully planted and tended by a distant relative of his daytime housekeeper-cook, Jenny. A wall surrounded the property. It had a street-side gate. Local people understood the barrier—as protection against a rising tide of teen-age vandalism. Inward-slanting wires topped its cement blocks. The high wall concealed the property from anybody—save men on power lines, or people discourteous enough to bring up and mount ladders and, of course, any people who climbed on the steep pali, across the Kalan—a thing very few considered; the dark, step pyramid rises were of a crumbly consistency.

Certain of Grove's possessions had arrived at night in small boats that made blacked-out trips from very large ones. The customs authorities were unaware of such imports. A few technicians had helped in the final phases of reconstruction—and returned to their widely scattered mainland homes, well paid by an obviously eccentric yet very amiable employer.

But Grove's home and his grounds were thought, in Waimanalo, to be the most open and accessible of any among the "cottages" of wealthy haoles—luxury mansionettes built on this windward side of Oahu for summer migration to the cool trades which the mountains blocked from Honolulu residents, rich or poor. The idea that Grove's ménage might be sinister would have been laughed at. And, once the work was done and the furnishing complete, Grove reinforced that concept by acts he thoroughly enjoyed. He became, in effect, the neighborhood uncle.

Scores of youngsters found that Grove not only liked kids but that he operated a part-time playground where you could learn a thousand things, such as how to walk on your hands, or juggle plates, or how to make like an acrobat—both on outdoor equipment and, when it rained, in a real gym.

He also lent fascinating books to everybody and didn't complain if they came back battered, or even if they never came back. He could tell wonderful stories, too; stories about wild animals and ghost stories that never left children actually scared, as well as true stories about people you still saw on TV, like Shirley Temple, long since grown up, and W. C. Fields, who was dead. But there were some kinds of stories he didn't tell.

Once Allan Mitsua, who had the features and skin color of a Japanese boy but red hair and blue eyes, asked Mr. Grove if he knew any spy stories. He said he didn't. And he told no war stories, either.

There were other things, too—kind things—that Mr. Grove did or was believed to have done, in Waimanalo and nearby. Things like the money that came by mail to the mother of a boy in his "gang"—a poor family who lived in the Hawaiian Homelands and didn't have a father. Mr. Grove never admitted doing such things; but they hadn't happened till he came to Hawaii.

There were a few special rules, however, and they were dutifully obeyed. Kids could come on any Monday, Wednesday or Friday, after school; and all morning Saturday—except when he was away, which he'd usually tell them about well ahead, and the other times when he ran up a blue pennant on his flagpole, under the American flag. That meant he wasn't to be disturbed. But it happened rarely.

Adults, too, found Grove a community asset, his suspected fiscal benefactions aside. He was willing, half the time and on short notice, to baby-sit. He got several boys out of trouble with the cops. He was a miraculous swimming teacher. He could even teach babies under three to swim. And at parties he often performed magic tricks. Even with ordinary playing cards, he could read minds. He taught many of his tricks to his gang, too.

And Mr. Grove took lessons himself—in Hawaiian and in Japanese. He studied Hawaiian with Miss Noe—Noe Roberts who taught history at Punaho and was a very pretty blonde; he studied Japanese with Mrs. Josephine Okuma, a widow who had been Miss Hawaii before she was married. The two ladies seemed slightly jealous of each other; but only slightly, Hawaii being Hawaii.

It was, then, a kindly and popular man who, at the moment, had fallen asleep in a chair, in a house on the beach where he'd lived for more than a year. And he was, in fact, precisely as generous and affectionate as he . . . deadly.

Three simultaneous events woke Grove.

The sun had cleared the Pacific, staggered into a ragged array of low clouds, climbed free and reached the point at which its rays, tropic-bright and very hot, pierced the oddly thick glass that protected his lanai, the local word for porch, and blazed on Grove's eyelids.

Smoke was rising from a slowly smoldering carpet at his feet—after an hour's endeavor by the red rim of combustion to do something really big with the fire-resistant material. It managed only to make a fume concentration thick enough to bother a sleeping, middle-aged man.

And chimes of a certain sort and sequence announced that somebody was outside the main gate, wanting in.

Grove woke and slowly gathered the nature of that trio of small torments. A fire extinguisher, fetched from the kitchen, did for the ambitious embers—and did nothing for the rug.

Merely getting up had solved the sun-smiting.

Grove opened the doors to the lanai after turning up the air conditioner. That promised to remove the smoke.

"I must," he said to himself, in a not unusual way, "get a better-smelling type of carpet."

Next he crossed the room and blew in the mouthpiece of

an old-fashioned speaking tube, waited, blew again and finally got a startled but firm reaction. "Oddie, FBI," a voice announced.

"Five minutes," Grove called back.

"This is official, Mr. Grove."

"You alone?"

"I am. Do I need guards?"

"No. But I need to finish my—ah—morning's morning."

"Oh. Then make it snappy as you can." The voice seemed amused. "Morning's morning!" Oddie's grandfather had used that one.

Grove stretched and went to a bathroom off a short hall. "Typical," he muttered, seeing his face in the cabinet mirror. He opened a window, washed, flushed the toilet and went to the floor below where he arranged a few things. He came upstairs calmly in three minutes and flushed the toilet again. He pocketed two toilet accessories.

Nothing in the present situation surprised him. He often fell asleep when very tired, in a chair, sometimes, and with a lighted cigar, occasionally. The results had, on several occasions, come almost as near to costing him his life as any other experience. Nothing to do about that, he had learned.

Grove possessed no faculty for setting a hypothetical alarm clock in his brain that would awaken him on the prearranged dot. He never woke up with an instant, ready-for-anything vitality. Following sleep, he would be somewhat feeble, a bit dull, not very ready to think about anything and probably not up to doing much, even under the greatest pressure. He could not, however, think of Oddie as a great pressure. He had taken pains to look over the local FBI head, long ago, and he had the man's measure, he felt.

Oddie was the embodied ideal of the Founder—a J. Edgar Hoover dream boy: nice, courteous and Christian; a YMCA athlete and religious service leader; a scoutmaster and an accountant. He was also a lawyer and handsome, in the square, empty, regular-profiled manner of male shirt models. He was top, or near it, in amateur squash. (Was there a professional sort of squash? Grove had marveled at the blank.) An A-one man, further, with a teacup, or a bridge hand, a vaulting pole (college, that was), gun, knife and whatever fast-draw dinguses were used in the FBI, currently. And dedicated. To the excessive degree of not being, so far, anyhow, married; dedicated over and above duty's call. Grove was a hard man to amaze; Oddie had come close.

At one period during Grove's covert watch, Oddie, disguised as a tourist, spent eleven successive nights at the Frisbie Tahitian show.

One of the Frisbie dancers, a girl named Maunamauna, aged sixteen, had become very much attracted to the mustached, fez-wearing Shriner from Valley City, North Dakota. The girl picked him, night after night, as her partner in the hula "lesson," an audience-participation event which broke up the spectators. The Dakota delegate (whose cheeks weren't really as fleshy as they seemed or abdomen as Masonic) studiously tried to be as inept as the other aging, overweight victims. But he improved—at first, perhaps, to maintain his role. Later, however, the lovely lass and her innate lasciviousness affected Oddie. His "hula"—and Maunamauna's—became wilder and very intimate: she had a banner-bright thing for him and he began to catch it.

Duty compelled Pilford Oddie to bear up. The FBI was close to a loss of face provoked by a lovely, licentious and plainly delinquent juvenile when, on the eleventh night, Oddie arrested sixth most wanted man, "Croke" Davis. He never again visited that night club or got in touch with the briefly bereft damsel. Grove had asked the lass.

Such was the devotion of the man now at the gate. Grove pondered the phenomenon with disapproval as he began undoing locks. He crossed the wooden bridge without glancing down, used another key and opened the gate—on Oddie, and two added but unannounced FBI associates, both Christian types.

"Well," Grove said, "come in."

Oddie had meant to. "I was just pushing your bell when my friends happened by." He smiled vigorously.

Grove merely nodded and led them toward the house. They didn't even realize they were crossing a bridge; all three were closely watching their host. "Been asleep," Grove said as he reached the first of his double front doors and sorted keys. "Glad to have you aboard. You're Oddie, local head, I believe? But—the other two?"

The Bureau chief held up the group to introduce them. "Porter Hollis and Dexter Mult." Both extra G-men (as Grove thought of them) looked their part: shaved, neat, eyes not quite blue enough, smiles like pasties, handshakes fierce—and both, ten pounds underweight for innocent citizens of their height. They were also professionally inconspicuous, even anti-conspicuous-looking, as if they had attained their job limit, in banking, say: tellers, whose computerized appraisal warranted no further promotion but whose rut-status elicited from others not so much sympathy as hazed vexation.

Grove, smiling happily, repeated, "Come in! Come in!" and swung the outer door.

"Lead the way, sir!" Oddie invited.

That was expected but Grove seemed not to know it. (If possible, you keep your enemy out front.) The three men followed, tensing a bit as Grove reached into a pocket—relaxing when he produced a small round mirror and a comb. He halted, trying to organize the tangle of his thickish, wavy hair. He could see by the stratagem that all three gave long, hard scrutiny to his many locks. And afterward, all three traded what were smiles and presumed private: the locks would be pie, if a time came.

As they entered the living room Hollis muttered, "Smoke in here, Chief."

Grove now employed the ruse of a stage magician whose illusion seems to have failed: an assumed embarrassment. The audience accepts it as an acknowledgment of blunder. Then the real trick is done—with doubled impact. He pointed at the yard-wide, sodden hole in his carpet. "Fell asleep. Dropped my cigar. Woke me up—the fire. Just moments before you gentlemen—"

"—barged in," Oddie finished. "Sorry."

"You'd like some coffee? I haven't had breakfast—"

The two subordinates eyed Oddie with the anxiety of people offered wine by a Borgia. Grove waved them toward chairs and indicated a door. "Kitchen, in there."

Oddie's mind went pocketa-pocketa. "See here, Grove," he said pleasantly. "Why not let Mult do the coffee bit while we get on with our talk? Though I take it you have a servant?"

"Not here. Day off." Grove looked uncomfortable. "I'll gladly have the java; kttchen's a bit of a mess. And I usually have cornflakes—" A wistful note, there.

Two and a half jaws dropped, Oddie having made the superior showing. Here sat a rumpled, ordinary man of middle age in a dirty, torn sports shirt, wrinkled slacks, and no socks, one who had red-rimmed eyes and needed a shave, but was trying to be hospitable—in spite of everything. This foggily genial character owned a quite large house on expensive property that was protected by a system of locks that a clumsy burglar ought to be able to pick with a bobby pin. He'd combed his semi-silver hair with a mirror about a half century out of date and a comb that lacked several teeth. A man just wakened, who had found a murder victim hours before, wanted cornflakes, for God's sake, and was, Oddie had been informed . . .

Ringling Wallenda Grove. Not R.K., as his mailbox said. The legendary Grove!

For a moment Oddie believed this fuzzy-looking codger had to be an imposter. The idea crashed across his mind so forcefully that he compelled himself to compare, mentally, the photographs of the famous agent with this older face. The wide-apart eyes checked. Here was the high forehead, the slightly snubbed but not stubby nose, the broad mouth, usually smiling, and the deep and delighted voice, all noted in the records. Exceedingly powerful but not large hands—Oddie could not be sure of the power element. Nor, so far, of a tendency to use them with great dexterity. Breadth of shoulder and thickness of body giving illusion of shorter person than an actual five-ten and three quarters. That, too, applied. Oddie, however, was still unable to believe the man now slumped in a leather chair had ever heard a shot fired in anger, not to mention broken into the Kremlin and committed robbery . . . among other things related by old-timers after a beer or two.

Mult went toward the kitchen, with instructions from Grove, who then smiled at the chief. "How'd you learn, so fast?"

Oddie, still on the verge of certainty he had made some sort of damaging blunder, gulped in relief. He answered, "Prints. Satellite."

Grove laughed heartily. "Be damned! Where'd you take 'em?"

"Handle and thumb latch of your gate. Ten minutes after you got home last night. Bounced them over this morning." He gave that restricted information out of grateful relaxation.

At that same moment, Grove's brain began to work properly. This dream boat was too perfect; nobody could be that near to ideal FBI type. But a good *actor* could, even probably would, overplay this role owing to his experience of public expectations. He was amazed he hadn't thought of it before; Oddie was an our-side double agent; a federal hermaphrodite; a trained impersonator; a much more informed person than Grove had hitherto assumed, among his additional qualifications. It took very little more time for Grove to contrive a test of his hunch.

"Satellite! For heaven's sake!" He seemed awe-stricken. "But—*why?* I was the first to find that body—whoever it is. Was. Ohhh! The throw? *That* set you off? Coy annoyed me, but I shouldn't have reacted. Out of practice."

Oddie was nodding. "The toss you gave Coy. Incidentally, Coy's ready to apologize. He lost his temper. Disgrace to the Bureau! He'll be back in Records for a year, at the least!"

"I'm the one who should apologize. I baited your man. And he had no idea of—my—well—past—"

"Very decent of you to take that attitude."

"What other? I'll write a note to that effect to your Top." Oddie again nodded with appreciation and Hollis almost beamed. Coy was his best friend.

Grove went on, brushing their thanks away in order to express a childish fascination. "Am I right, now? You got my prints and rushed them to Honolulu? Sent them via satellite to Washington—and got back the answer so fast you could be at my door in—"

Oddie wished he hadn't mentioned the print-sender even by inference. "Things are very swift—mechanized—nowadays."

"I know." Grove was humble. But he asked, absently and soon, "Which plant sent back the dope?"

"Eh?" Oddie wasn't sure what Grove meant.

"High or low?"

Grove seemed not to watch the FBI man. His eyes went out toward the brilliant morning. But he still saw what he had evoked: not so much a change in Oddie's color or in his facial expression as that less conspicuous thing—a subcutaneous effort to prevent surface alteration—a passage of spark-fast near nothing, as if Oddie's skull had gripped the muscles and capillaries that covered bone, to stop any shift in the external flesh. Only one who had learned the same control could discern it—a sort of non-effect.

Oddie was quite good at it—and quick, afterward. "I'm afraid I don't get you." Tone also correct, Grove noted.

Score one for me, he thought, before proceeding with his own, equally demanding charade.

"Hell, man! My obsolescence is showing! In the old days the OSS often worked with the FBI. Delivering messages, for instance—a poor analogue for the satellite bit, I must say. We called both outfits shops, plants, factories, what not. The Bureau was 'high'; we were 'low'—being 'underground.' "

He thought Oddie might check that—and get lost because it was almost true. And he did not want the other man to realize he had found him out: Oddie was FBI *and* CIA—wherefore more CIA than FBI. *What a cover!* Chitchat, he felt, was now in order: a quasi-official sort, related to the body in the Reef Tank. Grove began making not quite bright queries and Oddie fenced—in a patronizing way.

Mult came in with the coffee and served it before bringing another tray—of cornflakes: the box, cream in its waxed container, bowl, spoon, and a cup of sugar. The G-man set the second tray on the table beside Grove with a stare of revolted incredulity. He would have had the same expression if he'd been ordered to prepare and serve stewed toads.

Grove thanked him and Oddie said, "Let's get on with our business."

"If there's any." Grove smiled and poured cream.

"Maybe not. I'll be succinct and direct. First, why are you here?"

"I told Coy. The same reason all people have. It's a great place to live."

"You are not, Mr. Grove, by any chance—meddling?"

"Meddling?" Grove stopped heaping on sugar. *"Meddling?* In what, for pity's sake?"

"We thought it odd that you happened to be first to find—well—one of the CIA's people, in that tank, after you'd hung around the park, so long, so often."

Grove almost dropped his spoon. "You mean it actually *was—"*

"We'll skip the identity. Let's just say, it *was*, and not who. Did you, perhaps, expect it? *Something? Anything?"*

Grove looked at the man with a baffled expression. "What in the name of Satan are you guys thinking?" He spooned up cornflakes, talked and dribbled. "Napkin, please," he said to Mult, who went meekly to the kitchen.

Oddie let a moment pass and snapped the next question. "Explain, Grove, why have you taken such pains to make your business associates and your friends think you've been in Europe? Ignorant of where you really are, for a year and some. How about *that?*"

Grove slurped slightly, swallowed, and raised his brows. "Ever run a factory? Have you ever lived a vagabond life with circus people or gone touring on the road, doing magic? Then been caught in the office trap? A pen, where you are expected almost to *live?* With *routine?*"

"The lengths you went to weren't necessary to escape *that.* You could, simply, retire, right? Walk out, fly here and settle, as you've done. So?"

Grove spent some time musing before he answered, "Well, there's another reason for this." He waved a hand to indicate his surroundings. "I went to see Art Eaper, year ago and some. You know why?"

Oddie did not know. The director had held out that detail. Grove perceived the man's vexation and the fast thinking that made a fair disguise for his annoyance at his ignorance. "Assume I know."

Grove went on eating and trying by that to bring into the mind of the other such words as "codger" and "old coot" or some more recent synonym, "dad," say. The effort led to an extension of an already planned alibi. "I happened to be in Washington on business. A general I knew wanted to get my Warsaw plant to make some special toys for PX's." That wasn't exactly true; the general wanted Grove to make parts for a weapon and Grove had refused. But the man with four stars would, if asked, agree he'd asked about "toys," being a smart soldier.

"Just visiting the Pentagon got me remembering old times, and before I knew it I asked how to reach Art." That was fact. "Believe it or not I was thinking of trying to get back to the old game! Before I came to my senses I was down there in Axe's red cave trying to volunteer. He was mighty polite about showing me how out of date—how nutty—I was. When I got back to my limousine I began to wonder if I'd lost my sanity. I shook for hours. Suppose he'd accepted? Suppose I'd taken an assignment—fluffed it, for sure. The impulse made me wonder if I'd lost my buttons. Was such a fool fit to be in charge of *anything*—even himself? Does he need a head-shrinker? Or custodial care, say? *That's* why I came here and what I'm still trying to decide. It's been a happy period. In fact"—he meditatively spooned more cornflakes—"I'd about made up my mind. Not to go back to the rat race—my associates can manage the business—but just to let them know where I was—and to explain I've retired, but not why. Even that took longer than I'd expected. And, Lord knows, if you are trying to deal with my kind of problem, you certainly don't want anybody, business associates or friends, to know about it. Right?"

It might, Oddie reflected, be right at that. The story of visiting Eaper could easily be checked. And the information he had on Grove did not contradict his story. It wasn't exactly normal behavior, Oddie felt, but then, Grove had never been "normal," in other senses of the term.

Grove guessed those considerations as Oddie's face remained FBI blank but his eyes moved about, fractionally, seeing this, seeing that, from the brain behind. Inspiration made Grove abruptly stand and walk about, half laughing—as a change of the darting eyes followed.

"First time I've thought of your angle!" Grove exclaimed. "But it could be sound! I did go to a devil of a lot of trouble to set up this hideaway. The basic reason is the one I gave. But the trimmings, well, perhaps they were the aftereffect of that crazy interview with Art Eaper. If you see—"

Oddie saw: "You realized you wanted no part of the real thing—what you guys called cloak and dagger?—so you subconsciously invented a reason to act out an imitation? A frightening reason but a safe game?"

"Guess I did! Silly." Grove sighed. "Still, I've had a glorious time here. I've loved every minute, the way it is. If the FBI has busted the cover I set up—and set up in an old-time way, at that—it'll be a shame. I'd like to go on all my days living here as R. K. Grove, not R. W."

"We didn't 'bust your cover,' Grove. By the time the press and TV got to the park, you'd gone. So far as I can see, the chief won't want too much detail spread around, either, about last night's business. Security matter, as you guessed. I'll check on you. But as long as no pictures of you go out to the press or show on TV, so some old crony recognizes you and talks, I guess the Bureau will be more than content."

Here, Grove played another planned card. "Thanks. But look, Oddie. If things with me do stand as I set them up, *perhaps* I could"—his voice was childishly eager—"sort of *sit in,* somehow. I mean, for you. Keep the old eyes peeled. Always supposing, of course, that you have a continued problem here?" He hurried on, excitedly. "Does this check mean there will be something more afoot? Beyond the rubout of the chap? Was he working the park—on the lookout for some people or some dirty work, but got careless?"

Oddie relaxed a little more. "Afoot," "rub-out" and "dirty work" were responsible for that, phrases so dated as to be almost novel. And on that very account, he reasoned, they gave evidence of the old bird's probable innocence and certain incompetence.

If Grove's playing games, Washington had said on the computer-scrambler, *find out. Tail him for a week. And check his house. Notify us, any sign of his game.*

Oddie felt he had things pretty well cleared up now. He became what he believed was benign. "Well, Mr. Grove, we do know your record—from way back then. You say you offered to help out—another outfit—and were turned down. I'll be frank. In confidence, it was one of our men who was killed. You happened to be on the spot—to have been out here a good while, though. It wasn't *likely* that those items would add up. Coincidences are common as dandelions—but, after all—"

"Not much of a coincidence, friend. I have insomnia, at times. You might easily understand that—*memories.* I'm fond of animals and always was. My mother was too. The park fascinates me. So I hope I shan't be prohibited from my custom of—"

"Certainly *not!*" Oddie's laugh was like a small fall of icicles.

"I didn't know the deceased," Grove went on. "Never saw him in my life. I had no idea who he might be, but the coat *was* puzzling, I admit. And the rest. Something familiar I couldn't place. Not quite: out of style, I guess, way out of style. But familiar—"

The FBI man again nodded—to himself. "Well, that about wraps it up. Got it, Hollis?"

"Of course, Chief."

Oddie furtively waited for Grove's reaction, momentary perplexity followed by surprise. "I get it! Pocket tape recorder? *Brilliant!*"

"Something," Oddie said, "like that." He smirked; and

desmirked. "One last favor, if you don't mind: could we look around this place? Washington's orders and routine, as you'll appreciate. Though as far as *I'm* concerned—"

Grove seemed faintly annoyed but waved a hand. "Go ahead. Help yourself."

All three men moved. Grove finished his cornflakes and had a second cup of coffee. By listening, he could follow them through his bedroom, the library, the guest bedrooms, the baths, and the already Mult-searched kitchen. They reappeared to examine the lanai and various closets opening from the big, comfortable room where he sat.

Finally they moved to the door leading to the lower floor, a door visible from where Grove sat. Oddie tried the knob. Grove said, "Key's on the frame, up top."

Oddie nodded, found the key, opened the door, saw a stairway in darkness, looked for a switch and turned on the light. He started down—and came back very quickly. "What in *hell*—" He slammed the stair door.

Grove said, "Damn! I forgot it was loose! In *there,* eh?"

Oddie had lost ninety per cent of his FBI and nearly that amount of his CIA. *"Loose!"* he gasped. *"There?"* He gagged. "What in God's *name*—"

Grove rose, shaking his head apologetically. He went to the door the G-man had slammed, opened it, sniffed and closed it again. "The skunk," he said with calm assurance. "I was afraid of something like that."

Oddie tried to accept the unacceptable. "You mean you have a *skunk* down there?"

"But—what else?"

"*Why*, man? *How?*"

"That's it," Grove answered. "Exactly. Why? How?" He seemed preoccupied. He returned to his chair and sat down.

Oddie was enraged. "If this is supposed to be a *joke* . . . some kind of put-on . . . !"

"But it is."

"God damn it, Grove! *Explain!*"

"Well, I'll be glad to, far as I can." He shrugged and ritually prepared a cigar. "It's like this. Yesterday morning I went out for the mail. My mailbox is big because I get so many packages, mostly books, from the mainland. The local bookstores tend to be a bit slow at—"

"Skip local bookstores—"

"Right! Anyhow, besides the mail—I'd seen the truck stop and go on some while before I went out—there was this package, addressed to me but no sender's name and no stamps: wasn't a mailed thing. Naturally, not being a total idiot, I thought I better be careful about opening it."

Grove hesitated and gave the FBI man a you-know-how-that-is look. Oddie frowned a curt "yes" and thought the talky man must be getting senile. "So?"

"I took it to the shop."

"Shop?"

"If you will just listen!" Grove was plaintive.

Oddie clamped his lips. They vanished with that pressure. He waited.

"I have workshops, downstairs: carpentry and metal-work, and so on. I like to fiddle with things, make furniture, for instance, or new toys. It is my business, after all." He seemed to realize that was off the desired track. "Well, that's where I took it: the package, to open it carefully. But I didn't."

"Oh?" A miracle of sarcasm: "It opened itself?" Oddie asked.

"Right!" Grove beamed. "I was trying to think how to go about the job and feeling damned silly because I can't imagine anybody sending—rather, presenting—me with, oh, some sort of infernal machine, for instance. Bomb." He saw that first designation register as another antiquity and went ahead. "But the gate bell rang: the chimes. It was the dry cleaner. I'd forgotten it was his day. So I ran up—I had things for him. Jenny, that's Genevra Oopani, was in Kailua, shopping. Before I could get back down to the shop again, some folks showed up at the gate and buttonholed me—alms gatherers from the—Church of the Modern Saints of Lazarus. I *think* that was it. I got rid of them with a fin and had the gate almost shut when I heard a car smash, just up the Kalan—toward Sea Life Park. And that took me out again—to be sure nobody was hurt, of course. I felt I should go because, sometimes, others don't stop to help. Found it was more noise than harm. But I hung around chewing the fat with a driver of the car that the other one had whapped, a nice chap named Bissel or Kissel. He's a surfing champ and I've often thought of taking a shot at it. So we naturally kept yakking for quite a while—"

"But the *stink!*" Oddie had let the man ramble because he'd decided the absurd tale could also be checked out. His patience snapped when he felt he had sufficient detail.

For the first time, Grove was quietly but clearly hostile. "Do you want, Mr. Oddie, an answer to your question? Or no?"

Oddie found himself passionately wishing he had not given up smoking. He replied weakly, "Go on."

"That's about all, in any case. I finally got back below to the package and it was empty, with a hole clawed in its end. Which, taken with the faint reek I detected when I shined a flashlight into the box—carton, actually—made it clear there had been a live skunk in it, probably doped a bit, because I'd felt no movement, carrying it downstairs. Well, the shops connect with the conservatory and also with the hall and the stairs. I searched all over the place but the spice-kitty was pretty cute, because I couldn't find him. It didn't *worry* me, really. Skunks aren't—a trouble—if you don't molest them. I figured the thing was—a practical joke: but not—whose." He grinned. "Even, maybe, some old-time circus friend—just happening to recognize me. And sent the skunk as a calling card, say. I sort of half expect him to show up, soon."

"Oh, Lord Almighty," Oddie murmured.

"Did it?"—Mult interrupted with a sound of accusation—"go through *quarantine?*"

Grove stared; he seemed to need to reflect. Such mammals brought to Hawaii must be kept in quarantine for four months, owing to law: there is no rabies in Hawaii and the long quarantine keeps it that way. Grove finally said, "How the hell should I know?"

Oddie, who had been looking interestedly at Mult, turned to Grove. "Maybe the damned thing was *infected* with rabies, Mr. Grove. Maybe somebody was—is—out to get *you.*"

"Who? Why? Of course, some of the old-timers—our 'opposite numbers'—did survive—"

Oddie gave Mult a nod of praise. Mult basked as his chief rose smartly. "We'll come back when you trap the beast. Be careful, though. And let *us* have it—live or dead—when you nail it. And air the place out!"

Grove rose too, and said cannily, "If you have orders to go over my house, hadn't you better do it *now?* I mean, supposing there was something suspicious here—which,

Lord knows, there isn't—wouldn't I get rid of it, if you waited till I caught that critter?"

"Perhaps—" Oddie was shaken. He found a saving scheme. "I'll post a man here, of course, till you get the animal. Mult!"

Grove shook his head in a sorrowful way. "That's not up to the old standards, I'm afraid. You don't know what you'd be looking for, mainly because it doesn't exist. But if it did, I probably could conceal or destroy it, even with six G-men watching the house." Suddenly, he slapped his thigh. "I ought to have thought!"

"Yes?" Oddie was instantly suspicious.

"Whole façade's glass, down below! All you do is take the garden stairs and you can see everything without even risking a skunk bath. Any shop you want to go in, then, just say so and I'll open it up from outside."

Twenty minutes later Oddie returned, alone. He had seen the tropical plants and admired, even envied them. He had seen the well-equipped shops and smelled the faint scent some of them exuded where the locked glass doors met. But it had been sufficient to peer from the paved walk that lay between the transparent walls and the miniature cliff: all interiors were completely visible.

Oddie found his host now wearing a silk robe, shaved and showered, too. The robe was of many brilliant hues in odd-ball patterns: practically psychedelic and positively kook.

"Okay?" Grove asked hopefully.

Oddie grunted assent. His eyes ranged about as if he still hoped to find a dubious item. He finally started away and then stopped. "Nice place! Funny, though—it seems bigger, from the outside."

"But it *is!*" Grove smiled at the G-man's surprised look. "It has double walls—with glass wool between for insulation: foot and a half, all round. That saves a pretty penny on electric bills. Bills for my reversible air conditioning. Smart of you to notice. Can't recall others doing that. Well—"

The old ass was actually twinkling. "Post us on the skunk bit," Oddie said.

"Will do."

A brown, unmarked car drove away: a Toronado, as inconspicuous among ordinary Hawaiian cars as a fire engine—but very good on curvy mountain roads.

Mult, who was driving, finally broke the silence. "For a minute, there, Chief, I thought you might order us to go down into the stinkhole."

The comment had an effect on Oddie, both unintended and unconscious. He spoke crisply. "If the old fool hadn't glassed in his entire downstairs, I'd naturally have done the sweep myself. Not any need, none whatever."

When Mult said, "Right, Chief," it was without irony. He now had a conviction that Grove warranted no further attention and that Oddie was both thorough and obedient.

"We'll tail him a week or so, of course. Orders. Now and then and here and there. The Three OA thing. But I don't believe we need to waste our lives on it."

"Absolutely not, Chief."

They tailed him for seven days—using Three OA: Off and On when Operatives were Available.

The reports of the men who took those random assignments would be intriguing, Oddie felt—to any nut obsessively fascinated by other nuts.

Grove sometimes climbed the dangerous pali. These pleated and near-vertical cliffs, characteristic of Hawaii and some other volcanic islands in the Pacific, were dangerous. Their rock was soft and friable. Jungle growths on the vertiginous precipices weren't trustworthy for handholds. Trade winds stacked clouds against the upper reaches and to a climber such compressed murk was as blinding as any London fog. Even a skilled mountaineer always sent down intermittent falls of rock and rubble.

Following Grove when he climbed was impossible. "However," agent Pollar noted, "you can always get to the summit by car and on foot to be head of the subject when he tops out. Subject is expert at climbing and does it to collect rare, endemic plants."

Middleman noted, "Subject eats peanuts. Absent-minded type. Posted paper peanut sack at Ala Moana Shopping Center, in US mailbox. Arranged, Honolulu postmaster, for recovery. Lab exam of bag negative."

"Buys books in scores," Coppler stated in another report. "All sorts. Standing order for all new books about espionage. Likes who-done-its. Info from clerk, taken to lunch, a Miss F. Jones (see expense voucher attached). My identity not revealed. Grove also reader of various technical books."

Cooley: "Had four cases canned tomatoes sent to residence. What for? Should we follow up?"

Oddie read it all. The canned tomatoes he understood: he had looked into the subject of skunks and read that tomatoes were supposed to be best for the removal of skunk odor. With the news about the four cases of tomatoes, he called off his men. And the skunk arrived, dead, packaged tightly, a day later. With it was a note:

Gentlemen:

Caught the varmint! Here 'tis. They have more shooting power than you'd believe. Mr. Oddie was wise not to try to get in range of this baby. I did! Hired a professional janitorial service to clean my dump, air it, etc. Come by and chat any time now—we're pretty desmelled. Best.

Grove

Mult was ordered to dispose of the animal and its container.

Oddie by then was thoroughly annoyed at the whole thing. He guessed what none of his people ever did: the old boy had played tag with them on the mountains. Had himself a ball—even posting a peanut bag in a mailbox, for Lord's sake! What had Middleman expected when he got the postmaster to open that mailbox? Plans for the newest warheads on American ICBMs?

Oddie had not, of course, told his men they were tailing the "subject" to make sure he was not trying to *help* USA. They'd been free, as a consequence, to imagine Grove as anything they wished: a paid spy for another nation, ally or not. When Oddie called off the effort Middleman summed it up:

"The old guy is guilty as first suspected: suspected as kinky and now proven nearly certifiable."

The mailing of the candy-striped sack for peanuts had been one of Grove's double jokes. He knew he was being tailed, at irregular times. He found it very easy to spot his shadow. He knew people might be checking his incoming mail and that any letter he or Jenny Oopani posted might be recovered and read, too, even if that involved every letter they mailed or received.

So, when he posted a paper sack in the Ala Moana Shopping Center, he walked on a few steps and then seemed to realize that he'd done something typical of an absent-minded duffer. He turned around. That, he correctly believed, would force the man he'd already found to be on duty to duck out of sight. It did, and gave Grove his chance to post a real letter.

However, if that, too, had been observed, and even if all the letters in the box were opened and read, the one he had added would surely be resealed and sent on with the rest. It was addressed to a Master Clyde Williams, at 48 West Winter Street, in Ardmore, Pennsylvania. It bore no return address.

Such a young man existed but he was in prep school in Connecticut. So Clyde's father, sorting the morning mail, pocketed the envelope when it arrived. He sent it, registered and in another envelope, with a note for its next recipient, who, when handed it by his secretary, promptly arranged to call a third person for a brief talk.

Clyde Williams' father had once been in the OSS and he knew Grove. He now headed a law firm which represented various American interests of French corporations. Grove had long ago arranged with his old friend to forward communications addressed to "Master" Clyde to the French ambassador; and the lawyer had persuaded the ambassador to act as a delivery boy.

Even if efforts to make sense of the missive had been attempted, they would have failed. The letter was typed, rather poorly, on a worn portable and signed, "Your fond Uncle David." Its contents were those a boy of fourteen would presumably relish—in the judgment of an "uncle" who would not know that modern kids are unlikely to be much taken by rambling stories of fish, fishing, and of a visit to Sea Life Park, from an aged relative passing through Hawaii on his fourth world tour.

The person for whom the letter was intended, however, readily interpreted the tales. "Uncle David," or Grove, who said he had done some sea fishing, reported that sharks were thick in the Hawaiian waters, man-eaters and others. CIA and FBI, that meant. He hadn't yet seen the one species he had always hoped to all his life, a killer whale. The President of the United States read that as a Soviet or other Red agent. The uncle believed, now, he might get a chance, as the offshore waters abounded in killer whales. His main angling project, to catch a marlin or some other game fish topping a thousand pounds, looked equally good. Local charterboat skippers didn't realize he was aiming at a fish of that size, though they had asked him to talk of his angling feats in past years.

There were, with that, anecdotes about fish caught and fish lost and these, with the other matters, brought the President up to date on Grove. Of course, he'd already known about the body found in the Reef Tank; it had been on the front page of all major newspapers, along with the fact that an "R. K. Grove" had first spotted the corpse. He also now knew a multitude of other things about the dead CIA agent and Eaper's operations. This flood of knowledge came in steadily from Grove's chosen watcher in the tree. It made the President want, increasingly, to fire Eaper and order a CIA reorganization.

But as long as Grove had no idea of the nature of Project Neptune (the thousand-pound game fish) and as long as Eaper himself had no hard facts about Neptune—though he still speculated on the matter to his tape recorder—the President let the situation stand. Eaper now seemed fairly sure that there was no such project, and the occasional rumors were planted—to deceive him. If a genuine project existed, Eaper avowed, it would develop at a point far from Hawaii. The Reef Tank business proved that Hawaii was out. It was a macabre jest—but not sophisticated enough to trick *him!*

Grove's narrative about fish and fishing, propoises and whales, had a further impact on the President. Both the Soviets and the Chinese had, lately, become more arrogant than ever—acting as if they possessed a power not known to the free world. They were threatening the Atlantic Alliance in new ways, hammering on "Imperial America" in the United Nations, and behaving militarily as if they might soon enter West Germany as they had Hungary, Czechoslovakia, South Korea and South Vietnam. If that fresh and menacing position (not completely known to the public) rose from a dire operation called Project Neptune, the location and nature of it must be uncovered.

The President was very glad he had his "personal" agent in Hawaii. But he was not ready, yet, to take a new step. That might be a fatal error, he feared.

One man could never be relied on, he realized, to learn and report an unknown, devious plan of the Communists to develop some sort of menacing device.

What sort? The President smiled oddly and his eyes narrowed as they looked deep into thoughts behind them. Nowadays, the bright boys in science could describe any number of theoretically conceivable doomsday gadgets and blackmail weapons: chemical and bacterial horrors including instruments that might be used before their presence was even suspected.

He believed the USSR was honest in its effort to cooperate in limiting those possibilities. But he knew there was top-level opposition to that in the Soviet Union. The new leaders in China seemed rational but there were rumors of a hard core "neo-Maoism" group that used them as a front. And Hitler hadn't invented "the big lie." It had often been part of Red policy.

He sighed. But the alternative to Grove was Eaper. That incredible megalomaniac! Who thought he could manage American policy better than the government! Eaper and his minions would be a last resort.

7

DOUBT

A warm February night had followed a wet, cool period.

Grove drove a new station wagon into the park, cut the lights, switched off the motor and stepped down. Jerry, the watchman, was not in sight. An endless flow of the trades whipped rigging in the *Essex*, the more than half-sized replica of the vessel sunk by a sperm whale Melville later called Moby Dick and made albino, without any particular reason. The wind also drew rain sounds from coconut palms. It ruffled the feathers of sleeping boobies in sea grape trees around the turtle pond and produced, in sum, so much and such constant sibilance that the rush of three hundred thousand hourly gallons of clear, unfiltered sea water through the pipes and ducts which supplied this seaside wonderland could hardly be heard, anywhere.

Grove strolled toward Whaler's Cove, an artificial salt lake in which, five times a day except Mondays, pretty Polynesian girls paddled little outrigger canoes, whales leaped on command, and porpoises performed close-order drill in mid-air for human throngs with boggled eyes and dropped chins—thousands and thousands of air arrivals, cruise-ship passengers and other sorts of tourists as well as for polyglot locals and maybe, Grove felt, an occasional Russian or Chinese specialist.

As he approached the amphitheater where so much astonishment was so frequent, Grove paused. A porpoise named Ulu broached, saw Grove, made a birdlike sound and disappeared. Moments later, five porpoises (spinners, or Stenella, their generic name) flung themselves into the air above the lake, twisting round and round as they arced up, over and back in.

The man came closer.

The porpoises repeated their vaulting body-twirl. Grove opened a plastic bag and took from it a half dozen smelt, thawed that afternoon. He flung these delicacies into the cove and the porpoises surged to consume them.

Then Grove looked back. As he had expected, Jerry was now in view on the high road under the talus verge, watching. Grove waved. Jerry pushed his bike forward and mounted. The two men met.

"Nice night," the watchman said softly and with a smile. "What you doing? Training 'em?"

Grove laughed. "Sapphire told me how. Said it was okay."

"Oh?" The huge Hawaiian-Chinese was amused.

"They seem to like to see you show up," Grove went on, moving toward the Ocean Science Theater and causing Jerry to move too. "They react as if they were lonely—bored, rather—at night, in the empty park. I kind of got thinking about it when I dropped by: the way they'd greet you and put on flips and swim up, sort of grinning and hoping. It would be fun to feed 'em a little, I felt. So I asked Mrs. Abbott. Sapphire. Name fits. She said it was all right. But I feed them special smelt, a change for 'em that costs more than their day to day diet; they appreciate the treat."

"Now you get a big hand when you show, eh?"

"Every time."

Jerry nodded, pushed his bike. "I wondered. They've lately got to putting on fancier shows when I go by, too, though I never feed 'em."

"Don't have to; not every time. The trick's called 'operant conditioning.' The animal does something unusual, say. You want it to repeat that so you toss it a fish. When it tries some gambit, you don't want—no fish and you walk away. The next time, by chance, it tries the one you want, bingo! you toss it another fish. The porpoise catches on soon, and after that the right trick wins a fish reward. In time, only now and then are fish rewards required for the right trick. Funny! Like computers. Their binary system is a yes-no language, too. I enjoy getting this splashy greeting. So do they. The trainers use a whistle plus fish. A blast means correct, just like a tossed fish. No whistle means—wrong."

Jerry nodded. Together, they stopped and stared at the blue, dim-lit water of the Ocean Science Theater. An immense, curving glass wall contained it and faced a semicircle of rising seats so that spectators could see, both under water and above, all the action. That included demonstrations of how porpoises were trained and how they could use echo-location to find small items, even blindfolded; of how they could hunt up and rescue divers in trouble, carry messages bottom to surface, bring and return tools and many other feats the next brightest of living animals can do or learn to do.

Behind the curved glass front of the main tank and its mini-sea, those performers, in holding pens, were moving and splashing as they heard the men and tried to get attention.

"Porpoises," Grove said, looking back toward the still-heaving surface of Whaler's Cove, "are ham actors."

"Clowns," Jerry amended.

"Incidentally"—Grove started away—"I've arranged with the Abbotts to get a key for the deep freeze so I can store my smelt with the park supply to save bringing along a sack when I come by."

Jerry said, "Sure."

"If you like, when I don't make it here, you could give them a few."

The watchman at first didn't understand. Then he grinned. "So the porpoises you trained to greet you won't be disappointed when it's only me?"

Grove said in a rather embarrassed way, "Well—yes, I guess so." He made a dissembling sound. "I'm chicken-hearted about animals."

"I like animals too." Jerry braced his bike and took a cigarette from a pocket. The bicycle was now exposed by a floodlight and Jerry, Grove noted, had added an item. It was strapped to the frame, leather or perhaps plastic, with a long zipper and it looked like a tool kit. It would not likely be for tools, Grove knew; any number of tools were available in the work sheds behind the park offices. Jerry was wearing his weapon, a .45, as usual. So . . . what was in the kit?

Grove lighted a cigar and pondered.

Jeremiah Akaka Gong would not add anything useless to his bike. This had what use, then? He had been a detective and a soldier in an elite military cadre with an awesome record both in war and in the war on crime. It was as sure . . . as sure as Grove could allow . . . the watchman couldn't be *bought* by an enemy. He might be blackmailed by some means involving a life more precious to Jerry than his own, perhaps. And he might be tricked into an act by a friend, something that would serve an unsuspected purpose. But Jerry was not easy to fool, not innocent or naïve.

The corners of Grove's eyes crinkled in the half-dark, but his smile was rueful: it had been a long, long time since he'd been obliged to mistrust everybody.

His present situation differed from past ones, also: he had no explicit orders. He was alone, excepting for his old friend Elias Foth, minding the Eaper-tree, who forwarded information by devious and shifting routes.

It had included occasional details that could be used for curious ends. Grove could now get to Eaper in his deep lair, unhindered. By a swap of current passwords, Grove could buddy up with fifty major agents of the CIA in foreign lands. He could tell the admiral in command of the Pacific various orders not yet received by CINCPAC. But none of it was useful—since Grove's value depended on the certainty in all covert branches of the federal government that he was an eccentric idler only.

That, he had managed, or so he had thought, till now. But now, he wondered.

Did Jerry's new kit mean his cover was still suspect? Had Pilford Oddie enlisted the watchman without troubling to notify Eaper? Had Eaper arranged to recruit a night watchman in a distant park but felt the matter not worth recording in his diary? It was possible. A new thought changed Grove's smile—the thought that Jerry could have escalated his equipment on his own, after the finding of the man in the Reef Tank, but not soon, since the case had been added as a result of weeks of indecision, perhaps.

In that event, the likeliest, Grove felt, he would have to proceed with his present scheme very carefully. He might, indeed, finally have to learn what the tool kit held. A weapon? Radio receiver? Transmitter? Both? Tape recorder? If Jerry was a foe or even a foe's dupe it would be important to know the nature of the new gear.

Grove's present plan was other and urgent. The rumored January meeting by night in Sea Life Park, the news that launched these self-imposed endeavors, had not taken place. Grove had kept a thirty-one-night vigil to make sure. He'd often done so openly, but oftener, without his presence being known to Jerry. He would walk to the

Kalan Highway beside the park and slip into the natural cover there.

In January, however, a murder had taken place and the victim had been found in the Hawaiian Reef building. Grove had made his appearance too late to see what preceded that act. He could guess, however. The deceased and costumed CIA man had been drowned, elsewhere, and in bouillabaisse. That could mean the killers knew that he was, in some way, tagging or suspicious of them; if so, they'd taken considerable time to set up their grisly joke. Before Grove had entered the park that night, and probably when he had left his hiding place to make his presumed first arrival on his motorcycle, "they" had swiftly carried the prepared body to its place in the giant aquarium. "They" might well have been making their exit while he and Jerry chatted and scanned the magnificent, dark surroundings.

Nothing else of interest to Grove had occurred. If the meeting was to take place, if any such meeting had been and was still intended, it would now occur in February or even later. It might happen somewhere else, too, as the park and institute grounds were now equipped with three times the previous number of floodlamps. Also, since the finding of the corpse, Waimanalo police crusiers made several nightly runs through the area, at irregular intervals.

Eaper and his disguised minion, Oddie, had lost interest in the park. Grove stuck to it, stubbornly. He had a hunch that there had been a particular reason for selecting the park, granted the available date meant anything. The further fact that no covert watch was maintained by anybody seemed to suggest the Reef Tank business had the purpose of making the CIA and police positive the perpetrators wouldn't return. Grove saw that, both ways.

For some time Grove debated talking over the whole affair with Tack Abbot. Young Abbott had dreamed up the Sea Life Park and raised the funds to build it. Next had come the Oceanic Institute adjacent, and then his Brobdingnagian start on the Makai Range. Tack had been an officer in the Air Force and later held a high position on a presidential commission. He was building an empire in the Island State; and his name was a byword, there, with the best connotations. "Tack" was not derived from "sharp as a tack," which strangers often assumed, but was a shortened form of young Abbott's most favored cry, in all situations of stress: "Attack!"

He earned that nickname in prep school by his attack on studies and his performance (and loud abjurations) on teams, especially trailing teams. His Air Force record substantiated the nickname fully. And now his business enterprise and the swift expansion of "Abbott Associates" confirmed it, in a different area.

Tack's attacks, however, were not ruthless or necessarily frontal. He was a very subtle operator and his ends were as creative as lucrative. A graduate scientist and a passionate conservationist he was a man, obviously, to whom Grove could confide his mission, or part of it, his worries, or those centered on a continuing vigil. For, in spite of additional illumination, there remained routes from the Kalan to points in the park of utter dark where any number of persons could gather and be hidden. Police patrolling could be evaded, too.

But Grove had set aside the thought of speaking to Tack, for the time being. His story, even if he told it all, was very thin. He needed more facts to persuade a man as keen as young Abbott that Sea Life Park should have clandestine watching every night by trusted people.

Project Neptune, the strange code phrase that still appeared as occasional rumor in Eaper's shop, remained ghostly. Grove had tried to imagine what it could be and found his mind boggling over nuclear and other fantasies of vast magnitude, and at least possible in design, yet not of calm credibility. The project was probably sea-related—and that was all; even that was perhaps wrong.

So he had decided he must contrive a mechancial means for park survey by night. He had hit on an idea in February and gone to work. Now, in early March, one step remained.

Sapphire Abbott had assisted him in that—without knowing his aim to be anything other than what he claimed, one which Sapphire considered typical of their eccentric but delightful friend.

Grove drove a new station wagon into the non-public area and parked at a careless angle. It was early morning, sunny and hot.

The car was a Brigand Mark VII, conspicuously modified. On its dash (and an extension) were some two dozen extra knobs, dials, levers and buttons of several colors—not one of them standard instrumentation. Its windows, which he left open, and also the flooring of the rear area, were not of a stock sort, either. Its extra seat had been removed and the new, over-all floor was a foot higher than that of the regular model. A more than casual examiner could also discover that the windows, electrically operated, were not glass but something opaque: steel, in fact. The double flooring, which came flush with the tailgate, appeared to be of a firm material. It was carpeted with steel beneath.

There were other differences. The ignition lock was custom-built. A second and unusual lock protected the gasoline tank and a third made it impossible for anyone but an expert at burgling even to attempt to raise the hood. Before switching off the engine—which murmured in a manner any car buff would recognize as not that of the original power plant—Grove grinned at the elaborate dashboard. It had reminded him of what the operational side of Eaper's desk would surely look like. He got out, walked back, reached in and removed two baskets filled with plants. These he carried, one in each arm, toward a park gate marked *Authorized Personnel Only.*

It was five minutes past eight and the park would not open till ten—a glittering morning with the trade winds tirelessly at work. Some people could not long tolerate the windward side of Oahu because of those trades. Day after day and week after week they poured in from the sea and once a person began to be irritated by their incessant flow they became as maddening as a non-stop dental drill. The last owners of Grove's house had suffered that state, luckily for him.

Grove took his baskets to Whaler's Cove and on around the deep-water section where the whales were impounded between shows. He stepped over a low hedge that bordered an asphalt path. Pushing through some sea grape trees and avoiding a clump of thorny kiawes, he reached a weedy area seaward of the *Essex* at a point near the islet in the cove and opposite the amphitheater.

He had, weeks ago, asked Mrs. Abbott if she knew that a certain species of orchid, with fairly showy white blossoms, grew naturally at the edge of the sea, in its salty spray. Sapphire had not known. Grove had then offered to obtain and plant some on this lake edge where they would add decoration and make a novel conversation piece. Mrs. Abbott had eagerly accepted.

Now, with care, Grove began to set out a number of these salt-defiant exotics, many of which were in bloom. The performing whales and porpoises would insure ample dousing in calm weather—if, indeed, these plants constantly required salt-water bathing, which seemed the case, as they were never found in any other habitat. The site, left untouched by park landscaping and skirted by all paths, would not be invaded by tourists or molested by park gardeners.

An hour passed.

From beneath the last few, stiff-leaved orchird plants Grove withdrew a small apparatus. With great caution he installed it at a point where overhanging branches touched the cove's surface. The instrument was thereby hidden from all frontal angles. A few people might leave the blacktop paths for a close look at the orchids but his gadget was not visible from the shore, either.

Grove had made it in his basement shops. A float of balsa wood, painted with dappled greens to match the concealing leaves, was connected by an arm to a pen which traced movements of the float on a roll of graph paper, turned on a battery-powered drum.

A daytime record would be useless because of the shows, the acrobatics of porpoises and teamed leaps of whales. But it would run for ten days and nights without attention and he had marked the moment of twilight and of first dawn on the rolls of paper. It was a simple thing, much like a seismograph: it made a record of the waves that came ashore at Whaler's Cove. To protect it from the cove's inhabitants, especially the porpoises—who had watched the installation with built-in grins and amiable curiosity—Grove added a fence of steel rods, firmly anchored in the rocks on shore.

His "aquagraph," as he'd privately named it, was to represent himself. Its record of the waves in Whaler's Cove, with the record of another instrument at his residence, a recording anemometer that showed the approximate wind velocity at the not distant cove, would chart the nightlong size of waves in both regions. Of course, the porpoises would, at times, become playful, even without an audience —leaping in ones and twos, whacking their tails and landing flat, just for the hell of it. Such antics would leave traces on the aquagraph. But the now-trained response to any person passing the area *at night* would make a far more conspicuous set of waves; and these would be identifiable on the graph. He still encouraged that exhibition when he made visits, as usual, and Jerry now reinforced the porpoise "hello" by throwing fish to the cove inhabitants at least once a night, when he was alone. An innocent amusement, the watchman presumably thought.

Any night's evidence of human presence in the area would now be known to Grove. When he appeared, or Jerry, the aquagraph would record a sudden and special series of spikes, as the ocean dervishes came out, twirling, soared high, and arced back with a majestic splash. They did that over and over, hopefully to earn a treat.

In the absence of Grove, or other legitimate night visitors, Jerry's rounds were regular; these produced the telltale spiking but Grove could attribute it to the watchman by the time factor. Visitors, on night tours conducted by park officials, or passing scientists in the park for research, would also set the spinners and spotted porpoises flying. But Grove could quite easily learn from Jerry about such not-frequent events—and ignore their recordings. For Jerry usually offered, as chitchat and without questioning, news of those pleasant breaks in his solitary rounds.

If, however, the aquagraph should record the newly learned reaction of the porpoises at any time that did not match Jerry's rounds and if Grove learned that no other person had been seen by Jerry at the time, it would signify that somebody had entered unnoticed.

Any furtive intruder would, of course, come through the park while Jerry was touring the institute and Makai Range areas. The least illuminated route would be used, which meant avoiding the paved roads and paths, so passing Whaler's Cove. Who such persons might be, or on what errand, he still would have no idea, if he ever had a record at all.

Even when summer arrived and the park would be open several nights a week, Grove's instrument would serve on closed nights; and those were the likely ones for further park intrusion. He finished his installation and watched the pen trace waves caused by the trade winds and the added, miscellaneous signs of porpoise activity—random and easily identified. Then he straightened his back, aching a little from long squatting. He had already spread word, casually, that the salt-spray orchids would need his occasional attention. That was to explain later trips to change rolls of graph paper and, in time, batteries.

Eaper, he thought, with a grin, might like his gadget. But Eaper—the grin became a chuckle—would never think of teaching porpoises to make reports. Instead, Eaper would set up heat-sensors, people-smellers, sound-gatherers, or some other ultramodern apparatus. For the spotting of which, Grove reflected contentedly, Eaper's "playboy" foes would probably have equally sophisticated detection gear. Such people would note the leaping porpoises *too;* but not read what the animals were entering on the minutes.

A watchdog, in Grove's view, could always beat an electric eye. Mice, even, might be more useful than a mortar; and a scorpion superior to that gadget the director of CIA had mentioned. What the devil had Axe called it? *Mergator*—a thing Grove had never heard of before.

He stepped back and looked at the orchids. Sapphire would like them. And the spectators now filling the amphitheater would, too, if they happened to be people who noticed flowers, a diminishing breed. But some park visitors, some of the gardeners, sundry scientists and the Abbotts would, surely, come around the pond for a close look. Not able, however, to see the device a few yards away.

Satisfied, he walked away, noting the time. Saturday a week, he'd have to shift the tape and, that same night, check its spiky traces against Jerry's offered or extracted report of night callers if the "aquagraph" indicated the need.

He went over to the restaurant, nodding to several employees who recognized him, and drank coffee while buses roared into the parking areas and people in hundreds streamed through the turnstiles. He sat where his station wagon could be seen and afterward he attended the Whaler's Cove show, taking a seat on the topmost row of the amphitheater.

His purpose was to continue watching his station wagon, beyond the paved road that separated public from all other areas. These included the offices, laboratories, underwater-viewing rooms, miscellaneous gear and odd-shaped holding pools of the Oceanic Institute. Cars of officials, of secretaries and skilled workers, of scientists and their visitors, had accumulated in rows around the station wagon. Now and then an arriving individual would take a second look at Grove's vehicle and some would walk over to stare at the dashboard and its multiplicity of controls, for which the purposes could not possibly be guessed.

The distance was too great to enable Grove's recognition of faces. And the station wagon received more attention than Grove had expected. Most people were far too interested in things, these days, he believed; technology was becoming less blessing than a curse. Eaper himself was only a special variety of gadget-crazed contemporary man.

Sitting atop the amphitheater, his brown and silver hair teased by the trades that came from beyond Rabbit and Red islands, he occasionally but somewhat cautiously turned from the water show to scrutinize the distant parking area. The drama reached the point where whale leaps were about to start and Grove was ready to admit he'd wasted his time, when a man drove up in a tired and battered car, one with the fins of long-gone years. He parked and walked over to the refitted Brigand Mark VII to give it a very thorough going-over. A haole, a Caucasian, but Grove could see only that sort of thing: the medium size of the real or pretending car buff, his gaudy, Truman-type aloha shirt—perfect tourist camouflage—with a broad-brimmed straw hat that would hide his face, but again, was common enough as local headgear. Grove could see, also, that the man moved in a swift, athletic manner.

Not enough. He, like many others, could be a tourist who entered the park by the wrong road, not noting the markers, and left his car in the wrong area, as many did. However, the man spent more time than any of the others examining the station wagon. He went clear around it twice and even, Grove thought, swiftly tried to raise the engine hood. If that was so, the withdrawal was quick, and the full attempt was partly hidden by the hood itself. However, the man apparently did discover the windows were not glass, since he peered at length into their slots. But when he'd finished he yawned, walked lightly over the rutted ground, made a less lengthy tour of a Toronado (not the brown one the FBI owned), sauntered to the road, crossed it and strolled toward the proper park entrance.

Grove loitered after the show ended and the crowd dispersed. He studied a wall of gigantic lava boulders beside the amphitheater, and next several immobile sea turtles; then he took a rest on a shady bench. The man didn't return and drive off—which still meant nothing, or meant, if anything, that he was making the full park tour, a matter requiring at least a couple of hours for catching all the shows, making a Reef Tank circuit, devoting a period to the Polynesian Village and a side trip, as well as a look at various exhibits and displays.

A tourist, probably. Grove felt restless.

He drove home.

Jenny had one of his favorite lunches ready: creamed chipped beef on toast and prune whip.

Afterward, the large Hawaiian lady reminded him of his three o'clock date with neighborhood kids for their trampoline lesson. The prospect brightened Grove and his regular, post-instruction exhibition left him sweat-soaked but happier, as the youngsters trooped away, chattering about their own progress, or regretted fluffs and his marvels.

He showered and dressed again with his usual but unnoticeable care.

Jenny cleared up the bath, hung up his clothes and asked about dinner. "Be out again." Grove smiled. "So go on home."

He'd sent her home early, before or right after dinner, for several weeks now.

The big woman hesitated a moment. She knew Grove did not intend to go out, somehow. There was no mention of an evening engagement on the big kitchen calendar where he entered his social obligations, along with ideas for meals, notes about laundry and personal items needed, almost anything, including, sometimes, entries even a graduate of Kamehameha School couldn't decipher. She'd often studied those notations and decided they were abbreviations, for one thing, and for another, abbreviations of words in what seemed a mixture of other languages.

Jokes, maybe; on her; he made lots of jokes. So she'd never asked; that might be what he wanted.

There were, Genevra-called-Jenny Oopani knew, other possibilities. Mr. Ring Grove was a strange man. A wonderful man, too. She nearly loved him—in the way a mother or older sister loves. He was so kind to people and generous. And, then, his kids!

But he was eccentric. Sometimes he didn't come home when he'd said he would. He went away for a week or more, once in a while. He slept all day, at times. And occasionally he'd leave suddenly, return unexpectedly, not saying where he'd been or why he'd gone; but there might be signs of travel on his luggage—the fragment of a torn-off sticker that meant he'd been abroad. He'd even called her once, from Paris; and once from some other foreign city she'd never heard of.

"Business," he always said, with a calm smile that seemed to mean anybody would behave as he did and nobody should think it odd. He had also, recently bought the house next door and spent much time "fixing it up." Yet he didn't offer it for rent and still had a lot of "fixing" to do, he said. And he was sending her home early, now. But why?

Once at a big luau she had tried to find out more about her employer. Jerry Gong had come up with a drink for her and asked how she liked her "Boss."

"A lovely man! But somewhat strange."

In the middle distance, bamboo organ drums were playing and from the mat where they seated themselves they could watch the dancers, storytelling hands and arms, tileaf skirts swinging in the classic style.

"Strange? How?"

She'd told him a few things about Mr. Grove's absences, trips, carefully hidden philanthropies, his love of kids and of flowers. She mentioned the next door house and the endless hours he worked in it, doing what, she couldn't say. Banging and sawing away, she told Jerry. "An alone kind of man," she finished. "But always in happy moods, or almost always."

After a while she added, "Don't *you* find him—well—different, Jerry?"

"I don't think so." He was a little too casual, she decided. "Refill?"

"Coke, this time." She smiled.

Jerry left. Steel guitars joined in the bamboo orchestration.

And Jenny had thereafter contained her curiosity: it was

the best job she'd ever had and the highest pay—keeping house for a quite wonderful, very rich, but peculiar man. She needed the money. It wasn't her nature or tradition to pry. But she had noticed the news about the house next door made Jerry Gong's eyes turn vacant the way Chinese eyes do when a surprise needs hiding.

8

TRAP

Grove had prepared his supper, left the dishes for Jenny in the morning and now occupied the red leather chair in his living room. His feet were in slippers and they rested on a once-charred area of the carpet. It had been mended with a rectangle of the same material which, however, was darker and so easily distinguished from the original.

His book was the newest by the author of *The Cadmium Caper* which Grove had guessed Eaper had been reading. Grove did not hold all such fiction in Eaper's low esteem. Some of the tales contained ingenious ideas, a few of which Grove wished he'd known about when he'd been in situations still clearly remembered. He assumed Eaper read these books with the same idea, that of adapting a writer's invention to a real operation. That was doubtless why he belittled fictional espionage.

A few such books, like those of the late Ian Fleming, were based on actual experience in their field. This was also true in the case of *The Cadmium Caper* and previous tales—by a spinster author. What her real name might be was probably known only to her lawyer, her agent, and perhaps her publisher. Her pen name, Ellen Long, had become a household word.

Her narratives of espionage had a special style and also a central character who was female—a different damsel in each volume. But the faithful fans of Ellen Long were never put off by the change and, indeed, male readers probably preferred meeting the new beauty who appeared in every new book. Each one was gorgeous, clever, amorous, amoral and pitted against awesome forces. Each heroine became mistress of a new hero and, in addition, had several more erotic experiences owing to her profession. Her lover always understood them; he was on her side and under cover, too.

In the end, Ellen Long's lasses managed two feats: escape; and the downfall of some nefarious group. Her lover would also survive and, presumably, the pair would wed.

To have revived any heroine or hero lover for a similar set of events in a next book would not have been sensible for Miss Long; no one woman could be repeatedly and so violently in love with such an endless series of males. Miss Long thereby sacrificed the continuity that Arthur Conan Doyle achieved with one Sherlock Holmes. But her books had continuity of another sort. Each introduced a lady with a new name, who might be brunette, blonde, a redhead or anything between; but every one not only met and fell in love with a redoubtable male but also had harrowing experiences with sadists. And every one would encounter other men, whose expertise would rouse in her a skill and vehemence Miss Long described with blueprint exactness. To be sure, as Miss Long made evident, female spies are expected to use sexual attraction (with the expertise thus connoted) as part of the job.

Eaper, Grove reflected, had dozens of such agents as his recorded dictation made clear. He had inherited some of them from Canfield Ball, an admiral, nicknamed, of course, "Cannonball," and Eaper's predecessor. Axe mistrusted those left-over subordinates, whom he called "Ball's bints." The admiral's "bints," however, were the first source of the rumors about Project Neptune.

The book in his hands, *My Body Keeps You Free,* concerned a titian-haired number with a fully developed figure and the face of a girl of fifteen, among other intoxicants. Her name was Dorice Sleeper and she was in bed though awake, at page four, with a suspected enemy agent—in Milan, Italy. Thinking of "bints" was no great associative feat, it was a British word for doxy, and Grove went on to guess that Eaper mistrusted the female agents left to him when Cannonball retired, simply because Eaper had not, himself, supervised their training—an idea Grove refused to carry any further.

Returning to the book, he read on, casually, for a while. But his concentration increased when he reached a point at which Dorice Sleeper, presumed a West German defector, had carried out a fairly hazardous mission in Warsaw, Poland—and that fact was learned by the Soviet network in Poland. Miss Sleeper had then managed to hide in an old, disused bakery. The pursuit was closing in when her real lover—(not the "mighty Pole" or yet the "arrogant Cossack" of earlier chapters)—crashed into the ghostly, spider-webbed edifice with a stolen truck to attempt the lady's rescue.

As the truck burst in the heavy-studded, plank portals, Grove had a sensation of *déjà vu,* that is, of experiencing in the present something apparently from the past, but something impossible to recall save as a feeling. Grove then remembered having the same sense while reading other books by Ellen Long. It had been one element among several that had made him sure Miss Ellen Long—whoever she really was—had been in intelligence herself. Some of the classic techniques that appeared in her works were too correct to be invented: means of communication were among them, and ways of identifying other agents, along with places, often far from any tourist routes but described with an accuracy possible only for one who had been in them—and described with the exactness of a trained intelligence agent. These passages related to such matters as concealed alleys, connecting cellars, special exits from restaurants Grove had known, and truthful details of local police procedure.

Now, however, that sense of *déjà vu* was shifting. Elements of the new story grew less mystifying and, soon, quite obvious. The tatty, abandoned "bakery" where the heroine hid was like a certain unused brewery he'd known: the same bricked-up windows and similar "mixing vats" in the place where he'd seen a different sort. (The authoress hadn't researched early nineteenth-century breadmaking apparently.) Next, the building "across the street" was a pawnshop, disguised as a secondhand store, also a fact.

Grove read on, with absolute attention, which was unfortunate: it shut down his distant early warning system. He failed to notice that the sounds of the sea breaking regularly outdoors grew slightly louder: he read too fervently.

The door-crashing truck was Polish, driven by the damsel's lover, Malcom Burns, who resembled a TV star. The real-life actor named here was not known to Grove. The equally handsome spy rammed in, however, and told the endangered (but calm) Dorice what to do. On his truck was an iron lung, stolen (she was never to be told how) from the Warsaw Peoples Lenin Hospital. It was supposedly being sent, he informed her, to Monaco, for exhibition at the Monaco World's Fair of Surgical Progress, as a token of Soviet achievement in the field.

She got into the massive steel cylinder and Burns closed its neck opening. They took off, Dorice inside but able to breathe through a length of hose her lover had provided. Grove, by then, had envisaged the stratagem that would be used to cross the frontier and he was right, almost to the last detail.

Malcom Burns stopped the truck, after turning into a forest road, when they reached the border. Miss Sleeper was then obliged to conceal herself under the padded lining of the iron lung. Its proper closure was made and its pump activated. After that, no air entered and none escaped. The apparent emptiness of the interior could be observed by anyone who looked through glass panels, inset for that purpose. When they were halted by border guards, Burns explained, in Russian-accented Polish, what he was transporting and where it was bound. He also explained why the apparatus was working. The Polish soldiers and their Soviet superior could well believe that explanation—an embarrassed admission of a truck driver who was supposed to run the lung, from time to time, but who had dutifully got it going and now couldn't stop it.

The guards peered into the lining—amused greatly, but unsurprised by the Russian's dilemma, his lack of knowhow. They found and liberated a case of vodka in the truck cabin and opened a bottle forthwith. The Russian in command looked over the iron lung a second time and showed Burns how to halt the machinery. The guards then demanded that Burns share several rounds of vodka before departure. Since he could not well refuse, Miss Sleeper lay in the steel tank without fresh air, for a considerable time. When the truck finally departed and was cleared by friendly people at the other border, but in full view of the Poles, Burns raced away till out of view—and range. He had only then been able to open the lung and found the lady unconscious; almost dead by asphyxiation, and battered by the pump action, as well.

Grove went that far—and knew who "Ellen Long" was: Arthur Xavier Eaper.

He knew for many reasons, all of which could be summed up in one: only he and Art had shared the real version of this parodied "escape." Grove had skipped its humiliating details in his official reports and Art Eaper, whose face was saved, would be the last man on earth to mention his part in the affair. He reflected that, since the return from Ellen Long's books, with the sums for movies made from them, the translations and so on, had been reckoned by "her" publisher at more than four millions, Eaper had a nice thing going.

What he missed during those musings was a faint movement of air in a room where air conditioning caused no such draft.

He kept wondering why Eaper had chosen to do this stuff as a female writer, wondering if, perhaps, Eaper had furnished the material and some lady ghost the prose. Then he realized something else as he contemplated this absurd discovery.

There was a person in the room, a man.

That finding was easy, if belated.

Grove gave no outward evidence of awareness. His head, bent over the book, remained at that angle, though his eyes switched to a sugared and partly sucked lime on the table beside the humidor. He went back to reading and reached blindly for the lime. It was a lime, which he had been sucking, after sugaring the opened end. Feet approached on the rug, soundlessly, and Grove saw shoes that were badly made and of large size; the trouser cut was poor. That would mean a third major discovery of the evening, if it indicated what he both hoped and, perhaps equally dreaded.

He went on, not reading but seeming to. A chair halfway across the room was lifted by one hand, judging from its angle, and carried forward. The chair was set down facing Grove, who, absently, sucked the lime again and put it back, absently.

The intruder sat; and sat still. A long time went by while nothing else happened. Grove wondered why, and decided the other expected him to look up, eventually, or catch sight of the visitor in an eye corner and then look up and be appalled. Grove decided to play mouse to the other's cat. He turned a page, eventually, seemed to be caught by something else, looked up abruptly and reacted by gasping, half-rising and slumping down, the best he could do as turning pale on self-command wasn't within his capability.

He sat back slowly then, and stared.

The other man enjoyed the performance and when it was concluded—Grove drew deep breaths at the finale of his act—the man spoke.

"Good evening, Shrub. Tree. Maple. Bush. And so on. I'm disappointed."

His gun was steady: a Manasco-Windscale .44, the new Klokvik model they were making in the trans-Ural plant, heavy, but with an advantage. The silencer was not attached to it but included in it. Camouflaged, too, Grove noted—decent thought, to paint random patterns on a gun so it would not stand out in a wide variety of places, such as bushes or crowds. Neat, he felt.

Elbow on chair arm, and in no hurry; but he was changed, Grove saw. He smiled almost amiably now, and scrutinized the intruder: bullneck that became a dough head, the flat face of Siberia, pale irises and black-red beard, hands like mud pies made of mashed potato, fat-looking belly and huge feet. Feet that lacked the first joints of all ten toes, Grove remembered. This stewed-looking three hundred pounds of ugliness was Borotky Solentor and his favorite occupation was information-gathering with personnel removal, his score, unknown, but the known number sickening; and his methods, though numerous, were beastly and protracted, if possible.

"You've aged but you still look the same," Grove said without particular emphasis. "Like an albino toad, Borrie."

When he reached "toad," he risked death, but he added, "In spite of some excellent plastic surgery." And then, "Why are you disappointed?" The forefinger relaxed on the trigger, with that.

"Don't pretend you knew when I entered. You did not."

"Never said I did. So?" Grove's only sign of stress was the tapping of a foot.

"You were once a little less obtuse."

"Who sent you? That loveable mother of yours?"

Again, the putty monster almost fired. Again the reference was too unexpected and too knowledgeable to permit the intended flash that would disintegrate Grove's skull and decorate his wall with an instant Jackson Pollock.

"My mother sends worst wishes."

The man's tongue wet the big lips. Most Genghis Khan

types, Grove reflected, have thin mouths. This one, however, had the classic flat face and wide nose but not the mouth or the square body common to people of the Lake Baikal territory; his was the body of a decadent Buddha.

"Anything on the stove but murder?" Grove asked, not cheerfully, but near it.

"It depends. Justice—finally; at once, if need be. If not, you have a long night ahead, you cursed imperialist ghoul!"

"Naughty, naughty!" Grove shook his head. "Ghoul! Indeed! From *you?*"

The man actually snarled, to Grove's slight amazement: bad show, in the Ellen Long idiom.

"I am going to produce a small whistle and blow it, in time," the suet blob said. "It is not an audible whistle. Outside, a dog will hear and his hackles will rise. My assistants will enter. The soiree will begin—or, if you prefer, soiree and its morning continuation."

Grove responded in a calm, near-jovial voice. "You can shoot me, yes. But to do so might be foolish."

Silence. Solentor sat still and Grove tapped a foot monotonously.

Borotky Solentor had been the "dungeon master" of Beria's regime. Now, if Eaper's dictation was reliable, he was director and, by choice, chief torturer-executioner of the PPPG, a new branch of Soviet intelligence not known to exist except by three people in the USA apparatus. He was skilled in so many facets of his profession that Grove, looking at the living being, had difficulty in believing what he had known to be real. They'd last met a quarter of a century ago? About.

Solentor represented the unspeakable, the unthinkable, Torquemadan designs made more horrible by modern science. A Doctor of Medicine, a surgeon, who had never used his arts to heal; a clinical destroyer then, and the man who'd perfected some years back children-kidnaping and closed TV circuit parent-watching as the children began to die. The black genius who had accelerated brain-washing by a prior process of sex-washing: by—it was said—turning virile men into compulsive homosexuals before the next steps of mind revision were undertaken.

The dungeon master had long since earned an explicit trade name. In the Kremlin, in a few other Soviet bureaus, in some of the intelligence centers of other nations, it was known but rarely uttered. Men, the toughest, hated to hear it: *The Lever.*

To bear what he had been obliged to, Grove had finally found the means. With eyes on the fat frog and seeing through him to the book-lined, picture-hung, conventional living room, and beyond to the sea and the stars, Grove thought of the road to his means. For he had been forced to learn a way to endure mere existence, after his best friend, Rodney "Rumble" Russel, the famous M-ONE-K of Britain, had been caught by Arabs. The slow death of that brilliant and warmhearted man had been revealed to Grove by motion-picture film, mailed from Argentina. Watching that half hour of 8-millimeter film had almost destroyed Grove's value to his organization, to his nation, to mankind.

On the verge of madness, Grove had received his insight. Men who did these things, he realized, were more than sick and what they did was different from a purely professional effort to gain information.

The film that had all but defeated Grove without actually touching his flesh led him to understand the reason for its terribleness. If a sufficiently frightful series of torments could be inflicted and then made known to the enemy, he would lose heart and feel terror he could not master, become demoralized before he moved into some next action or assignment. Such an effort to frighten was that of *frightened* people.

Grove had then understood *Shrecklichkeit or* "frightfulness," fully. And ever since, he had known it as proof of fear. That led to his new strength. The way one resisted all such threat of terrorism involved moral courage, used against actual cowardice.

A minute passed. Grove asked himself questions while the Russian pondered. How did he get in with no warning? There had been warnings, Grove suddenly knew, noted subconsciously. A few odd sounds and a stronger breeze from the sea side.

Solentor now smiled. His big, steel-filled teeth were bared.

Solentor's use of those square incisors and heavy bicuspids was legendary. Filed to points and blades. So his smile was a reminder, a weapon.

"You are now, Grove, admirable," he said.

Grove's reply was pleasant. "I thought you were disappointed in me."

"I take part back. I must not pull this trigger? Or reach for my whistle and summon my team? It would be risky?"

"Correct."

"Marvelous. You are in a hopeless situation. You know it. Yet you tell me that I am. And so—hospitably! *Why?* Why so much acting for a bluff? Do you want to die—as you are going to? Have you—'had it'—at last? Or do you imagine that you may yet somehow gain an advantage? I wonder. I keep motionless to indulge you. Yes. And to ask the underlying thing, the psychology of your apparent—aplomb. It is, still, remarkable."

"You can talk," Grove answered calmly. "I can. But *fire?* No. Reach to get that silly whistle? No. So the question is simple. Which is worth more to your folks? Me, dead? Or both of us? Am I worth you? After my long years out of the business and in spite of your continued career? That, only that, is the question you must answer."

For a moment the Siberian was almost worried. Not by the bluffing words, however near to genius their projection and style, but by a small observation. Grove had not moved at all, save to talk, and to—this was the trifle that perturbed—keep tapping his foot, as he'd done from some point since he'd looked up at Death. Why that?

His deduction made him draw a breath and laugh in a way that Grove recalled, a way that had been added to files that perhaps still existed in some warehouse now the property of the CIA:

"The man's laughing style may assist in his identification as he seems unaware of its uniqueness. It is like the close-heard sound of a defecating cow: the little grunt of opening, the fluttered twitter of slight gaseous escape, the louder vocal grunt, the gush-noise of issue and the heavy plat of ground spatter."

Grove could guess the author of that footnote in the Solentor OSS record. By now, he surmised, that file must fill several drawers.

"I wonder," he said when the laugh came to its smacking end, "what the devil brought *you* here? I don't mean to my place—but Hawaii? Don't you trust your own people? Is the mission so important you feel obliged to quit your blood-soaked swivel chair in Moscow—"

Solentor did move, just a little: he lifted the forefinger of his free hand and, of course, noted that nothing dire followed. "The first agendum was to remove you, an automatic decision when I learned how you'd come out here to—live. And die, now. But we did not act at once because of a puzzle."

"Oh?"

"We have certain, let me call it, access to knowledge of the activities of your constantly retitled Composite Information Agency. Your CIA. Our various sources have told us, over the long periods after you were spotted here, that you were *not* CIA. What were you, then? At first, I had the impulse to order your removal in any event; old scores paid. But I waited."

"The plastic surgery," Grove commented reasonably, or with that seeming, "undid most of the damage you blame me for."

Solentor's eyes opened, he rubbed his face, lifted the weapon and then, perhaps realizing that his arm and hand motion gave a final proof of Grove's vulnerability, he half-lowered the gun. "I could not quite believe that your residence here and your means to conceal it—we looked into you from many angles as soon as I decided to delay your removal—were what they seemed. Very extreme measures, I'd say, just to allow an old man to retire so even his business associates and friends couldn't write or call. It appeared to me that you were on some mission, and one I determined to know."

"And what would it be, may I ask?"

Solentor stared as if the other were joking. "You do not really know? It is very possible but I must be sure." His voice dropped and he spoke half to himself. "You have failed to find out a thing." He corrected that—causing Grove inward excitement. "You are able to discover almost nothing. And our old friend, the director, Axe, is sniffing at ten thousand trivialities—in wrong places."

"Did you expect, then"—Grove was mild—"that when you called in your trained devils you could twist out of me a thing I have no knowledge of?"

"Haven't you? If so, we'd twist, as you say, that fact out of you." Solentor's thick lips parted in a smirk. "Your Joint Chiefs of Staff and your Security Council suspect my associates are perfecting some great but unknown—project. But they have no idea what, or where. And there was a time, Grove, when we held you in great admiration, which enraged us. You might still be—admirable. You would long have been dead except that, after Stalin, came Khrushchev, who was not vindictive but soft. I had recovered then. He told me, personally, to abandon our efforts against old enemies who had ceased to be active. Things have changed."

"I daresay," Grove interrupted, dryly. "K's softness. And Mao's wrath."

Solentor stared oddly. "When you found that fool, that trusting idiot of Eaper's in that big tank, I began to wonder anew—knowing by then Mr. R. 'K.' Grove had a middle name not initialed with a *K*. I advised my people over here to do some further looking. I found, among many findings, that you had become a smuggler. Of what? I asked myself. That is another thing to be learned tonight."

"Plants, mostly," Grove idly responded, "that I didn't want to declare. I'm making some horticultural experiments. Then I brought in a couple of pets. Which I didn't wish to wait for, over the four months of quarantine. Both of them, unfortunately, died; poisoned by a pet-hating woman who lives nearby, I think."

"And other matters you will not mention, easily? Explosives?" Solentor watched the effect—none. "If so, they are not in this place, I'm sure. You are too canny. Twice, also, you have picked up communications—yes?—from odd places." Grove made a swift note of that. He'd satisfied himself that Oddie's people knew nothing of the series of spots where messages from two men on the mainland had been left—by a carpenter living in Honolulu whom one of the men knew and trusted completely for the task slated: to deposit those sealed packages where instructed and without curiosity about their contents or their recipient. But Solentor's agents *had* seen him retrieve two of the reports, though which two Grove could not imagine. He felt humiliated. He would have to change that pattern, and explain why—always assuming he was to get an opportunity to do that.

Those thoughts were flashes and his response was delayed deliberately. He eyed the gross man who filled and overran the chair opposite and spoke with some amusement. "My mainland business is growing, and pretty big, now. As you certainly must know, industry in America differs in method from the sweatmills of Russia. But here we do a good deal of so-called industrial spying—to make sure the competition is not ahead of us and to learn what it plans."

Solentor nodded, looked irritably at Grove's tapping foot and considered ordering it to stop. He decided to hide his irritation, since the slight, insistent slipper-jigging was a barometer of stress that, otherwise, Grove had concealed with great effectiveness. He had magnificent control of his voice and face, Solentor mused, with envy. Grove guessed at those thoughts quite accurately.

"Whatever the United Socialist Slave Republic assumes," he went on, "whatever your agents have reported about me, as well—showing, of course, their lack of understanding of the subtle aspects of American commercial activities—whatever, I mean, you are trying on here—the thing you said nobody who ought to know about in America does know about, and wherever this gambit is located, if it is not a mere ploy—at least you ought to have sense enough to realize an old bird like me would hardly take it on by himself. So—why this call? You must be losing your old grip. Care for a cigar, by the way?" When the other man shook his head, Grove asked, "Mind if I have one?"

"No." Solentor saw Grove make the first sign of all-purposeful motion, a slight tensing for, in this case, a mere reach. "We have," the Siberian grinned, "made a fairly quick check of this room. We did it while you were banging about in the kitchen, getting your supper. While you sang old dance tunes, as my men reported. Americans are musical barbarians."

"You knew, when you came in, that there were no little tricks ready to hand? Your sort—or Eaper's?"

Solentor pointed. "Cigars. A lighter. Sugar in a bowl and a lime to suck?" He sounded revolted by that snack. "A cheap novel to read! A favorite chair, where you so often sit and where a third-rate rifleman could shoot you from the water, escaping easily, afterward."

Grove shook his head. "Nope. Bulletproof glass from that angle. I never entirely forget the drill. And I remember, still, that an old enemy might take a potshot at me."

"You Americans are insane in every way but your greatest madness is to believe you can hold back the extension of the doctrines of Marx and Mao, of Communism."

Grove smoked, smiled and said, "Oh, I don't know. You grabbed Middle Europe, sure. But you haven't broken its people. You and Mao's heirs still fail in India, Africa. And

Cuba is a tiny bit of Latin America. We're ahead of you in space, as of our recent achievement on Mars. You can't fight us, in all-out war. Of course, we ought to have taken Russia apart after the Second War. I recommended it to my superiors then. The main reason I opted out in '48 was their failure to get my point about defending liberty. Still—we've stalemated you, there, and everywhere, for years."

The summary was of an order often used by his leaders to spur Solentor. He replied, ominously, "The situation at the moment is, as you say, frozen. But deadlock is intolerable to us. A nation of sentimental, vulgar, ignorant, wasteful rich, cowardly empire-stealing, bourgeois people like yours will soon be humbled!"

"Red flag flying over the Capitol, you mean? A Politbureau replacing Congress? *That* bit? *Nuts!*"

Solentor turned a faint lavender. "You may have even been honest with me, Grove. 'Industrial espionage'—and what a filthy capitalist thing! So! If you have nothing else to add without pressure, I shall call in my men to be sure there is nothing."

Grove knew the time for sparring was about at an end. Solentor had his men ready, and he had means to summon them—an act that should not be permitted, if it was avoidable. He knew, too, that Solentor had wanted this private chance to study his former adversary, which was why there had been any time. He also had profited that way. He speculated on whether or not he should goad Solentor further and decided to try: one of them might, as a result, show his age—call it—more than the other.

"You told me you knew of my smuggling," he began. Solentor stared, not bothering to respond. "I mentioned the contraband: couple of pets and some—trees, shrubs, plants. I assume your men are under cover—as an extra precaution, even though my fence is high? Hiding under my shrubs and trees?" Grove grinned. "Just as I thought. Too bad!" His head shook slightly.

Solentor murmured an annoyed doubt.

"The planting," Grove sighed, "is partly of manchineel, some in every clump—and among all my major trees except the coconut palms, which are no good for concealment. You've surely *heard* of manchineel?"

Grove watched the other think that over, with interest. Had he any background in botany? Or had he, on some previous and probably murderous junket—say, to Cuba—learned of the species? Would it be wise to keep on needling the man with that invention?

Grove guessed, from Solentor's expression, that it wouldn't hurt. He began to talk like a lecturer and some of what he said was true. "You surely know that poisons used by Indians of the Amazon are made from gum-tree sap. And that the Caribbean Indians used to throw a tree branch in a stream to kill fish—which then had to be cooked thoroughly to be edible? You may even be familiar with the report of Gordon Bareter, the botanist, who had the bad luck to put a sleeping bag near a manchineel tree—on a night the wind rose? Their resin falls like that of the pepper tree—which merely etches the paint off parked cars. Bareter lived, though he never recovered his sight. And I *told* you, Borrie, you nitwit, that I had always taken precautions of some sort, knowing certain people, you topping the list, had not been sent long ago to a deserved grave."

He stopped. Solentor still had Grove pinned. But this dissertation had led him through a series of expressions that were as clear, almost, as speech.

Grove decoded them, first, as a hazy but incomplete recollection of manchineel, or, anyway, of poisonous branches that killed fish; next, a special doubt: Solentor's province was human nature and how to corrupt, pervert and destroy it, not—the realm of all nature. His doubt, as he then glanced directly at Grove, was like a silent question and answer, that decided Grove would be capable of planting his grounds with lethal trees. The third reflection appeared as movements of eyes toward distance, considering the men on duty outdoors—and then, with eyes nearly shut—the cost to him if he lost them, along with, perhaps, his chance of learning more if he shot Grove, and was left to escape on his own. In his concentrated state he let his .404 slant off target, slightly. A smile spread on the face.

Grove read it and said, "If you move your gun, what's right beside you, Borrie, will—hey! Hold it! Turn your eyes if you need proof—but for *God's sake, sit still!*"

Grove's tone was so real that Solentor did freeze and merely cut his eyes first toward the fireplace where he saw nothing and then in the opposite direction, where the thing he saw literally paralyzed him, eyes included.

"It won't do anything unless you move or I stop tapping my foot," Grove said mildly. "I think."

Solentor, bloodless, could not even breathe.

"We can talk, because it's used to that."

Beyond that cutting of eye Solentor called on no other muscle. He could not. His face became suffused with a crimson-threaded mauve that slowly turned fish-belly white. He did not breathe. It was like watching a speeded-up motion picture of the process of rot. Grove thought a heart attack or stroke might end his life; but the muzhik was tough. At last he drew in a slow, desperate breath. Exhaling with extreme care, he took a second disciplined gasp. His color improved, gradually.

What Solentor had seen and what remained in position at his side was a king cobra, reared to shoulder level, facing him with a darting tongue and spread hood. He tried to communicate with his stunned eyes, to ask mercy, perhaps.

"While your arm's beyond the cobra's vision," Grove finally suggested, "you better lower it and put that Klokvik on the chair, quietly." He saw resistance. "In time, your arm will tire and you'll have to lower it. The cobra will then strike. Besides, you are no longer aiming the gun at me"—an untrue but calm remark—"so it would be useless to snap off a shot, even if that's your idea."

Solentor actually began to lower the weapon with the perspiring care of a man trying to disarm an unfamiliar bomb. He let go of it, finally. Meanwhile Grove clarified the picture, lecturing, almost:

"My mother, you may know, was an animal trainer. She also had a so-called snake charmer act in the side shows with non-poisonous snakes, usually big but placid pythons. She was interested in the deadly species, though. And a long time ago some man she met who came from what was Cochin-China said cobras could identify people; knew their keepers, in zoos, for instance. One day I was touring the snake house in Washington Zoo and ran into a curator, a famous herpetologist—can't recall his name at the moment, unfortunately. I asked the man about cobras knowing people. He demonstrated the truth and scared the hell out of me. Cobras let him walk right past—but when I tried—*well!*" Grove swallowed convulsively and with no false effort. The experience had been memorable.

Solentor decided he had to try something. His position wasn't bearable. He whispered, "Will you deal?"

Grove smiled faintly. "What can you trade? Let me fill you in a bit more." He moved a hand toward his humidor, eyes on the big snake—and decided not to move further, or so it seemed to Solentor; though that act was pretense. Grove frowned and went on.

"As long as I keep tapping my foot, you are reasonably safe. This king cobra is among my smuggled pets. Twelve feet long, about, but never measured by me. They're said to grow twice that long. Cobras are suspicious snakes, as all herpetologists will tell you. This one, I trained to start up from the hothouse through a crawl hole between walls when I began tapping the way I've been doing. It means, food will be served. But to get its meal, live rats, usually, it has to cross from behind the draperies that close off the lanai to a point near me. You were on that path, and a stranger, so naturally it stopped to look you over. If I quit tapping it will strike, as it will if it sees you move. When it comes for dinner it knows I'll stand to get it—but I don't dare, with a stranger so close to it and considering its basic reactions." Grove now noted Solentor's stealthy effort to slide his hand toward the released gun. "Don't," he advised.

Sweat had begun to bead the fat face when Solentor got his first breath. It ran in tiny brooks, now; his armpits were soaked; and his clothing became a blotter for spreading stains. Grove would have liked to waste more time. But he was by no means certain how long the cobra would continue to inspect the unknown man. He hadn't even been entirely sure it would behave as it had; just fairly sure.

"I'll trade you on one basis."

Solentor almost nodded, remembered, and murmured, "Which is—?"

"You can talk safely," Grove reminded, "so long as you don't move at all. Well, I'll get you off this hook if you will tell me"—he looked away in thought and seemed not to be watching Solentor at all—"exactly the location and the nature of Project Neptune."

Solentor gasped, faintly. Then he flinched. Next his eyes screwed up as he waited for the fangs. At that very moment the cobra became bored and lay flat. Solentor peeped in frantic wonder because his sudden flinch had not led to the expected horror.

When he realized that Grove was looking down, he

looked. When he saw the great snake, hood no longer distended, crawling lazily toward Grove, Solentor leaped up and rushed toward the lanai where he let loose a hoarse shriek. Grove, meanwhile, sidled out of the leather chair around the arm farthest from the cobra and he also hurriedly left the room, but not in pursuit.

He heard expected sounds while he nervously procured from a closet and then tendered the cobra's meal. That done, he put a folding pen around the snake and the revolting dinner scene. He was aware that Solentor had left through a side window of the lanai, not needing to break a pane there. He was conscious that a motor right below the glassed-in porch had chugged briefly. He could identify other sounds, too, and their sequence. Men ran about, muttered and swore in Russian. A motorboat coughed. A dog barked. The boat roared and gathered speed, on a course toward Rabbit Island.

When the cobra's meal was half ingested Grove jockeyed the reptile and its folding pen into a box. The box went downstairs where he locked the whole business in a closet. He was not a snake admirer. He had not enjoyed training this deadly monster in its limited tricks. But it had saved his life, for one thing. And it had been the means of levering proof of a vital fact out of The Lever himself!

Project Neptune was real.

Grove returned to his living room, flopped in his red chair for minutes, finally lighted a cigar and decided to postpone the cobra's disposal for a while. Its value had been great; it was now zero.

He felt shaky, still, though a held-out cigar didn't show a discernible tremor. That, he thought, was something to be grateful for, not proud of. His hand might be steady but his *mind* was quivering like a plucked fiddle string. And he felt very cold, too. He tried to make apologies for it, speaking aloud: "It was a little tight there, actually."

Then he chuckled and not quite weakly, either.

At last he went out on the lanai and found what he expected. The windows at its ends were not of bulletproof glass, but ordinary plate, four large panes in each. One such rectangle had been removed from its metal frame, doubtless while he'd made supper though it might have been earlier. Replacing it was a now-dangling slab of rigid plastic that, if shut, would not be noticed save by accident or very close examination. It was removable. On the ground below was a fork lift, used as an elevator to reach the lanai. What he had heard, but failed to "hear" usefully, was the sound of Solentor climbing onto the raised lift. The draft he'd recalled, belatedly, came when the plastic window was opened.

Grove studied the setup for a while and decided these very effective means would not be used again. They would expect him to defend against such burglarious schemes immediately, with some diabolic counter, probably. So he could let that matter slide.

He stood on the lanai for some time, however, taking deep breaths of the air that came in through the opened plastic panel. Then he walked to the front of the porch and stared out to sea, wondering how Solentor and his men would be picked up—on the far shore of Rabbit Island, beyond doubt. He decided they would transfer to one of the Soviet "fishing boats" and head away on a course calculated to keep the island between their ship and the shore-based radar beyond the park. They could even transfer to one of the Soviet subs that frequently dogged warships coming out of Pearl Harbor.

He returned to the living room, then, shutting the lanai doors. He switched off the air conditioning and, feeling a need for comfort, lighted kindling under logs in his fireplace. He rarely used it and never had had an excuse of this sort. What sort? To calm my damn nerves, he admitted. Sitting in his chair again, he reviewed the visit and pondered the effects on his situation.

The next communication from his friend, Elias Foth, the tree-watcher, wasn't due for some days: ample time, then, to change the delivery system.

Grove was still humiliated at not having discovered he was being tailed, by other men than Oddie's. Of course, he had expected the latter; but he should also have suspected others might conduct a similar surveillance; he ought, in any case, to have caught onto it. A point for the enemy, then, and a point to keep in mind.

The visit had confirmed Project Neptune, a great gain. The importance of the visitor, together with various inferences drawn during the conversation, made Grove almost certain that Neptune involved Oahu; but what it was or where remained unguessable as before.

Solentor now knew Grove had heard the code name. He realized, too, that Grove was playing some game—the appearance of the cobra would prove it: an unpredictable move of a kind Grove, alone, would dream up. But, since the Communists also knew that Grove was not acting for any established American intelligence group, they would still be perplexed. Further, and Grove was ironically amused at the thought, Communists were easily led to believe the most preposterous things about Americans—as long as such things were vicious, infamous, crooked and ignoble. Solentor would doubtless be convinced that, whether Grove was effectively engaged in anything else or not, he was busy with "industrial espionage."

Neither had learned very much more of positive value. It was a compliment of sorts to be held up and interrogated by the alleged chief of a recently formed special cadre, the PPPG. The visit suggested, furthermore, that Neptune was an operation not only planned for and in preparation, here, but one that could not be easily moved elsewhere. Otherwise, why not transfer it instead of spending so much effort to try to find out the intentions of a middle-aged, onetime agent? That was a valuable assumption.

But when Grove tried to regard his part in the evening with some satisfaction his relish diminished in step with the effort. He wanted to tell himself he had come off well but increasingly felt that somewhere he had dropped a stitch, missed a point, failed to do or else to think of an item that he couldn't place. It made him restless and he walked around the room for a while, deciding to go to bed and then not to, since he was far from sleepy. A log slid from the dogs, smoking, and Grove went to the fireplace.

He set the screen aside and, with a wooden-handled fire tool that hung on a thong, replaced the log. Just after he had put the heavy instrument back on its hook Grove knew what had caused his vague sense of unfinished business.

He perceived it with surprise, and thought, as he often did, that his tardy recognition was a sign of age, of rustiness, of his folly in trying to do what he had undertaken. If his oversight was belated, however, the time lapse between Solentor's charge through the window to the present made it pardonable in a way.

Still, after setting the screen back and glancing around the room, he felt depressed.

His hands remained cold. He pressed them against the warm screen, remembering other times and places when, at other hearths, he had made fires for solace: fires of straw and of unknown wood, fires in a cabin during an arctic winter in occupied Norway, fires of peat and of camel dung, fires in a tropical village hut on the thatched roof of which monsoon rain hammered.

Ring Grove had always been a very lonely man.

9

HOSTAGE?

Grove was still squatting at his hearth when he knew suddenly his tantalizing and ultimately perceived oversight ought not to have been dismissed. He had caught a soft sound of footsteps. What had nagged him was the need to search his house to make sure Solentor had not left anything behind, or anybody. His rustiness was real and his position hopeless. He waited, not trying to move, for the command or the bullet he deserved. Quiet footsteps came close and halted.

A voice ordered, "Don't move."

He didn't. The voice was a woman's and husky; a little nervous, as if its owner was the one in danger. "Turn around slowly."

He did. She was young, in Grove's view, very beautiful—and stark naked. She walked forward till she stood in front of him. Her arms were lifted high, as if in surrender, which set Grove's mind stuttering. Was this Solentor's idea of—an ace in a sleeve? She had a fine figure and was tall; blonde hair curled down her back, very lovely hair; her eyes were deep brown and almost as wide-set as Grove's; a rather pert tilt of nose, a broad but not shapeless mouth, legs that, as he rose slowly and staring, brought the word "Ziegfeld" to his mind. A living houri, a personified odalisque. Her expression was intent but unreadable. The over-all result, in the word his gang of kids used, was kook.

That, finally, prompted Grove to say, "It doesn't make any sense at all!"

The naked girl relaxed a little, with that. She was, he thought, in her late twenties or early thirties but a girl to him.

"I am keeping up my hands so you will not shoot."

"Shoot?" That left Grove more puzzled then ever. "What in hell with? My cigar?"

"And so," she added, "you will know I'm not able to kill you."

"How'd you get in?"

"The way The Lever did. His men came with me ahead of him."

"I see. Well?"

"I need to explain."

"So help me Moses, you do!"

"I heard it all." She smiled briefly. "That cobra! It terrified him. I never knew he could be afraid, till then."

Grove gazed at her with a careful speculation unrelated to her sex or its complete exposure and excessive allure. "So you stripped before you showed up—to make me happy. Didn't you realize I know of women, as bare as you are, who have killed men?"

She kept her hands high and slowly turned in a complete circle. Grove reflected that all elevations were delightful; one expected that of Solentor's female colleagues. Facing him again, she said, "You must make sure I cannot do any such thing."

He nodded. "Don't think I won't!"

He rose and stepped up to her. His examination was professional, thorough, and conducted with no regard for modesty. Satisfied, he grunted and stepped away. "You can put your hands down," he said. She did so. The lady had not been in any way surprised or, apparently, embarrassed by his search.

If he had needed more confirmation of her background, that lack of reaction would have been ample. The first thing to do would be to get her dressed—rather, Grove decided, the second thing; the first thing would be to examine her garments before she put them on. He had made mistakes enough for one night.

"What's your name?"

"Esther Wilson—my real one."

"Well then, where are your clothes?"

The answer startled Grove: "On the boat."

There had been only one boat. He shook his head. "Solentor must have lost his mind? You came in—like this?"

"I was taken to your bedroom. There was a quilt—"

"I don't get it! Your boss never intended me to go to bed again, above the ground, anyway."

"No." She was silent.

"If you'll walk ahead, I'll get you a gown."

She did; when they returned, the woman wore a robe. She sat opposite Grove when he motioned her to do so. She said, "It isn't very hard to understand: me being here, naked."

"Suppose you try to enlighten a man who is evidently stupid, then."

"Will you listen? I mean—to the whole thing? From the start, for my sake?"

"Go ahead. I'll listen."

"I was a—well—a pretty crazy kid. I'm an American, incidentally." She looked at him with a sort of hope; he simply shrugged. "My mother died when I was nine. Dad paid me no attention. I ran around in my teens with the jet set's kids and went to Bennington, too. It's supposed to be—was supposed to be—the farthest-out girl's college anywhere. I was bored. I had an affair with a professor, finally, just to see how it was. When I found out about that—*how* it was—I broke if off. She committed suicide."

The words stopped; but Grove showed no reaction. His bizarre guest continued. "The lady prof left a note. I never had any idea even men could get that—intense—because of mere sex! And everybody acted afterward as if I was an absolute nothing. I went home. Dad lived in New York, when he wasn't with some woman or other. I was already fed up with the Park Avenue bit. I wanted excitement and that's how, finally, it occurred to me I could at least do one good deed in my life—even if it involved doing what was anything but."

Grove began to see ahead: "So you flew down to Washington and offered to be—"

"Father knew everybody. Including Admiral Ball. So I got to him and in a couple of weeks I was in the training camp. My God, I had no idea *anything* could be that rough! Not *then*. I stuck it out, partly because most volunteers didn't—and partly because some of the—*work*—*was* exciting—and promised to be more so, besides."

"When did you—graduate?"

"Almost six years ago. I was twenty-two. I had some special features to offer, after all. I'd been in school in

France—a convent. Father had hoped it would 'discipline' me." She laughed derisively. "So I spoke perfect French. In the training camp I learned Russian and German. You know what else, I gathered." Grove nodded coldly and she went on. "At first my assignments weren't much. An English physicist who worked in their A-bomb plants—a real dope. I was in Paris for a while. Hong Kong came later. And it was after I'd been in Hong Kong—I was an American buyer, according to my papers—I dated a cute guy, on my own, and against orders, of course. Well, I woke up once, in Macao—and the next time, on the trans-Siberian railroad. I was taken to Moscow and later met—your recent visitor. I had the two choices that you should be able to imagine."

Grove could, easily. It made him slightly sick. "So you chose to work for them."

"Who wants to die?" she asked quickly.

"A lot of people, men *and* women, don't want to. But do."

She twisted a strand of heavy, shining hair. "Sure. And later in their retraining center—I nearly did die. But I had the idea that, someday, while playing *for* them, I'd get a chance—" She gave him a pitiful look.

"Some people rationalize that way—under those circumstances." Grove shook his head as if at a disappointing daughter. "It never works."

Her dark eyes blazed. "It *did* work!"

A very pretty act, a very solid-sounding tale, he thought. But he said, "Meaning what, exactly?"

Her voice dropped as if she feared being overheard. "How did you hear about Project Neptune?"

That shook Grove. The information, such as it was, had come through what Eaper called one of "Ball's bints," women inherited from the admiral's administration. "Bint" suggested a type very different from the beauty sitting here. She seemed intelligent and she also seemed the kind of female who would be a bad risk as a wife: and why? Witchy, Grove decided.

"So *you* sent the code name?"

She nodded thoughtfully. "And that was found out."

"Oh."

They looked at each other for a full minute, a psychologically brutal encounter the woman lost. "And so," he prompted, "you went back to Moscow. Then what?"

"They told me all the way there the punishments I could be given after Solentor decided which ones."

"I see." Grove did. She went on in slow, horrified recollection:

"The Lever got everything he could from me, of course. About my work before they caught me. Most all of what I'd learned and transmitted about them. Nothing very damaging, I can tell you—whether you believe it or not. And then I was sent for more training." She could not go on.

He waited while she tried and said at last. "Okay. You betrayed them, and so on. How did you get here? And why?"

"When I was taken away to come here I had no notion of the purpose." This came out readily. "Just, I wouldn't likely last long, of that I was sure. I was flown—with some Russian agents—to Vladivostok. And sent on with them by ship to near here—they rowed, this evening—to your beach. I had no idea where I was, who you were, anything. I guessed it was Hawaii when I saw the shore from the fishing boat in which we crossed the Pacific—I presume you know about them?—but not much else. A while before The Lever ordered us in here, his men stripped me and brought me ashore. I was taken to your bedroom and told to stay there. You were in your kitchen. That was *all* I had from them. I left the bedroom when I found I could and tried to listen. I got cold and went back for that quilt. I did listen—and pretty soon I began to understand about you. See?"

"I think I do." Grove's mouth was dry. "You had no chance of getting out of the house. Borrie left no possibility of your running away. You were nude. He was going to use you to make me talk. He'd do that, by using you first. His boys would go into their act on you while I'd have to—"

"Yes."

Grove looked at her, looked away. "Typical," he said quietly. Then his voice became stern. "Just how badly will he want you back? How much, I mean, do you know that you can tell me?"

"Nothing important." Her tone was dreary.

"What about Project Neptune?"

"I wish I *did* have something more." She thought a moment. "Almost two years ago they sent me back to Hong

Kong on an assignment. One night my contact there—a man—ordered me to his apartment. He got drunker than apes—I didn't keep up—and he started boasting about his inside status. He said that something very big, very absolute was being set up to take over America. An operation called Project Neptune. He was sure it would make the commies top dog. I felt he believed that. But he couldn't add a damned bit. And I am sure he didn't know more *to* add—I can about guarantee it because I'm a girl, after all, and I know a good deal about when men are putting it on. So I took the trouble, a few days later, to get in touch with one of my former CIA contacts. Another woman—with about my rank, before I was snatched. We met in the dark and I don't think they even knew whether I talked to a man or woman—though I told them it had been a woman, when they—I mean—later. Anyhow, she didn't speak—I'd signaled her not to—and they don't know what I told her. We thought we were safe and alone, that night. She went, soon, and I stuck around and—that's all."

Grove stretched. "Like a drink?" He rose.

"Please." Her eyes shone briefly. Their light died out as he crossed the room and poured the drinks without noticing her. She raised her glass slightly. "To the liar you think I am, that I'm not."

Grove drank part of his whisky and stared at her thoughtfully. "Whether you've lied or not isn't important. What's important to me is, what the devil to do about you."

"I have a suggestion," she said—and stopped at his reaction. "Anyhow, it was an idea. Sometimes it works—I'm fun." She gave up. "They won't come back till they figure out some new gambit."

"No." He began thinking hard, paying no attention to her. It made her somewhat ashamed of herself. He seemed a nice guy and not all *that* old, she was sure. It was difficult for her to believe what she'd gathered from the overheard conversation: that this man had been an agent, too, and might be one still. One even Solentor feared—and for cause, she had found. She couldn't tell about him now and thought Solentor couldn't figure Mr. Grove either. Finally he did look at her, smiling a little. "What should I do, from *your* point of view?"

"I haven't any idea. When The Lever ran, I knew I was here alone. I knew somebody would likely take swift action—oh—blow the whole place up, for instance, just because I'd been left here. And I can see you don't think much of my kind of woman. Neither do I. So I haven't any real reason to care what's done to me."

"You're very beautiful," he replied mildly.

She raised her drink in another sad mock toast. "Thank you, sir." She reflected afterward and went on, "I worked for Admiral Ball of course—till they got me in Hong Kong. When I was sent back there I did try to get the word to CIA, as I said and how I said. By then, I knew the admiral had retired. I could tell you a good deal about what the Soviets know of CIA, and our other operations. But not much about *how* they know."

"You can do just that, later." Grove nodded. "But if you don't know who, what isn't very important. It would help, though. My problem is present tense. I can't just turn you loose—"

"Obviously."

"Why—'obviously'?"

"I'd have nothing to wear, for instance."

That made him laugh. "But I can't keep you here long either."

"Why? I mean—it's a charming house. At least, I thought it was till I got a peek at that snake. You keep revolting pets. Or is there just the one?"

His eyes were speculative. "Questions?"

"Sorry. You could turn me over to the police and I could probably convince them to put me in touch with the CIA."

"That's just the trouble. I have nothing whatever to do with the CIA and if they found you came to them from me, which they would, then—"

"I see. Then Solentor would learn, sooner or later, and suspect, as he did when he came here, that you were, after all, making an American effort for some outfit Solentor never heard of—maybe related to Project Neptune. Are you?"

Grove stared. "Not very smart."

She shook her head ruefully and Grove found he was wishing she wouldn't move that way: it made her hair shimmer and that led to an unwanted response. The disingenuousness of her question tended to strengthen his acceptance of her story. She had asked it spontaneously and for the manifest reason that she wanted to understand his status better . . . the better to judge her own. He thought of having her tell exactly what the others knew about American intelligence—and decided it wouldn't add greatly to what Solentor had made rather clear: the Reds had people who reported doings of the CIA and of the Security Council—which was more than enough to know. She could probably talk for hours and fake every word, too.

"Suppose," she said, "I was your runaway daughter, now. Any help?"

He shook his head. "I never had one. And the only possible man who could see you as a daughter would be your actual father."

He took her empty glass and refilled it.

"My real father—hardly thought of his daughter, at all. That was where the trouble started, I guess."

He abruptly asked a question, harshly—and was aware as he did that it was a personal and revealing act. "Were you ever Borrie's mistress?"

"Thank God, no!"

Grove was red-faced. "Sorry."

She understood. "We never mentioned his name if we could avoid it. The Lever, sometimes. By our superiors mostly—to keep fear churning in us. He was called The Head. I only saw him a few times—when they were deciding what to do with me." The inference she had drawn from his question at last had told her—without his intention—that he had appreciated her as a woman. As human.

Midnight had struck some time ago. The day ahead was going to be long and difficult. He would need sleep and he would have to be up in time to stall Oopani. The girl—Esther Wilson—was conceivably telling the truth, at least in the main. She was, however, possibly doing a very clever job, one set up against the chance that Solentor might somehow abandon his operation to her. It seemed very unlikely, though. The Lever had planned his execution, after he'd blown the whistle and after Grove had watched this woman die, slowly—before his turn came. The Lever used women-traps, exploiting empathy, chivalry, every human quality. But Grove could not see how this woman, in her state, would serve any end now.

The situation was ironic, whatever its real basis. Solentor would be furious over the girl left behind. But Grove was on a spot, too, owing to the same circumstance.

He sank in the red chair, almost oblivious of Esther Wilson. A plan formed. He wished, however, that he had found the answer he now needed earlier. "Esther," he finally said, "I'm going to ask you to come along with me."

She followed him to the floor below and watched as he cut a pair of handcuffs apart and, using the blowtorch, welded the halves to the ends of a long, heavy chain. He chilled the welds and next told her to go back upstairs ahead of him, still. He directed her to a guest room.

Its windows overlooked the grounds at one end of the house and fifteen feet down; its bath was adjacent to his own. The chain, she realized, was long enough to reach from the bed to the bath. She spoke hopefully. "You could keep me in your room, after all. Another pet—but nice."

"Come on!" Grove said with irritation. He attached the cuffs to an ankle and a metal bedpost.

She was permissive and then more than that. She let her borrowed robe fall open as she sat on the bed. "I won't let you sleep, then. I'll jangle chains like a ghost! I'll sing songs that nice girls never heard of, if there are any nice girls left." But she knew she was a fool.

"I won't even be around."

That scared her. Slowly, she pulled the robe rogether. "You mean, you'll leave me chained here alone?"

"Till I can get you somewhere else. If I can manage, yes."

Her terror was a mute facial contortion. It was shocking that human beings could be frightened to that extent; she had been broken, and broken again and yet again, as that rictus of horror stated without words.

He stood looking at her, silently. He knew all the truth about courage. Any human being can be smashed, forced to reveal any secret, however priceless, and brain-washed completely as well, *if he lives.* Some brave individuals manage, by luck, to die before their expert tormentors succeed. But if the torturer has the time and the skill, no one lives and keeps silent about what the other wishes to learn—no one keeps his identity, his dearest belief, his love of country or of God, if the dissuader has the time, if death doesn't thwart his objective.

"A brave man—or woman," he said to her, "dies a thousand times. Bravery isn't what we were taught, Esther. Neither is cowardice. I was brought up as an American, supposed to be fearless, and if not, a coward. It's a lie. A brave man is merely the one who, however badly frightened, keeps functioning, just doesn't panic. A coward quits as soon as fear looms. And all of us can be driven over the big wall. Fearless men are mad."

She nodded, her eyes fixed on his, her breath shallow and rapid. "I know. I do know. I was American-brave, once. Oh, very brave!"

He smiled slightly. "I realize it. And you'll be all right, here, while I'm out." He saw the rigidity returning. "Use your head! Solentor won't be back, or send anybody back, tonight. He wouldn't be that stupid even if he had the chance. Now *listen!* Don't flake off that way! I'll be back before daylight, or send somebody, to get you away. Solentor went out to his ship, or sub, and you must have heard his boat. My phones are working. He has no idea of what outfit I work for. A moron would assume that I'd contacted some of my people, in minutes, after he left."

Her eyes were reasoning again. "Did you?"

"Questions?" He frowned. "None of The Lever's people will barge in like second-rate robbers now. The next time they want in here, if there is one, they'll do a mighty cautious reconnaissance job. Don't you see why?"

She started to shake her head, then nodded. "That cobra."

"Yes. That cobra; suggesting that this joint may be fixed up with other surprises, even many, and as—unexpectable. You better lie down before you fall."

She lay back.

He moved toward the door, followed by pleading eyes; but the girl didn't say a word.

He crossed his living room slowly and went out on the lanai where he stood looking over the night-draped sea at the pale ridges and gouged trenches on the eroded slopes of Rabbit Island.

How should he tackle Jerry Gong?

Could he, even in this crisis, this need of aid?

Did he dare act on his likeliest assumption, that the park watchman was neither an accomplice of the police or of Oddie, nor a perhaps unwitting dupe of others?

No.

What bluff could be used to find out?

Not any Grove could think of, was the answer. He could take a gun, of course, and threaten. But, use it?

Grove had not carried a gun since his arrival in Hawaii.

His reason was simple. A man in an aloha shirt and slacks has no place to carry a gun that a professional cannot detect. The American public has been fed so many gun myths, by TV and movies, that not one adult in ten thousand, including those who own handguns, knows their limits and risks. Specially tailored clothes are needed to hide a gun from a pro. And the man who uses guns has one in his hand before his victim sees his problem. The fastest draw never beat the ready trigger finger.

More decent people, Grove knew, had been killed because they had guns and tried, too late, to get to them, than guns ever saved. How often do newspapers report the capture of an armed housebreaker, thief, mugger, rapist, or other criminal, by a citizen who had a pistol and got to it in time to make the snatch? The thought made Grove smile a little.

And yet, Grove knew, nothing but a gun would hold Jerry long enough for the talk he needed and the hoped-for answers. Jerry had a gun. . . .

He drove his rebuilt station wagon to the park.

Jerry waved as it stopped and cycled on toward the institute. Grove went to Whaler's Cove and watched the porpoises perform. They'd performed twice, at least, for other night-visiting persons, not expected or known, so far as he could make out from the graphs and from Jerry's accounting of authorized visitors. So there had been meetings in the park, alien presence, anyway, perhaps scouting prior to a meeting. It was possible that Jerry had known about those events. It was possible, if Grove's measure of the watchman was mistaken, or even if the meetings had involved Jerry and, say, some of Oddie's people, which events Jerry would not mention to him, their suspect, in that case.

After the porpoise greeting, Grove went to the Reef Tank but did not climb its spiral ramp. He waited in the dark entry till he saw Jerry riding back and then, keeping covered, he hurried toward the watchman, halted and crouched. Jerry braked and stepped from the bike when he came up. "Something wrong, Ring?"

Grove held up a finger, then pointed. He stole toward the cove and Jerry followed with the same quiet care. Obviously Grove had seen something that needed this guarded approach. When Grove held a palm up and stopped, Jerry did too. He also unsnapped the strap that held his Police

Special in place and slipped off its safety. Grove then pointed through a clump of trees to a lighter area, beyond. Jerry came close, bike supported by his left hand, and peered.

Grove took the .45 with the double skill of a trained agent and a professional magician.

Jerry reacted very quickly but apparently without great alarm. "Nice trick!"

"No trick," Grove answered and the watchman knew by the tone that it was, indeed, no trick. He leaned back on his bike a little and said, softly, "Okay. Then what is it?"

"Just that I have to have answers, right ones, to a few questions."

"Such as?" The watchman sounded perplexed rather than frightened.

"I hate to have to," Grove replied, slowly. "But I'm desperate and I *mean* that, all ways you can think. I want to know who you report to, besides the park brass, if anybody."

"Easy! Nobody." Jerry was steady and so was the bike he supported.

"What makes you suspicious of me, then?"

Jerry grinned slightly. "Am I?"

"I think so."

"Then you maybe can answer some questions I have." Jerry didn't allow Grove to break in. "A long while back you may recall I mentioned being surprised by a smell. Ylang-ylang blossoms, right?"

"I remember."

"Other things happened, that night."

"Yes."

"Such as you tossed an FBI man into the Reef Tank."

"So I did."

"Then the feds gave you a going over; tagged you, for a while, too."

"Correct. And put you wise to that?"

"No. Friends in the cops told me, a little of it, later." Jerry frowned. "Want more?"

"All there is." Grove gestured to remind the man of the gun.

"You planted some salt-water orchids, a while back."

"For Mrs. Abbott, yes. With permission."

"And another plant. Till I found it, I couldn't figure why you trained the porpoises to greet you that big way. But I had a hunch there was more to it than fun. And when I saw those new flowers and asked what they were and got told you put them in, I made a point of looking around that spot. Then it was clear."

"And you reported that, to whom?"

"I've been considering reporting it, maybe to my old friends in the cops. But I haven't yet. I sort of hoped you'd finally explain. I know you're working. I can't find out for who, not by any hinting around my pals. I almost put it to you, man to man, a time or so, recently. But—"

"I'm putting it to you, Jerry. You already know too damn much about me. If you've reported it, I mean to find out who got that word."

"How? If you shoot me, it'll be no good. If you don't—"

"—I could start operations aimed to make you tell me. In fact—you better begin walking toward the Reef Tank, now—"

"I suppose you could—manage," Jerry said slowly and with anxiety. Then his tone changed. "My . . . *gosh!*"

"My gosh—*what?*"

"This afternoon I went over my gun. And didn't reload it. Man, what a mistake! What a *lucky* one!"

"Very nice try," Grove replied grimly. Nevertheless he checked. The .45 was not loaded.

Jerry had then moved his bicycle a little. He looked at the deflated Grove with wonder. "The gun, as you saw, is empty. First time in years I've pulled that one. But look, Ring, the bike is now aimed at you. I can put one shot through the top bar—or blast you with buckshot, from the tool kit."

Grove nodded as if he already knew. His first reaction to the empty Police Special was astonishment and with it a swift thought that Jerry had deliberately allowed the little play that led to the gun-snatch because he was ready for it, expecting something of the sort. Now he tried to see what use he could make of a situation that either was—or was anything but—so slick that he'd ignored the possibility. He stared at Jerry in the half-shadow but the watchman, as far as Grove could make out, was as flustered in some fashion as Grove himself.

"I'm feeling ashamed," the huge man said in a low and embarrassed tone, "to make a mistake like that. And have it discovered by—another pro. But"—he grinned a little—"it sure was a fluff at the right time!"

Grove held out the Police Special, by its barrel. "You better reload it."

The other hesitated. "With two hands?" He shook his head while he replaced the weapon in its holster. "Not that."

Grove began to think this reversal of the situation might still suit his need. "If you haven't reported all you've learned about me to a soul, Jerry, maybe you'll explain why?"

"We'll go up to the restaurant level—you ahead—and talk. Okay?"

"Right." Grove walked and the aimed bike came in the rear. He heard clicks that told him Jerry was reloading the .45 and he sensed that the gun was being held either by teeth or else by the hand that also could trigger a shot through a bicycle bar or a spreading blast from what he'd known was not a case for tools. A wide-angle blast, in the event Jerry encountered more than one and decided to kill or maim them. Smart, Grove reflected, and about what he'd imagined.

At the level of the restaurant, which was open on three sides, Jerry gestured at a table in bright light. Grove sat where the watchman indicated and approved of the way in which Jerry parked the bike and came over with the gun to sit across the heavy wooden table.

"So?"

Grove shrugged. "So? For one thing, why haven't you reported me, if you're not lying? And my aquagraph?"

"Your—oh!" Jerry was silent for a moment. "You have been a friend, Mr. Grove, for a long while, right? You have been very kind to many people, in the Hawaiian Homelands and in Waimanalo, who are friends of mine; some are relatives. I have suspected you from the night of the found body. But of what? I couldn't say. I found your—aquagraph—and saw its purpose. But one more thing about that was clear. It was to tell you when other persons were in the park, besides me and allowed people. This meant you would not be here and even did not know when such people might slip in. You were not, then, *with*—whoever has made two visits. That I missed but the gadget recorded. So I am left to wonder why you want to learn about them. And who are they? Now, I think, you will tell me."

"I think I will," Grove answered slowly. "I only wish I

were certain beyond any doubt that you haven't spread the word on me to anybody."

"And why?"

"Because I'm acting alone. Because it is vital that nobody—not the police or FBI or even the CIA—know that I'm working here."

"I have not told anybody. Should I swear on a Bible?"

Grove shrugged. "While your gun's on me? No. I'm going to have to trust you. If I'm wrong about you, if you've lied, the result could be disastrous."

"Result for whom?"

"America." Grove paused and plunged. "Jerry, I am alone out here and I report to just one man. The President."

Jerry's eyes widened. His mouth opened and closed. He shook his head not in disbelief but as if to clear the brain within. "Why?"

Grove began the story.

He told it succinctly; but it took more than half an hour. He ended with an account of The Lever's appearance and of how that had been handled. He did not yet mention the girl.

Jerry had listened and occasionally nodded but asked no questions. About halfway through the recital he had done a thing that made Grove rejoice. He put away the .45 and sat with hands folded between them on the table top. At the end, he reached out one of those hands and the two men joined in an iron grip.

The Grove did explain about the girl. "You can see my problem. I can't keep her around. Jenny will be in, come morning. Oh, I could dope her and hide her downstairs for a day or so. But I have no idea of her—loyalty. Or the lack of any. You can see, if she's conning me with the idea of getting back to Solentor, that mustn't be allowed. In a way, she's clever. And, Lord knows, she's a dish! If she told the truth, if she was the one who got us word of this Project Neptune thing, and if she managed to survive yet not to give that away the second time they nabbed her, she's tough, call it brave. In which case, she deserves a chance to live—to get away and home free. Clear?"

Jerry nodded. He'd been half attentive at the last. "It will not be difficult," he said finally, "to take her off your hands."

"No?"

"My second cousin would be best, I think. Cy—Cyrus Ah Soo is resourceful. He owes me some favors. And a thousand bucks, too. He has property—interests—here and there. I'll ring Cy." The watchman rose to cross to the lighted phone booth. "You will meet him at your house in, say, half an hour?"

"Rather not, I think. On the thin chance that our friend the fat Soviet horror still has a watch or has set one up, by now. I'd think it would be better, at least more puzzling, if the girl was taken away by an unidentified person. Will this—Ah Soo—be able to manage that?"

"Certainly."

"Then, can he come here—discreetly—and get the keys? I'll tell him where I hid the handcuff set. And she'll need some sort of clothes. Five-six tall, about, and well proportioned."

Jerry nodded.

He was in the booth for five minutes. When he came back he said, "All set." Then he gazed at Grove with a beginning grin. "You'll have to tell the—President—that I have joined his Special Forces?"

"Yes."

The grin grew. It became laughter. "You are the damnedest man I ever knew!"

The response was serious. "We may both be damned, now."

Jerry cut the laugh. "But we shall try to prevent that. And two are better than one."

"Actually," Grove reminded him quietly, "we are four."

"Yes. And one in a tree and the other in the White House. I feel I'm dreaming. And know I am not. I thought the good days for me had ended. And suddenly, bingo! the best ones!"

"That's what they sure should be," Grove replied, "or else." Wearily, he rubbed his face. "Since you're in, I need to know about your experience, your training. I mean, I don't want to call on you for something that wasn't part of your drill."

Jerry began, then.

By and by Mr. Cyrus Ah Soo appeared, six feet two inches of muscle, aplomb and quick perception but few words. When he'd gone, Jerry continued. At the end he said, "I've probably left out a few things. However—"

"—however," Grove chuckled tiredly, "you have quite a

nasty repertoire. You could teach me a couple of tricks." He stood and swayed. "Gotta get some sleep."

"I could arrange to have other—cousins—keep a watch of your home—"

Grove shook his head. "I'll be okay. It would be wrong and I've made more than my quota of blunders for one night."

"Me too," Jerry said, and sat for a while as he watched Grove walk into the night. Soon he whispered an expletive in Chinese. No good. He tried Hawaiian. Unsatisfactory. He turned to USA-barracks and it was an improvement.

But nothing was adequate to express his amazement and elation.

The station wagon left the park and Jerry resumed his patrol, realizing he would need an alibi for rounds unmade and unrecorded: teen-age kids, he thought, who'd sneaked into the area and been caught and given a long, documented and very alarming lecture. That would appeal to his park superiors. As he rode on, Jerry was happiest over the fact that he had held back on reporting what he had found out about R. K. Grove. Somehow, he felt, he had practically known it would be a mistake to turn in his friend without proof of his menace.

Grove drove the short way home in an opposite state of mind. Why in the devil hadn't he trusted his instinct and just put it straight to the big Hawaiian-Chinese? What he'd done had been disloyal, ugly, and ridiculous, too, by sheer chance. As he garaged the station wagon and after the automatic door closed he was able to smile a little. Jerry would understand, after all. For Jerry was a professional and would know you cannot trust anybody, in certain situations.

The room occupied by the girl was empty. Grove tried to remove every trace of her presence—because of Jenny. As he did that, he realized no perfume lingered. He'd noticed none when he was closest to her. That tended to support ther narrative: perfume wouldn't be wasted by Solentor on a woman meant for slow dying, in Grove's presence.

He went to bed and lay awake, wondering about Project Neptune. It was real and it was huge; but it was still unguessable.

It would be, for a long string of days and nights.

10

TUMULT

Alfred and Albert Scopes were twins. Eleven years old, they were inquisitive, bold, attractive kids, wiry and freckled, redheaded, with projecting ears. Skinny, but far from feeble, reared in a suburb of Omaha, Alfred and Albert were, that humid midday, visiting Sea Life Park (and Hawaii) for the first time. They sat in the Science Theater and were dazzled by the acts of trained porpoises. They agreed, covertly, the young lady who announced the show should grace *Playboy* magazine—which they often examined after their elder brother Carl had finished with it. Examined away from the house, for safety and thus revealing a certain precocity, mental and physical.

The Scopes family left the theater, a little wet from splashes made by impish performers in the tank, perhaps on purpose. Elwin Deeter Scopes and his wife decided to look around in the gift shop and gave the twins funds for food purchase at the nearby restaurant. It was a blunder.

Albert and Alfred lingered briefly in the Sea Chest, bothering adults by merely being in the way. But when that area and its potential dwindled, they were glum.

"Mom," Albert said with disgust, "is looking at dress goods. Tapa cloth!" They'd already visited the Polynesian Village and knew even how tapa cloth was made.

Alfred followed his twin brother's next glance and saw what their old man was doing: examining paintings, and prints, in a different room. Mrs. Bessie Scopes was an indefatigable dress material shopper. Her spouse, an Amherst graduate and a CPA, was an amateur painter and an obsessive gallery-goer.

The twins left. With fast-melting ice cream cones they meandered through crowds, idly scrutinized boobies and turtles and so, by chance, came within sight of a gate bearing a sign: *Authorized Personnel Only.*

Naturally, they went through—and came out on a paved

road. Beyond were more buildings, several tanks with animals splashing, office buildings and other, obviously off-limits, constructions. Proceeding into the area, they passed cubicles where men were just sitting, or writing, or dictating, and a very complicated affair of tanks, underwater viewports in a two-story edifice that was locked.

Albert therefore turned his attention to unexplored regions—which included the gigantic talus slope and the massive, lofty cliffs that stood above, like steps of a giant's fort: other-planetary, in effect.

Nobody had stopped them or even, much, looked them over. Children of scientists and employees often wandered here while waiting to be driven home. In every research facility personnel changes produce wandering-kids changes. The twins had long since learned, moreover, that if you want to go someplace where you're not allowed the way to do it is casually, conspicuously, without haste and with the manner of authorized personnel.

For a while, then, the boys simply gazed at vertical rises of the pali and the frozen rock maze below it. Albert started the next effort by saying, *"Boy!"*

"Some rocks!" Alfred agreed. "Let's see if—a fence."

There was no fence here. The invaded area was out of bounds for the park's masses. And even those farsighted experts who had planned this vast, varied and growing complex hadn't thought of climbing boys, escaped from the park and parental contact, scrambling among the great stone shambles—sweaty, thorn-harried but game. Kids and adults, now and then, in other but identical areas of steep slope, green tangle and cliff, tried them; much of Hawaii offers even loftier and equally boy-provocative challenges, all hazardous.

When Albert-Alfred emerged above the green, flat tops of the tree fringe they scrambled onto a big polyhedron of stone, to rest. The view of the sea was tremendous and the islands made a spectacular, added attraction: the sea hues were ideal for a million home movie recordings—and endless sittings of friends, viewing "our trip to Hawaii."

Scenery is of limited interest to boys, however dramatic. After they got their wind back, they considered, silently, the possible advantage of moving up—where the rocks became smaller and lay at a patently precarious angle of repose. They decided not.

Their discovery was made coming down, and coming by

a slightly different route that seemed easier. The twins saw the object simultaneously: a drift of air carried it to the spot they were intending to reach by a pants-slide.

"Money!" they yelled.

It was. It was a single bill and its denomination was One Hundred Dollars, United States of America.

When they'd retrieved it they looked deeply into one another's eyes and said, in chorus, "We *both* saw it first." There was a silence. Another duet. "It's probably counterfeit." They looked toward the park. Albert said what Alfred was about to: "Dad'll know."

Their return to the Sea Chest—and to parents on the verge of rebuke—changed in tone when the bill was handed to the father.

"Where the *hell*—"

The ensuing palaver was heated and it was also overheard by sundry park visitors. Mr. Scopes, followed by spouse and led by dancing sons, ultimately went to the park offices and reported the find to Roy Hedges, who smiled, listened, frowned unaggressively and couldn't exactly figure out what to do.

A sort of escrow was finally contrived. Roy put the bank note in the safe, signed a receipt and smiled some more. Since the twins hadn't expected to possess the fortune, even if it wasn't counterfeit, the situation was satisfactory. They had found a hundred-dollar bill which, if unclaimed, would eventually revert to the Scopes family. Terrific!

Terrific—and a tale now shared by several secretaries, clerks, submanagers and such. Of them, two considered another foray—something that had not occurred to their boss, the sterling Roy Hedges.

These two, at 5:01 P.M. left the offices and took clandestine routes to the site, as near as they'd gathered it. Hepzibah Hiayama drove as if toward her home in Kailua and cut back on the temporary road that served the contractor's men now recommencing work on the Makai Range. Parking before she reached the institute grounds, the eighteen-year-old former Miss Pineapple made her way, with hardship, to a point much higher up the slope than that of the rich strike. Below her, silently, and to her left, Ahalamano Jones, a porpoise-training candidate who'd happened to be in the business building at the critical time, slithered through the tumbled boulders like a mouse in a rubble of cement blocks.

He found nothing until, as the twilight lost all muscle, he heard Hepzibah approach and saw both her expression . . . and her closed fist. He had no intention of doing more than asking. But that wasn't necessary. The charming girl said, unsteadily, "You scared me! Look! Could they possibly be real?"

She handed him two segments of a gold-colored bracelet with, in each, a very large, very green, very intricately cut . . . something. The gold didn't look like brass. A decent person, "Haha" Jones shrugged. But his eyes had a glitter that did not relate to the girl, however well she deserved it. Her subsequent near snatch of the fragments and hasty, bruising retreat downward were not really hysterical; merely conservative.

Before dinner, the Hiayama family, relatives and neighbors had heard enough to imagine that a fortune in money and gems lay scattered on the fallen part of the pali, there for the taking. A bill, of whatever sort, could have blown to the feet of the Scopes twins from any place; the park was on the windward side of Oahu, the side where the mountains diverted the trades and cooled their clouds into rain that fluted the precipices. On that side of the island, wind could carry more than bills for trips of circuitous and theoretically endless lengths.

The story of Hepzibah's find attracted another hearer, a local jeweler and member of the same church. He brought his loop, made a production of his scrutiny and announced correctly, that the fragment was part of a gold bracelet and the stones, not emeralds, but so what? They were tourmalines: perfect, clear, worth maybe nearly a thousand dollars apiece.

Haha Jones tried to keep his next intentions to himself. Unfortunately, he had two younger brothers, a quarter British, a quarter Spanish, and the same amounts part Hawaiian and part uncertain, who were very much like the Scopes twins. They followed him after supper on their bikes and watched him start sneaking up into the rocks, with two flashlights. Then they went home, to find the Hepzibah tale had reached there—with embellishments. It was being said "millions in money, gold and jewels" littered the pali behind the park-institute area—apparently cast away by robbers in a desperate flight.

One variation said that. There were, by 10 P.M., hundreds of other variations.

When Jerry reported for duty he was worried. The man he relieved told him the cause for the winking lights above the parked cars piling up on Kalanianaole Highway. Jerry made his rounds, watchful of the firefly swarm. It expanded and contracted, moiled slowly and put out pseudopodia. It wasn't his territory. Patrol cars were busy, keeping the Kalan open and getting stuck cars out of ditches. They tried to stop would-be climbers. Chains blocked all park entrances now; otherwise it would have been loaded with vehicles.

By two in the morning most of the seekers had given up and gone home. However, a skinny, dark girl with bangs and bright eyes saw a twinkle as she trekked down with her exhausted mother and picked up a golden brooch which was somewhat smashed but held nineteen pearls still.

The girl, Nomaua Dibble, was to appear the next week in an eighth-grade play. Her mother, a spouse-abandoned but deserving woman, was devoted to the "Insomniacs Club," a radio program that began at midnight on Station WWHH under the masterly direction of Mr. Hack Davis.

She got through to Hack Davis after long effort, since his switchboard was unusually lighted that night—or morning. Hack listened and his hardier listeners listened too. He had been skeptical at first of tales of "pirate treasure" on the pali near the park.

That view was modified when one of the tourists who had heard the Scopeses' first astonishment and had seen the bill phoned in that much confirmation.

Some of the peripheral recipients of Hepzibah's story then reconfirmed the lurid picture. The result became as certain as the then imminent sunrise. Before its manifestation, however, there was another happening.

Ever since the watchman had listened to Ring Grove's reason for coming to Hawaii, Jerry had been extraordinarily alert. Twice more, somebody had slipped into the park and remained for a long time, undiscovered and doing nothing he could hear or see or find a trace of. But Jerry and Grove were aware of the time of each entry and exit.

Jerry's mind was ready to accept anything novel though not, he had often thought, as novel as some things Ring Grove could produce—and suspect or look for. The finding of the hundred-dollar bill and the parts of a bracelet with the subsequent night's scramble of people greedy enough to take the chance was something new. And as he made his rounds Jerry watched the twinkling searchers and listened to the shouts of police and the roar of cars on the Kalan. It seemed to him he knew something else that might bear on this singular, insane business.

When it came to mind, which was about when the last searchers quit, it came hard. Three nights before, while he'd been cycling the park, he'd thought he saw a light on the summit of the escarpment above the institute. It had not lasted long enough to be surely identified and he had waited in vain for a repeat, dismissing it in the end as a freak reflection of car headlights turning on some curve of a side road, on the other flank of the pali. He had also thought, and he now believed it had not been much afterward, that he'd heard a frail, high scream from the same general direction. But he'd decided it was a wakened gull, or a similar bird, many of which gave out just such sounds.

He now and abruptly realized that if he had seen a light which originated on the summit and heard not a bird but a human voice, it might explain what had been found on the talus. A human being, hurled from the ragged skyline, would probably scream; if female, she would possibly be wearing a bracelet and her pocketbook might be thrown after her to erase all trace of the point of her dispatch. In any case, she'd lose it if it went with her and it certainly would burst open and might contain a bill of that high denomination.

The idea set him on the task of calculating the point where he had half seen the light and, as dawn made that possible, of trying to determine how such a hypothesized body would fall, and where it might come to rest. He could narrow the first problem to a matter of a hundred feet. The second, as light enough allowed him to study it, was more difficult. A human being, merely pushed from the summit, would come down a long way, hitting the narrow treads of what resembled a giant staircase and rolling off. Most of them were debris-heaped and sloped on that account. The victim, whether shoved or flung, would almost surely tumble to the talus slope itself, where momentum might carry it some added distance. Possibly, it might stop on one of the few setbacks that were fairly free of fallen rubble, wide, and level enough, to hold it.

With glasses, he began a search, moving about in the grounds for varied angles. It seemed to him that six or seven shelves in the many might stop such a coursing body. But if the theoretical victim were flung, by two men of moderate strength, the body would almost certainly clear the first half dozen setbacks and gain speed enough to bounce from the rims of those below.

With improving light, he searched such places but he could see no sign of a body. No wind-whipped garment showed—no splash of blood gone dark brown, and no other indication that gave substance to his hunch. He wondered what to do. He hated to waken Grove at this hour and he could not leave his post.

He was biking through the institute parking yard, still glancing upward now and then, when he decided to have a look at the slope above and behind the first cottage built there for scientific personnel with wives. It was actually bedded in the biggest rocks at the base of the steep slope. The flash of light had been somewhere above that first attractive mini-house—almost a thousand feet below. Kiawe-trees, bushes and a multitude of different weeds covered the first hundred feet behind the cottage. But once clear of the vegetation, he knew he could look around an extensive region and, at the same time, keep his patrol area in view, pretty much.

He went through the undergrowth fast, though the climb was steep. He felt, as he came out in the open, the way all Hawaiians feel about these slopes of graduated rocks, a fear. Masses of them could let go at any time. Rain could start such an avalanche, thousands of tons of it. Wind could; and they could be triggered by the tremor of a truck passing far below or the give of a rotted but temporary wedge. They were dangerous to climb—though the immense fringe of superboulders at their bases gave protection to land beyond. Every year the pali showed black, fresh swaths where a new slide had come partway down or down to the final barricade.

He could see nothing moving in his patrol range except where it usually moved in water—ponds, pools, tanks and the cove. He cast about and clambered around, peering into the poised, steep rock maze, sweating with unease. From time to time he made sure nothing had changed in the park-institute-Makai reach—more than a half mile long, now that they were building again. He was about ready to quit when a faint perception froze him. This time, he didn't have to run through his sense alarms like dictionary pages to know what it was.

A brief drift of air from his left brought a scent he instantly identified. But it was not the perfume of ylang-ylang. It was the smell of old death.

He found the body a minute later: what was left of a body after the warm interval, after that hideous, battering fall, and after birds, insects. A woman lay there, the remains of a woman. He bent over the windward side of an opening between two rocks that were almost as tall as he. She had been smashed almost beyond belief: bombs or artillery, alone, did such things to human beings. Her clothes were in tatters and only part of them remained. She had dark hair but not the coarse kind of orientals. Not straight, or wavy, like Asian and Polynesian hair. He had a moment of fright and then was sure his fright was due to error: it was not the girl his second cousin had taken from Grove's house. She was safe and on another island, he'd been told.

Jerry exhaled heavily in gratitude—and then almost grinned; Grove had shown a special concern for Miss Wilson. He had been very explicit when telling his second cousin Cy that the lady wasn't to be "bothered" by Cy or any other man and not allowed to run away. Subsequent reports from Cy were approved.

Jerry used a few moments for that and few more to note that the battered woman in the deep V made by the two boulders had been chic: the fingernails and expensive tatters showed that. She was without jewelry but he saw where rings had been worn on remnants of fingers. No pocketbook lay near, for plain reasons. One further finding startled Jerry: in two relatively unruined fingers she grasped part of a lei, hardly more than a scrap, and its brown flowers were ylang-ylangs. It was not, then, a lei she had herself worn but blooms snatched, at some final moment, from the neck or bosom of another person.

Jerry went back down, heedless now of starting a slide. He phoned Grove, who appeared in a remarkably short time and, together, they returned to the ghastly remains.

Grove studied them with a grim disregard of proximity. "People are beginning to climb the damn pali again," he said at last. "I don't know who she is. If it weren't for that lei, I'd call the cops—rather, *you* would. But ylang-ylang once had the meaning I told you, and could still have:

Mavis' daughter in Bangkok. I can find out, in maybe a day, who she was, if she's another of our people. Because they'll have been missing her, and looking, for a couple of days, anyhow. Till I know, I'd rather these crazy fortune hunters—"

"They probably have more to find," Jerry interrupted, gravely. "We can't stop them. Crazy to risk this talus, let alone the cliffs on up."

Grove thought briefly. "We'll have to conceal the—remains."

"How?"

Grove suggested a way and they acted swiftly.

When the first of the growing multitude ascending the treasure slopes drew near the site they passed without a second glance. The woman's remains had been wrapped in plastic dropcloths. Several heavy rocks hid the bundle. On top of them and caught by a smaller rock was a bird's feather plucked from a booby, along with evidence of what seemed its frequent use of the spot—a white spatter sufficient to account for what could not be entirely concealed.

Within an hour there was pandemonium on the Kalan. In both directions from the park, cars had braked, pulled over and come to rest more or less on the shoulders of the highway. For a mile, toward Waimanalo, and closing up on the Blowhole Observation Point in the other stretch, the shoulders were solid with vehicles.

By nine-thirty Roy Hedges was out of breath and close to a similar state in the matter of sense. A normal, all-day "gate" at Sea Life Park averaged five thousand heads, big and small. The parking facilities could easily accommodate cars and buses for twice that number. Judging by the auto incidence, there were, within the half hour after the ticket booths opened, some fifteen thousand people inside or eager to enter the gates. And of these, when the first show started, a large fraction had not remained as spectators. That portion had started up the talus.

Jerry and Grove had left long before, well aware that the search was going to go on and be big—but not remotely able to guess how big. Hack Davis had elicited the full story on WWHH only minutes before time ran out, that is, before 5 A.M.; and it takes awhile to prepare a gold rush even if the stampede doesn't require rounding the Horn. Even when it's a local affair.

Trent Ackley Abbott, called "Tack"—the dreamer-upper, fund raiser, designer and founder of the park, its associated enterprises and awesome intentions—was asleep. The phone rang and he opened occasionally smoky but very blue eyes. He raked a strong hand through curly hemp, that he had for hair, and called, "Get it, Sapphire, willya!" as the ringing continued. Then he remembered his wife had risen early and taken their three offspring to school over the mountains and was now, barring unforeseen digression, engaged in loading two Welsh ponies on a carrier hitched to their Number Four car for transport to pastures in Oolau.

Picking up the phone while scratching a chest that barely contrived to stretch far enough to reach his excessively broud shoulders, Tack tried to say hello and failed, owing to his not infrequent problem of speech impediment: a mere halt, not a stutter. Then he made it. "Yes?"

"Come to the park!"

Roy Hedges didn't have to give his name although the panic version of his voice was bizarre. Naval fighter pilots who survived such action as Roy had seen will surely have come close to panic. But those who survive will not have panicked. Hedges now was in panic, the cause, therefore, unimaginable. Tack had stood, by then, at his six-two, less the hair swirls.

"What's up?"

The phone talked. Tack began to smile. The smoke drifted from his eyes which, afterward, were fire-blue and, in that state, had a peculiar ability to make some people, cheats, liars, pork-snitching politicians and the like, think a tangible force was actually being projected from the blue gaze, one perhaps like a laser beam, but whatever, a deadly power. By the same token, the eyes (and the man operating them) gave the great and decent human majority a feeling that he exclusively emitted rays of kindness.

When he had listened to the point where Roy ran out of frenzy, he said tersely, "Be right over." Then he bent double, laughing.

The Abbott house was on the seashore, closer to the Makai-Range-Oceanic-Institute-Sea-Life-Park complex than the home of Grove and the vacant house beside it; less than a mile from the nearest element, the Makai Range, a science-fiction construction. But Tack was not right over.

Traffic crawled on the highway and more often stopped dead. Careless parking had already made the never adequate artery a one-way route. Cops were trying to get vacated cars off the pavement, with little help as few people cared to loiter even for a moment, once they were that near the gold fields.

Tack finally backed his Number Two car into a cul-de-sac which he created, partly, by crushing down shrubs. Then he walked.

When the structural oceanic Oz came in view, he stared, rotated a slow head and swiveled it: as far as the eye could see, cars. Up the road onto Makapuu Point, cars. Among them, people hurrying parkward, as were people at his Makai Range end. On the talus, on that unstable rock mass; people like flies. Thousands.

Absently, he helped a cop shove a Volks into somebody's plumeria tree. He walked on. The cop followed and grabbed him. "Look, mister. I need help, clearing this road! Emergency." Suddenly the officer's face changed as his voice dropped in deference. "Oh! You're Tack! What the hell *is* all this?"

"I dunno," Tack said.

"Got beyond control before we even knew it started."

Tack ran. He soon reached the office building where Roy now with Willard and Tim were staring at the human ant horde on the near-vertical rocks—an intent, insectile, many-hued multitude a mile wide or more. From that they looked to the park itself where regular buses and expected cars had deposited the morning's unprecedented crowd which, now, gave half an eye to the Whaler's Cove show from overspilling seats and the other half to the incredible mass climb.

"How do we deal with it, Tack?"

Will seemed near to cracking. Tack said, quietly, "Do we have to?"

"People are going to get hurt! Start a slide—"

"It isn't," Tim Baily, another top executive, said in a diffident tone, "our responsibility or our property. Though mobs of 'em paid admissions to get started up there."

Willard Benton, the fourth member of top brass, squinted with his usual amused look, one that hid shrewd eyes and a vast knowledge of the strange wonderland called Hawaii. "The gate," he said, "broke the record, a half hour ago."

"People believe," Tim added, "the fallen treasure is above the property. But, if it includes more big bills, they must think it's worth spreading out, where the crowd's too thick to push in for hunting."

"Has anything more been found?" Tack sounded as if that could not be the case.

Hedges gave the answer while the two associate execs listened in wonder, wanting to hear it again to be sure. "According to the cops and the boys trying to block our non-public entrances, two more bills, both hundreds, a solid gold cigarette case and a ruby earring."

Tack was silent—watchful and incredulous. At close intervals more or less determined by the nature of the steplike cliffs above them, gray rocks hung at the steepest angle their angular shapes permitted. Waterfalls had streaked notices in the pali during heavy rains. These trenched the mountainous face, and rocks the size of trucks sometimes thundered down those upended alleys.

Toward the upper part of the talus a multitude was moving, human confetti that reached apexes of loose stone, when some turned back or aside. Those more able or mad went on to the successive cliffs, acting evidently on the not improbable idea that the booty below was staked out and so certain of discovery but since it must have originated at the summit, chances were better for a find in the high shelves, recesses and gouged hollows. There, too, the vegetation was scarcer and the search easier—but the climbing was vertical for the most part.

Stupefying! Tack drew a deep breath and looked at Hedges, the man who worried about the vast flow of funds; the man some of the employees thought overly conscious of money and money above all. The man, actually, Tack mused, whose character, level sense, will, courage and education were responsible for the fact that the big dreamers in this multiple organization didn't go bankrupt. The biggest dreamer was, of course, Tack himself—whom only Roy dared defy; Roy was a relative, by luck!

Roy Hedges was budgetmaster of the Oceanic Foundation, which was the holding company of what Tack had dreamed and others—what was, and was to be. And Roy was the one now suffering most—the one whose desperation related to the fact that people above would be injured; Roy of the bloody skies of the Pacific and of carrier decks set ablaze by kamikazes; Roy Hedges—the one in thirty who survived of his flight wing.

It didn't surprise Tack but it moved him. Nothing would have made Roy more jubilant than the record-breaking gate receipts of that morning: nothing—unless some greater and truer value was interposed.

"We've got to get 'em down," Tack finally said. "Hell. They'll start an avalanche on a talus tongue; bound to, sooner or later, and it'll be slaughter."

As if Tack's tense near command had been heard, a police bullhorn thundered at the northerly corner of the vast property and bounced back from the stiff slope and towering cliffs, more clearly in echo than in projection:

"This is the police. All climbers will now begin a careful descent. All persons not clear of the entire area in one hour will be arrested and severely punished. You are breaking the law. Penalties will be heavy for all climbers not off the mountain in one hour. Come down! You are in danger! Every man, woman and child is liable to be *killed* at any moment! Move with the utmost caution on your return! But . . . *move! Down!*"

A repeat of the whanging threat and warning began. A second bullhorn, near the park's opposite end, took up the ad lib of a different police officer and this man was near to sobbing as he appealed. His voice, loud-bouncing at jet pitch, was so unmistakably driven by fear and so grief resonant that Tim said, "What an act!"

Will Benton, once MC of a very popular radio program in Honolulu, answered with a caustic flash, "That's not acting. His wife and kids are up there."

A little time passed. The bullhorns thundered. But very few of the clamberers moved down. In the park, a constant mass of customers clattered ceaselessly through the turnstiles. These, now, were not, in the main, hunters. They had learned enough from TV and radio to realize that the park was a perfect grandstand for what was sure to become an avalanche, or many, a cascade of rocks in thousand-ton or million-ton volume . . . mixed with people, for grinding.

The park restaurant was being stormed. Elsewhere, daily routines were slowly stalled. But the shows went on as they, too, became crowded with audiences waiting for the sure, terrible, reddening of an avalanche, or of many. And even the lovely lasses and handsome young man who swam with the porpoises, ran them through their amazingly brainy exhibitions, explained over PA systems and rode a boatswain's chair to a high spar of the *Essex* to put a handful of fishes into the maw of a whale that had leaped for the prize, straight up and twenty-three feet—all these people kept glancing at the crawling colored carpet of humanity high above. Scientists abandoned experiments to watch. Their aides, young men and women, doctoral candidates, came out to behold. Carpenters, repair men, cleanup crews, porpoise trainers-in-training, visiting scientists being escorted on a tour of the magnificent and unique instruments and facilities, forgot their purposes and turned to the mountain.

The heavy machinery preparing new foundations at the Makai Range fell silent. Their growling engines, squeaking treads, titan arms and maws stood still. Offshore, work and research vessels, twenty-footers and ships with the tonnage of Columbus' fleet added together, failed to leave Makai Range pier and the moorings. Their crews and the day's passengers, specialists in a dozen disciplines, stood on the decks, sat on gunwales, climbed rigging or found perches on huge ventilators, to look.

Binoculars proliferated and were passed from hand to hand in the multitudes ashore and elsewhere. The users would generally make a running report of what was beheld:

". . . woman with a baby in a squaw pack, way up. Looks pretty bushed . . . woops! . . . slipped!"

". . . can't be sure but I think there's a kid, oh, maybe fifty feet to the right of that hole we were looking at—that band-shell place, to the left of the dead-ahead notch . . . a kid found something! He's bending, getting it, straightening to see if anybody near him realized . . . What in hell, Martha . . . ?"

"My eyes always were better than yours, David." A pause. . . . "Now, tell me *exactly* where that boy . . ."

The people around Tack were making suggestions, none, so far, even hopeful. Additional bullhorns slammed threats and appeals.

"Might as well," Benton observed, "have tried to get people off the Klondike trail—by offering free peanuts."

Tack felt a presence and turned. "Hi, Ring! Know Roy, Will, Tim . . ."

Grove smiled. "Yes." Hands shook.

"The traffic woke me. Took near an hour to push through on foot. Terrible thing!" Grove said.

Tack nodded. "Trying to figure how to get them back. You can see what's certain to happen, sooner, later."

"Best thing might be a slide that trapped a few—and scared the rest. Anybody know where the jewelry and dough came from?"

Tim answered. "All we have is the latest radio bulletin. Somebody, woman, evidently, parked a Jaguar at the road closest to the summit. And fell—or jumped—or maybe just dumped her valuables. God knows why."

"Car belong to her?"

"Rented. But the police have a name. Maribel Dwelling, a divorcee, who's been living in a fancy apartment in the Tahitian Towers for six months. Not at home, though; missing; and she had plenty of dough."

Tack heard that for the first time. He scowled. "Then maybe she's—up there, too?"

Grove was surveying the human flies and calculating. The corpse lay in a boulder-enclosed niche. The hunt was, mainly, to the right of that place. But it would surely, in time, extend its greedy and shifting shape to the spot. He knew, now, the real name of the late "Maribel Dwelling" and her employer: Eaper.

His mind returned to the dilemma. A small cascade, however mangling or lethal to a few, alone, might start the rest downward, as he had said. Listening to ad lib suggestions for a while and finding them inadequate or hopeless, he finally spoke. "The slide idea is sound; no other practical way. Try to get up to them and bodily bring 'em down—even with regiments of the National Guard—and you'll have a shambles: no place to struggle with arrested men and women. But—a slide? With *burlap, chicken wire*—"

Tack whirled, instantly understanding. "And a chopper!"

"Kept out of sight beyond the summit. Yes."

An hour later a helicopter, wind-buffeted behind the crenelated rim, set down two men and their cargo. It left, then, to reload, piloted by a onetime Air Force captain who had been trained for the special uses of the sky-hung, clattering machines—Tack Abbott. With burlap and chicken wire, fifty fast-working people in the park garages had fabricated the "cargo." Now, battering through vegetation, Grove and Benton appeared, coming by car and on foot.

Even the highest and so, in general, the ablest climbers could not see the points from which the artificial rocks were launched. Their fall, by the time they hurtled in view, was fast enough to be convincing and their actual nature impossible to discern in the split second of passage. Their atypical crash and unusual bounce, when they struck, did not lessen their effectiveness. Those experts who saw them had been fearing what now was plainly occurring. The rest, the vast majority, lacked any experience at all.

"Rocks coming!" they shouted, and "Avalanche!" The bedlam grew.

"Ring's idea," Tack said later, "was a bit like yelling 'Fire!' in the well-known crowded theater. An audience doesn't need to see flames, after that. And a lot of these people did see an equivalent of smoke, at least. The uproar obscured the fact that our boulders bounded too far and didn't bang loudly.

"When I got the second load up, Tim had added a few bushels of chopped-up coconut hulls and some walnuts. Ring and Will were by then shoveling dust overboard, from behind trees. We added dry grass to the new junk. The roar coming up was remarkable; and when I took a peek at the sight below, the cascade looked so real it made me think for a second we were loosening up actual rock. There was plenty of panic; but you couldn't run, just freeze there. We knew we had them turned when the bullhorns began telling folks to take it easy and yelling out various safe ways down.

"Most of the able climbers, swapping greed for self-preservation," he went on, "not only started down but commenced helping stuck and petrified people, as they were trained to do. Still, it was late afternoon before the firemen, cops and all the organized rescue outfits got the place cleared." He saw the question in the faces of his family auditors, Sapphire and the kids, Edmond, Mack and pretty Layle. "Some were hurt, sure. Legs broken and arms, ankles sprained, cuts, brush burns, bruises. But not a soul crippled that I heard of and nobody dead, which is a miracle."

The cadaver was found by a sailor on leave who undertook to hide among the lower, biggest rocks. He saw some bird-marked flat stones in a deep crevice which seemed ideal. The area stank but the sailor was determined until he removed the flat rocks . . . and gave up his program to report.

That night the Honolulu police notified Oddie that a "Maribel Dwelling" had been found. Was she by any chance, the police asked, among the federal people under cover in the area? He said not. The (presumed) local CIA head had said the same. It didn't surprise the Honolulu cops. Plenty of young women with ample funds came to the islands under false names and for many reasons, of which some led to eventual suicide. The fragment of ylang-ylang lei meant nothing to the police and wasn't even mentioned.

Oddie did not add what he thought he knew. The killers had had to locate the body when the scattered valuables started an unanticipated treasure hunt. They had not expected it to be found, ever, Oddie surmised. He was not surprised that the plastic cover produced no fingerprints. It amused him, in a way, that the killers had gone to so much trouble to rehide their victim only to be frustrated when they'd originally taken pains to toss her pocketbook from the cliff top too.

He sent that word on to Axe and heard from him two mornings later. What he heard was what Oddie expected. In Eaper's opinion, this second killing of a CIA agent, his own, not a bint, meant that the playboys had doubled their effort to divert attention from Limbo Six. It also meant that the CIA people in Hawaii were very careless. Two had now been blown, and "erased" for good measure. Eaper ordered three of Oddie's group back to Washington for transfer and told Oddie that one more such killing would mean his own dispatch—to a far less pleasant post.

Oddie could not protest. He had spent a day disguised as a Chinese illegally hunting wild pigs, to set up a watch from a spot on the summit, near the road where the Jaguar had been parked; but he still could not imagine what had brought his female subordinate there. He had a fine view of the sea, the park-institute-Makai layout and the Kalanianaole Highway. He could see the mountainside from Makapuu Point to Waimanalo and beyond. A power line that came over a near crest and swooped down to the road and the park was the only work of man on that near-vertical vastness. Looking seaward, he observed the research vessels, the enormous pier, the barren islands —and water. The din of heavy construction at the Makai Range wafted up on a light breeze.

He decided "Maribel" had caught onto something. And they'd caught onto her—driven her car away themselves and carried her here, a dead passenger, he hoped, to fling her over. There wasn't any sign of what she'd been trying to do and the many signs of the false avalanche-markers had been explained in confidence by the police, whom Tack had informed.

The ylang-ylang flowers were identified by police routine and it was found many garden buffs had ylang-ylang trees and several made a hobby of forcing ylang-ylangs—and dozens of other trees and plants—to bloom out of season. Anybody could swipe enough blossoms to make a lei, or buy enough, probably, or have enough, either now or at any time, for a dozen leis.

That floral research failed to interest Oddie.

He decided his colleagues should pull in their horns, for his own sake as well as theirs. He told them to take a break, a vacation; and no one protested. Oddie could handle the routine: there wasn't anything of much interest at the time. No real meat, Eaper would probably put it, on his plate. Pilford Oddie tended to agree.

If events demanded it, he would be able to get his subordinates back in an hour or so. Chuck Davies, the FBI second in command (as far as anybody save the few involved were aware), could fill in, with his men. Chuck Davies was, in fact, the head of the FBI for Hawaii. Oddie had several subordinates who were supposedly FBI, too, and these had been FBI, once. Their CIA role was a "family secret," as, again, Eaper would say. And none of the FBI men who were only that were aware of the cover of others, let alone of any female colleagues.

Oddie was about to call Chuck when his phone rang and Chuck was put on. "Just heard you were losing some of the help."

"Come on over."

Chuck Davies was a heavy, rugged man some years older than the FBI-model Pilford Oddie, who was sometimes referred to as "Christ-and-Karate," or "Saint Oddball," or the "Judo Jesus," owing to his compulsive perfectionism. Davies was Welsh and barely tall enough to make the FBI; but nobody thought of him, afterward, as a near miss—he was good—and he was liked by people who merely respected Oddie . . . when they were not resentful of his holy meticulousness.

Chuck came in and sat looking at Oddie with brown, questioning eyes. "Anything about the recall I need to know?"

The CIA man stared slowly around the carpeted, tan-walled, impersonally furnished room, as if he might see something on the floor, in the bookshelves, on a settee, or pasted on the hung photographs of the Founder and others, that Davies would need to be told about. He shook his head. "Axe thinks we lost Maribel Dwelling because some playboys are trying to make us think they are very busy here."

"Neptune, still?"

"Neptune. Haven't heard the word for a month or more."

"You know what I think?" Davies was amused. He tried to light up a pipe while he said what he thought; it interfered so he gave the pipe priority while required. "I bet there never was a Project Neptune."

Oddie considered that with full CIA seriousness. "Could be. But news keeps arriving on *something* either the Soviets—or else the Chinese, or both, in spite of the hate act—are doing. You get it from England, Germany—the West, that is, even the French—and you wonder."

"*I* don't get that word, though," Davies chuckled. "What the CIA types of foreign countries including our so-called allies learn, that they send you people—or withhold—is a thing the FBI does not often have to deal with, praise God."

Oddie faintly frowned at the oath, which was a habit and made those who dared swear, sometimes, just to bug the man. "Axe sends the drift of things over to me. The British, especially, are very able, which a Welshman wouldn't agree with. They have—" He checked himself. "The number's in a special classification, sorry—but they have a lot of operatives inside the USSR and some in China, right where they can do the most good."

The heavy, square man blew smoke and remained amused. What Oddie knew that Oddie could not tell him was, perhaps, a good deal; but the very fact that a wall existed between his and the other's agencies seemed silly to him. "So?"

"Rumors. Bits and pieces."

"We're both in the bits-and-pieces business." Davies shrugged.

Oddie was always annoyed by Davies' attitude toward The Job. He said, with emphasis, "It adds up to the pretty solid information on Neptune. They could have changed the code name but the sum of it is"—Oddie had to think, before he waved his arm in the windowless, air-conditioned office, where the USSR and China lay—"the enemy is apparently up to some big operation, aimed at us. *That*—to be brief—is the point. Windesmere—you know who he is?"

"No," Davies replied. "But let me guess. A top man in M-1 or whatever the milords call it, now."

"Near enough. Windsmere, *not* the earl!"—Oddie flushed at the slip—"or whatever *his* title is—and the man's real name isn't Windesmere—thinks the Red world is rigging some sort of—superdevice that would wipe out America. He believes it. Eaper is running almost scared but you can't really scare the man." He ignored Davies' dark-eyed sarcasm. "I've scraped the barrel for the two years, going on, since Neptune came my way. And you have—and thanks. But what do I know?"

Davies answered for him. "That the muzhiks run fishing vessels around the islands to do the same work as our spy ships. As ours *try* to do, in their waters; and get sunk, one; captured, another. That their nuclear subs tag ours when they leave Pearl Harbor, and other harbors. That the damn fool submariners on both teams occasionally play chicken and sometimes ram, because it would be yellow not to stay on a suicide course longer than the other moron. Which has results the public is not told about. We know the Soviet seamen even fish, occasionally, just for laughs, I guess. And that they anchor offshore for swimming parties and to give their frogmen exercise; but you can't board 'em. We know that when you got those seemingly innocent beach boys to grab a Russian scuba man he was merely gathering coral specimens and turned out to *be* a conchologist. You did get onto the little game some of the people at the consulate were playing last year at Pearl—snooping—and several parties went home, fast. Et cetera, et cetera. But have you *any* harder information to back up this big-scheme rumor? Seems to me that by now it would be all set—which the missiles weren't quite, when we found 'em in Cuba."

Oddie had listened, as those accomplishments and non-accomplishments were summarized. He considered, and made up his mind to talk since he had authority for such decisions. "Well, Chuck, yes. Last month, a freighter in a fleet of Soviet whaling ships got off course and in trouble—fire. The crew took to boats and their pals, as far as we can tell, recovered all of them. But the hulk burned, even though there were explosions, and the Navy found what was left floating about. We've had the best people in related branches of science on the retrieved items, ever since. And we haven't gotten—they haven't—any clear concept even of their purpose."

"No fooling! Where'd it happen?"

"Philippines. Near them, anyway."

"Do they route antarctic whalers and supply ships past the Philippines?"

Oddie shrugged. "Not usually. But who can say what Reds will do? The unidentified ship maybe carried new gear for a Philippine scanning of some sort. Point is, when the enemy, by accident, leaves you parts of some very complex and, if assembled, probably *big* gadgets—elements your specialists can't make sense of—you're in bad trouble. We know the junk that floated had to do with high-frequency electricity, with communications of some kind, maybe by laser, and it was plainly designed for underwater operation. But the bright boys can't figure it better than that. The pieces were intriguing and suggestive but we didn't get enough parts, undamaged, to say more."

"On the bottom?"

"At close to a thousand fathoms? In soft sediments? We—the Navy, I mean—has deep vessels looking. So far, no success."

"Sounds either nasty—or smart."

"Smart how?" Oddie frowned with scorn.

"Suppose the whole affair was rigged—and what was found where the hulk sank was meant to be what it is—merely puzzling?"

Oddie's response was appropriately curt. "That's been considered, of course. Would the possibility keep *you* from trying to make sure?"

"No." Davies listened after that while Oddie explained

his arranged "vacations" and then said, sympathetically, "Hell of a place to look for some organized—'un-American,'" he laughed, "'activity.' Tourists come through by the million, visit all Hawaii. Groups of every breed alive! Japanese, African, Indian, plus all of Europe and our own folks, too."

Oddie agreed. "What does some doom-America operation require, supposing it is real and here, which I doubt? Must take a large number of people, all highly skilled. You can hardly set up anything of such a kind as we keep hearing whispers about—with a few experts, in a few weeks."

"Maybe you can—and we just don't know what that setup might be. The Soviets are technically pretty hot, as we seem never to learn."

Oddie disagreed. "What *I'd* expect would be many people, at or near the site, supposing it exists—and it's not here, I'm *certain*—because they'd need a good cover to be able to stick around and communicate or cooperate as required—*that,* or some group coming and going, with an equally suitable cover."

"Would you know," Davies asked, "if the members of, say, a Tawain Fisheries Convention came back to Honolulu as members of a Conference on Marine Engineering—and later the same guys, or some of the same, appeared as the Free China Moose, if any, or for an Oriental Ivy League Reunion?"

"We would," Oddie said. "We have specialists for just that. And several such groups *have* been looked over. I recently paid attention, for example, to a bunch of Arabs—the party of some oil-rich sheik—who are repeaters—always for a binge. I'll have to let them go, now. But they checked out safe. Eaper sent me an Arab-speaking—doll—who got herself a job in a dive. Those people patronized the best—" Oddie's tone showed distaste.

"Madame Sarah's? Nice spot! Went there myself with some friends, one night. Line of duty it was *not.*" He watched Oddie scowl before going on.

"The girl told us the Arabs spoke the dialect of their sheikdom, or whatever. She never met—dealt with the sheik himself as a—client"—this embarrassed Oddie —"but she knows all about Arabs. Wasn't surprised when two or three of them hurt her. They're like that, it seems. But she made it pretty plain that those so-and-so's were just having fun, away from their own women. Probably a harem apiece, she said. Desert goons. We got several sets of prints that way. Nothing in our files."

"Not the late Miss Dwelling?"

"No. She worked alone except for specially requested contact with us. Contact by very indirect means. She had a thing about the Soviet ships and subs and scuba divers, though. Surfer, she was."

Davies nodded. "So did lots of people outside the trade. I don't know how many reports we've had of alien scuba divers surfacing near the Red ships, and not *anywhere near,* too. So what? We checked out a few. Mostly they were kids and men with a handy dinghy the idiot reporters didn't see. And you can't hold a Russki who's sampling the local undersea flora, or just taking a dip, beyond three miles out. The sub and ship business is for Navy Intelligence, after all."

There was a short silence. The pair then went into a critical discussion of their long-time and elaborate efforts to find evidence of what might be Neptune—and now might have a new name: efforts without any success, if two killings were regarded as deliberate decoys.

The first was almost certainly that, since the dead man in Sea Life Park had worn clothes that had come into Soviet possession long ago, which was macabre and so, likely, a gag in the minds of its perpetrators. The second death could be anything.

The woman known as Maribel Dwelling might have been the victim of blown cover and killed by her discoverer simply to get rid of an American agent. In that case, the event was not an odd occurrence but an occupational hazard. She might even have been thrown off the mountaintop owing to somebody's personal motives. A couple of outraged wives, an enraged lover—the possibilities there were endless. For her work had involved relationships with many men and, so far as she had reported, all were "blanks"—that is, not engaged in covert work.

But they were male and her means of checking them could have led, as that means can in all walks of life, to a fatal result.

It was past time to shut up shop when they quit. The night crew had arrived in the outer offices. The two bureau heads had combed through scores of dead-end activities. Davies thought Neptune was a mere plant, a rumor kept alive to mislead those who heard it; Oddie was as firmly of the opinion that his area, Limbo Six, Hawaii, was not its locus; he was Oddie and he'd been vigilant.

The chunky man knocked out his pipe. "Ever checked back again on—what's-his-name—Grove?"

"Of course." This was one of Oddie's small items for pride. "I know Axe would, someday, put in an inquiry just to test *me*. So I had our people tag the old boy, four-five times, for a day or so, some time after we made that first check."

"And Arthur Xavier did ask?"

Oddie smiled thinly. "As I'd anticipated. And he was pleased to know I'd been on the ball. Grove is exactly what we first decided: a nut about privacy and all Waimanalo's Big Daddy. In fact—he's a nice old buzzard—considering there was a time when he was anything but nice. He is sold on Hawaii and may never return to western New York. His plant's well managed. He enjoys his little game of hiding out. But the notion of Grove getting into his old harness—is—well, ridiculous."

"I said so from the first." Davies grinned.

"I thought the same." Oddie's statement was not true; but, by now, he believed it—for the very sound reason that his subsequent checking had substantiated the original findings. And that one, final little gambit had, also, surprised Eaper, who thought he might catch Oddie in a lapse and was satisfied when he found he was not correct.

Davies left. Oddie locked up the files and followed.

Perhaps, he thought as he pushed an elevator button, he should have gone beyond having strangers ask around Waimanalo about Grove. But why? The more his men heard the plainer it became that a man who once had been sharp was now a soft-headed old *futz*. "Futz" was Oddie's second most disparaging term.

11

GOLF

After the latest election the Secret Service had worried about its task of guarding the victor when he reached the White House: he was a golfer and a good one. He had played on his university team and kept his game up during his years at law school. As a corporation lawyer, then as a candidate for the Senate, a senator and finally a governor, he had played at convenient courses frequently. He would be not only the best golfer ever to occupy the White House but, it was believed, one who golfed as often as Eisenhower.

Since the late Ike's incumbency, however, presidential security had changed. Assassination and other dire circumstances were responsible. So there was a great deal of anxious planning for the safety of the elected man on whatever courses he would play; but the planners had misjudged the new Chief Executive.

The inauguration came and went. No golf was played by the President in that month and those following until April. One April afternoon, however, the President called in the head of the White House Secret Service detail and announced he planned to play eighteen on the following Saturday.

"I suppose," he said, with a twinkle in his greenish-brown eyes, "you boys have been sweating."

"Well," Melville responded, "we've given it a good bit of thought. I wouldn't say—sweat."

"It takes a lot of men, though, to cover an eighteen-hole course—and a lot of time to hit eighteen."

"Part of the job, sir."

"Max, I don't expect to enjoy very many games—too busy. And I don't intend to play where you'll have to post an army on a weekend, or at any other time."

"I'm afraid—"

"You ever heard of John Boyer Wald?"

"The name is familiar, Mr. President, but—"

"He's president of AmcontAfro—a holding company."

Max clicked: *that* tycoon.

The President went on. "Jack took up golf some years back. He's one of those fireball types—which is why he got where he did. But he has a temper like lit dynamite—and he's vain in some ways. Who isn't? He couldn't play well enough, alone, to satisfy himself—even with the best pros for teachers. When he played with friends, he'd fall apart. Some do. But it made Jack Wald furious. He decided there were too many spectators for his blowups—they were funny to see. I should know! So—he built himself his own course. Called it Duffer's—ever hear of it?"

"Not that I can recall, sir."

"It's in Chesapeake Bay, on an island—most of which was fill to make the course and room for a residence and a clubhouse. Dandy layout. When Jack wants to play by himself, he can, since it's his. It's kept in perfect shape and twenty-thirty friends of his at most play there in a given week. I'm playing Duffer's—when I can, and no other links."

Max understood; he expressed his appreciation and departed. To make such an island secure required only a check of the people who worked and lived on it and a rundown of players and others visiting it on any day the President would be among them. Aside from that, a watch on an island was, relatively, a cinch. Max checked out "Duffer's Country Club" the next day, with colleagues, and came home happy.

The President didn't play much after that; but when he played, it was there as he'd promised. His game suffered; expectably and from lack of practice, people said. It suffered, however, in another fashion: he golfed now in a manner that was opposite to his earlier game and to his way of behavior in all other activities. He hit every tee shot, if the distance warranted, with all his might, not with a controlled limit to gain the accuracy attained by restraint. He took every chance possible, even when a dub would have chosen more cautious routes to the pin. His long putts were dispatched with the intention of sinking them and not that professional purpose of merely getting close to the hole. A once-conservative master, he turned into a reckless gambler.

From a customary score in the middle seventies, the

Chief Executive dropped to the high eighties, and even the nineties.

He seemed not to mind but, on the contrary, to enjoy the abandon which caused such deterioration of his score. It was as if he used golf, when he played, to let off pent-up steam. And that was the truth.

In his first year he got in just six rounds.

The game on which he embarked, in this next April, was his second for the season. He teed off in a foursome made up of a cousin, Oliver Wendham, a friend of the cousin, Mark Smith, and the Assistant Secretary of State, Jason Beekman. They used four carts but the Chief ruled out caddies. His cousin and the Assistant Secretary were excellent golfers. Smith, a redheaded, thick-chested man "in steel" who came from Bucyrus, Ohio, told the others he hadn't played in a long while and that fact was evident after two holes.

He was the only man unknown to the Secret Service guards on duty in boats and at shore points which enabled them to see any and every water approach to the island. Players already on the course, along with the permanent residents—grounds-keepers, caddies, a cook, houseboys and the rest—had long been cleared.

Max Melville had not checked Mark Smith. The President had saved him that by saying, "Old friend of my cousin Oliver, Smith is. They went to school together and see each other often. Mark's a keen coin collector—like Cousin Oliver—I never could see that hobby. Anyhow—"

More than enough, Max thought; any long-time friend of a cousin had to be okay, and beside, the Chief knew Mark Smith. That warm afternoon the air was still and damp but no showers were predicted till night. The few players on the links were well ahead when the presidential party teed off. No others came up to start, for an hour.

By the time the VIP foursome had holed out on the third green, the Assistant Secretary was miffed. The President had hooked a Number Three wood deep into a stand of high grass and insisted on hunting till the ball was found. Mr. Smith had sent a drive into a blind water hole at an amazing distance from the tee but he'd persisted in believing it was short of that and in the rough at one side—which caused another prolonged search.

That sort of thing happened several more times in the first six. Smith's long iron shot on the third had been straight but aimed so it entered a woods at the left side of the green where it was found after long effort. One presidential putt was so strong it had taken three more strokes to hole out; and all were made with great and now novel deliberation. So when the President suggested, apparently as a matter of courtesy both to the impatient pair and his cousin's guest, that the other two play ahead and he follow with Smith, the Assistant Secretary had been only too glad to accept; and Oliver Wendham hadn't debated longer than manners required.

The first twosome soon moved far ahead of the second. When they had done so, the President said to "Mark Smith," "Well, Ring. What's the emergency?"

"There isn't any, in a sense. That's the problem."

The President teed up, glanced down the fairway, took his stance, made several short fiddles with his driver and then, absent-mindedly using his original form, sent a straight ball two hundred and sixty-five yards down the middle. "You better explain that."

Grove stepped up to the markers. "You have *nearly* everything I got, of any importance. There's been no trace of Solentor since that visit."

"Which must have been something!"

"It was." Grove studied the fairway, got set and hit his ball within ten feet of the other's. "That," he said, "is what I was trying to do." He referred to the shot. They boarded their carts but sat awhile before pursuing the drives. "It *was* something," Grove repeated, grinning. "And it's something to think Solentor, in person, was on Oahu and may be still."

"I worry about Neptune."

"So do I. That's why I asked for this meeting. Many thanks, too, for arranging it. Because I now feel we ought to call the pros in. The CIA, anyhow. It's too big a risk to sit on, at my end, knowing what I know, alone, and what I don't, that's vital."

"You haven't a ghost of a notion—?"

"I have more information, yes, but what it means, I can't guess."

"We better move on so nobody overtakes us." The President grinned. "This private course has been very useful, before now."

They bumped out on the fairway and played steadily. Their conversation was interrupted only when the game separated them. Grove started it with his new information.

"It occurred to me that the big show, following the finding of money and bracelets—"

"Big show?"

Grove realized, then, exactly how busy the President was—and the result, that he skipped news he found of no relevance, such as the account, carried world-wide, of the treasure hunt on the mountain behind Sea Life Park. He described it and the President listened with fascination.

The intellectual ability of the man in the White House was once more made plain when Grove finished his narrative.

"The people who threw that girl off the cliff top assumed the body would be found—and didn't care. It would be identified as Miss Dwelling, whose real name and profession would be kept secret. That man in Honolulu, Oddie, thought the killers had been obliged to locate and conceal the body, first found by you and your new recruit—he must be quite a boy! Obliged to do that, in Oddie's view, because of the treasure hunt. The fact was, that treasure hunt had been the killers' purpose."

Grove putted and looked up. "There was that. Our opposite numbers would hardly toss away so much money and jewelry with, perhaps, unfound gems and more currency, from a mountaintop for no reason. They aren't fools. But they couldn't know that Jerry and I had seen the victim and hidden her. All they could learn was that the remains were reported found by Oddie and company. What the climbing mob collected and maybe some stuff they didn't, was taken for what it had been, the girl's belongings. By everybody except Jerry and me. The snatched bit of ylang-ylang lei told me more."

As tersely as he could, Grove repeated the Bangkok story of his near murder and the ylang-ylang "Mavis" who, then, had an infant daughter. He added word of the ylang-ylang lei found on the night the other body had turned up in the park's Hawaiian Reef Tank.

The President was quick about that too. "So our 'Maribel,' knowing she was about to be tossed over the rim of a near cliff, a thousand feet high, grabbed, from a woman present, the one thing that might carry a message to—our side? To Oddie or Eaper or someone. Damned bright! And brave as the devil!"

Grove nodded solemnly. "Yes, I think so. The daughter

of that Bangkok dame, a real beauty and a medium-expert fiend, too, must have followed her mother's custom. And been up on the pali that night with some boy friends of Solentor's. That's probable. Though the daugher might merely have had a penchant for that flower because her mother wore it so often, when she was a tot. It could also have been sheer coincidence. Or another woman using the old ylang-ylang identifier. But since the lass snatched it, I tend to see it as a signal."

"So you—and this Gong wizard—began to scout around. On the theory the mob hunt on the talus and the cliffs was staged?"

"I wasn't very quick about figuring it that way. But in time it occurred to me that you could very neatly pull off some other operation when the whole world was busy either on the talus and cliffs, or watching. It wasn't hard to guess, then, where such a business would happen. Upwind from the area toward which those hundred-dollar bills would be blown. At a considerable distance from where the jewelry would land, too. A stretch the mob wouldn't consider searching. That made it easy. There's nothing in that direction of the mountain flank but a power line, high-tension poles and wires, coming over from Honolulu."

"Interesting."

"Very. We had to scout carefully, not wanting their people to know we were getting warm, if we were. And we were, up to a point. They'd tapped the line. But," Grove added quickly, "it didn't tell any more. We could see that people had been up and down, from the park, usually, but sometimes from a spot on the highway nearer Makapuu Point, dozens of trips and maybe a dozen different men, by the tracks they didn't wipe out. There had plainly been some heavy gear up above the talus, near the high-tension line, too, for a while. But everything was gone by the time we searched—except the overlooked tracks, broken weeds and so on."

"They had to have a power supply, temporarily? And the treasure hunt thing was to—what?"

"Cover their removal of gear? Perhaps. Probably, even. But what were the instruments they had hauled up and removed? Transformers? No way to guess. And where did their cable tap go? Jerry and I made a big effort on that. No luck."

"No luck? Seems strange, with the other evidence so clear."

Grove nodded that their game should go on. They holed out, then teed up and drove again before he continued his report. "That area of Oahu is still on the windward side. Plenty of showers even in mid-spring. At the foot of the pali there's a lot of runoff. It would wash out the main highway along the ocean if there weren't culverts to carry it under the road to the sea. The park also has to return its salt water supply—three hundred thousand gallons an hour, constantly. We could find the place where the cable reached the road ditches, on the land side. Beyond—no chance."

"Rains, flooding, washing the signs out?"

"That, and the heavy construction at the Makai Range, next to the institute, which adjoins the park. They could have run their tap to the nearest culvert or to one a half mile away in either direction, and from there, under the road in any culvert and then, buried in sand or rocks, out to sea. A person who might see it would assume it had to do with the heavy construction, or research, in the area. It could be covered on the ocean bottom, easily, with rocks, or buried in sand, to a point where the depth would make it safe to run along on bottom. It could have paralleled the road and been carried back up and even over the pali. No way to tell *where* it went."

"Hunh." For ten minutes of play the President talked of other matters, when he talked at all; then, as they approached the fifteenth green he said, "What happened to that girl you caught?"

Grove smiled. "I wasn't told, exactly. Didn't want to be told. Jerry's second cousin didn't know who or what she was. Just that she needed to be hidden and guarded. No reason for me to have more dope. Regular practice of the system." At that, and very suddenly, Grove stopped a backswing to stare at the President without seeing him.

"Something?"

"Good *Lord!* Maybe there is! I think I may know how Ah Soo stashed her away!" He shrugged and resumed his game, saying, "Irrelevant, here. Just—a matter of interest. The guy may be cleverer than I thought—and using my *own* system! Golly!" He swung, topping the ball.

They went on. The President soon put an astute question about the tap on the high-tension line.

"Wouldn't the drawdown show up?"

Grove smiled a little. "I guess it did. The high-voltage lines serves a Coast Guard station, a radar installation, the whole Abbott complex, the electrically driven machinery at work there on construction, the street lighting in Waimanalo and the homes of maybe a thousand people—"

"I see."

"Well, there's this. Roy Hedges, an ex-Navy officer, incidentally, keeps tabs on costs for the Abbott holding company and it grows like—"

"I know young Attack Abbott," the President interrupted.

"Of course. Well, Hedges recently put in a beef to Hawaiian Electric about the latest bill. He claimed it ran over the possible top by several hundred dollars."

"At a special rate, that means a lot of juice?"

"Yes. The Coast Guard people were hit too. I don't know about the rest. It could be, their main splice drew current only from those two leads. We—Jerry and I—haven't made a close enough search to be sure of that. We don't want anybody who might be watching to see us up on the poles. We have merely made certain that they had equipment up above the talus—near the line. And that they had, for a while, a heavy-duty line down to the road."

They played a hole in silence.

On the next tee the President said, in a thinking-aloud tone, "You haven't suggested a *why* for all that—meaning you have no idea?"

"Right, Mr. President."

"Steve," the President corrected: it was what his intimate friends called him. "Could anybody else figure out—?"

"Figure what—Mr.—?"

"Steve."

"Steve," Grove said, dutifully.

"Figure out, say, the possibilities?"

"I doubt it. The setup has too many answers."

The President meditated aloud. "You want a source of power, high-tension juice, for a month or two—and that has to be managed in secret. So you have to steal it. It's vital—but for that period only. Right? It could be needed on land—or at sea. Nearby—or miles away—am I still on the beam?" Grove nodded, and he went on. "You aren't merely charging batteries or the like." He hesitated and asked, "Nothing visible at sea, that could be suggestive, I suppose?"

"Nothing that comes from the routine checks; radar; or other Navy and CIA reports. Nothing was reported on the surface in that period which wasn't supposed to be there, or at least *known.*"

"Behind the two islands you spoke of?"

"Nothing helpful. We had other people look around on Rabbit Island. Red Rock is too low and wet. Relations of Jerry's did the job. I'd say they were good at it. The seaward side of Rabbit Island has always been used—by assorted scientists, locals going ashore from boats and so on. I am sure Solentor was there, off and on. A submarine could bring men in close and the radar wouldn't show it up. But not much has been happening there lately. And nothing that would explain the power theft. No sign of electric or any gear brought ashore, that would use as much current."

"What about the sea bottom?"

"All that you can inspect—the shallow part out to the big reef—is apparently unchanged. Be dangerous to lay cable openly, there, anyhow. Too many skin divers and so on. A camouflaged cable, yes—or buried. Beyond the outside reef, though, lies the whole Pacific."

The President missed a chip shot. "If I call in the CIA what you've told me might leak. We've acted on your information and caught a couple of—incredible—traitors. One was an acquaintance of mine. You never know for sure; rather, you can't *always* know, what men may do for money—or because of pressure." The President shrugged off that disillusioning knowledge. "Let's assume, however, that the other side still has a pipeline into the CIA. So they would likely put an end to whatever is going on in Hawaii—or move it. I want to think this over, Ring. When are you going back?"

"Tomorrow?"

"Right. I'll get word on my decision in a few days. I need to talk to certain men, first." He saw Grove's disappointment before the signs could be banished. "Look, Ring. I'll do this for you right away. I've already thought of it. Nobody is more aware than I am of what it's like to carry a great nation on one human back." His smile was somber. "I have two close friends in Hawaii—men I can trust absolutely. Jake Palmer at Volcanos National Park—he's a geologist. I've know him from boyhood. And

Hank Balcom, in command at Kauai—the base where the subs rehearse war. An admiral, now, Hank. I'll get to them tonight and if you need help they will be set up to give it. Until I decide about the CIA, that is. But don't go to anybody else, no matter what, till you hear."

"Thanks—Steve."

"If we only have *time* enough!"

"That—is why I came direct. It begins to look like time is running out."

"I know." The President made another, remedial chip shot and the game went on.

The game of golf.

And the other game.

12

GLINT

Grove put a recently rented sedan in the garage. Another morning of cautious search on the raw land and talus beyond the park had been futile. In the week since his return almost nothing new had been found and what was new only showed more clearly how men had gone up and down the pali, dragging heavy gear, at night, until the treasure hunt enabled them to do whatever it was that required daylight. Minute fragments of cable insulation had been scraped off by woody shrubs, recovered and tested by Grove. Traces he had found on patches of sand and among trampled plants meant nothing more about those who had come and gone. Grove's gauge in the cove gave some of the times. It showed no recent action.

He'd received notes marked "Personal," mailed in care of the Abbotts as a precaution, from the President's two friends, the admiral on Kauai and the geologist on the Big Island. These hand-delivered missives were written in such ways that if they had come under hostile study they would have meant little.

Grove was invited to visit the research laboratories near the caldera of the Kilauea where a fire pit, Halemaumau, was in irregular but spectacular eruption. With the invitation was a phone number and that letter came, apparently, from another scientist, not Jake Palmer.

The note from Admiral Henry (Hank) Balcom had been Xeroxed as if it were a form letter sent to many people. It, too, was an invitation—to a charity dinner—and it gave a phone number with word that an RSVP to "Captain Houghton Defton" would be in order. That, Grove assumed, would be a non-existing officer at the base. But a call to that name would be a signal and get him through to the admiral.

He had replied by sending two picture postcards of hula maidens and a scribbled "Sorry, pal, my trip is too short to allow coming over to see you." The handwriting on both cards was disguised and the signature was "Steve Forman," which was not the President's last name but would suffice as receipts of the two very neatly designed invitations.

It was comforting to think he—and now Jerry—could call for help if necessary. But it was something less to receive word—by the revised route—that the gallant man in the White House did not want, yet, to bring in the CIA.

During the golf game Grove had had a shocking idea, and that he could and did try to check immediately on his return.

Esther Wilson, if that was correct, was perhaps "hidden" now, though after some interval following her first appearance, *in the park.*

Grove had taken many lunches in the park restaurant, recently, when he and sometimes Jerry had furtively searched the power-line area. An open-sided restaurant with Polynesia's thick posts, beams and high roofs, the service, cafeteria style to massive wooden tables of various sizes on two floor levels, it accommodated any possible fraction of the daily crowds wanting lunch or a snack before, after or between shows. This eating place gave a spectacular view of the park and the sea and its near islands. Like the gift shop, it was inside park limits and only paying visitors who wished to break their tour to shop or dine or people with passes were admitted.

Park executives and many scientists regularly lunched there: the food was excellent. There was a bar. Eight or ten girls served from behind the counters and three more worked as bus "boys"; the barman was male and Japanese. Grove knew these employees quite well—brothers of two of the girls behind the counter belonged to his gang. So he had noticed the new bus girl soon after she'd been hired.

Her job was to clear tables, remove trays, dispose of food left on paper plates, keep table tops pristine and clear up such inadvertent messes as dropped ice cream cones, infant food spills and the like. She wore the restaurant trademark, a cute, small straw hat. Her muumuu did not conceal her rather unusual width of hip and thickness of buttock or her similarly overdeveloped bosom. She had black hair, a huge mass beneath the absurd hat and a level fringe on her forehead; straight hair. Her eyes slanted slightly and her skin was golden, which, somehow, men called "yellow" long ago. Her profile was not oriental, a common result of Hawaiian racial integration, which is more than superficial.

Her name was Betty and her last name, when he asked, was Sato. She was as pretty, popular and amiable as the other girls; he'd often chatted with Betty Sato in the days before that game of golf. As he became acquainted with her in that casual way, he'd found himself, now and then, trying to remember a girl he'd known long ago whom Betty seemed to resemble.

It had not been a very important effort and he'd conducted it mainly because he disliked his habitual forgetfulness and tried to reduce its incidence when he could. The girl's aura, as he called it, certainly stirred some long-forgotten but sensual nerve. For several days, off and on, his self-questioning had been vain. Then he had abruptly remembered; Betty recalled a French girl he'd once known and loved, he guessed, as much as possible for him. Her name—Grove had to struggle a bit for that, even—had been (and maybe still was, with an added surname) Racquelle Eviant.

Racquelle was sixteen when her parents furnished Grove with a hide-out under their peasant farmhouse, which was near Lyons. He had used it as his base for five months. He was working with the Maquis in Vichy France, then, and Monsieur et Madame Eviant had taken a great risk to provide Grove that sanctuary. But they had done it gladly. Grove had saved their lives by killing three Nazi SS men who were questioning them, moments before he had made their acquaintance. Later he rescued their youngest son—the other two were dead in lost battles—when the boy had been picked up and was being carted away by collaborator neighbors, for Nazi "interrogation" meaning, of course, slow and hideous death. The Eviants' traitor neighbors had met a swift fate.

On the first night Racquelle came quietly into his candlelit snug underground quarters Grove was surprised. It was less than a week after he'd installed himself. He was startled when the trapdoor raised and he saw the girl, vaguely. He thought, as she came down silently and he reset the camouflage beneath the opening, that she must have a message. It was after midnight and he'd been reading to soothe nerves that needed such therapy, sorely. He wore no blouse or undershirt but was still in socks and corduroy trousers.

"Ah, Racquelle! It's late. You have a message?" All, in French.

"Yes, monsieur." She wore a woolen nightdress and was barefooted. "It is not of trouble. Or even urgent." She had smiled at him in a way that he'd begun to notice, during the past few days; not a proper way for a maid to smile at any man and, especially, a youngish, lonely and often frightened man who could do with the consolation of any trifle that could divert his mind from . . . yesterday, and . . . tomorrow, and all tomorrows there might still be.

"You'd like some tea? Coffee?" He'd superintended the lastest British parachute drop and some kind Briton had added a few luxuries to the arms and explosives that rained in feathery stillness from clouded skies, nearby.

"No, monsieur." There was a bed, nothing elegant, a mattress, two down-filled quilts, raised on planks a foot or so—a better bed than most of his people enjoyed at this time. She sat down there and very purposefully removed the soft gown. "I have a private message only. Please come and make love to me."

"Jesus!" It was, even then, strong, for Grove. He did not disapprove of profanity but rejected it as limiting and often in poor taste, a bad habit, therefore. He did not object to sixteen-year-old French girls being seduced by his colleagues. He had no such lenient view for himself because he was somewhat more responsible than the others—steadier than the times, indeed, allowed men or even warranted, in these matters. Racquelle was lovely, fully made, dusky of skin, with long, wavy black hair that looked heavy in braids or piled high, as now; she had wonderfully luminous eyes of an amber color and long lashes. Eyes she'd used, with effects he evaded, lately. She began to flush when he sat unmoving at his rude table where the candle stood in steady flame. He was speechless.

"I am not a virgin," Racquelle whispered. "The Boches —" She hunched her bare shoulders and covered her breasts. "I am not ill, however, like some. And not with child. It revolts you, that past I have had?"

The facts seemed irrelevant to Grove. He realized he was dangerously near taking a stride to her side. "You are only sixteen. Your parents, also—what would they—?"

She spoke after that with softness and a shy certainty. "They did not order me to come to you, because they would fear you might just reject me. I came because I love you, I think, and I know, at least more than enough to—don't you want me? Cannot you be a little thanked, a little eased from your—work—by a pretty girl?"

He said it again, slowly, "Jesus."

Five months of passion and wonder, of violence, terror, killing and of escaping death by seconds and centimeters. Often, in the later times, he had thought how perfect a wife she would be. If, he would amend, you could settle in the French countryside after surviving this war and be happy never to go anywhere else or see anybody, places or people that would embarrass your wife. She would try to acquire the graces of course. When she found that the great world at the levels Grove knew it was not a wonderland and that its paragons were few, male or female, she'd suffer. His French was Parisian and she tried from the first to imitate it. She was very proud; proud of him, of what she had to give, of the giving, and of his eloquent response.

But what would he do, where would he go, what would he want, including *any* wife, if he did live to know peace again? Probably the OSS would have a long task to be completed even if he were able to be part of that; one that wouldn't make marriage sensible, just a near-perpetual absence. Grove correctly guessed that. And while the OSS wanted him, he was theirs—much as the girl was his, while it was so needed, so wanted and so logical in its fashion.

When he was sent on a new mission, he had time only to say a little. "I may not return," he explained.

The entire Eviant family was present. His mistress, her two younger sisters, the young man he'd snatched from two traitors' wagon, *maman* and *papa*.

"You must not return, Louis," Racquelle said steadily. (Lord! He'd not thought of the name for an age!) "For us it is ended. We have loved each other. It would not be right to hope for any loving, again, between us. I shall marry if we are alive at the war's end. A nice young man. I shall be content. I shall not forget you. Nor will my father, my mother, Jeanne, Yselle or Robert, ever." The others nodded but could not speak.

Grove found one word he could manage: *"Darling!"*

It was all he did as a farewell. After the armistice he had ascertained that the Eviant family was well and farming thriftily; Racquelle had a beau suitable from every standpoint. One who soon married his love, his near love, one among the very few of the many.

What to Grove had been "the many" would have caused a fair fraction of men his age no more than condescending smiles. Their collective image hadn't appeared for many years and until the bus girl at the park reminded him of Racquelle.

Grove wasn't a prude. No one reared among circus people can be; a traveling magician, often with a road company as companions, won't be made more conventional.

Grove truly liked women, all ages of women, from infant to final hour. He liked *people.* There was in his manner and the feelings it usually though unconsciously expressed a certain appeal that other men noted and often envied but could not imitate. Physically, even as a younger man, Grove had not been very handsome. But his smile, the specific light in his wide-set, gray eyes, his deep, rolling voice, his self-confidence with the other sex that came from liking females, not their conquest, had impact. Taken with his constant proof of enjoying life and of appreciating, as well as furnishing, imaginative fun, his personality enchanted most females. They called him charming, dear, delightful, because he made them feel *safe.* He did not just arouse mother or sister feelings, but oftener, a magnetic, unfamiliar urge. Few men really like women as people. That was his basic appeal, perhaps.

But no one is liked by everybody. Sadistic females didn't see much in Grove. Masochists instantly knew he wasn't their type. They are a minority, fortunately, and most of his affairs seemed only that—partly because he could not look back on all of them with pleasure. There was Lisa Birch, for one, his assistant for a long part of his career as a traveling stage magician. Bright, pert, pretty and a devil as intimate partner; he'd considered marrying Lisa to make the lass an honest woman—and as a treasure, too—when he'd found she enjoyed other gentlemen wherever and as often as they became available and Grove's absence made her fun possible.

In his OSS days he'd lived with several ladies of a similar occupation and of various nationalities. Most of them took the intimate cover with the assignment husband-wife or even father-daughter. These girls and ladies knew such relations had to be as close as duty required.

Grove held nothing against prostitutes, either, a second characteristic rare among men. They were women to him; if they were honest in their terms and attractive, if he was attracted, he treated them as he did all other girls (or women) he liked; the fact that they rented (not "sold") themselves to live did not lessen his appreciation or alter his feelings.

However, he had never been able to exploit the appeal to which women responded so often, so warmly and so sure of their safety, as an instrument for professional purposes. He had often managed to charm information out of the lady agents of enemies. But he was unable to do it by erotic pretenses. He literally couldn't succeed that way. His superiors had soon found that out and passed him over as unfit for assignments that involved female conquest aimed at womanly betrayal. . . .

He had been very shocked to realize, on the golf course, that the girl who cleared away trays in the park restaurant was not physically reminiscent of Racquelle but that she brought to mind a lately seen beauty, called Esther Wilson. He had appreciated the President's tact in not pressing him when he'd made that discovery—if it was one—and had told Steve it was irrelevant.

On his return to Hawaii he found the expected, quick check did not answer. This Betty Sato might possibly be the lady Solentor had left him, without clothes and for the grim purpose she'd stated. But pretty Betty's eyes were black. Their color and slant could be managed—contact lenses and make-up. But as he made a point of chatting with her, it became difficult to believe Betty had so perfectly learned her Hawaiian "accent," that odd mix of accents which most of the counter girls had lost.

In the days he now spent trying to find useful evidence on the mountain toward Makapuu Point, in the spring sun's heat, slaving to remain invisible, growing less and less hopeful and always weary from those efforts, he kept changing his mind. Cyrus Ah Soo had said Esther was on another island—and perhaps she had been. Jerry, obliquely questioned, evidently assumed Cy's claim was still correct. Betty was fat. She had no more hesitation than the other girls about talking with him, at some length, and with the customary small jokes. Standing close, too.

Grove knew that if this Betty was Esther, this hiding place had been clever. Solentor's people might look for her, doubtless had looked and perhaps were still looking; but the public cafeteria wouldn't be a likely spot for their search. *Move away a block or so; change your name and looks slightly:* Grove's own formula for disappearing. If the bus girl was the onetime American agent and the twice-brainwashed captive of the Soviets, her presence might mean loyalty to America or that she was again, on the other side and alert on behalf of that side. And she might not be either.

He could not decide how to resolve this enigma—or fantasy. Black hair would be simple. Her Hawaiian locutions could be easy for the linguist his naked, short-term guest had claimed she was. And he found her resemblance to Racquelle, which had put him off for such a long time, wasn't facial except for a few trifles; it was owing to the fact that this Betty Sato, or whoever, *moved* as that long-ago girl had, *smiled* with the same warmth and the same special glow of eye—*attracted* him, then, in a way once very familiar. He discovered that with a slight sense of embarrassment because he had not expected ever again to feel toward any woman quite as he'd felt toward the French girl. He did, though, and at twice this girl's age, nearly! He couldn't help wondering if that wasn't a sign of male menopause though he kept obstinately trying to guess what the bus girl in the loose muumuu would look like if the wide hips, the extending derrière and the vast breasts were not substance but padding, and, imagined as removed.

One afternoon when he returned to the park after a final, hard and luckless crawl on the steeps in the power-line region he saw that Betty was preparing to go off duty. She finished some sweeping and now mopped up a spot on the asphalt floor. Then she took broom and the mop to their closet and he managed, by leaning awkwardly, to see her do something he still had not quite expected. She carefully wiped the long handles of the implements with a towel.

The dishes and trays she touched all day were, of course, put straight into washing machines.

Grove said nothing to her then. But he left for his home thoughtfully. If Solentor's people knew their lost lady was here, why would that clever lass be careful not to leave her fingerprints anywhere? On the other hand, did she suspect that the CIA, or somebody of that sort, might make a print survey of park employees, or even of herself in particular? Why?

It might be important to know. And it was interesting to be fairly sure, at last, that Esther Wilson was here and occupied by some cautious endeavor aside from that of staying hidden and unrecognized by him and maybe others.

The next day Betty was off duty he tried to find out from the counter girls what they knew about her. Not much that satisfied Grove, it proved. Betty had lived in Hana Maui, they said, till lately when she came to Oahu and got the cleanup job. She boarded with a big family in the Hawaiian Homelands, people who were known to several of the counter girls and who were sure of Betty's long-time residence in Hana. They said she "knew everybody"—it wasn't a large village, after all. If that background was false, as Grove believed, it was well founded owing, perhaps to the ingenuity and aid of Mr. Cy Ah Soo.

He told Jerry that night what he had learned and what he suspected. Jerry elicited from his second cousin, a few days later, the fact that Betty was, indeed, Esther. She had been "hidden" in the village of Hana for several weeks, at first. It was she who had suggested this different way of concealment. Cy hadn't told Jerry about it because the girl had begged him not to. And also because Cy had thought the whole affair was pretty clever, a bit of one-upmanship on his part in relation to Jerry Gong. Since Cy had no idea of the background of the lady he'd first unchained in Grove's house and provided with clothes, helped disguise for her appearance in Hana and later aided in her present imposture, he thought of it as a great joke.

"He'll keep it quiet," Jerry told Grove that night, "so no sweat, there. But what are you going to do?"

"That's a peach of a question! If we pick her up and she explains what's behind this bright idea, we may have to start all over, hiding her. We can't deal her in. Though I'd bet half of my dough against a single buck she's not working for them any more. But I've made mistakes before now. Suppose we just leave her as is for a while? I'll try, try a little, to get her to come clean. It's a mess! Suppose she now feels loyal to CIA, for instance?"

"Wouldn't she have sent them word?"

"Guess not. Nothing about her in the regular Eaper bulletins. There would be, if she'd made contact. Told 'em about me—us."

"I could get a—friend—to keep tabs—?"

"Let her sit, Jerry. We don't want any more aides. Can't have them: presidential order, remember?"

"My friend wouldn't need to know anything but just keep an eye on this Betty Sato."

"Not now. Anybody doing that could tip off somebody else doing the same. Right?"

Jerry agreed.

Some days later Grove came from his garage and found Genevra Oopani sitting on a shaded bench in the back yard—all two hundred and ten pounds of Jenny, all the serenity, the repose, the face that recalled a youthful beauty and still had a different loveliness. She was not aware of his arrival—or of the stunning portrait study made by the quiet traces of her character—her fondness, generosity and faint sadness, her wisdom, her—Grove had called it Polynesianness—a dignity, the innocent sexuality, the poise and her unspoken nature worship. (Did she still believe the story about Haleakala and the sun?) He never could know.

She was relaxing on a redwood bench, leaving scant room for another occupant and looking, with dark, shining eyes, toward the mountains. It made Grove look.

Maybe she knew by then that he was there. Maybe not.

What she was watching, Grove watched.

Over the tops of the near mountains, precipitous and vertically trenched, white, gray and ominously purplish clouds piled up. The trades kept adding to those already blocked by the sharp-topped, hidden crests. They came at regular intervals, marine cumulus, white as angel wings, spaced evenly, and almost of a size. Flat on the bottom but of varied shape, and when they were pushed into their predecessors they turned gray or mauve. As the compression increased the mass darkened. At a certain point their essence, moisture, congealed owing to the chill of altitude, very different from the warmth that rose out of the sun-steamed Pacific, whence they had origin.

At that height, the clouds rained.

From below, the rain appeared as glittering sheets, as dark shafts, as amorphous curtains that hid the jungle and bare stone. Through the panoply, light streamed in every degree of intensity from hot white to a dusky shimmer, light shaped by iris-opening of cloud and mountain into geometrical forms because the light did not bend; slow, hushed blocks of it slanted against the background. Grove looked and he thought, as often, of the praise heaped on Rome's golden light, or the Aegean's—and he knew that nobody had seen what light could be, who'd not watched the Hawaiian pali on such a day.

And he saw what fascinated Jenny.

"It's beautiful," he said softly.

She wasn't startled; she turned a little and smiled. "The rainbow? I am listening to it."

What an idea! he thought. Listening: to a rainbow.

Genevra said things like that. Perhaps they were things said by her ancestors, when they stared in awe at their new paradise, chiefs and princes, huge men in feather cloaks, handsome and impressive in a way lost to man now. Perhaps, when they looked at rainbows in the Hawaiian light they also listened—as the clouds came and thickened, darkened, spilled diagonal torrents into the light shafts that made, then as on this day, trapezoids of rain and curtains which then became waterfalls, silver torrents that fell for a thousand or two thousand feet from every murk-hidden notch in the summit line.

He tried it; he "listened" to the rainbow that arced above.

Its violet would be a deep and low tone, double basses and oboes; red, the brasses; yellow, the violins, high and wild and explicit, with violas and second fiddles harmonizing with orange woodwinds.

It stirred a memory. When he'd been a child, near to sleep, he'd sometimes heard massive, symphonic music, self-composed, marvelous, never repeating and very distant, long before he'd listened to a real symphony orchestra; when the only music he knew was that of the circus band, of calliopes, or of popular phonograph records.

He remembered that other, accepted marvel and wondered, now, what had produced it. Auditory imagination, perhaps—or some earlier, unremembered and chance hearing of symphony records which he had later recomposed in tempo with the rush of capillarial blood, giving an interpretation of his own, from its forgotten source.

Looking now at the rainbow, a resplendent arch with a hazy companion, and "listening" to both, Grove recalled those bedtime rhapsodies.

And a phrase came to mind: *music of the spheres.*

Suppose there was such a thing—a cosmic sonata, that only the innocent, or children, could hear nowadays? But music that Polynesians might always have heard, since, according to missionary and other haole views, they were more or less children?

He realized goose flesh had pocked him and that Jenny had turned, seen that and smiled.

For a moment, as he glanced back at the prismatic arc, the tiny pimpling stood out and he could hear the childhood rhapsody, with its massive orchestration. Then the sound ebbed, his flesh became smooth and he laughed a little at himself, but not quite with deprecation.

For Grove knew that man, in his modern, civilized state, scientific man, technological man, was merely at the edge of knowing. Science, however little scientists accepted the fact, was a beginning art. The most elaborate concept of the nature of reality—the farthest reach of telescopes, the minutest seeing of electron magnifiers, and the deepest insight so far gained—was elementary, tentative and crude. A hundred years from now an expectably vast extension of knowledge would also be regarded near to final, just as it was this day. But another next century would see all that prior knowing as meager and see its own, once again, as nearly whole.

He chuckled softly.

And the big woman answered that same way: "Haoles almost never know how little they know." She turned that into a great compliment. "But some, Mr. Grove, do guess."

They watched the rainbow a little longer. But he didn't hear it again.

Finally they went in. Lunch, Jenny said, was nearly ready. And she reminded him as she served it that, at three-thirty, his trampoline class would arrive: the multihued kids from the neighborhood, aged eleven to sixteen, who were becoming expert under his instruction. Fifteen boys and, by their special permission (with a little pressure from Grove), two girls, who didn't know they were being taught acrobatics by one of the world's former but greatest clown tumblers—a teacher who, at the lesson's end, gave exhibitions which he wound up with at least one new display, some combination of flip, flips or twists—tucked or layout—that no other "uncle" or "gramp," Japanese, Chinese, Thai, Portuguese or Yankee, the popeyed kids ever heard of could perform.

That afternoon as he watched Raymond Tatti and Joseph Wataln (who was East Indian) complete perfect tucked back-double-somersaults he thought that he would soon need a taller and bigger gym room, one equipped for flying trapezes, providing parents assented.

The kids would go for it.

But it was a bit risky. So far, nobody had been seriously hurt: sprains, strained muscles, a ligament pulled, but nothing worse. With trapezes, though, the danger increased even at low levels over mats.

Meantime, he held his breath while Timothy Chung, the recent scaredy-cat of the group did a layout back gainer safely, though he missed the padded steel rim by a margin technically adequate but, Grove felt, too small for kids. Whom you shouldn't tell that, he decided—unless they came out a bit farther.

Even with a trampoline frame padded, you can break your neck by a relatively minor miscalculation.

"How was that?" the boy demanded.

Grove looked at his gleaming, oriental eyes and great child grin. "Terrific! Try another. You drifted a trifle."

Tim tried—and came down dead center. Grove relaxed.

When his trampoline class had left Grove took a leisurely shower, dressed and strolled out on his lanai. The sun was near to setting—early on this coast where the mountains behind the Kalan were high and near. There would be sunshine in Honolulu for at least an hour more.

Grove gazed over the water through the special wall of glass on the sea side. He did that a good deal now, as if looking at the ocean could somehow lead to an idea of what might have happened out there, or was happening, probably beyond the reach of eyes or even of radar. The contours of Rabbit Island, to his right, were deep-dug by shadows, the white rock ledges emphasized by the last sunlight. The bay sparkled as usual and a small craft with a red sail tacked near shore toward Kailua. Earlier in the spring the Navy had put on an occasional show of bombing practice, using smoke bombs to show the accuracy of the circling airmen, or its lack. But there hadn't been any such sight for quite a while.

As Grove looked at nothing in particular, he saw a sudden and distant glint, offshore and slightly to his right. He took up binoculars, the kind used on ships' bridges, and tried to find the source. The flash came again but what caused it wasn't discernible. Anything floating and shiny, or merely wet, might return such a glint. But as he thought that he remembered he had seen it on two or three other occasions—just such a flicker in what seemed the same place, not far from Rabbit Island. And not, he thought, much beyond the long, irregular rim of white where the oceanic swells were smashed so the inside water was never exposed to the huge waves common on other stretches of coast and highly prized by surfers.

The distant sparkle could come from flotsam that had anchored itself beyond the outer barrier. It could be, and probably was, from a buoy marking a fish trap or a trap for crawfish that went by the name of lobster, here. But as Grove gave the matter uncertain thought while keeping the glasses focused, he realized that the previous sightings of a similar flash or two had occurred at about this time—when the sun fell behind the sculpture on the mountain summit: Nature's ancient anticipation, he had decided, and perhaps her present mocking of what often passed as art, these days.

This detail had at least one significance. If some floating object were fixed at the point he had noted, it cast back the sun's light only for a few moments and owing to a certain angle of the sun. He hadn't paid attention to the precise time before: every ocean is likely to bear objects that reflect a slant of sun as they rise and tilt on the waves—and any such that is anchored, or fast for whatever cause, may well be seen only for a brief time when the sun is right.

Nevertheless, this trifling discovery would need checking out. The need, Grove reflected grimly, was owing to the lack of any other leads, a lack which made his position almost intolerable. If, as he feared, the operation in progress (or completed!) could destroy America, or be used to threaten such destruction, just four Americans knew what he did about the situation and two more, who had been alerted to some degree by the President. It wasn't enough—not enough by thousands. Perhaps there would never be enough people in time enough.

However—he put down the heavy binoculars—this mere glint was out at sea and that was where the cable could have run—hooked to another, perhaps, in the maze of seaweed, gorgonians, coral, anemones and rocks on the bottom and so camouflaged as to be impossible to see there. The problem was, how to search the area where the glint had been seen without becoming conspicuous.

Maybe Jerry could help—Jerry's family and friends, rather. They had done several things for Grove now, and not asked why, or accepted compensation. They were proud of Jerry as uncle, cousin, whatever he was to them, and inasmuch as he had been a detective, if he wanted, now, say a woman hidden or an island combed they were delighted to oblige.

It would be awhile before Jerry came to work: Grove impatiently waited.

"How could it be done?" Grove had explained.

Jerry's answer was drowned out by a metal bellow from beyond the institute grounds, toward Waimanalo. He gestured with his head and walked his bike toward the park with Grove following. The din pursued them. Not until they'd entered the Reef Tank and ascended its spiral ramp for some distance was conversation at normal level possible.

"How come, working at night?" Grove then asked.

"Got to get the new foundations and walls up by the fifteenth," the watchman answered. "Contractor set up lights and pays overtime to make it."

That referred to an activity in the third area belonging to the organization controlling the park and the institute. It also owned and operated the Makai Range where the bulldozers, earth-moving machines and triphammers were now making the din in the darkness. The Makai, or Seaward Range, had a space age look. From it, a pier extended into the Pacific for six hundred feet. At its far end and at anchor nearby were three oceangoing ships designed for engineering and research operations. Beyond the ships and beneath the water at depths of two hundred, four hundred and six hundred feet three "habitats," steel and aluminum and glass structures, would soon rest, places where men would live for months at a time under pressures equal to the depths. Their future locations were already marked by lighted buoys.

Across the highway upon the pier an edifice was rising, one seemingly normal from the outside but, within, soon to be crammed with computers, delicate electronic instruments, chemical-analytical apparatus, spider webs of cables with varicolored insulation, pumps, mazes of plastic and metal tubes, teletypes and other automated devices of which some were highly classified—a scientific beehive so novel that most people now employed in its building could not imagine its functions.

What had been months of daytime activity now proceeded under floodlights: new tunnels were being excavated under the Kalan and a bridge high above it was being built to carry cables, tubes and traffic pierward; jackhammers resounded. Much of the clamor, however, rose from efforts to shift and fix the talus slope above so there could be no slip that might damage other rising structures. This involved digging a deep trench and erection in it of a barrier of ferro-concrete.

Pumps drummed, rocks dropped from cranes, heavy gear moved with the noise of tanks and blasting was sporadic. The world shook.

"What did you ask?" Jerry's voice was raised only a little.

Grove changed his question. "Is this—uproar—on schedule? I mean, was it planned for now?"

"What building ever is on time?" Jerry laughed. "In Hawaii?"

"You don't happen to know the original starting date?"

"Sure. Some steel company couldn't make the first date. Then plans had to be done over. The starting time was moved up again."

"And it was originally supposed to be?"

"January, you know, before they got going—daytimes. Way late. So—the night work."

"January," Grove mused. "I see."

Jerry frowned: what did he see? Because he was so much more than a watchman, Jerry guessed. *"They* planned to start—whatever it is—in *January?* The murder and all?" He rubbed his forehead with the back of his meaty hand. "But why?" Then he went on, quickly. "Because the *noise* would be a cover?"

Grove nodded. "Know anything about seismology?"

"Not much."

"Most people don't realize it, but Oahu has some hundreds of tremors a day. None sharp enough to feel. They register on delicate instruments, though. Five thousand years ago the island was actively volcanic; dying shudders of that are still going on. Suppose you wanted to do something that would make a pretty fair commotion but you didn't want anybody to learn of?"

"Something, in that case, not on shore?"

"Of course! Under water where it wouldn't be visible. Suppose it required running heavy machinery, blasting—don't ask me what for. All local seismographs detect tiny tremors constantly. The Navy, with all sorts of hydrophones, is listening for what goes on at sea. So you need some way to conceal the fact you're there, and operating, right?"

"Right," Jerry said softly.

"What would be better than this work at the Makai Range?"

"You checked?"

"No. I'm merely assuming the fancier seismographs won't work properly now—and the hydrophones must be deafened. Probably, all such gadgets are shut off or ignored while the Makai job is this loud—this earthshaking."

"If we could guess *where*—"

"We can guess some probable things. First, that it's around here. The uproar wouldn't likely affect gadgets at—say—Pearl Harbor. Or the anti-submarine hydrophones at Kauai."

"Sure. And so?"

"What I was trying to ask that was drowned out: how could we scout the likely area?"

"In boats."

"Out where I *think* we should look, first, is just beyond the barrier reef. But wherever it may be, I think a hunt has to seem anything but that."

"Why couldn't you take to sailing? Rent a boat. Or go fishing—troll for marlin?"

"Think it over, Jerry. Old man Grove takes up boating,

all of a sudden and after nearly two years. Assume, next, my hobby gets me near the action. Won't the site be watched for any such event, deliberate or merely accidental?"

"Disguise? I hear you're good at that."

"Not *that* good! The job could be pretty far out. A scuba diver could come up, board me—and find the mustache was false, so to speak. Who'd see the 'accident'?"

"Perhaps—" Jerry began, and was silent.

"Perhaps what?"

"I was thinking of some open-sea work with porpoises; Mrs. Abbott mentioned it when she brought guests up, a few nights ago."

"We can't put others on the spot."

"Ever see them do it—let porpoises out in open water?"

"No."

Jerry leaned against a thick glass window, oblivious to a shark that came over to inspect his back. "It's quite an operation. They take the porpoises out in big wells. Put them in slings and use a derrick to get them overboard; then let 'em go do whatever they've been trained for. Sound—for one thing—and bring up something to prove they reached bottom. One or more other ships are always around. And a big, iron-barred cage is lowered—which the porpoises come back to, and enter, on signal. You could get out there with a dozen people or two dozen—and not be conspicuous."

"Just how," Grove replied uneasily, "do I persuade Sapphire to make her animals perform where I'd want?"

Jerry pondered, then said, "Well, maybe, like this. You tell her you know of the free-porpoise experiments coming up. And you point out that diving animals usually retrieve the handiest item on bottom—a lost and sunken shoe, a cardboard box, a tool—rather than a stone, or anything heavy. They *can* bring up stones or a hunk or iron, but they'd rather scout around for some proof they went clear down that's easy to fetch."

"Logical."

"So—what? *You* lost something out there, wherever you'd like her to send porpoises down—on the wild chance they'd find it. Something valuable. Your wallet? With several hundred dollars? Sapphire would gladly go for that. After all, it's not a matter of any particular location, really. Where'd you *think* of looking?"

Grove reflected, "I happen to have one idea—a spot beyond the outer reefs but not too far beyond, where charts show twenty to twenty-five fathoms."

"Easy—for porpoises."

"I'll speak to her," Grove finally said. "Maybe. My hunch is mighty thin."

It was easier than he had expected, although it took somewhat longer.

Grove invited the Abbotts to dinner in town. They accepted—and twice postponed the engagement. Once because an unexpected group of VIP scientists had to be entertained, and a second time when Tack had to fly to California for a luncheon and back the same day, for him a common event. However, the three finally dined at Canlis' in Waikiki Beach.

During the meal Sapphire brought up the current, freed-porpoise work. "I have three that I'm letting go at once. And they actually compete with each other to see who can get down and back first." Trainers, Grove knew, and Sapphire, who trained trainers, often call their porpoises "who"—and not without reason.

Grove said he'd enjoy watching the experiment.

She said the day after tomorrow.

They ate steak. Remnants were duly put in a doggy bag for the Abbotts' dogs, cats and kittens. Then Grove asked where the work was conducted.

"Oh, out beyond the reef, around Rabbit Island."

"Could you do it, up my way?"

"Of course." Sapphire realized there was some reason for the inquiry. Grove was glad to explain.

His embarrassment wasn't wholly feigned because the tale he'd prepared was slightly absurd. He'd been trying to learn to sail one of the little craft so popular in the area: Sunfish and Sailfish. He said he went out early when nobody would be around to observe his clumsiness. He'd gotten too sure of himself and ventured well beyond the barrier reef one calm morning but it was not so calm on the other side.

"I flipped," he said with regret. "Well, I always wear a money belt." He *was* wearing one, now. "My business takes me abroad—and in a hurry, sometimes—I keep foreign currency in it, including gold coins—useful, abroad, for a traveler in a rush. Well, as we flipped, the belt caught in something—tiller, I guess. And it broke, so of course it sank like a rock. I got pretty good bearings, righted the boat, and came in."

"That," his pretty guest smiled, "is *exactly* the sort of thing they like to find and fetch up. A money belt!"

"Even though," Tack noted, "the chances of their finding it aren't great. Your bearings will probably be accurate only to—say, ten acres—and the bottom, out there, is very rugged: coral ridges and some deep holes."

"The belt probably weighs three pounds," Grove added, sounding dubious.

"They could bring that up, easily." Sapphire defended her porpoises. It was she, in fact, who'd first released and recovered a porpoise in the open sea. It was she, too, who'd first discovered that porpoises are capable of "original thought"—the only creatures on earth with the ability, except man, of course.

"Worth a try." Tack nodded as they rose.

That was how Grove came to be at sea, beyond the protective reefs, some days later. He and Sapphire with two girl trainers were in an open work boat. A much larger vessel stood by. A third, fast motorboat served the scuba divers who would be checking the porpoises. The iron-barred "return cage" was in position, held by cables let out from the big vessel.

When Grove said, "Right about here," the party had halted and the big ship had anchored. Three porpoises, Lani, Koko and Mahalo, were taken from the ship's well on stretchers, gently released, and given a signal to swim to bottom.

Now and again one then came to Sapphire's boat with a trophy. Some dives were fruitful, some not. She collected a variety of finds—a girl's bra, a waterlogged section of a life belt, two pieces of coraline rock and a plastic bag.

What interested Grove, however, was not the sudden appearances of animals with their trophies, but the bottom and the near surface. The water was very clear. With a glass-bottomed "scope"—an elongated box fitted with handles—he could watch the porpoises swim down and discern in blue-to-brownish shadows the dim contour. Since they were close to the place where he'd observed the glinting or flashing, from his house, he also kept an eye out for its source.

What he did spot was unexpected: a sudden drop-off of the bottom, a wide, blue nothingness which, as far as he could discern, continued out toward the open ocean as a valley. When he first saw the feature it meant nothing; but Sapphire sighted it with her scope too.

She'd been explaining things as they happened. Now her talk was more general. "Tack built the Makai Range here because of the clear water, and the fact that the bottom slopes steadily to more than a hundred fathoms—in three miles. The weather, and the relative calm, are important too. It's a miniature continental shelf, really, though not an actual one; with no dirt or pollution, too! And you can work here year round. No mainland water offers all that."

Grove had kept looking but he understood: "Mainland's east coast is stormy and foggy, a lot of the year; both coasts have dirty water. Winters, you can't work, much of the time. Here, though, with any depth handy—and few poor days—"

"Some years," Sapphire agreed, "not any." Then she said, "Oh-oh!"

"What?"

"See the deep blue trench down there?"

"Yes. Drops off like a cliff and continues on out."

They gazed; the work boat drifted about on its anchor. "Must be where that lava tube broke down," she said.

"Lava tube?" His voice sounded casual. But he then remembered one of the first books he'd read, on coming to Hawaii: a book about local geology.

Sapphire went on. "*You* know, Ring. You've been in one: the Thurston Tube at Volcanos National Park."

"This one must be a lot bigger. . . ."

"A lot." She peered again. "Comes halfway to the surface. It must have collapsed, here, because there's only that blue, deep gulch, from here out. We'll have a look at it someday. Jack Himberson told me the biggest lava tube so far known has a diameter of a hundred feet. This looks easily that size." She forgot the formation as Mahalo reappeared, with a find.

Grove was no longer able to see the supposed lava tube owing to the drift of the boat. But he was thinking hard. A lava tube was formed when hot, molten rock flowed downhill and began cooling, on the outside first, of course. The moving mass formed a crust that hardened and ceased flowing while its molasses-like inner contents kept running down until, not infrequently, they drained their outer crust. What remained was a hollow, rock-walled tunnel, like the Thurston Tube, which tourists could enter. It was some ten to fifteen feet in diameter, as he recalled. He had never heard of one a hundred feet in diameter. But he knew some were many miles in length. This one could therefore extend through, or under, the reef; not above it—or the fact would have been seen, long since, and charted.

Oahu was volcanic in origin, like all Hawaiian islands. The Big Island, Hawaii, was still being extended by volcanic activity. And the islands had been lifted and lowered repeatedly in geological time. There was nothing surprising, then, in this tube—except its size, perhaps.

Assuming, Grove assumed, the tube continues from this open end toward land, under the reefs and under the beach on shore, it would be more than a mile long. Lava tubes meander like river beds. This one might angle off toward Waimanalo Beach or Makapuu Point: a long, huge cavern, in that event, with a thick roof, buried by later lava flows and by the sea to just-found, open terminus.

What came to Grove's mind was a man-made but similar thing: the submarine pens the Germans had built near Bordeaux, on the Bay of Biscay, a hide-out that bombers never did destroy entirely in the Second War. Charges set by the Resistance people (and some OSS men Grove had known) also failed to smash those pens. If his present surmise was correct—Grove suddenly went white. It would be no great feat to build locks! The biggest nuclear subs could vanish into it, by night, with a friendly watch ship on guard. A Soviet "fishing boat"? A swimmer? Water could be pumped from a large section and air pumped in—even, air at normal pressure, given locks!

For *what,* then?

Nuclear subs don't need bases for refuelling. Conventional subs do, though. There could be a recreation center here for crews and even girls, since Soviet morality is less prissy than the official pose. Chinese don't bother posing. That would be mere spin-off, though. You could launch nuclear missiles from here in hundreds. Or assemble the elements for an operation called Neptune. His heart paused and then lunged as he considered that idea. Any such secret base would be closer to USA from the USSR by half the width of the Pacific.

Grove was almost sure, now. The Reds had found the tube with spy ships. They had explored it and decided to use it, years ago. How often had the Navy tagged—and lost—Soviet subs in the area? Submarines that were as often sighted beyond the legal limit—surfaced, their crews swimming, laundry on lines and all hands waving jovially? International law made such acts safe.

Heavy machinery employed to alter the interior of the tube—and necessary blasting, rock-hewing or lock installation could be managed without detection if, and only if, some big construction job in the vicinity served as a mask.

A huge undertaking at the Makai Range had been long set for January and put off till recently. January was the month mentioned when Grove had first learned of Project Neptune—from his tree perch; the date which had set in motion his own acts, ever since.

January was the month in which the CIA's man had been found dead in the Reef Tank at the park. The man had doubtless learned something which might have given away this operation. He'd been caught and held for a while, since he'd been unable to get his information to anyone else in the organization—and he'd been used for an eventual put-on, that Eaper was clever enough to see through, Eaper thought.

The faster his imagination raced the more feasible its pictures—providing the lava tube had some such form and dimension as seemed at least possible. To refit a cavern of the sort envisaged might take a great deal of work. His ideas grew to a deluge.

What would be easier than to replace a vast amount of water with air? The evacuated water, if pumped out at night, would be indistinguishable in the turbulence over the reef. Air could be pumped in at the same time, with precautions. A brief use of a periscope, while daylight was strong, would insure that no vessel was near enough to see, in the approaching twilight, some snorkel-like gear that, when the coast was found clear, would then be elevated as an air intake. The hypothesized periscope at the critical time might glint as it circled and so be seen briefly from the distant shore. . . .

Why, he next asked himself, the fantastic effort to get access to high-tension power for a limited term? That could also be answered, simply: for preliminary work enabling the installment of later types of machines. Electrically driven motors are quiet and they might be used for such purposes as pumping—with equally quiet turbines. But that setup would be safe only till Hawaiian Electric's bills went out. All signs of that use must by then be erased or, minimally, lead nowhere. Once an air lock was ready, work could proceed—any kind—so long as constant heavy construction on shore would conceal it. Its present, night-time continuation would help, too, and also serve notice that the Makai Range work would soon be finished, or at least this noisiest phase. The "January" plan had been postponed because of the Makai Range delays, surely.

Sapphire interrupted that torrent of thought. "Are you okay?"

"Am I—*what*? Oh!" Grove nodded. "Fine."

"You look pale. If you want to go in—"

He realized he was pale, then. "It's nothing," he said. "I always get a touch of seasickness in small boats, but it never lasts long. I'll be dandy in no time—"

She seemed doubtful but decided it was possibly correct. She would keep an eye out, to be sure. With relief, he saw her turn back to management of the crews and the porpoises.

The open boat drifted about on the swells and in the choppy backwash from the reef and its breakers. There was little wind and current; drift was unimportant, as the porpoises knew which vessel was which from their view of the hulls. He soon thought that perhaps he should accept the offer to run in or ask to be sent in. The location of Project Neptune had been found, he believed. What it was, others could determine; his duty would end when his idea was passed along and checked—rather, proven true.

There were surely eyes on the sea bottom, or their electronic counterparts, that had kept track of this porpoise training business. Fortunately it was an event those "eyes" or others like them had certainly watched closely in the past.

Porpoises were bright; but they could not tell about evidence of human installations at the open end of a lava tube—even if such evidence were there. It would more likely begin far inside the tunnel where only a very inquisitive and daring diver would come upon it—to his fatal misfortune. He was about to take up Sapphire's offer when sheer accident provided confirmation he scarcely needed.

Face glued to her scope, she called, "Here comes

Mahalo! He's got something!" In a moment she laughed. "Playing games with me! He saw me and he's moving to your side, for a joke."

"Right. Shall I take whatever he has?"

"Sure. He'd tease me with it, otherwise."

Mahalo's beaked head broke water, wobbling as the porpoise briefly played keep-away with Grove and then surrendered his trophy—a black rubber glove. "Got it!" Grove grinned. "Diver's glove." And he swiftly added, as Sapphire turned for a look, "Can I keep it? Souvenir?"

"Of course." Grove shook the glove and concealed it. Her attention was again on Mahalo and the hydrophone signaling device that sent the big, smart animal down for another grab.

Grove had acted quickly, though with no sign of excitement. The glove bore a stenciled symbol—for its owner, beyond doubt.

At first glance he had thought the marking was in Cyrillic, in the Russian alphabet. It wasn't. As he pretended to be absorbed in Mahalo's next descent he furtively examined the painted strokes. Roman numerals? No. The stencil used had slipped slightly but the result was clear: two Chinese characters, numbers, maybe, on what was certainly a diver's glove. He pocketed it. He was trembling a little.

This small bit of luck confirmed everything and it meant his part of the long hunt was finished.

Rather, all that remained was a phone call to either of the two friends the President had designated for exactly such a purpose. A direct call might, just might, tip off some unknown Eaper agent in spite of Steve's belief his staff was now clean. And the two intermediaries had special wires for any such need, Grove believed.

He felt a moment of letdown. It was followed by anxiety. If Solentor's people knew what he'd now learned they might destroy the tube—and perhaps all Hawaii with it. Or they might even be able to put Neptune in effect! How ready was it? What could it be? He sat sweating, then, hoping the clever porpoises wouldn't bring any other telltale object to Sapphire—and fiercely impatient for the trip to end. Soon, it did.

13

FLUNK

An engine breakdown delayed the return. The predicament was finally noticed, however, and the fast boat towed them in. Sapphire was sorry the money belt had not been recovered. Grove said the trip was worth the loss.

The sun was gone when they docked and he thanked Sapphire for an "extraordinary experience." She asked again if he felt well and, again, he said it was nothing. He waited about for a while, quite sure he wasn't watched but to give the impression that he was in no hurry. He could not be entirely sure his presence at sea had gone unnoted but he had done his best. Even so, there should be nothing in his behavior to make his opponents imagine his perfectly logical trip had been anything else, if they knew of it.

On the other side of the pali the sun shown. But Waimanalo was deep in its long twilight when he drove his rented car up to his garage. He pressed a button and a door creaked open. Meanwhile, he scanned the roofs and trees above his fence. He grunted. The phone wire no longer stretched from the power pole on the highway to his place. He ran in the car and shut the door—after one further glance that told him his premises had been entered.

Jenny had gone home early—her Volks wasn't in the garage or expected to be there. He thought of the tunnel but chose the open yard, after which decision he carried out on his back what seemed merely a large sheet of plywood. He braced it on the bridge evidently for a subsequent lowering to the workshops below. It shielded him while he crossed the lawn and unlocked his doors. But no shots came from the likeliest site for ambush, the steep, thicket-covered slope across the Kalan; his plywood shield would have flattened them, in any case: it had a steel inner layer.

There are more ways than one to skin a cat, he thought;

and grinned at this familiar use of hackneyed and dated phrases.

Jenny had left a note—about the cold chicken and apple pie. But he read it later. First came a series of efforts—and, next, spoken aloud, *"Flunked."*

Grove's regular phone line, cut at the power pole, was his only known way of communication, the only way known to his friends and to Jenny. There were three more means. A phone hidden in a workroom had been connected to the line next door, in the house he now owned. That instrument had been removed. They hadn't wanted to become conspicuous by dropping people's phone lines, he decided. But he was somewhat shocked to find the third line, its instrument even more carefully concealed and its wire running underground for a considerable distance, had been demolished.

How had they found that? The answer was, by looking very carefully, in the adequate time available for doing so. They must have moved when the porpoise work started in its special area. Started fast, to cut him off if a time for that had arrived.

As it had.

He went to the radio between his double wall—with diminished confidence. He switched it on and for a moment he was hopeful. In that moment, they located his band and drowned it with interference. So that was that.

To get the word out—word so important he did not dare think of failure—he would have to leave the premises. It was something that needed thought.

That was when he read Jenny's note.

Afterward, he checked the contents of a modest leather case to be sure everything was in place and in precise order. Then he ate some cold chicken and two slices of pie, with a glass of milk. He believed he could break out—but now it was going to be sticky, a valuable and calming word to use instead of many far more appropriate.

It would be well not to hurry. Waiting would be harder on them than on him, as they would not know what to expect. But they would also be given more time to prepare for eventualities which Solentor would guess as potentially many and bizarre.

Grove had determined, long since, where an ambush would most likely be set. To be safe, however, he had made additional arrangements. Before his garage door opened, now, for the station wagon, there would be a diversion. It ought, he had been pretty sure, to take care of expected but not certain fire from places across and above the road.

He could be out and going, if so.

Getting away afterward would require more surprises. They were ready for more.

He had eaten in peace and afterward he rinsed his dishes. He checked his protective devices and sat in the red chair, smoking a cigar. He then arranged to leave behind various special messages that would, perhaps, do the trick, if he didn't manage. He smoked two more cigars, while he read a stretch in *Tom Sawyer,* an old favorite for crisis time-passing. Then it was eleven o'clock.

He could guess what they were doing and where.

They knew, or near enough to it, that they must take all possible precautions against any attempt he would make to communicate with anybody again, ever. The situation was classical, tactical and yet one he should not have allowed to trap him. Rusty, as now was unarguable. He should have phoned when they docked. Collect, to the man on Kauai or the one on the Big Island. Not the White House. Steve still feared Eaper had a tap or an unidentified eavesdropper there. And Grove remembered Steve was on a trip, if the papers were right. A cruise to nowhere—a hush-hush conference.

He picked up the bag and made for the tunnel to the garage, resolutely.

A switch lighted it but the light could not be seen from the outside. Three boards in its wooden siding were levers and he pulled them. A red light came on as each board went down. He locked the house end of the tunnel—a false wall when viewed from the other side—and he did the same when he closed the opposite panel in the rear of the garage.

He set the leather case in the station wagon and made sure the thick grip was within reach. He started the motor and pressed buttons to raise electrically powered side windows of special glass.

Outdoors, a soft explosion sent an object sailing over the Kalan and into the thicket far above. It landed and burst into an incredibly intense light. That eye-shattering glare raged behind a row of rocks so the drivers below were not directly exposed; otherwise, there would have been accidents. Men in the area above that preselected target, however, looked, by instant reflex—and could not see at all, afterward, for some while.

Long enough so that when the electric door of the garage opened and the station wagon shot out and skidded into the northbound lane between a small sedan and a pickup truck no shots came from the dazzled group on guard exactly where Grove had expected them to be. The flare was a type used for air-sea search and rescue. It had been launched by a homemade mortar, carefully placed, concealed and aimed, long before.

He headed away from the park because the park was his destination, or his first one.

As he accelerated, he saw a car switch on its lights and start in chase. Grove tore through Waimanalo at a steady sixty, hoping for police pursuit. He raced up the first hill beyond the village, speedometer soon at a hundred ten and still climbing. The following car had lost some distance in the village, more on the sharp turn just before the golf course. Grove went over the crest of the next hill at a speed slightly lessened by its last pitch. He had, he thought, about ten seconds.

The station wagon braked as no standard vehicle could: it had almost overtaken some cars ahead. Meantime, Grove activated a special control and the original windows were replaced by steel sheeting. The car was stopped dead and off the road when the other swept past: three men in it.

They ignored Grove's vehicle because it had changed in appearance. It now looked, in the night at least, like a panel truck, waiting for a tow car, probably, lights flashing as a warning. Its rear end and sides bore large letters in red on a white background. They said:

JOE OPALANA
MEN'S TAILOR
1447 ELUA DRIVE
WAIMEA

When the pursuit roared on under the footbridge—as he could see, by its lights—Grove cut the flasher, backed, turned around quickly and took off in the opposite direction.

He regained speed through Waimanalo and his rear-view

mirrors indicated no tail, police or other. As he approached the park, he intended driving in. But that would be expected, possibly; in which case he and Jerry, too, would fail to achieve anything. He surged on.

The watchman, at first, thought it was teenagers: going past at that crazy speed and blasting their horn steadily, the damn fools. Then he saw the vehicle and knew otherwise. He leaped on his bike and shot from the cove as he soon heard and then saw the pursuers roar past. He ran to the institute where he unlocked a door and made a phone call.

Grove charged up the curves over Makapuu Point, grinning a little. There hadn't been any such plan; but maybe Jerry would get the message, anyhow.

On the long straight stretch of the Kalan, past the Hawaii Kai Golf Course the late Henry Kaiser had built, Grove saw them coming. It had to be them: in another car, he saw—one that had a radiophone. A car faster than the station wagon; so he slowed.

The car closed rather cautiously and Grove grinned again. They'd be uncertain of his capabilities, having surely by now taken a look at his dash and its battery of buttons and other controls, of which only five had any use. All the others, twenty-odd, were there to make anyone who'd examined the car hesitate about closing in on it. The man he'd watched making that extensive inspection from a top row at Whaler's Cove had probably been theirs.

Grove was waiting now for the long, open stretch just ahead and praying it would be empty, a prayer that was answered. Traffic at this hour was light; still, it was a break. In his rear-view mirror he saw fast, bluish flashes and heard the bullets from the muffled machine weapon hammer on the rear end, the steel plating. He accelerated into the straightaway and worried about his tires, about how much lead even they could absorb without coming apart.

They chased him and came up. Grove hit a lever, then another.

From an opened vent in the tailgate burst a tremendous volume of smoke. It expanded but seemed not to thin. Grove looked at the speedometer and decided there would be no sense in trying to slow and leap clear. Meanwhile the venting smoke blacked out a hundred yards of the highway behind, then two hundred and three, when it gave out. He pulled ahead and looked back by mirror, and then, after lowering a panel, by leaning out.

The chasing car had inevitably plunged into the smoke: no time to slow, even. Its expert driver cursed and tried to see the white center line. He could, for an instant, a few feet of it. Then he hit a stretch of something else: slippery oil. His tires made rain sounds on his fenders. He braked instinctively and professionally, stabbing the pedal and the accelerator, alternately. The stuff was slicker than butter and the car went into a lunging skid that took it off the road and into a ditch where it flipped. None of the three in the car was badly hurt but all were shaken. They slowly recovered, raised a reluctant door and managed to see the taillights of the station wagon as it raced toward the first zigzags around the Blow Hole.

The radiophone didn't work. They had a walkie-talkie, however: it did work—after they got it out of the jammed trunk. That took awhile. The long cloud of smoke drifted toward the volcanic mountains. Soon a car approached and passed, unseeing—a boy and girl's head on shoulder, in rapt togetherness. Two vehicles passed in the opposite direction. The wrecked car was off the highway and if seen was doubtless assumed to be parked, though it was actually on its side. One of the three urgent men took time to walk toward the place where the oil had sent them skidding.

Whatever it had been, it hadn't been ordinary oil. Every sign of it had already evaporated. To be sure they'd have privacy; the men now abandoned the overtoppled sedan, carried the walkie-talkie into the nearest cover, high grass hummocks and scrubby trees. They cranked a handle and talked.

A police car cruised past, slowed to a stop, then reversed. An officer got out and looked at the abandoned car, making sure it was empty and that no injured persons were nearby. He had used a big torch. He returned to his car, made a call and continued his patrol. The three men came back after that, and waited till the straightaway was empty. Then they lighted a fuse and ran. The sedan blew up and the shambles caught fire.

They were sure that a fire engine, if one came, or a wrecker, in the morning, if that would be it, would not have operators sufficiently expert or even suspicious enough to discover that the junk they would finally tow away had once possessed unusual capabilities. Its license would be missing and all its papers consumed.

That series of activities gave Grove time, more time than he had expected or knew of.

The switchbacks around Koko Head had to be taken slowly. He came up behind four normally moving cars as he reached the last rise of the Kalan. Shortly, the spangled megalopolis came in view: Hawaii Kai, Kahala, Aina Haina, Waikiki and the fire-tinted aurora over Honolulu. He stayed behind the cars as he drove down into the lights. A short way farther on, he slowed. Peering intently seaward, he realized, with relief, that Jerry had seen his passage, understood it and taken the step Grove hadn't dared count on, just hoped for.

There was no road or track where he cut off and thudded toward the sea, merely an open space, not yet developed, a place where heavy machinery had been stranded for months—waiting for fiscal resurrection. He drove behind a truck and stopped. He locked his car as he left and ran: the helicopter was waiting, lights out.

"Bob?" he called.

A man in the shadows of the rotor answered, "All set! Hop in! Here!"

Grove hopped. The copter had a seat beside the pilot and a longer seat, behind. Its bulby chassis was transparent. Grove could see the highway where the double-eyed traffic streamed. No pair of lights turned off in this direction.

He was aware of Bob beside him, of a door slam and of the racket as the outsize insect whirled its thin wings. It jumped into the air on a slant and started rising. Bob stopped a slow twist. "Where to?"

"Kauai." Grove named the Navy field.

The man shrugged and reached forward to switch on lights—exterior lights. Inside, it remained dark.

"No can do," the pilot yelled.

"Why not, for God's sake?"

The man held out a headset. Grove nodded, put it on, took it off, adjusted it and donned it again. The chopper was climbing and heading away from Kauai. Grove knew that course was wrong. Through the furry headphones the pilot said clearly, "Kauai, sure. Navy field, no."

Grove then understood the course: they would have to skirt Oahu before making a turn toward Kauai, more than a hundred miles to the west and a little north around the mountains. The course wasn't wrong, then; instinctively, he still felt misgivings for which he sought cause.

He was handed a mike. "Why not the naval base?"

"Radio's out." The man pointed and Grove saw a hole where some rectangular instrument had been removed from the panel. Exposed wires showed when the panel lights finally went on. Some were red and the pilot switched them off. In the remaining glow Grove studied the gap from which, evidently, the radio had been removed. Not a neat removal, he noted—seemed more like the result of violence.

Boats winked on the sea below. The muffled racket was unbroken. It had sounded, before he'd put on the intercom phones, like a child's stick, run along a picket fence, intensified a quantum degree.

So—what was wrong?

The pursuit and escape had left Grove more shaken than he had expected. Some unfamiliar sensation had smoldered below consciousness for a time. Then it defined itself. He had been scared; scared of dying; reluctant to risk it. This was novel. A middle-aged reaction? Certainly not the old and the often-endured dread that involved capture and what capture meant. This was, simply, the commoner thing, the human thing, that most people felt when they thought of dying.

A quick death had been bearable in the faraway past, even hopeful, if dying were part of the assigned risk. The other kind, well, he could face it—this new aspect of death, too; one which came to him because he had survived, lived long afterward, and happily. Now he was like all other men and his will to go on living was like theirs. He smiled—and the pilot, who'd given him some sharp glances, said through the phones harshly, "What's the joke?"

"Not used to these things. Fun, though."

"Oh." A long pause. "Yeah."

Grove studied the man's silhouette: dark hair, short, chunky, aloof and very tough-looking. Bob Barker was his ace in the hole—set up by Jerry. And described by Jerry as a quiet type and an expert chopper pilot: owner of three machines and employer of two copilots. Barker's business was carting tourists about the islands; rich tourists—copter flights are costly. Grove had paid, monthly and through

Jerry, a rather extravagant sum to be sure that a pilot and a machine would be ready, day and night, to go to and wait at the rendezvous long since chosen, against a time of need. Jerry had said it was all guaranteed; a ring on the phone and Bob's reliable services would be "go."

Up to a point everything had worked. But a man couldn't think of all possibilities—not Grove, any more, at least. He hadn't thought, for instance, to get a detailed description of Bob Barker—and the two other pilots hired by See-the-Islands Sky Tours. It had seemed enough that Jerry had arranged the landing place, the chopper and the ready pilot on a standby basis.

Grove pondered and the craft passed the last peaking height, the last deceased volcano. It took the proper heading. "What has the radio got to do with not landing at the Navy field?"

"Get shot," was the reply, "unless we can identify ourselves, coming in."

Grove thought that over. The pilot spoke after a time.

"You gotta give me another spot, pal."

"All right. Whatever is nearest the base. But where I can rent a car."

"Late, friend. Might have to wait till morning."

"That'll be my problem."

"Check. And over and out, son."

Now what the hell was wrong with that?

Several things made him uneasy. You could bring in a plane at the base, or a helicopter, with no radio, surely? Nothing secret about the field although what happened in the nearby war games, where subs played tag over a sea range, with hydrophones set out on the bottom, and umpires keeping score—that would be very confidential. But you could land, any cripple could, on the strips. They would keep guns on you till you emerged and identified yourself, perhaps.

But that wasn't the main element in Grove's feeling of unease.

"Be an hour," the pilot said, startling Grove slightly. "Chance for the old shuteye."

Grove had it, abruptly: not the accent; that didn't exist; not, anyhow, perceptibly. It was the words, the dated slang. *Pal. Friend. Son. No can do.* And now, *shuteye.* Not *sackout,* even.

He explored. "Lovely night."

"Dream-boat." The pilot gave him a smile. "Up at Kauai, though, nix."

"You be able to manage?"

"No pianola. But, sure thing."

"This top speed?"

"I'm flying, bud—can't chin. It's cruising speed."

He didn't want to talk; but he had already talked enough. *Pianola. Bud. Chin.*

The man looked older than the impression Jerry had given of Bob Barker and his team. Nothing about his boots, jeans, shirt seemed odd. A chopper isn't a costume thing, like a commercial passenger plane, Grove told himself. But those idioms had passed from common speech ten—twenty—thirty years ago. They could be regarded as contemporary only by people who'd learned colloquial American long ago—or from a teacher whose English —American, rather—was dated.

Or learned from records; *discs,* not tapes, he told himself.

Where was the heliport used by the company? Grove knew only that they could and did pick up customers on hotel lawns, on a few suitable roofs, in vacant lots—any open space legal and handy to their clients. The site that they had selected for Grove was a hundred times the necessary size but it was the first spot beyond Sea Life Park distant enough for an end he'd considered as very remote—that of an unexpected escape from hot pursuit. Grove had a thing about exits—the more the readier, and the less conventional the better.

Was it possible that they could have learned of this farout plan? Not through Jerry; but there were ways—ways that, again, Grove hadn't contemplated. A tap on Jerry's home phone might be one; a tail on Jerry might do it—one that led to Bob Barker and to overhearing or worming out this escape hatch. Had they even *used* this chopper service—and had the real Bob talked idly of his remunerative but unused charter, forgetting the pay included silence? Had a hired pilot talked?

Who could say?

Since the man beside him wasn't Bob, as Grove now knew—they had learned. And they'd set up their own means of spoiling the method. A man who, doubtless, looked enough like Bob to be mistaken for him in the dark, and was able to fly a chopper, was their very simple program. One who, assuming a watch or another phone tap, would rush to the empty landing place with its long-stalled machinery and wait to clobber the real Bob when he set down and also, probably, got out to wait for his passenger.

Grove laughed at himself without letting it show. The idea of a standby helicopter with a chosen place to meet had seemed, originally, so improbable that he hadn't even considered it could be discovered. His own phones had not been tapped: that, he had regularly checked out. But there were other phones, other means.

Bungling! Amateurish! Old-aged! Senile! Nitwitted!

Eaper would never have made so many mistakes or left such manifest openings: elephant trails, practically. Grove quit the indulgence of self-condemnation, soon, and considered his situation with intelligence.

He was in a helicopter which he could not fly. The man at the controls was his enemy. No gun or other weapon was in view—which meant nothing. Grove's suitcase had been tossed in the rear, out of reach, he feared; behind some other bulky object, he remembered.

He let out his seat belt and pretended to doze for ten minutes. He roused and stretched and groped with an arm. The bulky object was a chute pack. Far ahead the low stars couldn't be seen—clouds. He let an arm drop over the seat back again. The pilot was gazing fixedly ahead. Grove pulled the chute pack over to his side of the craft and examined it with his wandering hand. There was only one—which meant the pilot was not going to find it where he'd put it—that was his first aim. A small gain, Grove felt.

The chopper began to climb.

The island of Kauai lay beneath a greater island of clouds. Dimly and briefly Grove could see lights along the shore but these blanked out as they climbed. Grove was surprised to find the very crises which climb implied had completely erased his frightened interval and its surprise. The old feeling, the good one, that it was still possible to win and to live, had returned. And he was recovering old patterns.

Keeping the corner of his eye on the pilot, feigning a doze, he remembered a rule taught in OSS training: *Every tight spot is tight for the other side, too; find out how; find out their aim; find its risk to them.* Their aim was obvious:

to destroy the one man who could know the location of Neptune before he could inform others, who could not then be reached and removed. Their how was pretty evident, too.

A helicopter hijacking. What was the risk this bogus man ran? A crash? No. Then he had it: *one parachute* handy and, Grove felt sure, no others—handy, at least. Was he to be thrown out with it—a chute that wouldn't open? That might be difficult unless he was knocked out first. The pilot would hardly jump and sacrifice the aircraft. Or would he? Not his craft.

So perhaps the chute was for the pilot in an artificial emergency. The idea would be to dump him first and then jump by parachute near a place where his associates would find him—unless they knew Grove couldn't fly the thing or unless the false Bob made sure the craft couldn't be flown, before he bailed out. How would it read?

R. K. Grove had driven to the landing spot and left his (peculiar) station wagon there, conking the pilot and taking off alone (for reasons unguessable). He had crashed in the mountains (sea?)—someplace. What, then, about his house, which would be thoroughly searched, afterward, by the others, before the police heard of the stolen chopper or a dead, unconscious, even a missing Bob: he could be disposed of in the sea near the empty acres. Grove's house would burn to the ground before they found the shattered copter, Bob, or Bob's body. Jerry would believe things were going as planned—till much too late.

As he reasoned, the chopper entered the wall of cloud. Would they show on somebody's radar? If so, what would be determined? Some fools out in a private helicopter.

They were high in the overcast now—high enough so Grove could tell the difference in his breathing, eight thousand feet at least. What altitude was necessary to clear the mountains? He had studied the maps of the islands carefully and was sure that no Kauai mountain thrust much higher into this fudge than a mile, if that.

Was the added height to insure a total wreck—or a wreck in the jungle where it would not soon be found? The pilot was watching his instruments with great attention now. On Kauai was the rainiest place on earth—seven hundred annual inches and, some years, a thousand.

The helicopter was being buffeted by unpredictable currents. Hard trades hit cliffs below and were deflected upward here. The rotor sliced faster in the ragged upgusts. Grove waited and watched. The pilot squinted at his instruments, leaning forward, his hands showing tension. Grove chanced it, then.

"Just don't go for the gun," he said. "Or do you call it 'gat'?"

The pilot's head whipped around. Grove had no gun—just something that had pricked him slightly and pulled back; something that had stuck him in the shoulder where he couldn't see it.

"How's Solentor these days?"

The plane slid sideways and the pilot had to right it. He lost color.

Grove's voice was calm, firm. "I need only push this hypo plunger. Cyanide."

"Bob" looked around with horror.

Grove felt relief that he carefully did not show. He leaned across the man swiftly and found a gun in the far side pocket of his jacket. The pilot had been warned that Grove was tricky. But anybody could see he wasn't armed. Who'd expect a hypo?

Grove showed it to him; an open safety pin. A little one, at that.

The pilot cursed softly and continuously, but Grove held his gun and snicked off the safety. "That's the trouble with operators now. Got so many trick gadgets you believe everybody has 'em."

"Where do you want down?" The voice was shaky, mean, bitter.

"Just keep flying," was the answer. "At altitude. You think *I'm* nuts—*buddy?* I can't fly this thing. And you know where your people will be, so you could put it right there and I'd never know the difference."

"So?" Hope and malice in the other's eyes.

"I'm leaving. And don't try to stop me." Grove's free arm reached back and heaved the packed chute onto his lap. He examined it with care and began to put it on, changing gun hands as he did so, but never shifting his aim. He was aware, suddenly, that the chopper was turning. He muttered, "Hold it! *Right here,* where you were to jump, eh? Move!"

The chopper planed ahead in the fog. Its red and green

lights carved small caves of color in the surrounding whiteness. It flew straight. Kauai was small.

The back pack was set: straps under Grove's crotch fixed properly, shoulder harness pulled taut. To get his suitcase, he was obliged to half stand. He opened the case with his right hand, withdrew a knife and a coil of nylon rope, cut off a piece, put back the knife and tied the case to the chute—where it wouldn't bang the chutist. He could not fly choppers but parachutes were very familiar.

"How'd you figure me?"

Trying, Grove smiled again, *to stall.*

"You figure how I figured. It'll be a boffo, when you do." His free hand worked on the door latch. "A real hoot. Good night."

Grove dove out.

He spun slowly in the thick mist, tossing the gun to one side—no need of it now. His mind called numbers. At ten, he almost pulled the ring and thought better of it. He soon saw, briefly, a big radiance in the murk. Landing lights—or a searchlight, for all he knew. His counting continued. Seventeen, eighteen, nineteen, twenty.

His arms and feet had spread in the sky-diver fashion—which was known and practiced long ago, but not, then, as a sport. Acceleration of sixteen feet per second, slowed by the layout. At twenty seconds he yanked the ripcord.

A muffled snap, above. A tremendous yank. Then he hung in the sky, his leather case above his head, banging the shrouds. He untied it and refastened it to the canvas straps which held his body. So thick and so dark you couldn't see the canopy, just hear.

Then the chopper clattered near and again he saw a balloon of light, high above, circling.

The pilot was hunting and would hunt, all the way down to a level where there were—mountains, Grove hoped.

Twice the light-blob again came in view. Both times, Grove spilled air to hasten his descent, aware that he had no idea of the place he would land. It might be a crag that would break legs, or a cliff that would hit him and let him slide down, chute collapsing, for thousands of feet: wild country and rough, most of Kauai.

He was falling through cotton nothing; and soon, he decided, below the mountaintop level, because the pilot had given up his plan to rip apart the chute with the machine. Grove couldn't say whether the circling rotor would take that sort of beating.

Suddenly the mist thinned, then dissipated completely. Below was the sea.

He stared, appalled.

14

TRAP

He'd hit the water with the force of a foot-first dive from eleven feet, about. It was a chute of a type Grove hadn't seen, bigger, with gores.

The sea probably meant he was licked.

He looked left and saw only the ocean; right—and he gasped with relief: near mountains, breaking surf. He spilled air to get closer. There was just time to open the case for the knife. He splashed, went under, came up.

He cut the straps and the chute fell away in rippling billows. His case was freed next. It barely floated. But it was watertight: had to be—one never could foresee where it might be exposed to rain, or immersed. He swam the case toward shore, noting that the waves foamed nearer him and that a shimmer beyond had to be beach! Rocks, there, though.

As he moved in, he scanned the area. Not a light. Great, sharp-edged mountains towered into the murk and the beach ahead was enclosed by them.

Where the sea foamed he tried for footing.

Moments later he reached dry, sloping sand.

And he said, aloud, "Wow."

He opened his case again and took out a waterproof flashlight and the nylon rope—which he hung around his neck. He returned to the sea and swam out, to get the chute; he found it, held up by bellies of air, after a tiring search. He tied his line on it. He was winded when he got it back to land, but glad he was able to haul the chute ashore. Otherwise the wind and tide might have stranded it along the coast and in a place where he could not have recovered it but where it would perhaps serve as a marker. Now he took time to bury the canopy in sand. He thought he understood his location. He sat shivering on his sand pile at last, panting and looking about—and confirmed his belief.

Most of the major islands of Hawaii have coastal roads, owing to the fact that the majority of the population lives fairly near the surrounding sea; much of Hawaii's interior is mountainous. Molokai lacks such a road system, but Kauai, where he had parachuted, has as good a coast highway as engineering costs permit. However, there is a stretch of about twenty-five miles where no one lives any more, and where road building would be all but impossible. It is called the Na Pali Coast. The circum-island road turns inland at that point and avoids the impossible margin by many miles.

The reason is evident to any student of a map of Kauai. On the Na Pali Coast, precipitous mountains extend, one after another, into the ocean. They are joined on the land side by almost vertical valleys and their seaward edges drop into the Pacific. This formation is comparable to a row of axheads set together side by side, the blade of each immersed in the ocean and the inland juncture as steep as the angle of adjacent axheads would be. But the mountain "axheads" are thousands of feet high.

The sea in this region is usually rough and treacherous. So it is rarely visited by boat. And the dizzy valley-heads are even less practical means of access: descent requires the skill of an alpinist; and even such climbers hesitate since the near-vertical walls consist of loose rock. The sea-level vales are narrow, slope toward the water and are the product of eons of rockfall from the heights. Each is therefore a slanting isosceles triangle with a beach as its base and a crag heap in its apex.

The Na Pali Coast was, however, settled by Polynesians in ancient times and occupied by them into this century. Their outrigger canoes were fairly well suited to landing—in the rare but occasionally navigable bays. The coast is now called the "Valley of the Lost Tribes" for a strange reason. Scores of years after the Sandwich Islands swarmed with outsiders from America, Europe and the Orient, native Hawaiians lived here in their original manner, undiscovered and unknown to anyone except each other. That fact is evidence of the almost unique inaccessibility of the region.

Today the formidable shore is easily reached by helicopter only; and helicopter flights over Kauai, weather permitting, afford one of the most spectacular and unusual trips in the world. Choppers can land in some of the Na Pali valleys and people fortunate enough to be set down in them find abundant signs of the centuries of occupation by Polynesians. They abandoned their secret habitat, finally, at a time within the memory of living persons who say that life in those clefts was very hard—statements that will be readily understood by those few who have seen their former abode.

It was evident to Grove that the substitute pilot had intended to kill him, first, or throw him out alive, but not offshore where Grove had parachuted. He was to be jettisoned on the summit of the razor-sharp mountains where his body would never be found. If it had been sent hurtling into the sea, bullet in its brain, it might eventually have washed ashore; but dropped a mile or even a half mile inland, it would lie somewhere on the heights, jungle-covered, so the chances of his bones being found would be a million to one over the time span that bones would remain discoverable at all.

As it was, he would be trapped for an unguessable period, though he was sure the pilot had reported some version of what had happened—a true one not being likely, considering Solentor's way of dealing with people who failed to carry out their assignments. Most probably the false Bob would report that Grove was indeed tricky and that, in some imaginary scuffle, both the chute and his gun had gone overboard before he flung the finally subdued American through the door to his planned death; a yaw of the chopper at the critical moment would credibly account for the minor losses. The pilot would be fairly confident that Grove would never reappear.

However, though trapped, Grove was not without resources. He had food, weapons and means to light fire as well as to make various signals, among many other items; his case did not provide mountain-scaling gear at this time. But how to get out of and away from the Na Pali Coast would be a problem for daylight, in any event.

After a careful survey of the sea and the overcast he decided a fire could be risked. He gathered driftwood and dug a place in the sand for the blaze he then started. The sand he piled around the hole would serve for smothering the fire quickly and he felt that he would hear any searching chopper or sight any reconnoitering vessel in time to douse the fire before one could descend through the overcast or the other could get near enough by water to prohibit the risk. Strangers at sea would attribute the fire to campers who had been carried in by chopper for an eerie night's adventure; a few hardy souls did that. At worst, only a small boat would venture close, owing to the reefs and rocks—and he could defend himself from excellent cover in that case.

It seemed far more probable that by now Solentor believed his most dangerous opponent was dead.

Grove warmed himself at the small fire and ate some of his compressed rations. He drank from the bottle in his case although he believed each of these secretive gorges had a supply of water from the mountains; they intercepted the trade-carried clouds here to make the center of the island that rainiest-place-on-earth. He built a barricade of driftwood and stones which would help to hide him from the sea and he curled up on ember-warmed sand to rest, not daring to sleep.

The sun rose. His eyes took in the towering mountains on two sides and squinted into the sun high over an empty sea. Memory of the past night returned and he sat up, yawning, dazed and hungry again.

The overcast had lifted but not dissipated. It made a ceiling into which the mountains vanished. He found water at the upper end of the notch—a pool in a brook that ran to sea and was fed by a series of waterfalls of which only the lowest could be seen. Others, higher up, were lost in the clouds that supplied them.

Nothing was visible at sea. There was no sign of anybody aloft—always assuming anybody was looking for him, which was very doubtful.

At twelve-thirty by his wrist watch his usual early muddle began to clear and he said aloud, *"Nunc consideremus quid agendum sit."*

The Latin was not classic—not, perhaps, even correct—a sentence made up by a friend, in high school days, which had kept recurring to Grove under appropriate conditions. This was certainly one of them:

Now let's consider what should be done.

Grove tried to do so.

The sun, aided by the wind, began tearing the clouds apart—dissolving them from the bottom upward. In two hours the pali was wholly revealed and Grove stared up at the majesty that held him prisoner. On two sides, the knife-edge mountains soared to the sky and where they merged he saw the first of the series of waterfalls. As he stared, a few pebbles started and came down, gathering speed. Their rattle crescendoed until they struck bottom—reminders of the hopelessness of a climb.

He wondered if the Lost Tribes had been afraid here, even killed occasionally by rockfall. It would be a good idea to keep away from the base of these near cliffs. Thinking that, he made a slow tour of the once-inhabited triangle, which had an area, he guessed, of a hundred acres. There were signs of people, recent and ancient.

On the sand verge was a ring of stones, blackened by fires of visitors who didn't know how to make a fireplace and had probably burned hot dogs or hamburgers at this bad job. Beyond, in the tough grass and stunted trees, were stone walls that had once retained patches of earth for the cultivation of taro. Looking up from a new angle, he also saw what remained of more human handiwork: a broken platform with a few neatly placed stones still visible. Grove recalled the history of these people and shivered: a torture temple, he guessed—a temple for inflicting agony, for sacrifices of men or maidens to barbaric gods.

He could picture a Hawaiian noble on the pinnacle, a huge man in a feather cloak, wearing a helmet shaped like an old Roman's and carrying a magnificent staff. They had climbed these heights, even for fun, taking up fire spears to hurl down at night in blazing arcs for public entertainment. Grove traced the course and thought he could throw such a missile hard enough for a flaming descent of two thousand feet, clearing the steep edge so the sea would snuff it out.

He knew such imagining was a waste of time. He was not—had never been—capable of avoiding it. Born, he thought, with a wandering mind—or was it a mind that wandered more now, owing to age? He couldn't say. Then he could: daydreaming has uses.

If the people who had lived here so long ago could climb these sheer escarpments carrying spears and for fun, couldn't he? Did they make safe routes to follow? Probably, because they visited each other across the barricades—one group signaling it had a good catch of fish and the group beyond coming across to join the feast—bringing plantains, fruit or some other contribution over the high escarpments . . . men and women and children.

Grove knew it but decided a try at climbing would be a last resort.

Swim away?

If a spell of kona weather hushed the shattering seas, perhaps—by swimming out far enough to see where, in the miles of similar valleys he had descended. He could find a plank to float his case and swim from point to point until past the last barrier's edge. But that would require ideal weather and a long swim.

Meanwhile?

He thought of how Polynesians talked from valley to valley: sending smoke signals. Easy; but who'd respond? Solentor?

He was preparing a late lunch when he heard the helicopter. It was much nearer than he'd thought possible. The mountain swallowed sound, apparently. There was just enough time to bury his fire, grab his case and duck before the chopper rounded the nearest sea-laved precipice. He had chosen this position as the first act of his morning survey. It was behind a dense sea grape tree where the green, flat leaves kept moving stiffly in the wind—leaves the size of dessert plates. Through them he could watch, as he could part them without giving himself away, and there were boulders behind the tree trunk as a rude fortification.

The tree was low, about ten feet in diameter, and weeds grew under its twisted boughs, a sea grape that stood above the spot where choppers could and had put down, grassy and flat. When the snackering insect appeared, he was ready.

They would circle first but see nothing; then land—and come out fast. He would throw one grenade.

Suppose the people were tourists—or seemed to be? Women—or men dressed as women. The craft came in and circled as expected. It was identical to the one from which he had parachuted. At least, it bore Bob Barker's Island Sky Tour emblem.

He would not throw a grenade till the passengers had stepped down and, possibly, could disperse, before he was sure about them.

That might be fatal; the alternative might be murder, however.

Grove waited, horrified.

15

DILEMMA

Shortly after 2 A.M. and after Grove had dived into the overcast, an outside phone bell rang in Sea Life Park. It rang several times before Jerry could reach the nearest extension; he had been hiding out ever since he'd acted when Grove's station wagon roared by, its horn braying.

"Sea Life Park. Watchman speaking." He reached up and unscrewed the light bulb.

"Jerry, you bastard!" The voice was enraged or pained and also hoarse.

"Who's talking?"

"Bob Barker, you son!"

Jerry's big body hardened. "Okay. What happened?"

"He clobbered me."

"Who?"

"This guy who paid for the standby! Grove! The show you set up. I liked the dough but I don't like a bust in the head, not to mention having my chopper swiped."

"*Wait* a minute! He drove up in a station wagon—"

"The hell he did. He was *there.* I took less than fifteen minutes—dressing, warming up my chopper and flying it over to the spot. Just where you told me. I cut the lights and set her down. There's a car close, but no station wagon. You mean—?"

"Yeah. I *mean.*" Jerry's voice was flat. "It wasn't your guy. Go on."

"Try and stop me! Must have been two guys wanting the ride, then, and the other one—"

"There wasn't any other."

"So who conked me?"

"Go on."

"I'm trying! So I'm out cold! And when I came around —nothing. Chopper's gone. No sign of your pal. *Any* pal. I took a while, God knows how much of a while—"

"Where are you now?"

"Damn it! What does that matter? Okay. Across the road and up a few blocks—where there's a booth—and lucky to have the change. So I phone you and ask why your guy steals my chopper after he conks me."

"You okay?"

"*Who's* okay, with a fractured skull?"

Jerry thought for a moment.

The other man began to say, irritatedly, "Hello? You still there? *Hello?*"

"Go back to the field and wait. See a station wagon around?"

"No. I didn't look—scrammed. And next time I would get my brains totally knocked out. So no going back for me!"

"Okay. Stay around where you are. I'll be with you when I can get loose. Because my man got shanghaied—to where, God knows. But the chopper might—barely might—come back. Wait, Bob, for God's sake!"

"Oke." It was forlorn and grudging.

Jerry hung up. "Goddamn fool!" That was for himself. He turned on his flash and dialed. His number rang until a sleep-thick, female voice said a curt "Yes?"

"Mrs. Abbott?"

She was good at voices, and she woke fast. "Jerry? Something wrong at the park?"

"Tack there?"

"Wait!" In seconds, Tack Abbott came on. "Yes, Jerry?"

"I gotta leave the park. Can you send somebody?"

A moment. "Sure. What's the matter?"

Jerry had decided to say as much as he could. "Mr. Grove! Your friend?"

"Yes. He there? Hurt, or something?"

"Look, Tack." He fleetingly realized he'd never called the founder anything but Mr. Abbott. But he could almost feel Tack tensing with that familiarity. "You ever know all about Mr. Grove? I mean, that he works for some outfit in the government?"

Tack's interruption was calm. "He used to, Jerry—OSS. Long ago—"

"I'm telling you! He still does! Lately I've been helping him, in the park, nights. Got the porpoises trained to spot intruders. And there've been several. That mob on the pali—it was arranged to cover something and we know what. Stealing juice—"

"Stealing *what?*"

Jerry forced calmness and explained. After a bit Tack said quietly, "I see. And now?" He was told more things about Grove. Enough to bring sharp exclamations. Jerry added in an urgent tone, "Ring tore by, tonight, blasting his horn and being chased. I phoned Bob. He just rang me. Grove wasn't the first out where the development's stalled, below Aina Haina."

Tack was getting the picture. "He was trying to catch a chopper? There? To get away from *spies?*"

"Yes. The chopper and Grove are gone. Bob was conked and just came to. I'm taking off—with your permission—to be there, in case the chopper comes back."

Tack was more than awake. "I'll be over at the park myself, right away!"

"Not that!" Jerry moaned the words. "This phone could be tapped! Get out of your house with the family, fast! To some safe place and another phone. Then try to get a call through, somehow, to the President, if that's possible. If it's not—"

"What!"

Jerry realized he had to be clearer. "Look," he said. "Grove's been here on a job for the President of the United States. Remember that Reef Tank body?"

"I certainly—"

"Part of what's behind things. Grove's been trying to get answers. *Something*—very *big*—is happening here. Soviet. Chinese. Or both. What, God knows! *Ring* didn't know either. Only, it might blackmail USA."

"Right!" Crisp, now, attentive: military. Tack had been an Air Force captain—that was how he'd first seen Hawaii.

"Ring must have found out the answer today. I mean yesterday," Jerry said. "He was out with Sapphire and the porpoises—so it could be out there he learned." Jerry's voice caught, became a brief whisper. "They're coming in! Beat it with the family, Tack! Fast! Then call—"

The urgent words were broken off. Tack could imagine a phone left dangling in darkness. He could not know why Jerry had done that but only guess.

Jerry had heard the special talk of the porpoises, the big hello. That saved his life. As he left the darkened phone stall he saw the high splash that signaled the presence of strangers. The watchman started a long crawl toward the parking yard but not by a direct route.

Tack had hung up first, aware that any more talk from him might be bad news for Jerry. He looked at Sapphire. She stood steadily, waiting to hear or be told.

"Where'd you take the porpoises yesterday, and Ring?"

She said, "You know. Where Ring lost that money belt. He told us, at dinner at Canlis'. We didn't find it."

"What's there?"

"I don't—it's beyond the big reef— Oh! The lava tube?"

Tack nodded. "Go on."

She did. He thought briefly. "Wake the children. We're leaving. Don't dress them. No time."

She studied his face a moment and left the room. Their biggest car was on the way to Kailua before Jerry got to his own sedan, which was after he'd seen three men make sure he wasn't hidden in it or near it. They had gone away, angry and in a hurry. Because he'd unscrewed the light bulb they missed the dangling telephone receiver. When they moved behind the institute's main laboratory building Jerry went to his car like a hawk's shadow. They ought to have put it out of action but he watched and they had not; which meant that the other side wasn't working at its calmest and most efficient levels.

The car was parked facing out and on a slight slope that led to the one unchained exit or entrance, a standard position. He shoved it and jumped in, steered as he did that, and coasted down the road till he swung into the Kalan. From there it was a short run on a curving pitch past the Makai Range property where the road lifted. There he braked to a stop on the shoulder. Minutes passed before he heard a car moving and he started his motor as it drowned that noise. He drove a short distance beyond the first hill ahead, turned around, and came back at a fast but not spectacular speed.

Nobody shot. Probably nobody paid any attention. Cars passed there in both directions, once in a while. They had a walkie-talkie, however, and when they found his car was gone they'd relay the fact.

As soon as he got beyond their line of sight on the promontory called Makapuu, he speeded up. He had no idea what Grove had learned or even that he had learned anything. Tack and Sapphire would have even less of a notion and probably wouldn't do any calling till morning. Jerry felt he had sounded and been hysterical and Tack would know that. Well, he was still hysterical, he told himself grimly as he roared toward the place where he hoped Bob was waiting.

Jerry was wrong about Attack Abbott, and about himself too.

Tack left his home with his wakened three youngsters and his wife just because Jerry had been, not hysterical, but so incredibly *shook*: because of that, on account of the phone presumed abandoned, because of the blue, deep water where Sapphire had said the big lava tube was apparently opened by collapse and for related reasons. If whatever—rather, whoever—made Jerry leave the phone had overheard the call, maybe the Abbotts had minimal time to get clear. If the horror now blackly growing in Tack's mind and Sapphire's had substance, the situation was desperate.

Between them, Tack and Sapphire reached the concept of Makai Range heavy construction as a mask for enemy labors—the vast lava tube as a site, and other extrapolations at least possible. Tack used the rear-view mirror often; and when they turned onto Pali Drive toward Kailua he said. "I'm going to take a few fancy ploys in town. You check, to be sure."

He made the quick cornerings. She was sure, in time.

They pulled up at the Hedges home presently. It was dark. The door was locked and Tack pounded. Three young Abbotts in blankets moved up and Tack made a violent and almost mirthful sound that wasn't a word when he saw that his oldest son was carrying his .22 rifle: guarding their rear. The boy caught onto things fast, Tack thought.

Lights came on. Mrs. Hedges—Frances—opened the door.

"Duck the lights and don't let anybody turn on more."

"What in the—"

"Get Roy!"

"Right here," Roy called from the stairs and he added, as the lights went out, "Hey! What the hell—"

Tack wasn't very lucid in response. He gave orders as Roy came down the dark stairs. "Get the kids in bed again! Fran and Sapphire, you do that! Roy, if you have any weapons, break 'em out. If a car stops near this place, let me know, and keep it covered till you do—*can* you?"

Roy said, "Yeah."

"Okay. No lights! I'm going to phone from Roy's study. Let's all get moving."

Tack fumbled across the office and found Roy's phone. He dialed for the operator in a darkness that distant street lights only vaguely penetrated. He had already made up his mind on what to do.

The operator's voice came. "May I help you?"

"Yes. This is Tack Abbott. Speaking from Roy Hedges'."

His hope was realized. "Oh! Yes, Mr. Abbott. I *love* the park! And I was *terribly* disappointed when you didn't run for the state Senate again."

Fair enough. He asked her name and got it, sweetly. Marjorie Mahani. His speech impediment at first bothered him and soon vanished. "Marjorie, this is an emergency. I want you to ring the White House. Personal call to the President."

Her gasp was short. But her later words were only a little tremulous. "Right away!"

He'd be—Tack thought—having breakfast in bed; with his array of morning newspapers, relaxing before he dressed fast and went to the Oval Room, or wherever, to take the world back upon his shoulders.

The switchboard would be first; then the Secret Service, Tack guessed, and a male secretary, cutting over. He had met the President a few times as a state senator but Tack wouldn't indicate, as the president had, to Grove, that he *knew* the man.

"Tack Abbott here. Calling from Hawaii. I want to speak to the President—" He talked his way to a secretary. A male.

"Not now, Mr. Abbott. He's not officially awake yet."

"Look." Tack had dredged for it on the way over. "Can *you* see him?"

"If there's a crisis. Like a condition red, sure."

"Okay. There is. Tell him a friend of his named Tree, or Bush—is missing."

"Hey! What the hell— I never heard—"

"First initial, R. And if there's a line not monitored, to use that one."

The secretary muttered a protest and then said, "Very cryptic! I just say, 'Chief, a Tack Abbott is on the line from Hawaii with news about your old friend R. Shrub?' Well, I *will.* And you'll see the President *isn't* up, officially."

"I'll take that chance."

In another minute it came. "Yes, Tack?"

The man in the dark told the man at breakfast in bed something of what he knew of the local situation, guardedly.

Gradually, until the man with the green-topaz eyes, long stride and the calm, deep voice broke in. "Okay! I begin to get you. *Look!* We can talk freely on this line. I made sure, lately. You mean, if I'm right, that Ring Grove learned—something so important out there, he had to run before he could send the word out?"

"I think so."

"I do too." There was a pause. "Glad you got *me* first." The voice from the White House became quieter. "Next thing."

"Yes, sir?"

"Grove *is*—my man."

"I was told so. Jerry Gong, my park watchman, gave me this, half an hour ago."

"Nobody else knows that, except Ring, your Gong fellow, our man here—and now *you.* Don't let it spread."

Tack gulped. "Yes, sir."

"I'm going to start some action when we cut off. But Grove's cover must be kept—missing—and dead *or* alive. That clear?"

"Yes, sir."

"Now." The voice was worried. "Your situation is safe? Wife? Kids?"

Tack explained.

"Right. People will be around soon to take care of you. Stay put!"

"I'd planned to—see if I could help Gong—"

"Stay with the two families! That's an order. You sure Ring got his information out with your wife, yesterday afternoon?"

"No. But it *seems* that way." Tack added details.

"The CIA thinks the uproar on Oahu was a diversion. Ring did not. It's called Project Neptune and what it is God knoweth, only—unless Ring does. But it *fits:* lava tube, and so on. Big thing? Tunnel? Under the sea, you said?"

Tack repeated Sapphire's information and told about his own heavy building and its round-the-clock schedules. He heard the President's low whistle. "God! Keep that to yourselves. Tell Sapphire to hold it. If she's talked to anybody else—"

"Right, sir. It will stop there."

"Now. Stand clear of any action. Keep silence on Grove, on the big tube. That'll have to be a special operation. Those are also orders—Abbott. I'll call you later."

Tack hung up dazedly. In the dark, he leaned on his elbows, chin cupped, shaking slightly. Suppose he'd not called the White House? But he sure got the right man!

He heard Sapphire come in, whirled in the dark. He put down a gun when he made out her form.

"All right?" She asked it expectantly.

"A-okay." He smiled.

He told her, after they had kissed.

Jerry had waited. The helicopter came back at last—stick-on-picket din, lights cutting out when it was near. Below radar reach, Jerry thought. Bob and he were behind a dozer near the former landing place. The chopper descended like a giant praying mantis, bouncing after it thudded. The big rotor decelerated as the motor died. The hidden men closed. There was only one occupant; his silhouette was plain. He took his time, looking around on every side, in a way that seemed oversuspicious. Then sitting—not even releasing his safety belt.

Scared, Jerry thought; and not because of Grove. He gave Bob the agreed three nudges. The door opened finally and the pilot came down, looking over his shoulder fearfully.

Whatever or whoever worried him plainly wasn't around. He did not, however, expect ambush, which meant he was afraid of his own people. And perhaps meant also that his mission had failed: that Grove had gotten away.

Bob, who was the nearer, as the man began to walk, hit out—revenge in the blow.

"Jesus! You could of killed him!" Jerry felt for a pulse.

"Did I?" Bob sounded hopeful.

"No. Get him in your car."

"And call the cops, yes?"

"Call the cops, no!"

"No?"

"We're gonna talk to this bastard before we call *anybody*."

"Hey!"

"Take his legs."

Jerry's car was brown, a sedan, old and rusted, but there was no sound of age or decay in its engine.

Jerry made his call from the booth Bob had used. There was a smudge of blood on the dial—Bob's. Jerry grinned at that. In his case, no such smudge would have remained. He'd have wiped the place, automatically. Then he thought, Would I? And replied, Yes. Under this much—and this kind—of pressure, he'd have wiped his prints and the blood smear.

He made the unanswered call, smiling. Tack and the family had left. Thank God! The brown sedan departed. Five minutes later it would have been spotted.

Four men, one huge and toad-shaped, passed the bright rectangular phone station and moved on, in the occasional traffic, to the turnoff. With headlights cut, they went slowly across the flats. Their eyes became used to the darkness and the driver said, not in English, "It's come back, sir."

When they found that the man who'd claimed to be Bob was missing they began to curse.

The rhino-shaped man stopped that. "Varnik," he said, "is listed now. The finder will get the usual reward: rubles, dollars, pounds, gold. I want to see his body. Clearly, he failed, because why else would he run from here? Check the plane."

They checked. "Chute missing. His pistol."

Solentor nodded. "Quite so; almost expected. Grove jumped and left Varnik in the aircraft."

Somebody muttered, "How?"

There was dangerous anger in the response. "How? you ask. Pig! Idiot! Moron! *How?*"

A thin oriental in the party tried to assist his companion: "Varnik was armed. He has a good record. Speaks English in the American way. We had warned him the man was clever—"

Solentor's rage abated; it became thought. "That might be part of an answer. Varnik's wonderful Americanese. It was, the little I heard, a trifle obsolete. The slang."

"He learned it long ago, from old Ching."

Solentor apparently nodded: his neckless head moved, at least. "So. And for the past twenty or thirty years Ching has *not* been in the United States. Exactly. Which could have been Mr. Grove's first warning. Unless he had seen Barker which isn't probable; he would not, then, have gone into the craft. My fault. Two faults."

Voices tried to assauge that self-blame, obsequious voice. "Stop kissing my ———!" The Russian equivalent is lewd. "Mistake one: to rip out the radio. It should have been deactivated, only. Perhaps noted. Then, when G. got out by chute, Varnik could have informed us—and would have, if the pig-camel had not panicked. Mistake two: Varnik and his wonderful, antediluvian Americanese! So."

"We sabotage the craft? Fire?"

"Fool! Why? Leave it! You want to signal for more attention?"

"Sir."

"Now." Solentor moved his jelliness toward the car that had brought him. "I will think. I need some time. We shall therefore return. As usual—indirectly—to the hotel."

An hour afterward Ben Pakali, the night doorman of the Oriental Jade Hotel, went briskly to a limousine which had pulled up under the marquee: a Rolls, driven by a uniformed black. The doorman, who had learned much in his time, said to the emerging personage, "Salaam, sahib, salaam."

The prince was about fifty and big as two heavyweights but fatter. He wore a violent blue turban with a crimson stone in front. If it was a ruby, it must be the world's biggest, the doorman thought. From the gem three peacock feathers sprouted elegantly. The man's robe was a light blue and his shoes, soft leather, were also blue. The tints made his face look like a cadaver's. He stood on the pavement, finally, breathing heavily, and spoke to the chauffeur in English: the toplofty kind that the doorman usually heard from guests of the Oriental Jade.

"Thank you, Amherst. Won't need you any more tonight."

"Yes, Majesty."

That annoyed the doorman. The chauffeur was, after all, a citizen. And the way he said that "Majesty" was un-American, the night man felt. Too much kowtow. *He* wasn't so damn meek—colored, too—Hawaiian-color. But why the hell should color make a man crawl?

The prince was fumbling in the folds of his robe.

With that, the doorman put on his special look, a servile countenance. The purse was coming out, this time. Prince Ben Pak-Something-or-Other tipped only now and then, but when he did—he did. A hotel guest for the last couple of years, off and on, he got a big play from the management. He had the penthouse—and his staff was large, and largely male. Ben smiled and waited.

The cloth-of-gold purse was located, produced, and unsnapped. The doorman swung the big portal open. As the prince went toward it he held out a languid hand.

"Thank you, Your Majesty," the Hawaiian said with a flourish and a salute.

He bit his tongue as he felt the tip, a coin. Half a buck? Old Fatso went in, trailing across the deep carpet in the lobby toward the elevators like a sailboat tacking.

The doorman looked at the coin. It was gold, solid gold, a double eagle—a term he learned only the next day.

And he was not entirely mollified, even so.

We lease their goddamn desert, he mused as he stood outside in the brilliant night beneath the marquee. We drill the wells, install the pipelines and the pumps. Then we pay 'em billions for the oil.

Lousy Arabs!

It did not occur to him, or to the management and the regulars at the Oriental Jade Hotel, that their frequent guest from Oman-El-Brazaan was not an Arab, not Moslem, not a man with any religion. Nobody ever searched a map for the kingdom called Oman-El-Brazaan; if they had done so, they'd doubtless have found an "Oman"—and thought themselves privileged to know its full name.

The prince had carried letters from the British Foreign Office on his first visit. He had deposited a fortune in the Bank of Hawaii upon that arrival. He paid for his suite even in his many and sometimes protracted absences. Finally, he talked—in Arabic—to the Arabians in his entourage. The house detectives had checked that out. The British papers were said by the Honolulu consul to be in order, furthermore. Only the signatures, in fact, were forgeries.

16

RUN!

The chopper came deep into Grove's hidden valley and hung on its rotor. From the sea grape canopy Grove could make out a pilot, but not clearly. The craft executed a slow circle; binoculars momentarily glittered. It moved up the cleft as far as the narrowing cliffs allowed and came back rather swiftly—to Grove's relief. The pilot was plainly satisfied the search of this canyon was futile because he went whacking out to sea, around the dividing mountain and into the next slot.

If it had landed, Grove thought, he could have taken care of the pilot: there wasn't anybody else aboard, so far as he could make out. He was on the verge of leaving cover when the sound changed.

The machine returned and hovered. Grove saw why: his banked fire was smoking. As the chopper settled, the pilot could be seen clearly—and Grove ran out.

Jerry was smiling—tightly. "Get aboard! Hook up the gear. Great idea, the smoke signal."

"Signal!" Grove snorted, climbing in.

"Where to, boss?" The chopper rose. They put on the intercom mikes and headphones.

Soon the machine clattered through large clouds and emerged with the largest part of the island coming into repeated view.

Grove mentioned the Navy field on the island. "There's a man who can send some information I have, to the right person. The President. I didn't tell you that—couldn't. What in *hell* have you done?"

The big Chinese-Hawaiian shrugged. "I didn't do much, Ring." He described his actions beginning with the time Grove had driven past the park. He explained how he'd heard from the real Bob and left the park to wait, the return of the machine, the capture and his later chopper-search.

He was interrupted shortly. "Do you think Tack sent the word?"

"Can't say. Didn't have much dope at the time. I only knew you were on the run, then. Told him you'd been working for the President and to call him. And to scram. Which he did. Tried early this afternoon to get Tack but nobody knows where he or his family can be reached. So he did get away. Being Tack, though, I suppose he'd be trying to find out more about the situation before bothering the President."

Grove looked distressed. "That could mean sudden death. If he—no. He wouldn't connect Sapphire's and my junket with what I found."

"Hardly. Who could without our facts?"

Grove turned slowly and stared at the watchman. "You just said you got added dope, later. What? And how?"

"Need some minutes to explain, exactly."

"So, find us a cloud and take the time." Grove started and then said angrily, "You and Bob snatched the fake pilot? And exactly how much pressure—"

The watchman-now-pilot found a cloud and turned in surprise. "Would you have minded how much—in your OSS days?"

Grove faintly smiled. "Old, soft. Shoot."

"We didn't have to use hot cigarettes on that Ivan boy. Soon as we got him to Bob's and the gag came out he began begging us to hide him. It wasn't us, but the fear we might turn him loose that had his guts churning. So—we just threatened to do exactly that. The guy was ready to spill all, in exchange for protection from Solentor. Must be a lovely character!" Grove's eyes turned a hue new to his friend, pale and vacant. Jerry went on.

"He knew a lot more about Neptune than people at his level are supposed to know. A thing that happens in every outfit I've belonged to."

Grove nodded agreement. "Like what?"

"There's some sort of underwater cave the Reds learned about years back. Off the Makai Range. Subs can get in and out. The rock opening is on rails and moves back and around. In the cave. A steel lock, next. Then, the main quarters. What you figured?"

"About."

"We were in a hurry, I thought—"

Grove answered thoughtfully. "We are. But I need all

you've got before we make contact with our Kauai man. The admiral I spoke of. Once the word gets to Steve—the President—people will move. And the more they know about what they're up against, the more likely—"

"—the residents—will blow it up?"

"Or use it."

"Thought about that. Ivan is no nuclear whiz. His picture wasn't totally plain. But he said this. They've towed subs from a Chinese or Soviet port and the subs are now stashed in the cave. They're nuclear things—enormous h-devices with special packing, he thought. The idea is—and I guess they're about set to do the job, now—to move them to our West Coast and sink them deep. With nobody looking and where nobody can find 'em. When that's finished—and it won't be long if Ivan had the dope—they'll be able to tell the USA that, any time they want, they can touch off a series of these super-mines and if they do, he claims, it'll be good-by America. It could throw the whole Pacific ashore to the mountains and wipe off the West Coast population. The rest, though, I thought was phony."

He looked at Grove.

An answer came after a moment. "It's not. In fact, a friend of mine explained how just that might work. You reminded me of it." He pondered. "Remember, years back, Khrushchev's people detonated a pair of monstrous h-gadgets in Siberia? Hundred megaton things, tamped with lead so they yielded about half that? At the time, Kennedy was President. He said the tests were purely for scare purposes and the things had no military use."

"I more or less remember."

"My friend wrote Kennedy to put him straight. With the right elements in the jackets around them—and because our weather moves west to east—a suitable number detonated offshore would not just send a tidal wave over the coast to the mountains from Puget Sound to Lower California. It would make a radioactive cloud that would slowly move over the continent with the weather drift. The fallout would be hot enough to kill most people in the USA, Canada and part of Mexico."

Jerry was staring. "But when it got on to Russia—and China—?"

"That's the point of the special jacketing." He saw the perplexity of the pilot. "As that cloud passed over the mainland of North America its fallout would be deadly.

And there'd be too little time, on the East Coast, to take any effective steps for the masses in the area, or even those in the Middle West. You'd need special filters and special pumps to bring air to deep shelters. That, or stored air, enough for several weeks for each person. But when the cloud went on across the Atlantic the fallout level would have declined greatly."

"Nice," Jerry murmured.

Grove went on, thinking aloud to get ready for his call. "Probably a lot of people in Great Britain, France, middle Europe would die. Certainly, millions would get radiation sickness. But Moscow doesn't mind other people's troubles. And as for China—Peking boasts it can stand a loss of hundreds of millions. The USSR and Red China would have a far less serious fallout to deal with. And more time to get ready. The top people would *be* all set, of course."

Jerry didn't respond but his expression was sufficient.

Grove cogitated for a time and then asked, "Anything else that 'Ivan' told you I need to know? Rather, that others need to?"

"Maybe. They had to borrow—power to get that cave—"

"Lava tube," Grove put in. "That's what I saw out with Sapphire Abbott and the porpoises."

"—to get it ready for the last operation," Jerry continued. "Put up the fake rock pile. Make the lock. Seal off some cracks. So they could put in diesel power or steam or whatever they did. And bring in the towed subs. They'd been sunk and anchored offshore in special spots for a long time. If we could have traced that tap on the power line above the park, we'd have been home sooner."

"But we couldn't. And they knew that." Grove again reflected and finally said, "That makes it pretty clear, I guess. If there's not anything else?"

"Nothing I think of. We pumped him dry. But I thought part of what he said was crazy. Though he wouldn't change his story."

"Not crazy."

"Hard to believe. Did JFK?"

"Did—oh! When my friend wrote him the super-bomb tests weren't mere fright-makers? I saw Kennedy's reply to him. A long letter. Glad to stand corrected and promising to go over it with his scientific advisers. JFK was that kind of a man. And a quick study. So's—the one there now. I hope to God he is! And that we'll give him time enough so he—or his advisers—can come up with a workable scheme."

"If they knew I'd picked you up—"

"I doubt if they could know. Not for sure, at least."

"Could they pull out?"

"I don't see how. Personnel, maybe. But they won't—with what's hanging on the chance for success—not till the final moment they're sure it's hopeless."

"If they blow it?"

"No Hawaii," Grove said bluntly.

"The cloud?"

"Bad. But it would be concentrated. And half the Pacific to cross. Still—" Grove started to unclasp his mike and then asked, "What about the prisoner. That 'Ivan'?"

"On his way to Molokai. Bob has a hunting shack in the wilds there. He'll keep Ivan secure till he hears."

"Good." Grove smiled and added, "We are in a hurry now."

Jerry moved the throttles. The clouds thinned as the chopper descended.

Kauai was not very distant; green, sungilded and beautiful. Jerry began craning his neck and Grove realized, abruptly, that hostile aircraft weren't unthinkable. Solentor had everything.

Grove peered until Jerry made a thumb-up gesture. Minutes passed and then Grove grinned; he would have asked the question sooner . . . in ordinary times.

"How come you can fly one of these?"

"Last job I tried for required the drill. And the last flight I made in one was final for my buddies."

Grove didn't reply. Nothing to say.

They went over the shore and climbed a wooded hill. Then the craft cornered an escarpment and the world dropped sheer beneath. It was strange—like riding a pendulum, Grove thought.

Then he gave up watching and he ordered his thoughts as carefully as he could before they reached the field.

Jerry was making palm-up signals to the men below. He frowned as he gave Grove more facts. "I got leave from the Honolulu Police, early in the Vietnam thing. My military career ended out there. In a chopper. A VC rocket. So I was back in the cops."

They landed noisily but gently.

Armed marines surrounded the ship. Grove opened a window and said mildly, "Will some of you guys tell the base switchboard operator to contact Captain Houghton Defton?"

A sergeant answered, "No such officer here, mister. *Look,* you guys—"

"Just *try* it. The name's code."

There was a short and mystified discussion. A marine was dispatched to the operations building. He soon ran back. Grove leaned out again—an improbable passenger in a chopper that had no right to land on the field. "I'm to tell you," the marine said, and started to salute as he spoke. He checked that uneasily. "—that the man you want is not here. But if we can do anything for you, sir—"

The other marines were stunned.

Grove looked at the ranks of fighter planes in the distance and the military helicopters behind them. "Thanks, soldier. And please thank whoever told you to help us out." He turned to Jerry. "Need gas?" Jerry nodded and a tank truck soon rolled up alongside.

The sergeant said, "Would it be too much to ask how come a couple of civilians get such service?"

"Yes," Grove replied.

The sergeant nodded. "CIA? Oh well. Top 'em off, fellows."

A hose was unreeled. Gasoline flowed into the chopper. The men on the ground stared and shook their heads. Presently Grove called, "Could I get to—the man I wanted—by phone, a private wire, from here?"

"Not unless you are God. The gentleman's on a submarine and the sub's silent. If you can wait till day after tomorrow . . ."

"We can't."

Jerry spoke to Grove in a low tone. "If I'm flying this crate again, where is it to?"

"I can't decide. Gimme a minute."

Grove pondered. They might get to his home; no communications even if it hadn't been burned down by now. They could hardly expect to use the development area again—Solentor would have that covered. Helicopters could and frequently did land in the park. But that idea was not appealing. Russian vessels had radar. He knew his jump off the Na Pali Coast could have been seen and, likelier, his lucky rescue. So the airports at Kauai and Honolulu would be under watch. All Solentor had to do, Grove reasoned, was to keep himself and Jerry from getting to a phone to call the man on the Big Island. Not the President—save as a last resort—because Steve had set up this route for emergencies. Should he phone the geologist here? Would it make sense to call Oddie if his other contact wasn't on hand? Was there that much rush? As long as a chance remained, Solentor would take it—try to stop the ideas in the minds of Grove and Jerry, and perhaps Bob from going any further.

Suppose they asked for fighter plane transport to the Big Island?

Solentor could anticipate that possibility, surely. Already had, probably. The best thing would be to phone from this base. He started to loosen his safety belt and heard a siren sound. A jeep now roared toward the chopper from an HQ building. The siren didn't make its first zoom to top pitch; halfway, it died out. The jeep braked hard but Grove knew the message it was bringing.

"Phones went out, just now," the captain beside the driver of the jeep yelled to the sergeant. "And I guess the power just went too."

It gave Grove an idea of how fast Solentor worked, of his desperation, and of his extensive personnel. It also indicated that the chopper and the men around it might come under fire, any minute. His mind charged. If your goal is world domination, you have to be ready with every sort of protective measure, even such sorts.

Grove glanced at the man topping off the tanks. He was all but finished. "That's plenty," Grove called.

The sailor nodded and screwed the tank's top in place tightly, leaping back on the truck afterward.

The sergeant was muttering to the jeep-borne captain. He turned to Grove and Jerry. "You have anything to do with this power cutoff?"

Grove knew it had to be very quick now. "Not us!" he called. "We're taking off at once! And have your men scatter—there might be firing, any second."

The captain was puzzled. Grove made a sign to Jerry and yelled, "And now hear this, too! We never landed. If they insist, well, we never made a phone call. Okay?"

The chopper roared. Uniformed men stepped back. The

truck rushed away from the chopper and its exhaust. The men below were scattering and the jeep was heading off the strip.

"Low," Grove bellowed above the engine and rotor din. "And fast! Out to sea."

Jerry nodded and followed the—unneeded—suggestions.

"Can we make the Big Island?"

Grove did not ask that until they had skimmed the contoured hills of Kauai and until Jerry had gestured with a thumb. Grove had agreed—so they'd climbed into the large, spaced but convenient clouds above the sea.

To the delayed question, Jerry replied, "Have to refuel for that trip."

"Not good."

"Getting on in the day," Jerry offered later as they circled around in the misty cumulus.

Time passed. Their intercom was open but they didn't seem to have anything to say to each other. Jerry was waiting for Ring to determine what to do next.

"Seems idiot," Grove finally said in a musing manner, "not to be able to figure out how to get to a phone."

"Solentor is figuring all the ways we could try, and how to prevent us."

"Yes."

More time passed. The chopper sometimes lost a cloud but quickly found another. Jerry began working their way back toward Oahu, his idea, but Grove didn't object. Grove finally asked, "Could we skim in toward my place and, if it's still there, hang low? Dive into the sea and swim ashore with the chopper preset to go on, climbing and seaward, till it ran out of gas?"

"No communications in your place, you said."

"None. But beds. And food. If we could make it seem we came in for inspection and decided not to land—after dark, of course—we could get home safe—maybe."

"Maybe. Unless they have a squad there to meet us."

"They wouldn't. Not at my house. They might have burned it but I doubt that. Too obvious. Conspicuous. They have men on the talus, above the place, and, for sure, a ready-group in both directions, along the Kalan. Not on the grounds—they might expect people to be looking for us, there."

"So we do it. Swim ashore. Get in your place. And it's a rattrap, from what you said."

"Not quite. Because there's only one really good place for a bunch of people to keep watch for a car or what not coming from my place toward Waimanalo. Several vacant lots with thick Australian pines. Given some sleep, and with a predawn start—from my place to next door and thence, by swimming, to that woods—where we could maybe put the surveillance out of action—and even borrow their transportation, which they won't shoot at, right away—"

Grove looked at his friend, who shrugged. "Stopping in the village to phone, then?"

"Well—no. Making a break for the airport."

"And another reception committee?"

"Well, perhaps we could avoid it, for a few moments." He hesitated and nodded to himself. "We could look over the one possible Kalan post before we got some sleep."

Jerry realized that Grove was about finished and he wasn't at his best. He thought he understood and Grove verified what he'd been guessing.

"If Neptune is more or less the thing I think it is—the problem of how to—well, defuse it, say, is beyond me. Take the Navy and a lot of specialists, submariners, nuclear people, frog men, Lord knows. A lot to explain. And it's got to be the President who decides the team that takes charge. The Reds may blow it—and all Hawaii—clean off the Pacific, given the opportunity. If Eaper had the news first he might make one more fumble, and one too frightening to imagine. Anybody may fail. But it's got to be Steve who's briefed for the decisions."

"Steve," Jerry repeated mildly. "Yeah." Later he said, "How far do you want this damned chopper to sail after we jump?"

"Miles and miles. Possible?"

"We better move in, then. It'll be plenty dark when we get off Oahu."

It was.

They came around Makapuu at top speed and low. The chopper stopped and hung when it was opposite Grove's property. The house was intact and dark as was the one next door. Jerry jockeyed in close and then back out to sea a ways as if for deliberation.

The chopper sank to within a few feet of the swells. Two forms dropped in the night and splashed. One carried a leather case. The machine leaped upward then and, with locked controls it moved on a rising and somewhat wobbly course toward the east and the empty Pacific.

Two men swam ashore, taking pains to be unobtrusive. Wet, cold, they nevertheless scouted Grove's house and the adjacent property with great caution before Grove recovered a buried key and they entered through an end door on the lower level. Grove led the way upstairs. He crossed the living room without a sound and as if he could see clearly. Jerry admired that. He was relieved when Grove came back and handed him a gun. They waited a long time before they went to the bedroom and changed to dry clothes, Jerry's very tight. Grove provided food; cold, ample.

Jerry insisted he make the planned scouting trip. He borrowed trunks and left in the manner Grove showed him, through a tunnel to the vacant place next door, through it to the far yard, across that behind trees, some recently planted, and over a wall. From there, Jerry went carefully to the shore and waded out. Then he swam—toward the lights of the village and those on Kaneohe Point, beyond.

Grove was asleep when Jerry returned.

It took time to rouse him. Finally, however, he seemed awake enough.

"They're in the Australian pine woods, all right. Quite a few of them. They have some vehicles or at least one, up near the road. I didn't get close enough to make it all—too dark—too liable to bust a twig and get shot. I'd think, if we hit their beach just before first light, we might take 'em. You said so—and so far, you've guessed right. Which relieves me far more than surprises."

Grove made a sound of comprehension and fell back. Both men had alarm clocks and the clocks were set for the same moment of action.

Grove snored.

Off and on, in the guest room, Jerry dozed. Any slight sound roused him and the wind made many. He tried to figure what better way they might have found for their aim—and failed. He was dry, warm, fed, resting and alive—so far.

When his alarm clock buzzed he shut it off in three seconds. He stretched and wondered how much longer he would be—alive, even. His own clothes were damp, but they fit.

He went to meet Grove and found him dazedly trying to

shut off his humming clock. Jerry took it and cut the sound. As they ate in the darkness Grove seemed to come alive and awake, inchmeal.

When they left he was all there.

They traveled over the route Jerry had taken some hours earlier. Grove still had the leather case—to Jerry's slight wonder. They both had guns which went into waterproof bags before they started this third swim for Jerry and Grove's second. They made it to the near edge of the tree-covered lots and got into the woods without trouble; without trouble, because both were skilled in such work.

Once set in a suitable thicket, they waited for daylight. When it was sufficient, Grove touched Jerry; they moved apart on planned courses soon beyond sight of one another. Already traffic on the Kalan, not more than a hundred yards ahead and beyond the woods began growing heavier. Peculiar, Jerry reflected, but the whole world was behaving normally while threatened with an end to all normality and while the state of Hawaii might vanish, any second.

It occurred to him as he crawled forward that traffic wouldn't be normal on the highway if Tack Abbott had taken any effective steps. The thought made his sense of responsibility almost overwhelming. Then that weight was shunted aside by a more immediate demand. A guard—or one of unknown numbers—posted to watch the shore, was visible doing that. Jerry was behind him. He began to study the ground and tree trunks, the fallen limbs and needle carpet between himself and the man's back; he was fair-sized and had an automatic pistol. Jerry had no intention of shooting.

This was a drill he knew. The man watching the shore and sea did not even sense danger until hands closed on his throat. He thrashed for a while and then his body bent stiffly for a time. After that, he was dead. It had not been very noisy although the pistol thumped when let go. Jerry snaked it into the woods and hid it, his ears and eyes elsewhere. There could be a second man on seaward watch: and there was, Jerry soon gathered.

The man whistled, perhaps because he had heard the sounds of his struggling comrade or perhaps because that whistling was standard operating procedure. Jerry didn't try to respond to it. But he moved very swiftly to another spot. When the second man showed and saw the fallen form, he acted as Jerry had expected, hurrying up after a glance into the dense woods and kneeling to see whether the other was dead, merely hurt, or perhaps taken sick. With his left hand clamped on a preselected limb, Jerry swung out like a silent ape and used his gun butt. Then he turned away from the shore to hunt for others.

Grove, meanwhile, had crawled toward the place where he was sure the main operation would be based. A double track led into the casuarina woods from the Kalan. It wound between trees until it reached an opening where a car could turn around. Grove had made a careful study of his environs and found this road and turnabout long ago. He had smiled at the discovery; for the car-wide, double track led nowhere beyond. Yet it was plainly used a good deal. It came from the highway and where it ended a car could not only be turned around but would be hidden from the Kalan. It was, then, a teenagers' refuge for petting. It would never be used in daylight. Any would-be user in dark hours could find it pre-empted; an earlier vehicle would be spotted after the second turn from the highway. The intending driver would then back out and find a different spot.

There was a place on the shore in the opposite direction from his house equally ideal: an abandoned, decaying cottage surrounded by coconut palms up which and around which once-ornamental vines and shrubs grew rankly. Grove had bought the house next door to his own because it furnished a far better means of getting into the water, at night, than his first abode.

Nobody could keep watch of the ocean beyond it, effectively, in the dark. But the three sites Grove discovered, of which two were now known to be in use and the third surely was, had shown him that a constant and lasting surveillance of the nearby land area and of the only road exit from his first property was possible. To get clear, unnoticed, under those conditions then became a problem he went to work on. One solution was the station wagon. The other, a tunnel to the next-door house, certain rearrangements of its interior and some additions to its landscaping.

He had delayed that work until he began to feel he might need means for departure from his home of a suitable nature, always granting there was observation and that it would be by professionals, who would want their presence to remain unknown to the public. And, of course, to Grove, hopefully.

His crawl through the woods took time. Twice he saw the evidence of posted men—but he merely evaded those locations. Australian pines are not, actually, conifers. They are more closely related to oaks. However, their leaves are like needles, they are thickly branched, grow densely and quickly, and they shed a carpet that is like that of a pine forest. The land they covered here was unimproved, which meant that the boulders and lesser rocks that had rolled from the talus over the place long before the Kalan had been constructed were still in their original stopping places.

Better cover would be hard to find. Grove slid through the gloomy trees till he came up behind a rock where he could look into the opening at the end of the auto track. He smiled, unconsciously, when he did so. Solentor had excellent ideas for concealment and for maneuver, too. Excellent.

It did not surprise Grove to see the ambulance. A man lounged on each side of the white fenders—an armed man. In the front seat were two others. Grove saw one was a hunchback and knew his identity, instantly. He was a little older than Grove. He occupied the driver's seat in fact and metaphorically. The very tall man beside Rauchamb was a Chinese and that did not seem surprising. Grove had never seen the hunchback, Georges Rauchamb, but that Nazi collaborator had infiltrated the command of the Provençal Resistance to the terrible cost of certain of Grove's friends.

As he crept closer Grove realized their humdrum talk had become different and staccato. He began to gather its purport even before he reached a better hiding place. The ambulance also served as a communications center! One with a wave length or some other system that would not be detected.

The hunchback's speech was hoarse and had a frightening quality. The fake or modified ambulance looked normal—on one of its two stretchers lay a motionless figure, a dummy, Grove was sure. No evidence of the electronic gear showed.

What Grove heard was spoken in bad Russian and he had come in on its beginning.

"Nothing so far," the muted loudspeaker had said. "Not a sign of movement inside. No light flashes. Zero."

Solentor cut in, then, apparently speaking from a distance, as the volume was fainter. He sounded unsure, for him. "How many men are within rushing distance?"

"Rush that house?" There was shock in the response; Grove's expression was fascinated.

"May come to that. The area check is all negative?"

"Yes, sir."

"Both sides of the properties? No move in the bay?"

"Nothing, nothing at all, General."

"Good. You will stand by." A pause. "Station check," came the command.

The check astonished Grove. Seventeen posts reported in alpha-beta succession; their positions were not stated.

When that rapid, many-voiced string of negatives ended, Solentor said, "We've lost touch. They may be out and running." A pause. "Georges?"

"Sir?"

"Your present disposition?"

"Vehicle C at assigned post. Men on both outer corners of area. Two on seaward watch. If targer appears we are ready to destroy. If other movement occurs, will pursue and strike. Any order change?"

"None."

Solentor went off the air. The dwarf descended, speaking English to the men leaning on the fenders. "Send Overti and Han on a sweep of these damned trees. Tell them to look for signs of recent disturbance. They hardly could be here, but we won't take chances."

The men pushed into the thick foliage and separated. They soon came back accompanied by two mixed breed thugs, square, rudely made men who looked silly in aloha shirts—but weren't silly, in fact. The hunchback cocked himself to protest. The corner guards hadn't gone straight into the woods. But he realized why they had come back: to pick up binoculars Rauchamb hadn't thought to send his shore guards.

Grove was near enough to see the hunchback's pique at his oversight, and his near failure to bawl out men for his lapse. He had to vent his temper on others. "Han," he said to the oriental who'd been loafing, "go with them."

Three men were thus ordered into the pines. A sharp snapping sound made them stop. The hunchback smiled with hate. Then, meaning to exhort greater caution but actually instilling fear, he said, "Remember, dolls, if it is

Grove, he is cunning: I know of him. His companion, the park policeman, is not a simpleton either. If they are in the wood, you will need maybe more brains than you have. But I, for my own reasons, and the director also, would appreciate a gift of Grove's body."

He made that speech, Grove thought, for another end, too. It would give anyone who'd perhaps broken that branch, time to get windy or become confused, to hurry, as the crack would expectably result in a rush. Very smart.

Grove knew Jerry had been coming to see why he was late for the rendezvous. Now the bad luck of a branch-crack had set three men out for Grove's friend. Two remained. Rauchamb clambered back laboriously to the front seat. The other man was looking up to see if the hunchback would let him enjoy that comfort.

Grove took out of his case a smooth, silver-bright, steel ball bearing, two inches in diameter, heavy, and something that required practice to throw well. Grove had been practicing for a lifetime on throwing this along with many other, mostly ordinary things. He hit the guard in the temple and dropped him instantly.

The hunchback caught a peripheral impression. He slid out of the seat to the other side of the vehicle and down like a broken snake. He knew the guard had fallen but not why. Georges Rauchamb acted on the one fact for a single goal: saving himself. He had no accurate idea of the nature or the direction of the attack, if it was that. And Grove, already rolling under the ambulance, watched legs turn this way and that as Georges tried to find a target for the gun he certainly had drawn.

From the woods came the quick and double booms of a .45. That galvanized the hunchback. Grove was out and behind him while his legs stood tense. Grove had grabbed the man before he was aware of any presence near his vehicle. The gun was twisted out of the hunchback's hand. Georges was powerful and skilled but his warped back was a handicap and in any event Grove wanted no fight. A karate chop left one of his arms hanging limp and when he whipped the frog-shaped man around Grove saw the eyes identify his attacker even as he composed the blow to the jaw that dropped the man.

Grove looked about and found a stone the size of a basketball. He returned to the hunchback. He had not killed a man in a long while, but he raised the rock to destroy this deadly, hated traitor. He felt a moment of something like shame though the execution was due a thousand times over. To leave Rauchamb alive was a sin. Yet could he be inactivated and perhaps would then, someday, face justice less summary? The rock slammed down.

Grove was going into the woods when he heard a chuckle. It came from Jerry, who had watched Grove's last act of discarding a rock. Covered with dirt and pine needles from rolling on the ground, bloodied, bruised, Jerry still laughed. "I got all those three. Shot two. The third kind of dropped from a tree. A surprise. He died, after a scuffle." He was still panting and trying to conceal that. He watched Grove retrieve his ball bearing and he studied the hunchback. "There are people who wouldn't believe it of you, Ring."

Grove shrugged and jerked his head at the ambulance, taking the passenger's seat, after Jerry said sure, he could drive it. He slipped behind the wheel. "Where to? Phone?"

The ambulance bumped toward the Kalan. "No. Airport."

"Airport, for God's sake?"

"Yeah. Full speed. You know how to switch on the siren?"

Jerry knew. They gathered speed as cars jumped onto shoulders to evade their careening approach. To zigzag wildly past the golf course and on to Pali Drive took minutes but involved twice as many near misses of other cars as those minutes. Grove wondered, evanescently, if he'd been wise to let Jerry drive and he saw a red light at the Pali intersection. Jerry jumped it, then, drifted the turn.

Grove hadn't known you could drift an ambulance; maybe Jerry hadn't, either, and was merely finding out.

"Why can't we make your damn phone call?" Jerry asked. Then he answered himself. "Never mind. I know."

Grove nodded. "Seventeen parties have been posted by Solentor, at what points he didn't broadcast." Grove was watching traffic plowed open by Jerry as they roared up the mountain thruway. They might have a tail, soon; as soon as the post they'd put out of action failed to answer there would be a general alarm.

That happened as the ambulance lunged to the tunnels. A crackling voice called, "Station Gamma—do you receive me?"

Grove considered faking. He couldn't talk like Georges.

He didn't know the passwords. They'd catch on in a few exchanges. Instead of stalling, he turned to the black boxes on the floor in the rear and began to throw switches. He got one that stopped the noise. As it ceased, the ambulance shot out the second tunnel, siren at full banshee, accelerator floored. And Jerry pointed.

Grove saw what Jerry meant. Along the shoulder of the road dust and gravel bursts rose as if magically. Machine gun bullets were making the neatly spaced puffs, fired from above the tunnel mouth, but not accurately. In seconds they were out of range of that group.

Grove apologized. "If I weren't an old-timer—and a lazy dope—I'd maybe know how to use this equipment. Get somebody to alert *my* guy—say. But what I know about electronic gear you could stuff in a pool ball."

Jerry missed a Buick, an ancient Rambler, and a cement truck before he could even shake his head. "Better as is. What if the cops chase us?" He sounded eager. They were going down the mountain at just above a hundred; Honolulu would soon come briefly into view.

Grove climbed into the rear of the ambulance and found what he thought he might: two white outfits—trousers and blouses. As Jerry drove, Grove was knocked about, but he put a pair of white trousers over his slacks. Then he climbed back and helped Jerry into a coat when the lunging scene allowed it.

They picked up a possible tail on the last mile of the International Airport freeway. They were sure when guns flashed from men in the tan Continental. So they skipped the red light at the airport turn; the others tried to, but traffic that let the ambulance roar through closed against the mere Continental.

"There will be a next party at the airport," Grove said. "But maybe not at the charter plane end."

"Got the money?"

"Sure." Grove reached for his case again.

Jerry then executed a complex and illegal run through the mazes of the parking area and pulled up at the far end of the roofed walks and the building behind them. Before they leaped out, they donned white caps. Grove grabbed his case and they raced into the building with a furled stretcher. Jerry went to the counter of the Royal Hawaiian Air Line. A girl at the counter had seen them coming. "Is somebody ill?"

Jerry said, "Where's Mac?"

The girl, Japanese, turned toward an office. She called, "Mac." A Texas-tan, cowhand-gaunt man appeared. Jerry took the roll of bills from Grove and was startled to see that the top ones were hundreds. "Got a plane out there ready to go?"

Mac was puzzled and in no haste. "Hi, Jerry. What's this? Hallowe'en?"

"We want out—and up—and to the Big Island, Mac, before people come in here and start machine-gunning the place. Name your price. But let's go. Sheila can hold down the shop. We're just in a kind of panic. Legit but not to talk about. My friend will square the whole bit—"

The man named Mac took about five seconds to decide. Having done so, he said nothing. Instead, he ran for the swing doors that opened on the gates and then led through the gates to a standing Beechcraft. Jerry and Grove leaped aboard. The two props began turning before Jerry got the steps up and the door fast. Mac was talking to the control tower about an emergency—ambulance case—and his need to be cleared.

The flight took nearly two hours, owing to weather and stacking. But it was an uneventful trip and Mac had radioed for a car. Jerry and Grove started for the Volcanos National Park at the best speed of the rented sedan. Mac was arranging the paperwork to let them leave Hilo at once, if required.

When the local traffic thinned and the road was straight on its steady rise, they took stock. "Nobody got in the air to chase us," Jerry said pensively, "but we ought to take a peek now and then to be sure they haven't sent out a Hilo posse. Nothing in the mirrors. What about the wild blue and so on?"

Grove leaned out and gazed up. "No bogies. No friendly craft either. Blue yonder is all." He looked closely at Jerry, who had taken the wheel again. "You got a big swelling on your cheek and it'll be a gaudy purple pretty soon. And then there seem to be a few cuts here and there. Blood ran out and congealed. Were you in some sort of accident?"

"Nearly," Jerry replied, deadpan. "Man fell on me from a tree—big as I am. He acted peeved about it—tried to kill me, in fact. Foolish." Jerry allowed time to pass. "He was the one that got killed."

They slowed slightly to a show of respect for the speed limits of Kurtistown.

Grove then resumed the game. He didn't have to wonder why it was played. Other times and under other stresses—though never with such a magnitude of responsibility—he had played the game, waiting to get a signal that would send him and his companions on errands sure to involve assorted risks or waiting holed up under shelling: lots of times, lots of places.

"You ever drive an ambulance before?"

"Not exactly," Jerry grinned, his eyes fixed ahead; the car was doing almost ninety.

"That's a comfort! I doubt if you'd ever have gotten a case to a hospital alive."

"Another kid and I once borrowed a hearse. Never forget it! In California—where we knew a stretch that runs straight for maybe twelve miles."

"The other kid survive too?"

"Yeah. Well, that hearse had more speed then a gun-shy goose. Turned out later it was also used as an ambulance. We tried out various other things too. We finally got stuck and we had a long wait for a hitchhike home. Nobody was glad to see us either. But I still remember the general capabilities of that wagon! What hospital's ambulance was it, incidentally?"

Grove looked at the road. It poured at them like a jet-powered, endless javelin. "The lettering on it referred to some St. Mark's—or St. Luke's—Clinic."

"No such thing."

"Naturally. But what cop would realize that, for sure, in time to catch it?"

"No cop."

"Anyhow," Grove said after a further pause, "I don't ever need to go over Niagara Falls in a barrel. I know how it feels."

Jerry chortled.

It grew cooler though the day was bright and the hour midmorning. Eucalyptus trees thinned; tree ferns replaced them and reminded Grove of the Thurston Lava Tube, which he had twice visited by a meandering steep path through a forest of such ferns.

They swept up the slope of the volcanic shield. Ohia trees appeared, their scarlet shaving-brush blossoms showing here and there. Grove began to contemplate the meeting with Jake Palmer. Unless Palmer was also away. He could think about that if it happened.

It would be Dr. Palmer—and the President hadn't said what Jake stood for. Jason, perhaps? Or would it be for "Everything's Jake"—a nickname earned by a habitual expression! No matter, Grove thought. Would he live in the Observatory itself or have a house nearby? Grove didn't know and had not had a chance to ascertain since he'd been given the name.

One thing was sure, Dr. Palmer would, recently, have had a phone installed, a second phone surely. A phone put in a bedroom, or some other place where it could be used and the user would not be overheard. The installation would probably be known to his colleagues. And his refusal to explain it would lead to ribbing, no doubt. But the fact that it was connected to a special instrument in the White House would not be imagined.

Palmer might use it for trumped-up personal calls—to nameless pals, or perhaps he and his old friend Steve chatted, now and then.

Jerry had been glancing at his silent companion.

"You know, Ring, you've gone to more trouble and spent more time trying to make a phone call than I ever heard of! Some woman?"

Grove laughed. "You must admit the opportunites have been limited. Service is poor on the Na Pali Coast. The admiral was away, for a poker game or something. There were problems, and I needed your company before I could tell my party about things."

Jerry slowed for the turn into the park. "Been here?"

"Yes."

In the past year Grove had covered all the major highways in the state and many of the minor routes. He had familiarizied himself with the park road system, which is provided with gates so the crowd driving in to see an eruption can be kept out of danger areas. His trips to Kilauea had been made in quiescent periods. He knew Halemaumau, the legendary home of the Pele, had resumed eruption recently.

As they sped past the Volcano House—a motel set on the rim of Kilauea's three-mile wide caldera—he saw the countless steam vents and, beyond, massive smoke from the fire pit. He'd heard it described as "Hell" by people who'd never been in the latter place, as yet. Others rather vulgarly referred to Halemaumau as the drive-in volcano.

Jerry turned off at the Observatory driveway and Grove stared. The vast caldera lay before them, plains of cooled black lava hills, some now forested, smears of sulphur-yellow and ochre, with steam plumes everywhere. But the smoke vented massively by Halemaumau was of diverse tints, illuminated underneath by fires unseen from here—intermittent, reflected orange fires. A man stood outside the building, yanking at something he wore.

Grove hurried up, passing the man's car, its door left open. The man yelled, "Give me a hand!"

Grove did. The fellow was dressed in heavy clothing, neck to shoes—which had very thick soles. At his side on the lawn was a helmet, like an astronaut's. He'd been attempting to free a stuck zipper. Grove took over, realizing the suit was an asbestos and fabric coverall. When the zipper yielded, its wearer muttered thanks and shurgged out of the garment. Underneath, he wore shorts—and sweat; nothing else. He dashed to the car for two metal jars with long handles.

"Gas samples." He smiled. "Much obliged." He ran.

Grove charged into the building behind him; he was, plainly, one of the vulcanologists—a brow fit for any egghead, nose long, with a reading-spectacle mark, eyes amber—intent, hurried; he had to be grabbed to be halted.

"Palmer?" Grove said. "Where'll I find Dr. Jake Palmer?"

This amused the haste-prone scholar. "You'll find him—if that doesn't mean reach him physically, or talk with Jake—in Halemaumau. Where I've just been!" He waggled his jugs. "Got to get these in the lab." He went.

Grove chased and overtook the man a second time. "I believe Jake has recently installed a private phone. Know where it is? It's an emergency situation—"

The stranger took that with more aplomb than might be expected, even of scientists who deal with volcanoes. He set down his thermal containers and shook his head. "Emergencies are what happens, around volcanoes! I think Jake *did* install a line for his own use, a while back. But all the phones here went out not long ago. My lab assistant drove over to tell us."

Grove's disappointment was great.

His expression aroused sympathy in the other. "Happens occasionally here. Lady Pele's a pretty busy goddess now, and telephone lines can be snapped, you know. Charley, my assistant, went off to try Volcano House, and around. A repair crew will come up from Hilo on the double, when word goes through." He was trying to be decent. "Incidentally—your name is—?"

He asked, was told, and said, "I'll be damned! The second one!"

Shaking his head, he picked up his samples and trotted toward the lab. Something sure was biting that guy! he thought. Grove had fled back through the hall while his name was being repeated.

Jumping into the car, he explained the new problem to Jerry and added, "Let's go over where Palmer's at work. Maybe we can get to him and brief him—while the repair people are on the way. If, when and as."

They passed the car-dense parking yard on Halemaumau's rim. From a railed wooden platform nearby, people gazed down at the surging lava pit and across to the cinder cones standing in the heaving lava. These black, steep pinnacles rose from the red-hot lava floor almost to the rim, a hundred feet above their black mouths. And the pit smoke eddied and rolled across a desert of shimmering pumice beyond the overlook and the cars.

They drove past the tourist-crowded grandstand, past the parking area and through the acrid smoke. Clear of that choking stretch, Jerry pulled off on a shoulder glittering with pumice, drifted there like brown snow. Grabbing his case, Grove led the way over a shoveled footpath on naked rocks. They passed large signs warning that all persons who entered the region did so to their own risk and skirted the rim of Halemaumau to a point far from the safe public edge—a point where the heat could be felt, where the massive cinder cones could be heard whoofing as they ejected heavy clots of lava, and burbling as they maintained constant fountains. Lava rose higher than this rim, fell back, and slid in bright rivers down the cones. There it spread and darkened into sludgy scallops with red edges. The black floor of the pit was cracked by a hundred seams which opened and closed, revealing the molten red beneath the changing surface. Waves of dark lava hit the cliff walls of this near-circular abyss and broke into crests and spume of fire. Red lava poured over precipices in falls and ran in rivers, like the issue of a gut-slit blast furnace.

They slowed. A hundred feet beyond, several men labored. They wore the heat-resistant clothing and the helmets like that of the man at the Observatory and they were hoisting or lowering some heavy object at the edge of the volcano. Grove signaled them to wait; they paid no heed. The verge at Grove's side was split away from a solid edge. Hundreds of tons of rimrock leaned out, balanced, hanging, and liable to drop into the molten pit at any time.

Through that cleft Grove saw the cause of concentration up ahead. A man on a boatswain's chair was dangling halfway down the vertical wall, a situation demanding the absolute attention of his colleagues. To Grove, the descent was incredible. How could any man bear being lowered closer to the molten, seething floor, and nearer to the gobbets shot from the giant fountains of lava, almost directly under a great slab of split-away rock? In the heat, the noise, the fumes.

They sat down; Grove's state was apparent; he had to stop.

"They do it all the time," Jerry shouted, to override the volcano's din. "Learned more about volcanoes here than from all the others in the world."

Jerry would have gone on. But Grove was now looking back along the trail with a strange fixity. Three men were approaching on the your-own-risk path. They were some sort of Arabs, Jerry saw, without surprise. People from everywhere thronged Hawaii: Japanese in kimonos and obis, Hindus in dhotis, nothing was unusual.

These were robes and turbans. Their leader was an outsize fat man with peacock feathers topping his headgear. So why was Ring staring? Just then he turned to Jerry.

"Let's take cover behind that rock pile at the rim!"

"Why?" Jerry looked at the foreign tourists again and shrugged. But he followed Grove to a heap of slaglike stone that hid them from the trail. "What's the matter?"

Grove moved to Jerry's ear to reply. "What the matter is, I've made my last mistake."

"Hey!"

"The wires that were cut. By an earthquake?"

Jerry reacted swiftly and peered around the rocks, at the Arabs. "No!"

Grove was already opening his case. "There's also the thing that scientist said at the Observatory."

He had to shout although Jerry was less than a yard away.

The earth quivered in response to tumultuous rhythms of Halemaumau. Cinder cones spouted white-hot fountains and steam hissed in many places below them as if a hundred safety valves were trying to reduce the pressure in as many overloaded boilers. Occasional damped explosions accompanied the ejection of molten rock which had choked the throats of the black, immense cones; with each such hoarse but giant cough the impediment was hurled aloft. It separated into brilliant shards and glittering chunks that fell back onto the seething floor below the incendiary steeples.

Grove risked a quick look from the cover of their rock pile. Two Arabs preceded the huge one and now, emerging from flowing clouds of smoke and steam, came two more, wearing turbans but otherwise in Western clothes. He thought he saw the head of still another man pop up from behind a rift on the barren area and at the side of the trail opposite the pit. He wasn't sure. Dropping back close to Jerry, he explained.

"I was the 'second' somebody, that scientist said. It didn't occur to me that he meant another 'Grove' had been asking if a Grove had been seen around here. Probably one who said we were brothers. They got here ahead of us, Jerry. And they're coming for us now. Five of them."

Jerry still had his gun. He leaned around the rock heap and fired twice. "Missed!" His word was drowned.

Grove began unpacking his case. To Jerry's stupefaction, he produced wrapped sandwiches and held one out. "Jenny keeps fresh ones in the refrigerator," he bellowed, smiling.

The two Arabs in the lead had halted and looked to their right when Jerry next peered from a different spot. He got off two shots and both men crumpled. It made no sense. Then it did. Jerry ducked and gestured. It made no sense, again, to see that Grove was actually eating his sandwich and had set out fruit on a paper napkin. However, Grove did look after another bite.

Jerry had aimed two shots at one person yet both leaders had fallen. Now Grove could see why. A man was running in the open toward the Arabs and as he ran he fired. Both men in the rear were shooting at the runner and so was the huge Arab. The exposed stranger did not manage to stop the three, though one in the rear staggered as the stranger fell and lay still.

Jerry ducked back and looked wildly at Grove, gesturing with his gun. "Solentor?"

Grove nodded. "I'm sorry—"

His face taut, Jerry made his next try. This time, however, he stood up to aim at the waddling Arab. He failed by a split second because he'd wanted to be sure. The Arab's weapon flickered and Jerry fell back, slowly. Blood poured from his forehead and Grove, seeing, was sure he'd lost his friend.

He gave one more glance at the enemy and saw the rear guard cut down. He heard, as if distantly, a machine gun but he could see no one firing. It broke off in the midst of a next burst. Grove knew what that meant! The gun had jammed; one operated by somebody using a periscope, Grove dimly thought, since nothing human had been visible in the place where the firing stopped.

Solentor, alone, cleared the last wraiths of steam and came steadily toward the rock heap. Grove sat again and resumed eating. He did not try to think of the identity of those who had helped to kill four of the five Arabs. There was no use in speculation and apparently they were only two, one now killed and the other frantically trying to get a jammed weapon working.

In this pandemonium of volcano and this unaccountable exchange of firing, Grove swept every emotion from his mind. He could not let himself look at the body of Jerry. He must not speculate on the completely unexpected help. Waiting for his enemy, Grove set his bitten sandwich aside and picked up a lime. He shook sugar on it from a shaker.

Solentor rounded the rock heap, smiling. He squatted behind it and took in the action of the other man. He was briefly astonished and to a degree that showed on his heavy, outsized face, which now had a darker tint that matched his flowing costume. He held his Lvov Mark Ten on Grove steadily and bellowed, "Just sit where you are."

Grove nodded. The weapon didn't appear to faze him. He glanced down as if he was going to suck his lime and decided not, apparently. They looked at each other for a few seconds. Grove's wide gray eyes were calm. The other's were wild, which Grove interpreted as a very grand thing to see in this last moment he expected to live.

Solentor shoved the case out of Grove's reach. "You probably won't mind being killed," he said, "considering your success." Bitterness clenched Solentor's massive features. "And my failure," he added.

Behind them, a cinder cone huffed out a clot of lava the size of a locomotive. The overhanging section of cliff split away with an earth-shaking sound that caused Solentor to glance toward the place for an instant.

He did not glance back.

The green, fruitlike object in Grove's hand was, this time, a plastic imitation, one that was filled with concentrated lime juice, a product sold in most supermarkets. Squeezed lightly, it would squirt a slow and measurable stream. Squeezed hard—its small opening would jet the concentrate like a water pistol.

The highly acid liquid shot into Solentor's eyes. He jumped away in shock, tripped on his robes, lost his turban and continued moving backward to get his balance or to keep away from Grove; perhaps both.

Grove was on his feet and ready but he saw what was certain. Solentor, blind, howling, backed a step too far. Grove rushed to the rim and saw the massive body plummet, strike the lava, cast it in high waves and sink into a molten sea.

He turned back slowly and went toward Jerry just as Jerry began to try to sit up. Grove covered the short distance and knelt beside him. Jerry rubbed his scalp, looked at his bloodied fingers, leered at Grove, and said unevenly, "He should of aimed lower."

The wound was deep and bleeding hard. It seemed, to Grove's touch, prickly—bone-sharp.

Then a voice called thinly. Once more Grove peered around the slag heap but with great caution: one of the men with Solentor might be, like Jerry, hit but conscious.

What he beheld was the most astonishing thing of all that had happened in the past two or three minutes. Beyond the motionless and fallen Oddie and the fake Arabs another man stood—a man in a Panama hat, a lightweight jacket, shirt, tie and tan slacks. The man was looking down at Oddie and he held a peculiar weapon.

Grove tossed his case into Halemaumau, glanced at

Jerry and left him for a moment to go to meet Eaper. Axe behaved as if he were greeting a colleague in the next office, at the hall drinking fountain.

Grove couldn't say anything. But Arthur Xavier Eaper could. The director of the CIA spoke in a sonorous way, looking down at the body of Oddie. "He was one of ours," said the director. "He was on the team."

Grove felt slightly and inexplicably faint. Eaper's weapon distracted him then: it was a machine-pistol with some sort of periscopic device. Trust Axe, he thought crazily, to have a fancy model you can fire without exposing yourself, providing its complexity doesn't make it jam.

Eaper continued in a manner neither sacred-faked nor mortician-fatuous. "How the devil do *you* happen to be here, Grove?"

The question removed the traces of faintness. Eaper and Oddie had got on Solentor's trail, somewhere, somehow, before the Russian reached Volcanos Park, by a a small margin, as Grove could see. But Eaper hadn't any idea of how or why he and Jerry were at the same point!

"The night watchman at Sea Life Park," Grove said as the director waited, "is a pal."

"I've heard." Beneath Eaper's social caste, Jerry.

"We—well, went on a sort of binge. Wound up here. Then those Moslems started shooting at us."

"I saw it." Eaper nodded solemnly. "And the big one *happened* to fall?" He smiled insinuatingly.

"He—ah—tripped."

Eaper was informative. "That man—and those Oddie gave his life to attack—were fleeing pursuit, hot pursuit—by myself—and my team. I strongly suspect, Grove, when the leader, the large man, tried to force you to share your cover, he was killed deliberately. Your rusty judo was still adequate, since he didn't expect it, eh, Ring?"

"You could," Grove admitted, his eyes narrowing slightly, "put it that way."

"You didn't—ahh—recognize the man?"

"That sea elephant? Should I? Who is he?"

"Nobody you'd recall, I see."

Grove cut it out. "My friend is hurt." He turned, gasped and rushed to the unevenly approaching Jerry. Taking an arm, he murmured, "Say nothing, we're both drunk, plastered!"

Jerry got it—besides, his stagger was real.

Eaper watched Grove help Jerry along the path. "Drunk as a goat," Eaper said disgustedly. "You look like the devil too, Grove! When you're cleaned up and rid of the hangover, get in touch. I'll be in Honolulu. Number's in the book. Not the address."

Eaper smirked at the ingenuity of that and resumed his equally common look of distaste as the pair tottered on, toward a sudden rush of men in neat clothes who shouted with pleasure that was sickening, to see the chief in one piece.

Grove got Jerry back in the car and bandaged the wound with a clean handkerchief and a pad made from Jerry's already ruined shirt.

"What in hell was all that?"

"I haven't any idea," Grove replied; and he started the car.

17

WHICH?

Grove drove to a hospital in Hilo. The doctors looked at the wound and kept Jerry there for observation. It had been a very near miss, with bone splintering and concussion that might affect him later.

Part of an afternoon remained. He phoned instructions to Jenny and had to listen to some incoherent talk about the big quake near the park. Grove had an idea about it, but the evening papers said little he understood. An eruption of the explosive type had occurred off the Makai Range at noon. Fortunately nobody had been harmed as the pier had been vacated because of some hush-hush scientific work planned for the evening. All vessels were at sea. The Kalan Highway had been closed off immediately afterward, and the park had been evacuated by the Makapuu exits. Reporters, as of now, were not permitted in the area. Offshore waters were similarly forbidden. Oahu's last eruption had occurred about five thousand years ago, geologists estimated. This one was minor and quite possibly induced by some secret military experiment.

Grove wondered.

He bought some new clothing, took a room in the Sherman-Demoiselle and slept well, that night.

In the morning he found Jerry looking great—but confined to bed for another few days.

Grove decided it was high time to deactivate his windward side premises, granting certain facts.

He took a regular plane and rented another car at the Honolulu airport.

Honolulu seemed in its ordinary state of tourist-native, slaphappy chaos.

The drive over the pali was, as usual, gorgeous, and, as usual, refreshingly cool.

Waimanalo was tranquil also. No public signs of whatever it might have been.

And when he parked outside his garage things were quiet there too.

He had expected anything but that—armed guards, a burned-out ruin, not the silent shapes of two empty and adjacent houses. He took out keys and made his way in by the tunnel. He noticed that a couple of lights were burning and, by that, gratefully assumed that Hawaiian Electric had restored his lines. His regular phone, when he listened, also buzzed invitingly. He would make some calls as soon as he attended to even more urgent matters.

That effort required the best part of an hour. He was sweaty and dusty when he finished and he sat down, sniffing. But his house was now innocent of novel props no longer necessary. He'd had breakfast at the hotel and a free snack on Aloha Airlines, so he wasn't hungry.

He was ready now for a cigar.

He reflected, as he smoked it, that there would be—remnants, say—of the Solentor group, people not yet able to arrange transport. They might, conceivably, come snooping here, in hopes of tardy revenge.

Very well; he had another leather case ready and he procured it upon that thought.

His gate bell chimed.

He went out, crossed the bridge and lawn to open the gate. An Air Force major stood there, at attention.

"Mr. Grove?"

"Yes, I'm Grove."

The major extended an evelope, quite a thick one. "To be delivered by hand, sir."

Grove gawped.

The major saluated and left.

Grove locked the gate, then the doors, and examined the envelope. It bore no markings except for his name. He took it to his metal shop, using the outdoor stairs, and opened it with routine precautions. Nothing blew. So he looked at the last page for a signature. He found one.

Steve

He read the lines just above:

My gratitude is beyond expression. The world should know that one man saved freedom, all alone. What I have asked may be too much. If it is, say so. I shall call you as soon as I am able but after you have received this.

Yours,
Steve

Grove carried the letter upstairs, lighted a fresh cigar and turned to the first page. When he had finished he walked to his lanai and stared toward the sea; his emotions and thoughts shifted behind his wide-set, gray eyes much as the ocean at which he looked unseeing. He arranged the points in the letter neatly to achieve calm:

One. Tack Abbott had gotten word to the President. So the ordeals of Grove and Jerry had not been necessary. Or had they? Grove saw a value in their long race, Solentor prevented from a desperate act. And dead.

Two. The lava tube had been blasted open by picked men from Hank Balcom's command. The flooding that followed had wrecked the interior and drowned its occupants. Divers had found fifteen tow-submarines, two larger subs rigged for towing, enormous workshops and storage areas, all wrecked. The enemy's plan was vulnerable if discovered, which was why such ingenious and extensive efforts had been made to prevent discovery.

Project Neptune, in sum, was drowned, wiped out, finished.

Three. Eaper was on his way back to Washington.

Axe never gave up his theory that Neptune was happening elsewhere. When Tack Abbott blew the whistle I told Eaper enough to get him on his way by supersonic plane to Oahu. Owing to the efforts of the late Pilford Oddie, they did get on Solentor's trail and, thank God, in time.

I shall ask Art Eaper to resign. He'll be only too happy when he learns that I know about his books . . . and also "hers." Thanks for that! What do you think about Bernie Bergman as director?

Grove thought it was a great idea.

Four.

I believe it is feasible to sit on what we know about Neptune. The whole area was blocked off on the night of the blast and flooding and for most of the day following. The park, highway and so on went back to normal late that day and all further recovery efforts will proceed from the sea end of the tube, behind a very tight screen of ships. The news media have no information of any definite sort. Our cover story looks to be satisfactory, an explosive but minor quake, and hinted to be due to the need to recover some nuclear weapons lost because of the quake. The sort of affair that happened in and off Spain years back.

Five.

If we can keep the actual nature of Neptune a secret we will have a tremendous lever against Mainland China and the Communists who covertly assisted in that horrifying effort. The Reds aren't going to bring their devilish scheme to world attention. But they will know that we can, with absolute proof, whenever America chooses. It will be a very useful lever although both governments will play innocent and blame each other, whatever the facts.

Six.

This means you two would have to agree to a silence of indeterminate length. The Abbotts and Foth have done so. But you have a right to demand that the whole Neptune Project be given immediate release and, with that, the honor and acknowledgement you, especially, deserve.

It was up to Grove and Jerry Gong. At that Grove smiled a little: the President knew what their answer would be. If Neptune could be kept secret for such use—and Grove began to think that was possible—neither he nor Jerry would demur.

Seven. The President had come to a next point he found very difficult. Grove riffled through the pages for the exact words:

I asked you, up in Buffalo, to undertake a mission for me that proved vital beyond imagining. You carried out that mission. I have just asked you if you will waive a richly earned public honor. Now I ask more, with a feeling close to shame, one certainly of humbleness. Would you, Ring, for the rest of my term and another, if I am re-elected, be willing to act for me again on any similar matter—or one dissimilar—should an occasion arise when I needed you?

Grove sighed. He would, of course. As Jerry would, and the Abbotts would too.

The eighth item was simply Steve's statement that all costs of Grove's operation would be repaid from a special fund, including a reward to Jerry and another to the tree man. After that came the paragraph that began, *My gratitude . . .*

He returned to the red chair and sat for a time. In view of the plan to keep secret the uncovering and ruin of Project Neptune, certain loose ends ought to be caught up as quickly as possible.

Jenny came in, at that point, and started cleaning up what she called "this shambles." Grove wondered what she would have thought if she'd seen the whole house and all it had contained before he "defused" it.

The phone rang. Grove took it, hoping it would be Steve. It was not.

Bob Barker was angry, almost incoherent. "Where the hell have you and Jerry been? For the last two days I kept buzzing every number I could think of . . ."

When he had the chance, Grove broke in. "We've been away."

"I know that! In my chopper. Where is it?"

"Where's Ivan?"

That stopped Bob for several seconds. "He got loose from where I stashed him on Molokai. I didn't think it was possible. Anyhow." Bob's swallow was audible. "He tried to climb down a cliff to the sea, or, maybe, jumped. I dunno. The Molokai police have the body and don't know where it came from."

"I see. Look, Bob, no sweat. I'll get to you on that tomorrow. Meantime, have you talked to anybody else about—anything?"

"Of course not. Jerry made that clear enough. What *is* it all about?"

"That's the point."

"Anything to do with the big uproar around the park?"

"I don't know what that's about, myself," Grove lied calmly. "But I do know the man you took to Molokai had nothing to do with it. And he's no loss. I'll tell you a bit about him, tomorrow."

"Okay."

Jerry had said Bob was a very solid man and it sounded that way now. His next question was unemotional. "Where do I pick up the chopper?"

"We lost that."

"What?"

"Let me know what it costs to get another, a new one. And how much business you will lose till a new craft is delivered. It was my fault and I'll send you a check the minute you give me the figures."

Bob asked how his helicopter had been lost and presently realized that, too, was something to be kept under wraps. "Incidentally," he told Grove when his protests and queries ended, "your station wagon is still out on that empty development."

"Thanks. I'll pick it up later."

Grove was glad the police hadn't done anything about the station wagon standing amid the dormant construction machines. He'd be able to dismantle it too. If anyone had tried to tamper with it a fire would have started and in a short time it would have become so intense that such a person or persons would have to back away while the vehicle melted.

He sorted the accumulated mail.

A many-times-forwarded letter from Warsaw, New York, about the plant; everything fine there. Appeals for funds. A note about a boy in his gang from a grateful mother. Some advertisements. And another note that startled him. It had been mailed on the previous afternoon and read:

> Some friends of that big, dangerous man through whom we met showed up at Hana, and I decided to move. Cy got me a job in the park where I thought you had recognized me. Wrong? An Arab shiek who closely resembles our friend (oddly!) has twice visited the place

and met a girl I once knew when she was in my trade but worked for the competition. Very exotic. The other day she set fire to a slip of paper that I snitched by taking her ash tray. It said "Polonia Hills Motel, Falls Church, Va." Where she'll be, later? Also, our big acquaintance is rumored to be working, maybe without the knowledge of his bosses, on some *oriental* thing. I tried phoning but no luck. Came by and will again but meanwhile this note in case you are interested. We didn't have much time for me to tell you all I knew, when we met that once, did we? Incidentally, about that dame in my former trade but for the opposition. She always wears a lei of flowers I don't know. Sample enclosed that fell off in the restaurant. Hope this is useful and that it wasn't a mistake to mail it. I've been worrying. Because you know I owe you my life. I wish I could spend the rest of it thanking you. I haven't known many *kind* people, I guess. With love. Me.

The gate chimes sounded again and Jenny hurried over the little bridge and through the gardens to answer. She came back to find Grove holding a single, dead blossom in his hand and shaking his head in a bemused way.

"It's your girl friend," Jenny reported. "Very beautiful. She hopes you'll see her."

He looked up. "I have no girl friend."

"No? How would you describe the lady you had here one night, quite a while ago? In the guest room. Where she left a long gold hair which this girl's matches exactly?"

Grove flushed as Jenny showed amusement.

"I found it, yes," Jenny laughed. "It did not belong to either of your two teachers. One has black hair. The other is a blonde but with shorter hair." Jenny described the girl waiting on the garden bench; beyond question, it was Esther Wilson. He half rose and sat down again. He wanted to go out and welcome Esther. He thought of the hackneyed bit about old fools being the worst sort. He told himself he wasn't that old.

Jenny watched his indecision with disapproval. "You know what you are?" she finally said.

"What?"

He was stunned at her reply. "You're a coward."

Grove's eyes began to twinkle as he weighed alternatives.

A hostage to fortune and, if that, no coward to Jenny?

Or the lonely bachelor's ways that would certify his status with her as a coward, which he even might be, or at least have been.

Which?

His smile told Jenny which.